WORDS
UNSPOKEN

Books by Elizabeth Musser

FROM BETHANY HOUSE PUBLISHERS

The Swan House
The Dwelling Place
Searching for Eternity
Words Unspoken

OTHER BOOKS

Two Crosses
Two Testaments
*Two Destinies**

*Not yet available in English.

WORDS UNSPOKEN

ELIZABETH MUSSER

BETHANY HOUSE PUBLISHERS
Minneapolis Minnesota

Published by Bethany House Publishers
11400 Hampshire Avenue South
Bloomington, Minnesota 55438

Bethany House Publishers is a division of
Baker Publishing Group, Grand Rapids, Michigan.

Printed in the United States of America

Library of Congress Cataloging-in-Publication Data

Musser, Elizabeth.
    Words Unspoken / Elizabeth Musser.
       p. cm.
    ISBN 978-0-7642-0373-2 (pbk.)
    1. Young women—Fiction. 2. Traffic accident victims—Fiction. 3. Automobile driver education teachers—Fiction. 4. Psychological fiction. I. Title.

    PS3563.U839W67   2009
    813'.54—dc22

                                            2009004740

DEDICATION

This story is dedicated to
my brothers and their wives:

Jere Wickliffe Goldsmith V and Mary Chandler Goldsmith
Glenn Edward Goldsmith and Kimberley Gartrell Goldsmith

Merci, Lord, for my bright, mathematically inclined, computer-whiz brothers who have loved and helped their dizzy sister for all these years.

Jere and Glenn, thank you for being strong men who hang on to Jesus and raise your families to know Him. Thank you for two decades of love and prayers in our missionary journey and thank you for getting married and giving me another wonderful gift: beautiful, godly sisters-in-law who are truly sisters to me! I see Jesus in all of you, and I love you all so much.

—Elizabeth

PROLOGUE

The hail came from nowhere. The sky turned dark gray, as if a shade had suddenly been pulled down over the highway. Lissa felt her knuckles tighten on the steering wheel as the hail pounded the windshield.

"Leave it to Tennessee to give us hail on an otherwise perfect spring day," Momma said lightly.

She isn't worried, Lissa thought, *so why should I be?* The cars behind her on I-75 had slowed to a crawl, disappearing in the rearview mirror.

"Anyway, I think that a substantial scholarship to a small liberal arts college is worth considering. I know you have your heart set on an Ivy League, but I was frankly impressed with this small school."

"There's so much to think about, Momma. It makes my brain hurt."

Momma laughed. "One day at a time, Lissa."

Now the hail was hitting the windshield so forcefully it popped.

"This is freaky."

"Yes. You better slow down, Liss." Momma's voice cracked.

7

The hail thundered all the louder, harder. Glancing in the rearview mirror, Lissa wondered where all the other cars had gone.

"I think we should pull over. This will pass in a few minutes."

Lissa pushed on the brake, too quickly, and the car slipped and swerved precariously to the left. She saw the white dashes separating the lanes blend into one. *How can I measure a safe distance from the car in front if there are no dashes? It's all one twisting, curving, blurry line.*

It didn't matter—there were no cars ahead of theirs.

"Lissa! Slow down!"

The car was almost perpendicular to the highway. What had her driving instructor said about correcting a skid?

Turn the steering wheel in the direction the car is already going.

She turned the steering wheel, and the car slid in the opposite direction, zigzagging across the highway. A car passed, slowly, slowly on her left.

That man looks really scared, staring out the window at me.

A horn blared. Or was it the hail? A car crept by on the right. Then one swerved out of the way on the left.

This is what it feels like to be completely out of control.

The hail popping on the windshield echoed the sound of her pulse in her ears.

How will I go to college if I die on the highway in a freaky storm?

"Slow down, Liss!" Momma's voice was a whisper, a terrified whisper.

Lissa forcefully pressed down on the brake, and the car slid again— now they were hurtling to the right, toward the cement wall of an underpass. Lissa watched it move closer, closer.

We are going to hit the wall. It is covered in graffiti, and we are going to hit it.

The car righted and slowed as the wall drew closer. The sound of hail stopped momentarily under the cover of the bridge. Lissa was vaguely aware of the screeching of brakes. Closer, closer.

The car slipped out from under the bridge, the hail pounded again, the white lines began breaking up. The car finally came to a halt in the emergency lane.

Lissa let out a sob, head down, hands trembling on the wheel.

She sat with her mother in stunned silence, hearing only their labored breathing.

"Thank the Lord," Momma whispered eventually, seconds later. Or minutes? She reached over and gave Lissa's hand a pat. "There. Good job, sweetie." She flashed Lissa a weak smile.

Lissa continued to tremble. She couldn't release her fierce grip on the steering wheel.

The hail stopped as suddenly as it had begun, and the sun blinked through the clouds. Cars whizzed by, spraying the windshield with fresh rain.

"Honey, scoot over to the passenger's side. I'll drive."

Still Lissa sat, her hands on the steering wheel, her seat glued to the upholstery.

"Scoot over, sweetie. I'll come around."

She met her mother's eyes briefly; they shared a smile of relief. Other cars sped by. The wet pavement shone, glistened, a rainbow of colors in front of them. Lissa slid to the passenger side, admiring the violet blue that momentarily dressed the pavement, while her mother walked in front of the car and quickly opened the driver's door.

At the same moment Lissa saw, with a glimpse in the rearview mirror, a truck trying to pass a car, the car swerving, slipping, and skidding as she had done minutes before. She saw it as if in slow motion, the car sliding across two lanes, coming toward them, toward her mother. The scream started in her throat and exploded, "Momma!"

The car slammed into theirs, throwing Lissa's mother twenty feet ahead onto the pavement of I-75.

CHAPTER ONE

~

Lissa woke as usual to the sound of the voices. Sometimes they only whispered faintly, a vague accusation. At other times they shouted, furious, demanding.

As she glanced at the alarm clock, her foggy brain registered seven thirty. How many times had she hit the snooze button? She swung her feet out of bed and planted them on the hardwood floor. She stared at the small oval rug just to her left. The intricate needlepoint pattern displayed a rush of color—pansies and butterflies. Lissa concentrated on the blending of the muted yellows and bright fuchsia. She counted to ten, stood, and made her way into the bathroom, massaging her temples with the tips of her fingers. She threw cold water on her face, grabbed a towel, and blotted her face dry. She reached for an elastic band and pulled her tangled hair into a ponytail, wrapping the elastic around once, twice, three times.

Back in the bedroom, she lay on the rug beside the bed and forced her way through fifty sit-ups, staring at the imaginary spot on the ceiling, the one she had willed into existence so that she could report it to her therapist. Routine, routine.

Down the stairs and into the kitchen, still panting, she turned on the kettle, took a sachet of tea from the little cardboard box, and dangled it into a mug. She added two lumps of sugar. As the kettle began to whistle, she lifted it from the burner and poured the water into the mug, watching the steam rise. She opened a cabinet and grabbed for a box of cereal. It didn't matter which one, just as long as there was enough sugar to perk her up. Then the hot tea would kick in.

Her father's empty mug sat in the sink. She studied the thin-lined stain of coffee inside the rim. The dirty trace it left spelled out for her *You're late.*

"Lissa! We're leaving in ten!"

"Okay, Dad," she whispered to herself.

Sitting on a stool at the breakfast room counter, she leafed through the booklet once again. She knew it by heart—which had in no way kept her from failing the test three times before.

Today would be different, she told herself.

No, it won't. Today will be like the last 423 days. Dark, depressing, sluggish, morose.

Today had to be different, she told herself, thinking of the letter that sat on her bedside table. *When are you coming to see Caleb?* it had asked.

Her stomach cramped. She imagined Caleb there in the dark, waiting for her.

Today had to be different.

"Good morning, Lissa," Mrs. Rivers's voice called out from behind a stack of books.

"Good morning." She forced a smile, walked behind the circulation desk to the gray metal cart loaded with books. "I'll start reshelving."

"Thanks, dear."

Lissa pushed the cart along the aisles, reading the book titles slowly, almost tasting the ingredients in the ones she knew so well. *Rebecca, All the King's Men, Things Fall Apart.* She grimaced. That one described her life perfectly.

Eastern Crossings. She had never heard of it. She carefully opened the cover, then snapped it closed and reshelved it.

Returning to the circulation desk, she offered, "I'll pick out a book for the elementary reading today."

"That will be fine, dear." The librarian's voice sounded sugary sweet, sweeter than the cereal Lissa had eaten that morning.

Quit feeling sorry for me!

But why shouldn't Mrs. Rivers look at her resignedly, when one of Lissa's favorite tasks was choosing and reading a children's book for the first graders who came to the library on Friday afternoons?

"I'll need to leave a little early today, right after story hour."

"That's fine, dear. Your father phoned to say he'll be picking you up. Driving test?"

"Yes, ma'am."

"I'm sure you'll pass this time."

Mrs. Rivers didn't mean to look pitiful, but Lissa knew her thoughts. The girl who had graduated in the top five percent of her class from this very school should not be shelving books in the school library. She should be getting an education from Radcliffe or Princeton or Harvard or Williams, or perhaps Georgia State. Somewhere.

Failure. Failure.

Seventeen first graders arrived at the library, giggling and whispering. It pained Lissa to study their bright, inquisitive faces.

I used to be like them. I used to want to know everything. Now I just wish I could disappear.

The children found their places on the rug and looked at her expectantly, eyes wide, faces solemn.

"Today we're reading a story called *Madeline*. It takes place in a faraway land called France." She began to read, giving voice to the characters in the story.

It always surprised Lissa that her own voice sounded warm and full and calm, when inside the voices were not.

Failure. Your fault. Give up!

"I'm afraid you didn't pass," the young driving instructor said when Lissa cut the motor and sat with her hands folded in her lap.

She didn't meet his eyes.

She bit her lip and nodded and murmured, "Thanks anyway."

She started to get out of the car when he said, "Miss, I don't mean to intrude, but you say you've failed the test three times?"

She nodded again.

"Well, if you don't mind me saying so, I know you can pass. It's not that you don't know how to drive. It's just you're so doggone nervous." He cleared his throat.

You're doggone nervous too, she thought, but the sarcasm stayed in her mind.

"I know a man who's really great at helping kids who are afraid of driving. He runs a school. He's kinda old, but he's good. Been teaching kids to drive for thirty years now." He fiddled in his shirt pocket where *Department of Motor Vehicles* was stitched in dark blue thread, pulled out a card, and handed it to Lissa.

She stared at the card and murmured, "Thanks."

The young instructor shrugged. "I'd give him a call. Couldn't hurt."

Lissa waited at the curb for her father to pick her up. She thought of him as a jovial man, big and brash. He used to hug her to his chest and slap his hand down on the coffee table and let his head fall back in boisterous laughter. He did these things still, but it was all pretense. The arms that closed around her, the big, muscular arms, felt stiff, unbending—a wooden hug that gave no comfort—and his words were equally wooden: *Lissa, that's enough. We will not talk about it again. Do you understand?*

She felt the pain gnawing her from the inside.

Your fault! screamed a voice.

So loudly that for the moment she couldn't hear the one whispering *Not good enough.*

Her father's gray BMW rolled into the parking lot. Lissa painted a calm expression on her face, but she was sure he could read it nonetheless, before she even opened her mouth.

The image in her mind was still there, though blurred. She was giggling; her father was tiptoeing through the house, pretending to be befuddled; her mother hummed softly in the background. A bright, airy, happy memory. The tune she could hear even now, that softly hummed tune. Lissa reached, physically, with one hand for the image, trying to grasp it before it evaporated. Even after the image disappeared, she thought she could faintly hear the giggles.

Then she realized it was the panting of the BMW's powerful motor as her father pulled the car up beside her.

He gave her the big, hopeful smile. "How'd it go?"

She shrugged, climbed into the passenger's seat, not meeting his eyes. "I failed."

His smile faded, and the wooden arm reached over and patted her on the back. She felt the heaviness of the silence between them. She closed her eyes as they drove toward home, and she willed herself to hear the soft melody again.

Instead, the voices whispered around her head, pecking at her like a bird on a windowpane, pecking. Then suddenly they were shrill—a siren, the teakettle whistling, the burglar alarm at the neighbor's house. They made her head ache and throb! She rubbed her temples.

"Lissa, you okay?" Her father was staring at her with that perplexed expression on his face.

What could she say? What was she allowed to say?

"Sure, Dad. I'm fine."

Back in her room, she collapsed on the bed, arms dangling off one side, legs off the other. She turned her head to the side, and with her right hand pulled open the drawer on her bedside table. Reaching underneath a stack of underwear, she clasped the little brown bottle of pills. Thirty-two of them, carefully saved. That should do the trick. She picked up the bottle, let her fingers close around it, and imagined pulling off the small white cap.

What about Caleb? a small voice whispered, wooing her back.

Yes, Caleb.

Rolling onto her back, she reached into her jeans pocket and pulled out the little business card. It was crinkled in the middle. *MacAllister's Driving School*. An address and a phone number. *I'd give him a call. Couldn't hurt.*

She set down the bottle, picked up the phone, and dialed the number.

MONDAY, SEPTEMBER 21

One more year until retirement, Ev MacAllister told himself, leaning forward in the chair to tie his shoes. He did not dwell on the thought. Truth was, he loved his job. A vocation, he called it. At first Annie had thought he should look for something better than sitting in the passenger seat with nervous kids. Eventually, she had understood and accepted it, even embraced it.

He stood up with a grunt, thankful that they had agreed and flourished in that idea for so long after the accident. Could it be almost thirty-five years?

His first client drove well, a sixteen-year-old girl who was meticulous, careful, and focused. Easy. The next client was waiting for him by the mailbox of the dirt driveway that made a loop in front of his old Victorian home. The sky was cloudy, a surprisingly cool nip in the September air.

Ev always gave his clients the benefit of the doubt, refused to judge by appearances. But after observing kids for so long, he could read them with amazing accuracy, and what he saw in front of him was spelled out on the young lady's face as if she were holding a sign.

I've failed this test several times and I'm scared to death and I'm begging you. Please help me.

She wore jeans and a bright turquoise T-shirt. She had pulled her tousled brown hair into a loose bun and secured it with a long spearlike instrument, and the hair stuck out and strands fell down around her face. That face held an injured look, fragile; thin, dark circles around large, dark, expressionless eyes. He thought briefly that if she'd gained ten pounds she would be very attractive. As it was, he wondered if she could be anorexic.

"Good morning, miss," he greeted her, holding out his hand.

She offered hers limply, not even bothering to disguise her resignation.

"You must be Lissa. I'm Ev MacAllister. You 'bout ready?"

She nodded, met his eyes briefly, then stared at the ground. "Yes, sir."

And he imagined her thinking *Just my luck to get some old geezer.*

She looked up. "I'm only here for the free evaluation. I'm not sure I'll be taking lessons."

"That's fine, young lady. See how you feel after today. If you want to continue, you may."

She nodded again, her hands stuffed into her jeans pockets. "How long does it usually take to help someone?"

"All depends on the person."

"I see."

"But I can tell you that in over thirty years of teaching, only a handful of people couldn't get over their fears."

She glanced up at him suspiciously when he pronounced the word *fears.* "I need to learn to drive again. It means everything to me."

"Then we'd better get to work, wouldn't you say?"

For one brief moment, Ev saw what looked like a flash of determination in her eyes, before she turned them down to stare at the pavement again. That was enough—the look in her eyes brought back the memory of an old, familiar aching. He felt the lurch in his gut, ignored it, and walked toward the car.

"Okay. Thanks, sir."

"You'll be driving Ole Bessie today. The blue Ford Escort over there. We'll take a few loops around the driveway first, just to see what you know, if you don't mind."

The girl didn't smile.

She's a serious one.

"I don't mind."

Lissa took in the surroundings as she walked over to the old car. The house sat perched on a hill at the end of a wide country road with a view of Lookout Mountain spreading out in front of it. A spacious green carpet of grass out front bisected the semicircular dirt driveway. The house was white and needed a new coat of paint, but it looked neat and clean. A wraparound porch led to the front door, and the roof was black and gabled. Flowers grew rampant around the house and in window boxes.

Two other cars, a red Buick and a white Impala, were parked beside the light blue Ford. Painted along both sides of the Ford in dark blue lettering was the advertisement: *MacAllister's Driving School.* Mr. MacAllister wore a blue seersucker suit that almost matched the color of the car.

Lissa studied him curiously. He was tall and lean and stood erect, as if he had been in the military. His thick silver hair was abundant—definitely not military—and he wore old blue and white tennis shoes that seemed incongruous with the rest of his appearance.

She liked him. He seemed confident and calm, and something else. Kind. Yes, that was it. Kind, with a sense of humor.

"Okay, Lissa. A few bare essentials before you take the wheel. I know you've heard it all before, but it never hurts to review." He pointed out the accelerator, the brake, the turn signals, the rearview and side mirrors. He mentioned that the faster the car was going, the more sensitive the steering wheel was to the touch, and easier to turn.

He glanced down at the sheet of paper she had filled out with her personal information.

"I see you used to drive. Is there anything you'd like me to know before we start? Any past experiences I should know about?"

She shook her head too quickly, swallowed, and stared at the ground.

"All right, then. Let's get in." He opened the door to the driver's seat, and Lissa slid in.

The upholstery was dark blue, worn thin in several spots. Lissa noticed the single brake pedal on the instructor's side. Mr. MacAllister got in and closed his door, and the noise made her jump, for no reason.

She pulled on her seat belt, turned the key in the ignition. As Ole Bessie gently rumbled to life, Lissa heard the voice.

Your fault.

She willed herself to block it out, released the brake, and pressed lightly on the accelerator, checking her mirrors. She drove slowly around the circular driveway in front of the big white clapboard house. Once Mr. MacAllister leaned over toward her and adjusted the steering wheel, just barely, when Ole Bessie's tires veered slightly off the dirt driveway and onto the patch of green grass.

After the third lap, he said, "Okay. That's great, Lissa. Just pull to a stop over by the hickory tree."

As she braked she noticed, with another feeling of relief, that his pedal brake mashed in automatically with hers.

———

Well, I'll be, Ev thought to himself. In spite of her scared, anemic appearance, the girl handled the car with ease as she drove around the semicircular driveway.

"Lissa, you did just fine. Now let's just go down the road a little ways, and that will be enough for today."

She gave him a questioning look. "That'll be all?"

"We don't want to overdo it. Little by little, you'll get your confidence back."

She pulled out onto the wide road in front of the house and started slowly down the hill.

"I like to go easy the first lesson. But for your second lesson, would you be ready for a drive on a small road—not much traffic?"

"Yes, sir."

"On Wednesday we'll go over to the Chickamauga Military Park. It's convenient, with wide roads that curve around easy, a low speed limit, great scenery, relaxing." He glanced at Lissa. "Altogether a good place to practice."

She nodded.

"My philosophy is to get you back on the road again as soon as possible. I don't believe in spending hours driving around parking lots. Makes you feel like you're on a merry-go-round."

She nodded again as the road opened up before them.

"Just go straight on ahead for about a mile or two, and then we'll turn around at the filling station and go back to the house."

The clouds had evaporated; the sky was that intense autumn blue that Ev loved. Lookout Mountain towered in front of them. In fact, from their position miles away on the road it looked as if they might drive right into it.

"Do you mind telling me your driving history, Lissa? You say you've failed the test several times?"

One hand, the right, tightened on the steering wheel almost imperceptibly, but Ev saw it.

"Um, well, I had my license and I drove a lot. But . . ." Now the left hand clutched, the knuckles whitened. "But there was an accident and . . ."

"You've been afraid to drive ever since."

She glanced at him. "Yeah, that's pretty much it."

"So what we need is to work on building up your confidence, young lady."

Her hands relaxed, and she took a deep breath. "That would be great, sir. Yes, that would be great."

Ev let the screen door slam as he came in from the porch. Six thirty-five. He needed a glass of lemonade. The weather had decided to turn muggy, and Ole Bessie did not have air-conditioning.

Something about that young woman irked him. Bothered him. No, scared him. Hurt him. There.

Back on the porch, he settled into the rocking chair with the glass of lemonade. He took a long sip, closed his eyes, tried to shake the image of the scared young woman, skinny with hollow eyes. Hollow, desperate eyes, begging him for something.

Begging him for life.

As quickly as he admitted it, he saw her. Tate. Little Tate as a round-faced baby, sparkling brown eyes. Tate at five, mischief written across her pudgy cheeks and in the crease of her brow. Tate at ten, stomping out of the room, furious with her older brother. Tate at fourteen, taking her first sip of alcohol . . .

Stop it! he told himself. What good did it do to relive these things?

He stood up, said out loud to himself, "I'll be glad to help her if I can."

If I can? He had helped so many others. Of course he could!

What about Tate?

Nothing he could do about Tate. Nothing he could have done, he corrected himself. He closed his eyes, took another sip of lemonade, walked to his little office, and sat down at the desk, where he scribbled a note to himself before going back outside. Time for his next client.

———

Lissa sank onto her bed with a groan.

You see, Caleb, I am trying. I swear I'll come to see you soon.

She let her eyes travel around the room. Nothing had changed since the accident seventeen months ago. It would be good to move forward, make a few changes, as her therapist had suggested. But she could not. Every single item in her room, every pillow and book and photograph, every trophy and award, was stuck in place as if it had been glued down. Somehow it was simpler to let them stay there and taunt her, remind her of the other life, the *before* life. A constant reminder of what had been and what should have continued.

Lissa lifted her head from the pillow and forced her body out of inertia. She walked over to the desk, the clean white desk with its three drawers, the desk that the cleaning lady dusted twice a week so that no one would know the neglect. She looked at the photo of the gelding, his chestnut head held high, a blue ribbon attached to his bridle and floating out in the breeze. Lissa herself stood beside the horse, an elated smile on her lips, her black riding hat pulled down on her forehead, her hair swept into a bun underneath. She studied the picture in a way she had not allowed herself to do for so long. *Carefree.* Even then, what a rare emotion to be displayed on her face.

A surge of joy rushed through her before she could stop it, exactly like the feeling she had had at the moment the photographer flashed the picture. She remembered how the gelding shied, jerking her up, and how she laughed so easily.

Stop it! the voice reprimanded.

With a stiff hand, Lissa turned the framed picture down on her desk, and that one simple gesture felt harder than lifting a fifty-pound bag of horse feed.

Glancing to the armoire on the other wall, she went across the spacious room, reached up with one hand, and touched the gold-framed photo. In this one Lissa wore a sparkling evening gown, pink taffeta on top, closely fitted, showing off an attractive bustline and small waist. The gown flowed out in soft pink petals to her ankles. A strand of pearls around her neck and a string of dangling smaller pearls from each ear completed her accessories. Her lips spread in a wide smile as she clutched the trophy. Beside her was Momma, beautiful gray-eyed Momma, her ash blond hair swept off her bare shoulders, her blue sequined dress sparkling. Momma laughing, looking like an older sister. Laughing and proud of her daughter.

With a swift gesture Lissa knocked the photo over so that it landed with a slap on the top of the armoire. There. She had done it.

She went back to her bed and lay down.

What good did it do? Tomorrow Helena would come to straighten and clean. She would right the fallen frames, dust them carefully. Unless Lissa could bring herself to say the words, pronounce them convincingly— "I don't want these in my room anymore"—the pictures would be there tomorrow afternoon when she returned from the library, their golden frames shining, the smiling faces taunting, calling her back to when life made sense.

Lissa remembered holding on to Caleb and saying over and over, "It's going to be all right. We are going to survive. I swear it. This will not destroy us, Caleb. We are going to survive." Her arms were tight around his neck; she felt his warm breath and held him tighter.

Had she said those things? Did she still believe them? Now she was the one longing for arms to close tightly around her and swear to her, swear to her on everything under the sun that things were going to change. She was going to make it, and these terrible voices would stop. But there was no one around, only the bright, cheerful yellow walls and the bed with its yellow comforter and the desk and the armoire and the china cabinet with ribbons and trophies lining its shelves.

Why did she expect her father to walk into the room now and grab her in his all-engulfing bear hug and hold her there until she had wept on his shoulder, and say, "It's okay, Lissa. You are safe with me"?

How she longed to hear him say that. She longed for his robust laughter, the way his dark eyes twinkled merrily, the sparkle of someone who knew how to appreciate life. But his eyes looked dull now and, if she let herself admit it, angry. Brooding.

She shuffled through the mail he had left on her desk. Three more college applications. A letter from one: *Dear Miss Randall, Based on your fine academic achievement as well as your impressive extracurricular activities, we are pleased to tell you that you have qualified for the scholarship to . . .*

She picked up the framed high school diploma that sat on the desk and lifted it above her head.

Lies, lies! Failure!

She threw it forcefully across the room, where it hit the door to the bathroom. She heard the glass shatter and then tumble onto the soft blue bath mat.

Lissa formed the words in her mouth, repeated them out loud twice, the same words she had longed to pronounce to her father for the past seventeen months. "Stop trying to recreate my life, Dad. That life is over. Do you hear me? Over. Stop trying to make it okay again. It will never be okay again."

She sank onto the bath mat beside the broken glass and took the little card out of her pocket. *MacAllister's Driving School.* For some odd reason she smiled, seeing in her mind the tall, older man with an abundance of silver hair, dressed in a seersucker suit in spite of the muggy weather. She remembered his bright blue bow tie and his dirty blue and white tennis shoes.

So what we need is to work on building up your confidence, young lady.

"Yes, please," Lissa said aloud.

CHAPTER TWO

The day began in typical fashion. Silvano Rossi arrived at the office early and clicked on the machine to start the coffee—the *real* Italian espresso. None of that weak muddy American stuff. He was ready to begin the day! The other offices at the publishing house were still dark. Silvano prided himself on arriving first; one day soon he'd get noticed. Eighteen months as a measly assistant editor at Youngblood Publishers was long enough. Hard work, long hours, and offering a steaming cup of perfect Italian espresso to the boss when he walked in were part of the recipe for him to be making a decent salary before he turned twenty-eight. He liked recipes!

Coffee in hand, he walked past the office door of Mr. Edmond Clouse, senior editor at Youngblood Publishers, and nearly tripped over a small, dark bundle sitting on the floor, smack in his way. The coffee sloshed onto his hand and then down onto the package.

"*Oh, la miseria*, Leah! When did you put this package here?" He cursed the absent secretary out loud in Italian as he set his cup of coffee down and hurriedly searched for a napkin.

Quickly Silvano blotted the drops of coffee from what turned out

23

to be a small burlap sack. What? Why in the world would Leah—the world's most meticulous secretary—leave a thick burlap sack in front of the boss's office door? Did she think the company was in the animal feed business? Books, they dealt with books, not burlap! Good thing he had found the bag, and not the boss. He'd move it out of the way and let Leah know. A little leverage never hurt.

Silvano lifted the bag off the floor. That's when he noticed the label marked *Special Delivery* with the address of Youngblood Publishers hanging from the thick twine that held the bag closed. It felt like a ream of paper inside . . . and then it hit him.

"Of course, you idiot. *Certo!*"

He took the burlap sack, carried it to his desk, and carefully unknotted the twine. He reached inside and pulled out a rectangular box. It too was bound with twine. With shaking hands, Silvano slid the twine off the box, opened the lid, took out a thick stack of papers, laid them on the desk, and began to chuckle. The chuckle turned to all-out laughter. Silvano was thankful no one else was around to hear him.

"*Certo!* Of course."

He stared at the first typed page. *Novel #6 by S. A. Green.*

Essay Green, he'd thought the name was the first time he'd heard it mentioned.

An author who refused interviews and book signings, who never appeared in public—no picture available of her, no biography. Just an amazingly well-written novel every five or six or seven years. The woman was slow, but hey, no one was complaining. Her sales always leveled off around 400,000.

A round of champagne for all the staff when a burlap bag arrived! A new novel by S. A. Green meant big profits for Youngblood. The public loved her, and Silvano understood why. He had read her books, every one of them, as a young intern.

Her biography was sketchy at best. Female. Age unknown—presumed to be in her mid-fifties now. First published book, 1960, immediate success. *Eastern Crossings.* A small novel with a powerful punch. Dark, dark. The thin paperback had made its way into the back pocket of every college kid. But the woman wouldn't give interviews.

Her next novel had not come along until almost seven years later, with not a word from her in between. *The Equal Journey.* This book was 723 pages long, a family saga of life in an unnamed communist country. The book's style was completely different—third person narrative. Long, descriptive phrases. Chillingly beautiful. As seamless and haunting by its length, a winding river, as *Eastern Crossings* had been in its bleak first-person portrayal of child refugees and prostitution.

Again, the book had become an instant success. The college kids were now married, and they couldn't carry this tome in their jeans back pockets. Instead, it sat beside their beds, its hardbound cover hidden beneath the glossy dust jacket that portrayed a mass of people looking vacantly into the sky on a cold evening.

The story of the author S. A. Green went on like a fine spy novel. An untitled manuscript appearing without warning in a burlap bag, years after the last release, the novel almost faultless, the editing minimal. No wonder. The lady took five or six years in between each work of art. She had plenty of time to get it right.

Now he, Silvano Rossi, held the manuscript of her sixth novel in his hands. This manuscript was rather short at 263 pages. If he hurried, he could get a ways into the novel before anyone arrived. Just a sneak peek and then he'd pack it back up.

Thirty minutes later, he was still turning the crisp white pages, placing each one facedown in the pile to his right after reading the double-spaced typewritten page. He surprised himself by needing to clear his throat once.

Amazing. How did she do this? How?

His predecessors had always been happy to leave well enough alone. Let the novels sell. It made the publishing house a bundle. And the lady was loyal. As far as anyone could tell, she'd never sent another manuscript to another house. So no one worried about the refusal for interviews or signings. No one wanted to look any further.

But Silvano was curious. What did this lady do with her money? Where was she hiding? Why did she hate interviews? And how could a nutty woman write a book that made his heart race and cramp at the same time, that felt like a long skinny finger jabbing into his soul? In the year and a half that he'd held this job, he had read—or at least started to read—over three hundred manuscripts, and not one of them had caused this kind of fluttering in his gut.

By the time Silvano heard the voices of his co-workers, he had replaced the manuscript in its box, retied the twine, and put the box back in the burlap bag. He made sure he knotted the twine in the same way it had arrived.

"Hello, Silvano. Early as usual." Eddy Clouse wore a dark suit, perfectly cut to enhance his large frame. Imposing, polite, shrewd. Loud.

Americans were always loud. Couldn't they learn to communicate without involving the whole room?

"Yessir."

Mr. Clouse entered his office with Silvano following, his boss's coffee in one hand and the burlap bag tucked under his arm.

"Mmm. Smells great. Thanks, Silvano." Leaning over his desk, his boss flipped through a few memos, his square face with the heavy jaw turned down.

"My pleasure, sir." He set the coffee on Mr. Clouse's desk.

"Perfect," the boss said when he had taken a sip. He gulped down the espresso and motioned to Silvano. "What have you got there?"

"I found it outside your office this morning. A burlap bag."

Mr. Clouse's head jerked up. "A burlap bag, did you say? *The* burlap bag?"

Silvano nodded. "Looks like it, sir."

Mr. Clouse sat down in the swivel chair. Clear blue eyes looked up expectantly, and a smile twittered on his lips. "Well, let's have it, Silvano!"

"Looks like another masterpiece, sir," Silvano commented, placing the burlap sack on the desk. He noticed a slight flicker of annoyance on his boss's face.

"You've opened it?"

"Oh no, sir. Just admiring the packaging. You know—my first peek at the publishing house's lucrative mystery writer. Mystery writer who doesn't write mysteries." He chuckled awkwardly.

"Yes. Yes. Fine then. Thank you, Silvano. That will be all."

As he had expected, Clouse dismissed him. No help needed. No thanks, no opinion asked. He existed only for espresso and midlist authors. Well, now he had just what he needed to move up in the publishing world. Evidence. Finally, arriving early had paid off. A photocopy of S. A. Green's manuscript lay at the bottom of his slush pile, hidden by a dozen manuscripts that would never be read.

You're on your way now, Silvo. Espresso, gelato, Roma. This is good. E Buono!

Immediately he heard another voice in his mind. *You are good, Silvano, buono! Buono! Yes, yes, that is good!* The nun at St. Jude's Montessori School hovered over him. At four, Silvano's English was limited but growing. Thank heaven for Maria Montessori—the woman whose face was on every lira! Way back in the early 1900s she'd founded her schools in the poorest district of Rome, insisting that all children could learn. St. Jude's employed her methods; the nuns took in some of Rome's poorest and educated them in Italian and English.

This is your destiny, Silvano. The Blessed Virgin has answered our prayers. You have been chosen. You will bring honor and wealth to the family. You will go to America!

He had studied hard, had worked through three phases of the Montessori school's curriculum so that at age twelve he was ready to move to America. America! The land of opportunity! His English was impeccable. Yes, the average American recognized a faint accent, but only a few could identify it as Italian.

Bring honor to the family, Silvano; bring honor.

It echoed in the recesses of his mind.

No matter how long it takes.

He gave a stiff smile and thought *Now I'm on my way!*

———

The wind outside the little house in Montpellier was blowing fiercely, but no one seemed to pay any attention. Huddled around the small coffee table, the women bowed in prayer. Janelle thought she might fall asleep from weariness and, ashamed, was thankful for the chance to close her eyes. So many sad stories, whispered in French and Arabic.

"He hasn't paid child support in three months. I don't know how we're going to make it. Before, with his pitiful salary, we barely made ends meet. Now, impossible."

She recalled an evening last year when the same lady had shared in front of the whole group of friends and her husband, "Well, you know he doesn't make much more than minimum wage. He never has. So obviously we can't go."

Janelle had winced, for the hundredth time, at the typically demeaning remark. Now the husband was gone. He'd gotten so tired of it that he had simply walked out of the house.

And honestly, that was what she felt like doing at the moment. Standing up in the middle of prayer time and walking out, saying, "I am very sorry, but I'm too tired, and I quit." Wasn't almost twelve years enough time to invest in this ministry in France that was doomed from the start? *I quit!*

She opened her eyes to stop the barrage of thoughts, to shake herself out of the torpor. It didn't help. What she kept hearing over and over were two little words: *Go home! Go home! Go home!*

Perhaps she even said it out loud because, instead of staying for the usual half hour after prayer time to chat, eight minutes later every woman had left her house. She was alone, finally.

Every bone in her body was tired, weary. *Don't grow weary of doing good, for in due time you shall reap. . . .*

But in truth she *was* weary, and not just physically, not just from raising her kids in a different culture. Oh, yes. She was tired. But the weariness had settled into her mind and then traveled down into her heart, her very spirit. The fight had gone out of her. Maybe the faith too. Oh, how could she even tolerate such a thought!

She didn't have the strength to fight the nagging voice. She longed to go home, to the Georgia red clay, baked and cracking under the summer sky, and the music of the grasshoppers and katydids and the blinking of the lightning bugs on a muggy September evening. She wanted to sit on the porch, resting her head in her father's lap, the feel of his warm hand seeping through her cotton shirt and onto her back. She wanted to be a little girl again.

Life in this country had cost them too much. She and Brian had prepared for it, trained, spent their energy and zeal in the land, and now she was weary.

She peeked in on Sandy and Luke, sleeping soundly, left the house, and made the mile walk to the graveyard alone. Her pilgrimage. She knelt by the grave, cleared away the wilting flowers, and replaced them with a potted bright red geranium.

"I miss you," she whispered.

How in the world could she go home? Life here had cost her everything, but if she left, who would come to replace the flowers on the grave? Janelle trudged back toward the house. *Go home.*

––––––

Ted Draper was going to make it big. The graph for the Dow Jones with its erratic ups and downs was like the machine in the hospital that registered heartbeat. *His* heartbeat was the stock market, and at the present time it was soaring. Company benefits! He checked his commission runs. Over 600,000 dollars in production credits by mid-September, with several of his biggest deals forthcoming. He would easily reach the million-dollar mark in commissions before the end of the year, qualifying him for the company trip to China.

Lin Su had always begged him to make the trip again. Job pressures and little kids—and spending too much money on other things, he admitted to himself—had kept them so busy that they had put it off for way too long. But now it was going to happen. This, he thought to himself, made his hard work, his overwork, worthwhile. A trip with Lin Su and the kids to her homeland.

"Hey, Ted, the line's for you. The big client," Janet, his secretary, whispered while holding her hand over the phone.

"I'll get it in my office," he answered.

The big client. The big break. He smiled, self-satisfied. With this conversation, China was sealed. Well, maybe that was a bit overly optimistic, but it wouldn't be long.

"Hello, Dr. Kaufman! Ted Draper here . . ." His voice oozed confidence and adrenaline. Ticker tape, the graph shooting skyward, Dow Jones over the top. He had made it.

When Ted walked past the open cubicles of the younger brokers, the appropriate silence ensued. Awe. Yes, that was it. He was one of the firm's top brokers. At the ripe old age of thirty-two he had already passed many of the older brokers.

The year 1987 was turning into an amazingly profitable year, as had the preceding five years. It was the right time to get rich as a stockbroker. If you were willing to take risks, which Ted was, and if you were very bright, which he was, and if you could keep your cool while trading, which he could, then you were cut out for the brokerage business. In five years he had risen to the top ranks, and so, when he stepped into the room, the aura of awe followed him.

"Hey, Ted!" a younger broker said. "What have we got today?"

Ted shook hands, nodded eagerly, slapped a back. "We've got those three new junk bond issues coming out. Get on the phone and you can become a millionaire too!"

Go, go, go, Ted! All the way to the top! And don't you dare stop to look back!

———

Katy Lynn Pendleton checked her face in the rearview mirror as she pulled into a parking space at the Capital City Country Club. She retrieved a tube of lipstick from her purse and spread it across her lips, satisfied with the bright pink color. She reached across the seat to lock the passenger door. The minute the engine was cut and the air-conditioner went off, she almost melted. She estimated the temperature at ninety with enough muggy Georgia heat added in to wilt the most stalwart hairdo plastered with a thick layer of hair spray.

She gave a long sigh as she shut and locked the door to the driver's side and placed her keys carefully in the side pocket of her purse. She closed her eyes briefly and recalled walking into this same beautiful old sandstone building sixteen years ago for her wedding reception. The limousine had driven them from the church and let them off at the front door. Hamilton had looked perfect in his black tux with the white shirt, the gray bow tie, and the red rosebud boutonnière.

"You are absolutely exquisite," he had whispered as he helped her out of the limousine and paused to give her a long kiss. "Let's get this over with so the fireworks can really begin."

She blushed even now with the memory. Then she cleared her throat and walked determinedly to the same front door, the heels of her low pumps making a *click click click* on the smooth pavement. When she reached the door, a black man in a blue suit opened it for her, tipping his hat.

"How ya doin' today, Miz Pendleton?"

"Okay, Tom. Hot enough for you?"

"Yes, ma'am." He smiled his wide smile, the same one that had greeted her on that wedding night. For only one second their eyes met, and for that second she wished she could throw herself into his arms and sob on his shoulder. Instead, she kept her head up, played the part.

But as she stepped into the building, Tom called out softly behind her, "You gonna make it, Miz Pendleton. You're a strong woman. You gonna make it."

Katy Lynn felt the prickle of sweat on her brow even though the dining room was almost chilly from the air-conditioning. She surveyed the other women and felt both at home and as if she were from a different universe. They had so much in common, and yet, nothing at all. Or perhaps they were all pretending too.

She thought of Tom's reassuring words, *"You gonna make it, Miz Pendleton."* Well, Tom should know. He had seen it all during his forty-one years of service at the Capital City Country Club. Nothing caused him to raise his bushy black eyebrows anymore. "Human nature's all the same, Miz Pendleton. Rotten at the core."

Of that she was sure. So why the heck was she dressed in her creamy yellow suit, preparing to have lunch with her five friends, eating perfectly arranged chicken salad on a plate of porcelain? Why didn't she just tell them all the truth, spit it out in between a bite of chicken salad and a sip of vichyssoise?

If she could just keep going, she'd survive. She had survived many things, and this was simply another test of her resolve.

"Katy Lynn, you look just so pencil-thin in that outfit. Where did you find it? Saks? Or Lord & Taylor? They had the most divine sales at Saks last week!"

"Has everyone seen the article in the *Journal* this morning? That poor woman—having her whole life displayed on the front page. I always thought her husband was a crook. Nothing but a crook."

"Well, we've just booked a flight to Hawaii for spring break. The kids are thrilled. Their first time. This will be my fifth, but you get such a nice feeling every time you fly over the islands."

"We're thinking of Greece. A cruise."

Katy Lynn nodded with each tidbit of news, chewed slowly, forcing every bite down in spite of the large ball of fear that almost completely blocked her throat. "Delicious," she murmured at just the right time.

Her friends, her dear, dear childhood friends, did not notice the paleness of her cheeks beneath the painted pink blush. *Thank heavens they enjoy talking so much about themselves. They won't guess.*

"Katy Lynn, you've been quiet as a mouse. What delightful piece of gossip do you have for us today? You've always got some tasty morsel."

She cleared her throat, set down the fork, swallowed with difficulty her last bite, and said, "I think I'm getting a divorce."

Five pair of eyes stared without blinking, forks went down, friends made little humming noises in their throats.

"And if you believe that," Katy Lynn whispered after an appropriate time of silence, "I've got a wonderful little plot of land to sell you off the coast of Africa!"

The girls relaxed and laughed, pursed their lips, jabbered back and forth. "Honestly, Katy Lynn, why we ever take you seriously, I don't know!" Giggled. "You are always trying to shock us, but I didn't buy it for one second."

She relaxed and smiled. "Of course not. I didn't think you would."

Keep up appearances. Play the game. The expression on each face was priceless. They had no idea.

CHAPTER THREE

"Lissa! Time to go!"

"Coming, Dad!" She hurried out the front door, a brush in one hand, a bagel in the other, then stuffed the bagel into her mouth as she opened the car door and sat down. She pulled on the seat belt, then brushed her hair into a ponytail, wrapped it around her fingers, and secured the makeshift bun with a clip.

"Ready for another day of work?"

"Yes, sir." She took a bite of the bagel.

"And you're having another driving lesson after you finish up?"

"Yes, sir." She chewed slowly, swiped at a few crumbs.

"Need me to take you there—over by Fort Oglethorpe, isn't it?"

"No, you don't need to drive me, Dad. The instructor will pick me up at school around five. He'll let me off there too, after the lesson—at six thirty."

"Then I'll be waiting for you at six thirty."

"Thanks." She took another bite of bagel and stared out the window until she found the courage to speak. "Dad, I don't know if you saw it, but we got word about Caleb. I was wondering if maybe we—"

"Lissa, we have talked about that subject enough. I thought I told you not to bring it up again!" Her father's face reddened, his voice boomed through the car.

She flinched. "But, Dad, we've never settled anything, and I have to give an answer. . . ."

"You know good and well that I have already given an answer. It is settled." His eyes had that familiar, furious look.

Lissa shuddered. "Yes, sir."

Silence reverberated throughout the car for five minutes as her father drove down the winding road taking them from Lookout Mountain into Chattanooga. Then, as if his outburst had not occurred, he turned to her, smiling, and said, "Did you see the mail I put on your desk yesterday, Liss? Three more colleges. Good offers."

"I saw, Dad."

"Well, I hope you can find some time in your *busy* schedule"—he glanced her way and chuckled—"to fill them out. That's what that little counselor told you, wasn't it? Set some goals, have a routine. Movin' forward, girl. That's what we gotta do."

"Yes, sir."

He let her off in front of the school building, and she pecked him on the cheek—like a five-year-old.

She watched the children getting out of cars, waving, rushing with their books to the elementary school. She smiled to herself as Amber, her favorite third grader, blew three kisses to her mother and then ran toward Lissa, calling, "Miss Randall! Miss Randall!"

"What is it, Amber?"

"I finished it! I finished *A Little Princess,* and you were right. It's the best, best book I've ever read."

"I knew you'd like it. Sarah is a wonderful girl."

"She's courageous."

"That she is, Amber."

Lissa watched the little girl disappear down the hall. Precocious, eager Amber. And Sarah Crewe, the little princess. Sarah, the girl with everything. Sarah, who lost it all and kept her dignity and compassion.

She had wanted to be like Sarah when she was nine, Lissa reflected. *And now's your chance.*

What a nice thought, Lissa mused. What a nice, positive thought.

The old man in the light blue Ford was waiting by the curb in front of the administration building when she came out. She liked the snapshot view—a silver-haired gentleman in a suit, sitting in a blue Ford—that was in the foreground, while out behind loomed two beautiful magnolias and a few maples just beginning to change colors. If she looked to the right, down the hill, there was the soccer field with the Tennessee River running right beside it. A beautiful, peaceful setting, all in the shadow of Lookout Mountain, the mountain of her youth, the place where she lived. The huge picture windows that made up the west wall of the library gave a breathtaking view of the river and the mountain, and it came to symbolize for Lissa not only her past but also the rest of life—what was out there to be discovered.

She reached the Ford. Mr. MacAllister stepped out of the car and shook her hand. "Hello there, Lissa."

"Hello, Mr. MacAllister."

"Time for lesson number two. How are you feeling today?"

"Pretty good. A little nervous, I guess."

"Well, as I said, today we'll just work on confidence building. First we'll drive around Chickamauga Park. Make sure you feel secure with the basics again. We'll take it nice and easy."

"That sounds good." She got in the passenger side of Ole Bessie and put on her seat belt.

As he drove, Mr. MacAllister looked over at her periodically, asking questions. "So you work at Chattanooga Girls School?"

"Yes, sir."

"Well, you look more like you'd be a student there."

"I'm nineteen."

"And what is your job?"

"I help out in the library."

"I see. Got any plans for schooling?"

"You mean college?"

"Or high school."

"Oh, I finished high school. Here. This is my alma mater."

"Really? Well, it's a fine preparatory school, that's for sure. So have you thought about college?"

"Sure, I've thought about it. But I don't have any plans right now." She kept her hands in her lap. "I hope you'll understand, Mr. MacAllister, but I'd rather not talk about college."

"Sure, no problem." He let a few seconds of silence hang between them, then asked, "So tell me, Lissa, what do you enjoy?"

She knew he was trying to make conversation, but she couldn't do it. Her father's angry outburst from the morning had pummeled her like a sound beating. "To be honest, Mr. MacAllister, there's not much I enjoy right now."

———

When they arrived at the visitor center of Chickamauga National Military Park, Ev parked Ole Bessie in the empty lot, cut the ignition, put on the parking brake, and opened his door, motioning for the young woman to move into the driver's seat. She gave him a tight, nervous nod and opened her door, but with difficulty, almost reluctantly. Simply walking around the car to the driver's side seemed like an effort for her, as if he'd asked her to hike all the way up Lookout Mountain instead of just drive around in a park.

He waited until she was buckled in and said, "You just start out nice and easy. Remember the rearview mirror, the turn signals. Just keep to the speed limit—thirty miles per hour. Real slow."

"Yes, sir."

He watched her knuckles. She didn't flinch.

Ev wondered what exactly had happened to make her so nervous. He was thankful there was not another car on the road, a straight shot. "We'll do what they call the Chickamauga Battlefield Tour. Just follow the signs marked by a pyramid of cannonballs. Takes you around through where the Battle of Chickamauga took place, past all the monuments.

September 20 and 21, 1863. A hundred and twenty-four years ago, almost to the day. Have you been here before?"

"Yes, sir, several times. When my eighth-grade class studied the Civil War, we spent a whole day here. I find it fascinating. All the history."

As she eased Ole Bessie into the lane, Lissa sat straight up, and her face became intense. Now the knuckles clenched the steering wheel.

"You're doing fine."

She nodded, eyes boring into the autumn day on the other side of the windshield.

"You've got good speed, Lissa. Keep it at thirty."

Up ahead was only blue sky and evergreens. "We'll pass the wide open field and then take the fork to the right."

She swerved so suddenly he did not have an inkling it was coming. Suddenly she was heading directly toward the large cement statue beside the road.

"Lissa, keep your eye on the road. Slow down."

Lissa heard his words, listened to them filter through her mind, but other words were crowding in.

You'll panic again. You'll see. The cement wall is right there, there's graffiti on this one too. You're going to crash into that statue that commemorates the death of soldiers. Dead, all dead, dead like your—

She tried to control her breathing, but she felt a suffocating heat. She wanted to let down the window, but didn't dare take her hand off the steering wheel.

"Lissa!" Mr. MacAllister's voice was sharp, clear.

She felt her foot press more solidly on the accelerator. The car lunged forward, then she stamped on the brake, and the car skidded, shrieking in protest. Her hand, the right one, started shaking. Soon her whole arm was trembling as she gripped the steering wheel. It was happening again. They were going to wreck.

"It's fine, Lissa," Mr. MacAllister said as he gently pressed on his brake and reached over with his left hand to straighten the wheel. His voice was calm as the car slowed, swerving off the grass and back onto the road. "You can do this, Lissa. I know you can."

He let up on the brake. Her speed slowed from forty-five to thirty-five and then thirty. The trembling in her hands and arms eased slightly.

"There's a little parking lot up here on the left. Why don't you pull in there, Lissa?"

She was still shaking when she stopped Ole Bessie near a cannon.

Mr. MacAllister let out a long breath. "I'm sorry, Lissa. That was my fault. We went a little far today."

She nodded, staring straight ahead.

"Everything all right?"

"Fine." But she doubted she sounded convincing. He was looking at her knuckles. She forced herself to loosen the grip on the steering wheel. The hands were taut, the veins clearly visible, she knew, but gradually the whiteness left.

"You seemed apprehensive when we went by that monument. Is there anything particular that is upsetting you?"

She did not allow the expression on her face to change.

Anything in particular? Oh, not much. Just the graffiti on the wall and that look of astonishment on Momma's face and the sound of the thud. The horrible sound of the thud when the car struck. The splattering. The blood on the pavement. The scream that lasted only half a second. The silence afterward. Only that. Nothing more, sir.

When she didn't respond, Mr. MacAllister turned toward her and said, "Lissa, I will not let you fail. You hear me? I am taking care of you. You will be fine. If you have anything to tell me that might help, that would be great. But you don't have to say a thing. We're not in a hurry."

Lissa nodded and closed her eyes and thought of Caleb. *Oh yes, we are, sir. Yes, we are.*

"How was the lesson?" Dad asked when he picked her up in front of the school building.

"Okay."

"Just okay?"

"Yeah. Barely okay." *I could've killed us both. It could've happened again.*

"Well, I imagine it will take a little time."

"Yes, sir. I'm sure you're right."

Liar!

She said nothing on the drive up the mountain. Arriving at their home, her father parked his BMW in the garage beside the yellow Camaro, her car. It sat there unused, another nagging reminder of failure.

"I ate dinner with a client. Want me to fix you something?"

"No, thank you."

She quickly made a sandwich and went to her room. She tossed the mail from the colleges on the floor and picked up a letter that had arrived today.

Hey, Liss!

How are you, girl? Hanging in there? School's great. Sophomore year is a blast. You know the ropes, everybody's happy to see you back. I like my classes too. Calc III, physics. Computer science. We'll be working on Apples. Okay, I know these things aren't your cup of tea. Literature, languages . . . fine.

Please, please come for a visit. You should be here. You'd love it. Girl, you were made for academia. And the guys aren't bad either. Not bad at all.

You better write me back with the latest gossip from our dear alma mater.

Love you, Jill

She set the letter aside, got out the notebook—the one the therapist had given her and told her to write in when she was tempted to "spiral into despair"—those were the words she used—and began to write.

September 23

They all think I am crazy. I am not crazy, even if I hear voices. I am working this out. On paper. Right here. One day it will be over and done. The therapist wasn't all that helpful, but one thing she said is very true. "Learn to quiet the voices and you will learn to live again."

This proposition seems logical and the exercises she suggested pertinent. The difficulty arises when other voices crowd in—specifically my father's. I cannot understand his complete inability to face truth. He says we've discussed Caleb way too much. But it has never really been a discussion. More like an ultimatum. He'll murder me with his silence, with his plastic smile covering over the horror. He is stuck and refuses to move, and I am stuck with him.

Lissa replaced the notebook in her desk drawer.

Helena had come today. The frames were righted. The wastebasket with the shattered glass in it had been emptied.

We're building confidence.

She walked to the armoire, took down the framed photo of her with her mother, and stuffed it in a drawer, far below the notebooks. Then she did the same with the photo of her horse. "I'm sorry, Momma. But for now, I have to do this. If I am going to learn to drive again, I can't have you staring at me."

These are logical thoughts. I am getting better.

Liar, liar.

———

Ev's friends called him a prophet. It had actually started as a derogatory term. He recalled the first time it was used, thirty years ago, the day the Russians had launched Sputnik. He'd been talking to his friend Bud, who worked for the license bureau.

"That teen came to his lesson high on something. He cursed me up and down when I told him he'd fail if I had anything to say about it. I thought he was going to drive right into that brick wall. I don't think that kid should ever get his license. He'll be dead faster than you can say lickety-split. Or he'll have killed someone before he turns seventeen."

When Bud passed the kid four months later, Ev had had a premonition of trouble. Then, only weeks later, the news flashed across the radio stations—a teenager involved in a hit-and-run accident, killing a mother of three.

"Whaddaya think you are, Ev?" Bud had asked him, with a mixture of mistrust and awe. "A prophet or something?"

But it wasn't hard to see the truth. Two minutes in a car, and he knew who would be a safe driver and who wouldn't.

This new client, Lissa—he watched her climb into her father's BMW—would not be a good driver. In fact, she scared him. He rarely felt nervous with the teens. He knew the routine well. He didn't take them onto the street until he was sure they could handle the car. But she had fooled him. Obviously she had experience driving. In some ways she was poised, mature. Why did a cement statue beside a country road send her into a panic?

He cut the engine of Ole Bessie and got out, walked beside the redbrick school building to where the library was located, at the end of a grassy courtyard.

A thin woman with glasses and a smile greeted him as he stepped inside. "May I help you, sir?"

"My name is Ev MacAllister. I'm Lissa Randall's driving instructor."

"Oh, hello. Nice to meet you." Then she frowned. "I thought Lissa had her lesson an hour ago."

"We just finished. I let her off here. I, um, I don't mean to pry, ma'am, but Lissa told me she went to this school. Graduated from here."

"Yes, she did! One of the top students in her class. She was planning on attending an Ivy League college up East. A fine young woman." She frowned again. "So you don't know her story? I thought since you're teaching her how to drive again, she would have naturally . . ."

"She mentioned an accident, but she doesn't seem to want to give any details."

The woman's face creased. "Why don't you have a seat, Mr. MacAllister?" She motioned to an overstuffed chair.

"This is quite a place."

"We've got the reputation for the most complete—and comfortable—school library in the state of Tennessee." She held out her hand. "I'm Jennifer Rivers. I've been at Chattanooga Girls School for twenty-three years, and I've seen a lot of students come through this school. Many of them arrive as first graders and leave as young women, ready to face the world. Some more ready than others. But in all my years, I have never known another girl more prepared, more poised and mature than Melissa Randall."

She cleared her throat. "Until the accident, that is. Lissa was president of the Honor Council. Gave an eloquent speech at graduation—got a standing ovation from her peers. You know, that's not that easy to do among a group of bright, cutthroat, Ivy League-bound young women.

"She hadn't decided on her school, and it was getting very late in the game. She could have gone anywhere. She even had one offer for a full scholarship—to a smaller college in Tennessee. But she was undecided. So she went on one last college tour with her mother, the week after graduation. On their way home . . ." Mrs. Rivers cleared her throat again.

"They'd been up East, driven hundreds of miles, and then they were only a little ways outside of Chattanooga—on I-75. Lissa was driving, and a bad storm came up—you know how it is around here—hail the size of golf balls. The car skidded, and Lissa got it stopped in the emergency lane by an underpass. Her mother offered to drive, but . . . but she was hit by another car as she was getting into the driver's seat. Lissa watched her mother get thrown down the highway."

Mrs. Rivers took off her glasses and wiped her eyes. "She got the car stopped; they were fine. Lissa kept them from wrecking, and then her mother gets killed walking around the car. How tragic is that?"

Ev nodded and found himself staring at his shoes. One of the white laces was coming untied. He let out a long sigh. "Now I understand." He did in fact remember reading about the accident in the paper when it had happened. "Thank you for telling me."

"After that, Lissa just seemed to give up. She'd always been a very private person. You know—very bright, almost too bright. I'm afraid something snapped. She quit seeing friends, tore up her driver's license, stopped riding her horse. A lot of people around here really love Lissa. We certainly are hoping she'll pull out of it."

"Yes, well, I'm hoping to help her. Looks like you are too."

The librarian gave a tight grin. "Yes. Good day, Mr. MacAllister."

"Good day, Mrs. Rivers."

"You're deep in thought, boyfriend. Anything bothering you?" Annie's playful tone jostled Ev out of his reminiscing.

He set down his glasses on the coffee table and turned to his wife. "Hello there, young lady."

She came and pecked him on the lips.

"Nothing too much. Just a client."

"Want to tell me about it?"

Annie plopped down beside him on the sofa. No-nonsense Annie. What would he do without her? He told her what he had learned about Lissa.

Annie shook her head, wrinkled her brow. "A terrible shame. I vaguely remember reading about it." She patted Ev's hand. "You'll know how to handle her. You always do."

"Hmm. Yes. I don't know why this one seems so heavy."

Annie took his face in her hands, as if he were a child. She brushed his hair off his forehead and kissed him softly.

His sixty-five-year-old wife, the one who had worn pants to class in college when all the other girls were in cashmere sweaters and wool skirts, hadn't changed. He reached for her, ran his rough hand over the smooth cheekbones, touched the slight wrinkles beside the laughing eyes, the eyes that read right into his soul.

"I say you need to be thinking about retirement, young man."

"Why would a young man think about retirement?"

"Maybe his eyesight is going."

"Nope."

"Maybe his joints are aching—too much sitting in that old car."

"Joints are fine, Annie."

"Maybe his heart is getting just a little too soft around the edges."

"Quit trying to read my mind, girl. Anyway, you think we've got enough money coming in for me to just quit my job?" He winked at her.

"From my latest look at the finances, we're doing just fine. It's about time for you to buy that motorcycle and ride off into the wild blue yonder with your girlfriend."

He gave her hand a squeeze. "Someday soon."

They sat for a long time with her head resting against his shoulder, her hand fiddling with the crease in his pant leg. The truth was he knew exactly what was bothering him, and Annie would figure it out before long.

Tate.

CHAPTER FOUR

Janelle held the ink pen in her hand and stared at the empty page. She tried to think of something to write and winced, remembering all the times she had filled every inch of the blue aerogram with tiny cursive, explaining in detail all the events of the past days. Exclamation points. Requests for prayer. Questions. News of the children. The economic letter that folded into an envelope could never hold all the news that she scribbled home quickly at the end of a full week.

Now the page was bare. What to tell?

Dear Mom and Dad,

Well, the rentrée is over. Kids are back in school. Fourth grade for Luke. Sandy was pretty nervous about starting first grade. She has the hardest teacher in the school. They'll have to buckle down and study a little! But they've started the year well and are happy to be back with their friends.

She set the pen down. She'd skip the news about Sandy's squabble with her best friend and Luke's disappointment in not making the soccer team.

We will have our first planning meeting for the church Christmas play next week. I've got quite a bit of preparation left to do.

She set down the pen again. Normally she enjoyed the project. Not this year. It exhausted her just to think of the play. She stared at the letter. Her writing was large and uneven. Like her heart. She sighed, stood up, and went to the door.

A walk to the cemetery. Again.

The bright sun warmed her. The crisp breeze of the morning had melted into a fiercely sunny afternoon. She liked that about the south of France—the Midi, as the French called it. The blinding sun pierced her with its intensity, as if forbidding any shadowy thought. She breathed in the scent of lavender, sweet as perfume, that greeted her as she passed the green plants with their skinny stalks holding fragrant pale purple flowers. She leaned over to smell the basil in her herb garden, the healthy green leaves ready to be plucked and washed and slivered onto vine-ripened tomatoes.

She left the yard and walked down the cobbled street, past the olive trees and the vineyards. She loved this time of year—usually. The vines laden with fruit. The deep violet color of the Muscat grapes, hanging pregnant from the vine.

I am the vine, you are the branches . . . You will bear much fruit, bear much fruit, bear much fruit. I am the vine. . . .

What fruit, Lord? She felt a sting in her eyes as she observed rows and rows of vines, carefully tended. In a week, two at most, it would be time for the *vendange*. The harvest was coming late this year. Janelle stooped over and plucked one ripe grape from its bunch. She started to plop it into her mouth, then changed her mind. Even Muscat grapes tasted bitter to her this year.

She entered the ancient cemetery, where stone markers testified to hundreds of years of burials—hundreds of years, and this one only 738 days old. When would she stop counting? She knelt on the ground and touched the petals of the red geranium.

"You should be starting kindergarten," she whispered.

Things will get better once the rentrée *is over,* she told herself. *This is always a hard time of year.*

The day dragged on, a long lazy afternoon, punctuated at times by a gust from the mistral. At three o'clock she made a cup of coffee and stared at the half-filled aerogram until her eyes went blurry. What was the matter with her?

Go home! Go home!

The phone rang, startling her out of the torpor. She answered automatically. *"Oui, allô?"*

"Allô, Janelle?"

Lydie. Again.

"Thank goodness you're there," Lydie continued in hurried French. "May I come by? This *rentrée* is absolutely *un catastrophe!* I need to talk to you about Généviève's teacher. And about Charles. He's been gone every night this week. . . ."

Janelle wished that just once Lydie or another of her friends, these ladies with whom she shared and prayed and worked, would ask how *she* was dong. Didn't they realize that the *rentrée* meant fresh grief for her? Over two years since they had buried little Josh in the ground, but still her heart ached, a hollow hurting that nothing seemed to fill. She was too tired for this! She wanted to go home! She did not want to listen to Lydie.

She willed a prayer to form on her lips, but it died before it was birthed. After Lydie left she would buy the last school supplies for Luke and Sandy. And fix dinner. Yes, dinner.

Her mind was a fog of vague obligations. She closed her eyes and pictured the grapes, ripe, full, juicy, ready. At one time, that had been her life. Not now.

The doorbell rang, and she went to answer.

———

Ted Draper walked into his office, sat down at the desk, and smoothed his hand over the cherry finish. This new baby had cost him 3,500 dollars, but with all the money he was making, it didn't even cause his wife to blink. They were getting rich! Rich! He checked his commission run and smiled to see it had risen to 625,000 dollars in just a few days. A few days! He caressed the sleek silver frame holding the photo of his family—taken by the most expensive professional photographer in Atlanta. Lin Su looked stunning in her black and red kimono, and the kids were picture-perfect cute.

Ted allowed himself a minute of deep satisfaction. The years were paying off. He had started out in the Atlanta brokerage firm Goldberg, Finch and Dodge, selling to individuals—the bottom rung of the ladder. "Dialing for dollars," they called it. His goal was to call anyone who had a pulse. It didn't matter how much money they had; as long as they were alive and could answer the phone, he would call them, talk to them, offer them his services.

Ted excelled at dialing for dollars. He had a smooth, generous voice, plenty of charisma, and a real personal interest in the smallest client. Soon he was dialing for thousands, and the clients on the other end of the line had bundles of money to invest. The biggest break had come a few weeks ago when Jerry Steinman, the wisest and oldest broker in the company, announced that he'd be retiring. Jerry liked Ted, saw potential in him, and decided to refer his biggest clients to him. Ted was more than happy to accept.

"The guy's smart, gregarious, charming. He's got an eye for profit. He'll do you well."

Ted had heard Jerry's presentation to Dr. Kaufman. Jerry Steinman's clients trusted their retiring broker implicitly. Before Ted knew it, he was dealing with million-dollar portfolios.

That was how the reclusive novelist S. A. Green became his client. He fiddled with the file folder on his desk, opened it, and recalled Jerry's comments on the novelist's sporadic career.

"Just be patient, Ted. Stella"—that was what Jerry called her—"will do you right. Invest well, and you'll make plenty of money too. She's shrewd but careful. She doesn't trust many people, but if you do her well, she'll trust you. In the almost thirty years we've worked together, she's been very generous to me. I'm handing you a fine little jewel. Just be sure you handle it with care."

A jewel? Jerry was a master of understatement. More like a gold mine!

Ted flipped through the folder and studied S. A. Green's assets. Strong stocks, reliable mutual funds, wise investing over many years that had paid off. The lady was worth a fortune. By quick calculations, Ted figured that Jerry made over fifty grand off of her assets each year, and that wasn't counting the years when she released a novel. Amazingly, Jerry was handing him the account just when Miss Green's new novel was coming out. That was very good news!

Ted reread the short message that Jerry had passed along to him.

> Jerry—Terrible shame about your retirement. Who do you think you are, leaving my accounts in the hands of this young whippersnapper? I'm trusting you on this, Jerry. You know better than to get on my bad side.
>
> As for the money, this Ted Draper should be receiving the advance check from Eddy Clouse soon. You know the ropes. Make sure Mr. Draper does too. Put the whole amount into the foundation, please. Blue chip stocks, mutual funds. As always. I know this is repetitive, but I imagine Mr. Draper will read this letter too.
>
> Thank you, Jerry. I'm putting a little something in the mail for you— hopefully it will make your retirement all the sweeter. Don't make me sorry.
>
> Your friend,
> Stella

Ted wondered immediately what "little something" Jerry had received from Stella. He didn't dare ask. But when Jerry came by his desk later in the afternoon to discuss the different accounts, Ted asked the other question that was bothering him.

"Jerry, what is this foundation that Stella Green is talking about? It looks like the great majority of her royalties go straight into the Stash Green Cash Foundation. What is that?"

"You know, she's never told me. I send the money, and I don't ask questions. That's our deal."

"You think it's legit—all that money going into a nice little non-taxable foundation?"

Jerry Steinman took off his black-rimmed glasses and dangled them on two fingers, brushing his hand through his thinning gray hair. He rested his elbow on Ted's desk. Ted studied his face, lined with years of fording bull and bear markets, dispensing wisdom, making tough calls for clients; Jerry carried the worry and tension on the inside, far down in his gut.

When Jerry didn't answer, Ted continued, "Hey, what's percolating in there?"

"I'll level with you, Ted. You're going to be her broker, so you deserve to know this. The woman is an enigma. Maybe she's simply paranoid, maybe it's just that touch of genius that makes her such a darn good novelist. I don't know. I've chosen to honor her wishes to remain anonymous to the world and not to meddle with her affairs. That foundation has baffled me since its inception years ago. But the way I see it is this: if there's something shady going on, no one's found it out for all these years. She's not just eccentric. She's smart. Everything I've done for her has been completely aboveboard."

"Of course. I understand."

Jerry relaxed a little, gave a tired grin. "Don't be intimidated by her. She's got a lot of hot air and"—he added with a wink—"a wicked sense of humor. But it's nothing that an intelligent, savvy young guy like you can't handle. I think you'll grow to appreciate Stella."

Ted certainly hoped so. Maybe someday he'd receive a "little something" from her.

"Jerry, you're the one who's taught me through the years that it's best to meet my clients face-to-face, that it gives me a chance to read their minds, understand how they spend their money. You think I could go meet this woman? Where'd you say she lives?"

"Didn't say. I'm a hundred percent sure she won't invite you to her house. Perhaps if you write her a note you could convince her to meet you in some out-of-the-way spot. Don't be too eager, but write her and see what she says. Let her set it up—whether it's a meeting in a restaurant or simply a phone call. Follow her lead, and you'll be all right."

Later that afternoon, Ted sat down to compose a letter to the novelist:

Dear Miss Green,

I consider it a great privilege to be handling your accounts. Jerry Steinman is a dear friend, and I appreciate his confidence in my work. I assure you I will do my best to handle your portfolio with utmost care.

My normal procedure is to meet with new clients to gain a better understanding of their goals for the future. Would there be a time and place we could meet?

Congratulations on the new novel. I look forward to working with you.

Sincerely,
Ted Draper

Stella. He chuckled to himself, remembering the character Stella from *A Streetcar Named Desire.* All he could see was that poster of Marlon Brando, looking like a pent-up stallion in the role of Stanley, and Kim Hunter playing the pitiful Stella. She'd won an award for the role, he recalled, along with Vivien Leigh in the role of Blanche DuBois. 1951. Before he was born, but he enjoyed watching old movies. Jerry's description of this Stella sounded nothing like the self-effacing, weak character in the movie.

He wanted to meet this Stella. *Yeah, me and about half a million of her fans.*

Jerry came back by the desk, looked over Ted's shoulder at the letter, and slapped Ted on the back. "You'll hate her at first, but give her time. She doesn't need a lot of pampering. Just do her right."

Ted opened the portfolio that belonged to Dr. Harold Kaufman. Fifty-three years old, prominent neurosurgeon, made a bundle. Jerry had written the doctor's profile: conservative, blue chip. Ted had met the man. A bit frenetic—too much energy, too much money—Dr. Kaufman rarely even looked at his portfolio. All that mattered was that his stocks were going up. His secretary kept up on every detail, though.

"Hey, Ted!" A colleague peeked his head into Ted's office. "What you got on that new junk bond?"

"It'll pay off, don't you worry."

Not for Stella Green or Dr. Harold Kaufman, but he had other clients. The risk takers. For instance, Coleman Little. Now there was a profile he liked: speculative, high risk. This junk bond was perfect for him. Time to start dialing again. China, here we come! *Go, go, go!*

———

Silvano finished reading the manuscript at two a.m. He almost wished he hadn't. This novel was different from Green's other ones. Private. Intimate. Personal. Better.

No, not better, but something. There were phrases that haunted him the next day. He couldn't get them out of his head. Especially the one about the subtle way a bad habit—that's all it was—twisted its way into the protagonist's life. The way it slipped into the story on page 109, right when he was cheering the protagonist along, stopped him short. Foreshadowing, and not just within the novel. He felt again like a finger was jabbing him in the chest and yelling *This is a bad habit! Be careful!*

Problem was, he could not figure out exactly which of his habits was the culprit. Every other ad on TV was warning about lung cancer. Well, he wasn't a chain smoker; surely just three cigarettes a day couldn't be the problem. Lying—yes, he'd told Ed Clouse that he hadn't opened the burlap bag, and no, of course he had not mentioned making the photocopy. Was that stealing? He preferred to call it borrowing—and for a good cause. He might be young and inexperienced, the bottom rung of the ladder, but he had ambition and he had vision.

This is your big chance, Silvo!

He knew what the others at the office whispered about him. Brash, macho, obnoxious, overconfident, arrogant.

He was Italian, *per l'amor di Dio*! He grew up in Rome, and when you grow up around beauty—art, women, sculptures—you learn to appreciate the finer things in life. He may be young, but he'd lived long enough to know that his ideas were usually the best. He was going to go places whether this publishing house liked it or not. People would learn to respect Silvano Rossi.

They had to, and soon.

You are our only hope, Silvo. For the family, for our honor. You go to America—the land of opportunity! Papa's sister has done it—worked hard and escaped poverty and made more money than she could ever have hoped in Italy. Papa is not here to do it for us, so it falls on you—the oldest son, the smart one. Honor and money. You will take care of us, yes? Anything can happen in America!

He glanced at the calendar—September 23—and imagined his mother in the little tourist shop by St. Peter's, selling postcards and trinkets, rosary beads and key chains holding tiny dangling replicas of the cathedral. And gelato. It had almost hit a hundred degrees yesterday in Rome. Yes, Mamma would be scooping out gelato, then brushing her hand across her sweaty brow as the ice cream dripped from the scoop onto her blouse. All the while smiling, not showing that inside she was worrying if she could pay the rent at the end of the month.

That image sealed it. Somehow he'd find Miss S. A. Green and get an interview. Then he'd sell it—to *Persona* magazine, perhaps, or *Life*. Dirty journalism, some would call it. Who cared? He wasn't planning on staying at Youngblood forever. He had other plans. For the honor of his family.

He glanced at the photocopied manuscript on the little bedside table. Ignoring that jabbing finger, he switched off his lamp and went to sleep.

Silvano looked in the mirror the next morning. He wore a well-cut Italian suit, Italian leather loafers, and a silk tie; his face was slightly tanned, and his thick black hair was combed back like the Italian star of yesteryear, Rudolph Valentino. He headed to the office, arrived early as usual, made the espresso for himself, and reviewed the work for the day.

An hour later, Leah stopped by his desk. She wore her habitual dark blue suit—a rather inexpensive light wool jacket and skirt. He'd often wanted to get the tight-lipped, middle-aged secretary into something more becoming. She could be a lovely woman, in a Gucci suit with the right makeup and a few accessories. She didn't have enough self-esteem.

Leah whispered, "Boss wants to see you, Silvano. He seems riled."

Silvano brushed his hands over his suit, straightened his tie, and walked the hundred feet from his small cubicle to Ed Clouse's office. "Yessir?"

"Oh, hello, Silvano. Yes, come in."

"Can I get you your cup of espresso?"

"No, no. Not right now. Have a seat, Silvano." The boss cleared his throat. "Listen, I just got off the phone with Frank Blanton. He's irate. Says you chopped his manuscript to pieces without any forewarning. I gave you Blanton because he's a good author who needs minimal editing. What gave you the idea to rip the thing apart?"

"It wasn't good, sir," Silvano stated simply, but with authority. "I've read his other work and I've talked to Deborah about her editing of his previous manuscripts. Usually they are clean, but this one wasn't."

"You should have given Frank some warning."

"I figured he's a pro—he can take some serious criticism."

"Yes, but with the deadline we've got, he says he'll never have time to make all the changes you suggest. It won't be ready."

"Mr. Clouse, ultimately it's Youngblood whose reputation is on the line. You've always said we will not keep publishing authors if their work doesn't continue to meet our high standards. Frank's a great author, but he's written a bad book. I'll work with him, and we'll get it ready for spring."

"Spring is too late!" Ed bellowed. "If you can't get this straightened out in the next few days, I'm going to stick Deborah back on it, and that will not make me happy. You understand?"

"Yessir. I'll call Frank."

"Don't make me regret hiring you, you hear me?"

Silvano felt the burn climb up his face. "Yessir."

He stalked to his desk, cursing Frank Blanton and Ed Clouse under his breath. Someday this lousy publishing house would wake up and realize just how much he had to offer and then it would be too late for them! Who cared about that dried-up mystery writer, anyway! He had his hands on something much more lucrative. Soon enough, Eddy Clouse would be begging him for suggestions. And his main suggestion, the gut feeling he had ever since he read the first page of S. A. Green's unnamed manuscript, was *Find the woman, interview her. See what makes her tick. She's amazing. Find out why.*

———

Katy Lynn came back from the grocery store to an unlocked house. That meant that Gina was home. "Gina! Gina!" she called up the stairs while setting the brown grocery bag on the counter.

No answer.

"Gina, could you come down and help me unload the groceries from the car?"

Still no answer.

Exasperated, Katy Lynn climbed the stairs and marched into her daughter's room. Typical teenage disorder surrounded her—clothes on the floor, schoolbooks tossed onto the bed. The bathroom door was closed.

Katy Lynn hammered her fist on the door. "Gina! Do you hear me?"

No answer.

"Open the door, now!"

"Go away, Mom. Please just leave me alone." Gina's voice was a hoarse whisper. She'd been crying.

Katy Lynn's tone softened. "Gina, what's the matter? Can we talk?"

She thought of the ice cream and other frozen goods thawing in the car. She did not have time for Gina's melodramatic antics.

"Not now, Mom. Please."

Katy Lynn left the room and went back to the car. She had a fifteen-year-old daughter and a forty-one-year-old able-bodied husband, but she always unloaded the groceries. She wanted to strangle them both. Then she caught sight of the ripped-open envelope and the letter beside it, lying on the kitchen counter. She picked it up and slid the letter out.

Dear Gina,

I need to tell you something that will be hard to hear. I wanted to tell you in person, but my schedule is crazy, and you need to know.

I won't be coming back to the house anymore. I've filed for a divorce. I've gotten an apartment not too far from your school, so you can stay over on the weekends.

I'm sorry to write this to you. Your mother and I have discussed this and think it is best that we divorce.

But I want you to know that I love you. I really do. The problem is between your mother and me—it has nothing to do with you.

I love you, Gina, and we will talk soon.

Dad

The scoundrel! What kind of way was that to tell his daughter about the divorce! He'd promised to come over tomorrow night so they could talk, the three of them.

Katy Lynn ran back up the stairs and banged on the bathroom door, panicky now. "Gina! Gina! Open up. I'm sorry about your father's letter. That was not how we had agreed on telling you. Open up, sweetie. Let me talk to you."

Several minutes later, the door opened and Gina stared at her mother with hollow eyes. Without a word she held out her arms for her mother to see. "I feel better now."

In bright red welts on the insides of Gina's arms, Katy Lynn read the message. *I hate Dad.*

One more interminable dinner with her father. Lissa wanted to grab the newspaper from his hands and hurl her plate of spaghetti in his face. *Talk to me, Dad!* She had tried to say this, even scream it, hundreds of times, but it never got past the catch in her throat. The anger proved to her that she was at least alive, that the icy numbness that invaded every inch of her being could sometimes change to fire.

Your father has a different way of grieving, Lissa. You have to give him time and space.

The therapist's words had seemed wise a year ago, but now they drove her crazy. All she asked for was a minimum of communication without his hiding behind a copy of the *Chattanooga Times* or the *New York Times*.

She heard voices in her head, but what did he hear? Nothing! He filled his ears with static—from the radio, the TV, the hi-fi. Now with the new video device he could even program it to record shows and watch them at night. Denial. Her father was in denial. She might struggle with debilitating depression, but he was worse.

At least I am trying, Dad. I am trying. I went to that counselor, I take those little pills. I'm relearning to drive.

Lissa glanced at the back page of the newspaper—an article about a football player from Penn State. She hoped her father would not read that one. Then it would be a conversation about "When you get to college . . ." and "You need to seriously consider those scholarships . . ." and "Lissa, you can't just sit around at that little library table all day. It's not healthy."

Healthy or not, the library was where she wanted to be. She felt safe there, surrounded by shelves of books, the books of her childhood and teenage years. Here in this house she felt trapped, imprisoned by her father's refusal to communicate.

She wanted to grab his shoulders and shake him and yell at the top of her lungs, "I am sorry she died! It was an accident, don't you know! Even smart, obsessive, perfectionist daughters make mistakes. Say something to me! Forgive me! Or do you just want for me to die too? Is that it, Daddy? Do you want me to disappear? I'll leave!"

She wondered at times if his obsession with college was in fact a desire to be rid of her, so he would not have to face his daughter—the girl who was responsible for his wife's death—every morning at 7:27 on the hardwood steps of the house on East Brow Road.

Sweetheart, don't let yourself get overwhelmed by the details. Just take it one day at a time.

Momma had understood, had read her mind as if Lissa had handed her a documented version of her diary. Momma had recognized and admitted that her daughter had a screw loose in her overactive brain. Intellect cost something. It cost Lissa sanity. And friends.

I did not ask to be born smart! They all thought it was easy for me to succeed, to make the grades, to be the best. No, it was hard, it was torture. All I wanted was to be normal.

Lissa took a bite of spaghetti.

Never good enough, never good enough. Failure. Failure.

If only her father would talk to her, she might stop hearing those other voices in her head.

CHAPTER FIVE

FRIDAY, SEPTEMBER 25

In the predawn light, Ev sat on the porch, a cup of steaming coffee in his hands, rocking back and forth, back and forth. Together with the Almighty, he awaited the sunrise. In September it peeked over the oak tree at the far end of the property. He preferred December, when it rose in the open vista of the front yard, illuminating Lookout Mountain far in the distance.

In the stillness of the dusky morning, Ev began his day. He called it the journey inward, the preparation for everything that would open up during the next twenty-four hours. He settled his mind, took a sip of coffee, and watched the sky shed its darkness—a yellow streak, a pinkish-orange ray of light.

Ev spoke out loud. "If you don't mind my saying so, Lord, this is a particularly beautiful sunrise. Thank you for giving me eyes to see it. Thank you for another day. You made it; I will rejoice in it."

He forced his mind clear of other thoughts and waited. Stillness, he had learned, did not come naturally. He practiced it. Sometimes, as he waited, he heard the Lord's voice coursing through his spirit almost audibly. Other times he heard nothing, but he felt filled up and satisfied and understood.

Eventually he voiced his concerns for the day. "Lord, it's about Lissa. You've known it for all of time, that in this September of my life she'd show up on the curb and need to learn to live. I do want to help her. But I'm getting older, and my heart is weak, and I don't like to feel afraid. You know why I feel afraid. You know I don't like it a bit. I'm betting that you have something up your sleeve. So be it, but I'm warning you, Lord. It may not come without a fight."

He gave a long sigh, letting his breath out as if he were practicing yoga. Another sip of coffee.

Then he moved through the other people on his list. First of all, Annie. Always Annie. Then the kids and the grandkids. Then the others, the students, the prisoners, the little girl they sponsored in Ethiopia, the patients at Good Shepherd Rehabilitation Center, the young couple at church who were getting a divorce. Mrs. Avery, the neighbor who needed help with her car. On and on, a stream-of-consciousness conversation with the Almighty. Ev prayed, eyes opened to the dawning day.

––––––

The cup of espresso sat in the middle of Eddy Clouse's desk, the innocent alibi in case someone came in earlier than expected. On the other side of Eddy's spacious office, Silvano poked through the file cabinet that he had unlocked with a paper clip and a magnet—a little trick he had learned as a schoolboy. *G.* He shuffled through the manila files—Golding, Good, Gould, Grandfeld, Grant, Green. Green! S. A. Green.

He took the folder from the file cabinet and hurried to the photocopier in the back room, which he had already turned on. Immediately he began placing each paper from the Green file under the heavy top. The whirling of the machine magnified the beating of his heart, and he glanced over his shoulder, feeling a mixture of guilt and excitement. Again and again he pressed the start button until soon thirty pages were neatly stacked in the receiving tray. He clicked off the copier, then the light in the little room, and pulled the door shut. With the photocopies safely tucked in an envelope under his arm, he stuffed the *G* folder back into its rightful spot between Grant and Groenburg in Eddy's filing cabinet, pushed the drawer shut, removed the now lukewarm espresso from the boss's desk, and walked into his own office, where he stashed the envelope at the bottom of his slush pile.

Fatto! Mission accomplished. A self-satisfied grin formed on his lips. Tonight he'd have some very interesting reading to do. He could hardly wait.

———

Lissa waved good-bye as the third-grade class left the library.

Amber ran over and gave her a hug. "I'm going to read the rest of the book tonight! I can't wait, Miss Randall. *Misty of Chincoteague* is my favorite book of all time!"

"I thought you said that about *A Little Princess.*"

Amber furrowed her brow. "Well, Sarah is my favorite people heroine, and Misty is my favorite horse heroine. That's it!"

Lissa chuckled a little. "Then I won't dare mention *Born to Trot.* You know that Marguerite Henry wrote that one too?"

"I know. I'll check it out next week. But first I have to finish *Misty,* and then *Sea Star* and then *Stormy, Misty's Foal.* Did you know there were three books about *Misty?*"

"I do know, and I've read them all! Now run on—your class is already out in the hall."

Lissa watched the child leave and felt a chill shoot down her back and legs and then that old familiar ache in her heart. Ten years ago she had been Amber, excitedly choosing books to check out of this library each week, listening happily to Mrs. Rivers's suggestions: *A Wrinkle in Time, Tom Sawyer, The Secret Garden, A Little Princess.* And the *Misty* books— all three of them. In the third grade she had fallen in love with reading, and that had been the only love story of her life. Until Caleb.

———

Stella Green read the letter from Ted Draper, written on stationery with the heading *Goldberg, Finch and Dodge.* She folded the paper in two with a frown and absently scribbled on the back. She didn't much like the tone in his letter. Self-confident. Overconfident. But she trusted Jerry Steinman. He'd kept every one of his promises to her, especially about the foundation. He'd faithfully and fiercely guarded her desire for anonymity. He'd completed the business triangle—Ed Clouse, Jerry Steinman, and Stella. Too bad he'd decided to retire. She let out a sigh and traveled back more than thirty-five years to when the happy, complicit partnership had begun.

The shrill ringing of the phone called out to Stella as she picked a hand-ful of raspberries off the bush outside the kitchen. She tossed the berries into the sink and wiped her hands on her apron before picking up the receiver. "Yes?"

"Mrs. Green? May I speak to Mrs. S. A. Green?"

"Who is this?" she spat out, sweeping a hand through the wisps of hair that clung to her perspiring face.

"Well, nice to hear your voice, Mrs. Green. My name is Samuel Ernst from the Washington Post, *and I would like to schedule an interview with you—"*

"How did you get my number?"

"Your publisher gave it to me—only because I assured him it was for an important interview for the Post.*"*

"Don't give interviews!"

"Yes, I've heard that, Mrs. Green."

"Miss Green."

"Excuse me, Miss Green. But this is the Washington Post, *and we thought that since your book has become so popular, you would naturally be interested in answering a few questions from your public."*

"I am not interested."

"It could surely help with sales of the book. It's already skyrocketing, and your publisher believes that a little personal history would push it even further along."

"Not interested."

"But I'm talking about . . . about money and . . ." She heard him think-ing, trying to come up with something enticing. "Fame."

"Did I ever say I was interested in money or fame?"

"No, ma'am, but I thought—"

"Well, you thought wrong! I'm not interested in anything at all you have to offer, and I am not available for an interview, and do not call again or I'll send the police after you for disrespecting my privacy! And you tell that publisher that if he ever gives my number out again, I'll send my next manuscript to his biggest competitor! You tell him that!" She slammed the receiver onto the black phone piece, wiped her hands across her face, and started out the screened back door.

Then she turned in her tracks and went into the office, searching through a mound of unorganized papers until she found the business card.

Youngblood Publishers, Inc. She had scribbled a phone number under the printed address. Now she picked up the receiver and dialed the number impatiently.

After three rings, a woman's voice answered, "Youngblood Publishers, Edmond Clouse's office. How may I help you?"

"I need to speak to Mr. Clouse! Immediately!"

"I'm sorry, ma'am, but Mr. Clouse is in a meeting. I can take your number and have him—"

"You tell Mr. Edmond Clouse," Stella spat into the phone, "that if he ever wants to see another manuscript from me, he'd better come to the phone now!"

"And who may I say is calling?" the secretary, obviously intimidated, asked.

"Tell him whoever you want, but you get him to the phone!"

It took the woman two minutes and twenty-two seconds to locate the editor, which gave Stella ample time to load her ammunition.

"Miss Green?" A man's voice came on the line, out of breath. "Is that you?"

"You bet it's me, Mr. Clouse, and I'm madder than a hornet! I thought we had an understanding. You promised me there would be no phone calls, no reporters. And you let some hot shot journalist call me at home and ask for an interview! I have a good mind to take my book and move to another publishing house right this very instant."

"Miss Green. Forgive me. Please let me explain—"

"I don't want any explanation, you hear me? I want anonymity. Now

I'll have to change my phone number before that thieving reporter gives it out to every sleazy journalist out there. Do you understand me?"

Edmond Clouse replied meekly, "Yes, ma'am. I am so sorry for the mistake. I will call the journalist immediately and have him destroy the number."

"Oh, it's too late for that. You certainly are a trusting soul. Break your promise to me and expect someone else to honor his? The only person in the book business that I ever want to hear on the other end of the phone line is you! And that is to tell me how the book is doing and what the royalties are. Is that clear?"

"Very clear, Miss Green."

"Good." She slammed down the phone.

Stella couldn't help but smile at the memory. She and Ed had both been young, inexperienced. Still, he was a good publisher with a lot of business sense. He'd suggested Jerry Steinman to her for her broker.

"If you really want anonymity, Miss Green, let Jerry and me deal with the paperwork. We'll send you monthly reports if you like."

She could not complain. The plan had worked well for all these years. The foundation was thriving. But she wanted to make absolutely sure that the young, talented Mr. Ted Draper understood the rules of the game. She picked up the phone, flattened the crumpled letter, and found the phone number.

After two rings, a man answered. "Ted Draper."

"Mr. Draper. This is Stella Green."

"Stella!" he sang through the line, his voice warm and assured.

"Miss Green."

"Excuse me, of course. Miss Green. Thank you for calling. It's good to hear your voice. How are you today? And how may I help you?"

"You may help me by stopping the sweet talk and getting down to business. I need to know I can trust you, and I do that better face-to-face."

"Tell me when and where to meet you, and I'll be there."

She smiled with satisfaction as his voice became professional. "You know Chicago?"

"Like the back of my hand."

"The Berghoff, 17 West Adams Street. Lunch, 12:30 next Tuesday, September 29. Be on time. I don't tolerate lateness."

"Yes, ma'am. I'll be there."

"Good." She mashed the button on the phone until she heard a dial tone.

He seemed compliant. But one could never tell. Better to meet him in person. Much better.

————

Perspiration dripped down Janelle's back as she waited in the Marseille airport for Brian's plane to arrive. Fifteen minutes late. She was sitting in a low metal chair in the big open room, watching humanity pass by. The screen announcing the flight still proclaimed *Retardé* without saying how late it would be. She didn't use to feel afraid when Brian flew back and forth from Algeria. Now, with the latest events of violence, it was only natural to be anxious, she told herself.

But that wasn't the real reason. For most of their twelve years in France she had never felt terror, a debilitating fear, a premonition of tragedy at every turn. Before, she trusted. Now she panicked. If something happened to Brian too—

This line of thinking was preposterous!

Fill your mind with things above.

What things?

God is good, God is love.

God allowed my son to die!

She fought the tears, blotted her eyes with a handkerchief, and concentrated on the people walking by: veiled women wearing the *hijab*, brown-skinned men ushering the veiled women around, a French mother pulling her small children close as she cast a suspicious glance toward the men.

This was the new France, with its open hostility between the *maghrebins*—the North Africans—and the French. Distrust. The feeling every Frenchman had, but most did not utter, was something she understood all too well.

Go home!

The North Africans were not going home, of that Janelle was sure. Home now was France, no matter how unwelcome the second generation of *maghrebins* felt. What did the young North Africans know of Tunisia and Algeria and Morocco? Janelle wished that Brian's work with the radio station didn't take him away so often, didn't ask him to fly over hostile waters in the Mediterranean. She used to love the adventure, anticipate the all-night prayer vigils, the clandestine meetings, the hurried supplies shipped to Algeria and Morocco on a boat.

Not now. Intrigue, danger, adventure. It all terrified her. What she wanted most of all was to have Brian, Luke, and Sandy sitting with her around the table, enjoying a delicious meal. Happy, healthy, safe. She longed for this. Was it so hard for the Lord to answer? Did she not deserve this after what had happened?

I cannot think straight right now, she had confessed finally to her parents yesterday in the aerogram, sealed shut with a crease and a lick of the flap. *Everything about life seems hard. Very hard.* Now she wished she could reach through the postal services and retrieve her letter. It would only make them worry more.

She realized she was nibbling her lip. She brushed her hands through her hair and glanced back at the listing for the arriving planes. With a sigh of relief she read the one word she longed to see: *Arrivé.*

Ole Bessie was parked by the curb when Lissa walked out into the late September afternoon. Beyond the light blue car, the sky boasted a perfectly cloudless deeper blue, almost sapphire, with Lookout Mountain standing off to the right.

Mr. MacAllister, who was bending down beside Ole Bessie to talk to a young boy, had replaced his seersucker suit with a striped button-down and a pair of khaki pants held in place by leather suspenders. His tie was a strange shade of burgundy, and the tennis shoes were still dirty, blue and white.

Lissa smiled as she watched his animated conversation with Eric Dudley, who lived across the street from the school and routinely came by to taunt the girls.

"Well, Mr. MacAllister, she's a real beauty. I guarantee she's worth a lot. My dad sells cars and he knows." The boy frowned. "But if you wanted to sell it to my dad, you'd have to take the sign off the sides."

"I'll keep that in mind, Eric," Mr. MacAllister said, shaking Eric's hand. "See you later."

"Good-bye."

"You're making friends quickly," Lissa commented, coming to the car.

"Hello, Lissa," Mr. MacAllister said, going around to the driver's side and getting in the car. "Yes, well, he looks like a rascal. Caught him trying to take something out of another car, and when I confronted him, he came up with quite a tale about his father's car business."

"He *is* a rascal. You've got that right." She opened the passenger door and climbed in, put on the seat belt, and took a long, slow breath. Mr. MacAllister started the ignition and Ole Bessie was off.

"I thought we'd head back to the park today."

"All right." She was careful to keep her hands settled lightly on her lap. No clenched fists, no white knuckles.

"Back in the early 1800s the town of Chickamauga was just a big old plantation. Cherokee Indians lived nearby, peacefully. They helped General Jackson win his victory over the British in the Battle of Horseshoe Bend. I guess you studied all that?"

She knew Mr. MacAllister was trying to calm her down, make her think of things other than her fear of driving. She glanced at him, thankful.

"Yes, I remember the guide mentioning something about that. But I really don't know anything else about the Cherokees."

"They called this area their home—called it Crawfish Springs, named after one of their chiefs. They lived here peacefully all throughout the first three decades of the 1800s—until they were driven out in 1838. The Trail of Tears."

Lissa felt a tiny prick of perspiration form above her lip. She had studied that. Massacres, cruelty, blood . . .

"A terrible mistake by the American government; a blemish, a scar on our national identity, even if we try to cover it up . . ."

He said something else, but Lissa did not hear him. Her attention turned to the brown billboard in front of them, directing traffic into the right-hand lane for Chickamauga National Military Park. She didn't want to get back into the driver's seat. Instead of the sound of Mr. MacAllister's voice recounting history, all Lissa could hear were the voices.

Failure! All your fault! This is your trail of tears.

―――――

If ever there was a day to drive in the park, this was it. Silently, with a fullness of satisfaction in his heart, Ev complimented the Lord for His continued extravagance on this perfect early autumn day. He also prayed that Lissa's self-confidence would grow, buoyed by the bright sun and the trees making friendly shadow pictures on the pavement as the light seeped through their leaves.

Ev parked Ole Bessie in the lot beside the white-columned stone house that was now the visitor center. Three cannons sat in front of the stately home. The American flag rippled in the breeze. Deer grazed on the other side of the street. Four other cars were parked in the lot, none of them near to Ole Bessie. He had chosen carefully.

"Okay, Lissa. It's your turn." He opened his door and got out.

Lissa unbuckled the seat belt, opened her door, and walked around the front of Ole Bessie. When they were each in the opposite seats, she looked at him, blinked her deep brown eyes, and pulled the seat belt across her lap. Her eyes were dark with agitation and a hint of fear. Her posture changed, she stiffened, and her knuckles became eight miniature mountains as she held the steering wheel, then reached for the key in the ignition. In that moment, Ev made a decision.

"Wait, Lissa. Hold on a second." He swiveled so that he was turned toward her. "Why don't we back up a little, start over. Let's pretend you've never been in the driver's seat before."

She gave him a quizzical glance.

"Pretend you know nothing. Pretend . . ." He searched his mind for something to convince her. "Pretend you're the heroine in the most beloved book in the school library. She's clever, she's capable, she's even courageous. But she doesn't know how to drive. *And that's okay.* She's not a failure. She just doesn't know. We're at the start of the novel. Can you do that for me, Lissa?"

He watched her hands, so tight on the steering wheel. The delicate face lined with tension and fear, the way she held her shoulders so taut and stiff. The girl was terrified. She was staring out into the distance, hearing him but seeing something else.

Ev tried to imagine what she saw. He'd found the article of the wreck on microfiche at the local library. A terrible tragedy. What did Lissa see now?

He spoke softly, still turned toward her. "There is a delicate balance that eventually becomes innate when driving the car—the push of the foot on the gas pedal. The lifting. The slow release and the pressure on the brake. The light grasp of the steering wheel, the touch of the finger that flicks on the turn signal or the windshield wipers. During their first driving lesson, my students always wonder how in the world they will master so many details at once."

She looked over at him. Her forehead was an accordion of wrinkles. Such a young face to be wrinkled! Her eyes were glassy brown. He thought she might cry.

But then Lissa took a long breath. The shoulders slumped a little; she released her grip on the steering wheel and folded her hands in her lap. "Okay, Mr. MacAllister. I'm ready. You tell me what to do."

He relaxed too. "The first thing you do is you pay attention. That is the law of driving, Lissa. Paying attention."

———

He knew. Mr. MacAllister knew why she was afraid. Somehow he had heard of the details of the wreck, of that Lissa was certain. And relieved, actually. She would not have to recount it in all its gory details. He knew, and what was much better, he understood. She wondered briefly if the man read minds. No one else could have told him what the voices screamed at her. Yet he had said it, plain, simply, with the kindness of his pale blue eyes seeping into hers.

She's not a failure. She just doesn't know.

Lissa picked a character immediately—the heroine of *Rebecca,* fragile, scared, inexperienced, naïve. But smart! "Have you ever read *Rebecca*?" she asked.

Mr. MacAllister smiled. "Loved that novel. So you've chosen Ms. Du Maurier's unnamed heroine?"

"Yes."

" 'Last night I dreamt I went to Manderly again.' But don't take the analogy too far, Lissa. You are going to learn without all the mystery and heartache! Agreed?"

She gave him a half grin. "Sure."

"Today, all we're going to do is practice getting in and out of Ole Bessie. In and out, in and out. You start in the passenger's seat and you walk around the front of Ole Bessie and you get into the driver's seat. You close the door. You lock it. You put on the seat belt. You start the engine. And then you turn it off. You repeat these things again and again and again, until it's the most normal, natural reflex in the world. Can we do that?"

Lissa's eyes filled with tears, but it didn't matter. Mr. MacAllister understood. He read minds *and* he was a psychologist. Back to the scene of the crime. She would go back there and further back and even further back, until each time that she moved from the passenger's seat to the driver's seat she didn't see an image of her dead mother, doing the very same thing.

———

Safe. Together. Peaceful. Janelle let the words soak into her spirit as her hands soaked into the warm suds of the sink. Dishes! Many, many dishes to wash. Some women complained about the daily chores of cooking, but she thanked God for the familiarity of mundane tasks. Cooking, eating with her family, and washing up afterward showed progress. She set out to do something, and she accomplished it. With a job where spiritual results were impossible to measure, at least she had housework.

She leaned against the counter, wiped her hands on a dish towel, and listened to the children conversing happily with Brian about their first weeks of school. Sandy squealed in mock protest as her father tickled her under the chin.

"So, my princess, you have already gotten one *Bien* and one *Très Bien*! We should celebrate that your ogre of a *maîtresse* is warming up to the princess."

"Daddy. Some other kids got good grades too. And actually, she's not as mean as everyone says. I think I might like her. . . ."

Let life stay simple for a little while, Lord. Let us be busy with book satchels and homework and teachers' meetings and good meals around the table. Just for a little while, please.

An hour later Brian cuddled up beside her in bed, his long arms holding her around the waist. She shifted and turned to face him. His face was playful, like an eager little boy awaiting a gift. She pushed the hair out of his eyes and traced her finger along his lips.

"Hey, there," he whispered, and kissed her neck softly. "Thank you for taking such good care of the kids, getting them organized. And for a delicious dinner. And for being here beside me tonight." He gave her a little squeeze. "Two weeks is too long, isn't it?"

"Too long," she agreed.

Tomorrow they would talk of his trip. Tomorrow she would tell of the heaviness. He knew it, anyway, had heard it in her voice each time he called home, no matter how she tried to disguise it. But they had learned through years of traveling and separation how to deal with his "reentries": no meetings the first night home, no deep discussions, just time as a family, a good meal, and, after the children were tucked into bed, a little celebration of their own, a mutual giving to each other, with joy. For the next hour she didn't hear any voices except his saying, "I love you. I love you, Nelli."

———

Annie found him sitting in the swing on the porch, lost in thought. He had not even bothered to go into the house to greet her when he returned from the last driving lesson. He needed to think. And pray.

"You've got that worried expression on your face, Ev. Same one every time you finish a lesson with that girl. What's her name?"

"Lissa."

"Yes. Lissa. What's the matter?"

He nodded to his side, and Annie sat beside him.

"She can drive—she just can't live. She's stuck, and I don't know how to help. So much potential. But maybe it's not the right time."

"She have another panic attack today?"

"No, not today. Today I earned my reputation as that old eccentric driving instructor who has such unorthodox ways of teaching." He watched Annie's face crinkle into a smile. "We concentrated on some very, very basic things—like walking around the car and getting into the driver's seat. She's not ready to go any further than that. She's just so fragile."

Annie stood and came behind him, arms encircling his shoulders, resting her chin on Ev's head. "Why don't you invite her to dinner? We've done that before. Remember Angela? And that poor boy Charley. You said his IQ was lower than the score he'd gotten on the driver's test. But you saw potential."

Ev sighed, took a long breath, reached up, and placed his hand over Annie's, giving it a squeeze.

"Mr. MacAllister." Her voice was reprimanding. "You are letting this girl get to you. She is not your burden. You're too old to get all worked up over a student."

"I thought you called me your young man."

"Well, right now, I'm calling you old, and I'm telling you to let that girl be—or I'll force you into retirement, you hear me?"

He chuckled. When Annie got desperate, she made threats. "You will? Because I want to help a scared teenager? I don't believe you, Mrs. MacAllister. I don't believe you for one second."

"Humph! Then have it your way, but invite her over. Let me see what she's made of—maybe that would help. It's worked before."

"Yes, it has." Ev squeezed her hand again and watched as she went back inside. Annie, bless her soul, had her own unique, unorthodox way of helping others. Perhaps that was what Lissa needed.

He'd almost told her the problem. He'd almost pronounced that one word that would explain everything.

Tate.

Silvano settled himself in his favorite chair—the only one in the small den. Despite the shabby furnishings, his little apartment in Decatur felt like home. Framed prints of Canaletto's and Guardi's representations of St. Peter's Square and the Coliseum hung on the wall. A framed black-and-white photograph of his family—all of them together: Mamma, Silvano, Daniella, Sophia, Roberto—sat on a small table beside his chair.

He spread the photocopied sheets in front of him like puzzle pieces, got on his knees, and studied each one. The folder was thick with newspaper reviews and magazine ads for each novel, as well as Eddy's scribbled notes and sales figures. But correspondence with Miss Green was slim. Search as he might, he found no street address or phone number on any of the royalty statements or bank deposit slips. Just a post office box: P.O. Box 6765, Chicago, IL 60607. He jotted it down. How did one go about locating a post office box?

A photocopied memo scribbled on Eddy's personalized stationery named one other person.

> *Jerry,*
> > *Please deposit as per last statement.*
> > > *Thanks,*
> > > *Eddy*

That memo was dated November 6, 1979.

And finally, Silvano found a short letter written on stationery with a header.

> *Jerry Steinman*
> *Goldberg, Finch and Dodge*
> *Life of Georgia Building*
> *600 West Peachtree Street*
> *Atlanta, GA 30308*
> *Phone 404-237-9938*

> *Eddy,*
> > *Miss Green's portfolio is in fine shape, growing steadily. She will be pleased. Enclosed are all the reports for you to send to her. I have mailed the monthly statement to the post office box as we agreed.*
> > > *Jerry*

And a phone number! Silvano poured a glass of red wine and congratulated himself.

See Mamma, it isn't as hard as we thought. This is my big chance!

Almost immediately, a line from Miss Green's new manuscript floated through his mind, something about paths deviating and the protagonist's need to make sure the road he was following ultimately led in the right direction. He frowned subconsciously, took another sip of wine, and brushed the thought away.

This is my chance. Buono.

CHAPTER SIX

"Thanks for stopping by, Jerry," Ted said, standing briefly and reaching across his desk to shake the broker's hand. "Have a seat." When they'd both taken a chair, Ted continued. "Miss Green called me yesterday. I don't think she likes me too much yet, but at least we've arranged a meeting in Chicago. Lunch. She told me not to be late."

Jerry chuckled. "You'd best heed her advice. As I said, it'll pay off. Be charming, but be cunning. Show her you understand the brokerage business and her personal account."

For the next half hour, Jerry went over the foundation in minute detail, the stocks, the bonds, the mutual funds, the past trading history. "Just call it a briefing." He winked at Ted, stood up, and shook hands again.

"Thanks, Jerry. For everything."

Jerry leaned over the desk. "Rumor has it that you're selling quite a few of these junk bonds to a couple of your high-risk clients."

"That's right."

"I've watched you come along, Ted. You've had some hard clients, and you've handled them well. You're a good broker, but don't let the money go to your head. Watch those junk bonds—I don't think they'll spell success in the long run. This bull market is about to turn bear, I'm afraid. It's been strong for seven years. Can't last forever. "

"Is that why you're getting out, Jerry?"

"I'm sixty-seven, and I've got a wife, three grown kids, and seven grandkids. They are why I'm getting out. I've been a broker for over forty years, and a bear market never scared me away before. I'm just giving you a little friendly advice. Be careful. Leveraged buyouts and all the junk bonds make me nervous. You've read about the illegal insider trading. Just keep your eyes open and your head clear. Right now may not be the time to take the big risks."

Ted nodded enthusiastically, his mind on S. A. Green. "I hear you. Don't worry, Jerry. Thanks for the advice."

"And remember, I'll still be around for a while—planning to come in on Wednesdays and Thursdays. And if you need anything when I'm not here, you can always call."

"Thanks, Jerry. Thanks a lot. Have a great weekend."

Ted reflected on Jerry's words. The seasoned broker wasn't the only cautious one. The continuing bull market had at first stumped the analysts and then made them wary. Ted fiddled with his pen, twirling it between his thumb and forefinger. Junk bonds didn't scare him at all. Plenty of Americans wanted to play high-risk games. If it wasn't with junk bonds, it would be with something else.

The eighties were all about takeovers—dueling companies scrambling for money to buy each other out, creating junk bonds to sell to overzealous clients. The profit provided the capital needed to buy out the competitor. The Dow Jones was speaking the language of newly issued stocks—called IPOs—and the new age of computers. Incredible, how those stocks were soaring. The public was eager to buy into products that were going to change the fabric of American life, maybe even life on the whole planet. Sure, people tended to be a bit overly optimistic, even euphoric. He tried to be honest with his clients.

"Bull markets don't last forever," he'd remind them. But the truth was that he believed 1987 was going to be the best year yet, and junk bonds provided the perfect way to increase his income.

That and a visit to see Miss S. A. Green.

SATURDAY, SEPTEMBER 26

Janelle pulled herself out of bed with the alarm, feeling the weight of a new day descend upon her, heavier than the stuffed backpack that Luke hefted onto his back when he left each morning for fourth grade. Brian had risen early, very early, as was his custom, even on Saturdays. Janelle could barely stumble downstairs in time to get the box of cereal out for the children.

Go home!

She ignored the voice and yanked the covers up on the bed.

Go home, she heard later, as Sandy fretted over her spelling words in between bites of soggy cornflakes.

"Sandy, you know how to spell *être* and *avoir*. This is just a review. We went over that last week." Janelle tried not to sound exasperated. Not this early in the day. "Hurry up, or we'll get there after the gate is closed."

Sandy frowned and grumbled something and then trudged back upstairs to get her pink *cartable*.

Luke called up to her, "Would you pick up a little speed, sis?" and slung his backpack over his skinny shoulders.

A nine-year-old should not have to carry a backpack that weighs fifteen pounds, Janelle thought. *And children shouldn't have to go to school on Saturday morning!* She hurried out the door with the kids.

"Bye, Mom," Luke said, taking off at a trot to meet up with his friends. Having his mother drop him off was no longer acceptable.

"Bye, Mommy," Sandy said, hugging Janelle's neck and kissing her cheek as the car stopped in front of the elementary school. "Have a good day. I love you."

"I love you too, sweetie," Janelle whispered through the catch in her throat. Sandy scurried through the gate and ran to catch up with her classmates.

Go home, Janelle heard again as she left the school. Her stomach got that awful lurching, and she wished that Brian had not rushed off so early for his meeting. Back at the house, she read his hastily scribbled note: *See you around five. Great to be home!*

Yes, she felt thankful too. Glad the family was complete.

Go home.

She sifted through yesterday's still-unopened mail—a bank statement, a form letter from missionaries in the Philippines, and a notice from their mission, informing them that they were behind on their monthly support. Yes, she was aware of this.

Sitting at the little wooden breakfast table, sipping a second cup of coffee, Janelle skimmed through the missionary letter, filled with reports of what God was doing in another corner of the world. Children being fed, families learning a skill so they could provide for their own, several hundred people converting to Christianity from another religion. Statistics and information, glorious information of lives transformed and dear people serving God in hard places.

She set it down. She had not written a prayer report for six months. What did she have to say? *I struggle to get up in the morning, I hear accusing voices all day, and I ache for my dead child.*

Josh! She closed her eyes and saw him there beside her, a beautiful, laughing toddler. Then the horrible image of his little body floating face-down in the pool flashed through her mind. She clutched her stomach, and the sobs escaped, rushed out, like the gushing waters of the Lez after last week's sudden rains.

"Lord, it sneaks up on me and overpowers me—this grief." She spoke out loud. Then, to herself, she admitted that way down in the depths of her soul lay the true culprit, a writhing, slithering reptile, ugly, hideous. Anger!

"I'm angry with you, Lord." This came out, as always, in a whisper. "I love you, and I am so thankful for my family, and I know this is where we are supposed to be, but I'm having a hard time trusting you. And I hate the anger."

Cradling the coffee mug in her hands, she climbed the stairs and walked down the narrow hall into the tiny room they had made into an office. She looked at the desk she and Brian shared, strewn with mail to answer, Bible studies to prepare, a half-written Christmas play. She left the office quickly and stood frozen in the hall, unable to decide. Correspondence? Impossible. She physically could not get herself to write a letter. The play? Not one creative thought in her head. She would surely write the saddest of tragedies today. The study? No.

She walked past Luke's room, peeking in at the hastily made bed with the Star Wars comforter and the array of Legos lined up against one wall. She came to Sandy's room, paused, went in and sat on the bed with its Barbie sheets and the horse statues with real horsehair manes and tails. She let another sob escape, looking across the narrow space to where *his* bed had been. Now a brightly painted armoire stood in its place, an armoire she had purchased at the used-furniture store and painstakingly painted in pinks and greens and blues. Sandy had helped her stencil on the little white flowers.

Janelle knew the signs of depression, knew that the circle of grief could not be hurried. She even knew what she needed to do—what she must do—right now. She stood up from the bed, walked back down the stairs, left the empty coffee mug on the kitchen counter, grabbed her keys, and walked to the front door. She went outside, shutting and locking the door behind her.

She walked quickly, reciting Scripture, speaking out loud to the Lord. "Yes, I am hurting. Yes, I am angry. But, Lord, by your strength I am going to fight this. Just for this morning."

She walked around the little subdivision, then out into the field across the street, veering away from the road that led to the cemetery. As she walked, she whispered, "When I am weak, you are strong."

———

Katy Lynn observed herself in the mirror. The blue silk dress she'd chosen brought out the color of her eyes—"a cloudless sky in autumn" was how Hamilton had once described them. Why did he have to crowd into her thoughts now? She needed to concentrate on the fund-raiser for the symphony. But every time she tried to put on the mascara, her eyes welled with tears; she blinked, and then the mascara left little black exclamation points above her eyes.

Her life was ripping apart, and all she could think about was mascara!

Keep up appearances. Show the world you are strong. He will not get the best of you.

She sprayed a mist of perfume on her neck and wrists, then placed the strand of pearls around her neck and rummaged through her purse to find the right color of lipstick. These ludicrous, maddening details kept her sane, she thought, just as Dad used to say. "When your heart is heavy, engage in the mundane. Let the small details take your mind off the hollowness for a few moments." Whatever else Dad was, he had a way with words, she thought bitterly.

Katy Lynn walked down the hall to Gina's empty room, went inside, and stared at the bright blue- and white-striped walls, the perfectly coordinated bedspread and overstuffed pillows, the bathroom door, half opened, with the matching blue towels hanging on the towel racks. She winced a little. She certainly wasn't going to leave Gina alone tonight, not after she'd carved her feelings into her flesh. Her daughter's skin-deep cry for help definitely made it hard to keep up appearances. Everyone could read their family's story on her daughter's arms. So be it.

At least tonight Gina was safe at Caroline's house. Bill and Ellen had assured Katy Lynn that they would be there. Not that the parents' presence downstairs could stop Gina from trying to harm herself again.

Katy Lynn planned to call the shrink, whatever his name was, the next day. And the lawyer. And the private investigator. Hamilton thought he'd get away with this. Well, he was about to find out how wrong he was!

She picked up her purse and headed downstairs, inspecting herself in the mirror by the front door. She licked her finger and wiped it across her left eyebrow to remove a tiny smudge. *You are a mess,* she admitted. *But no one else has to know it. Not yet at least. Not yet.*

"Good evening, Miz Pendleton. You look mighty nice tonight."

Katy Lynn handed Tom the keys to the Cadillac at the valet parking lot of the country club.

"Thanks, Tom. You doing okay? How's Charlean?"

"She's getting better after the hip surgery. Shuffling around, pleased as punch to have her man giving her some attention." He chuckled.

"You tell her I asked about her."

"Sho nuf, Miz Pendleton, I will. Thank ya. And you?"

"Making do, Tom." A car drove up behind her. "I'll see you later."

She walked into the carpeted hallway of the club, greeted by the faint sound of music. The party had already started in the downstairs lounge. She hurried across the foyer and down the winding staircase.

"Katy Lynn! You look smashing! That blue is so you!" Lanie rushed up to her.

Katy Lynn managed a smile. "Thanks, Lanie. You're the one who's gorgeous. You look about twenty-two in that dress."

Thank heavens for petite, brunette Lanie with the sweetest smile and kindest voice on planet earth. A true friend.

Lanie grabbed Katy Lynn's arm and pulled her into the women's restroom. "Is it true? Hamilton's asking for a divorce?"

"How did you hear?"

"Chad told me last night. Hamilton called him at work. Wanted Chad to represent him, but Chad said no. What's gotten into him? That's insane!"

"I'm afraid some cute little thing at his office has gotten into him," Katy Lynn replied bitterly.

"He's seeing someone?"

"I'm pretty sure."

"What are you going to do about it?"

"Well, after I get Gina to the shrink and pay the mortgage on the house and finish planning the Christmas gala, I'm gonna make his life, and *the other woman's*, absolutely miserable. Just you watch."

Arms looped together, Lanie and Katy Lynn walked back into the downstairs lounge, where men and women dressed in semiformal attire were sipping martinis and biting little pieces of bacon-wrapped shrimp off colorful toothpicks, laughing and talking about trips and cars and money and the Atlanta Symphony.

Katy Lynn joined a group of friends by the mahogany balustrade. She made polite conversation and ate her share of spiced meatballs and jumbo shrimp. But she longed to run up the steps and out into the parking lot where Tom stood sentinel in his blue jacket and cap and let him hug her tight as he'd done when she had come running to him thirty years ago, a lost little girl looking for her mother, who was happily lobbing tennis balls over the net on the court down the hill.

———

Lissa knew exactly why she'd accepted the dinner invitation that Sunday night—one less excruciatingly painful dinner with her father. She slipped on her black sandals and ran a brush through her hair, not bothering to fasten it into a ponytail.

"You look nice, Liss," her father commented as she came down the carpeted stairs. "Where'd you say this couple lives?"

"Off Highway 2 in Fort Oglethorpe. Near the Military Park."

"Seems a bit strange that your driving instructor would invite you to dinner."

"He's nice. He said that he and his wife like having young people around. I don't think they get to see their kids and grandkids very often."

"Yes, well . . . And you're sure it's not a problem for him to bring you home?"

"That's what he said."

"Maybe he'll give you a little free lesson in night driving! Before you know it, Liss, you'll be zipping up and down Lookout Mountain after dusk."

Lissa stiffened and felt her jaw clench. She glanced at her father—dressed in the impeccable business suit. His six-foot-two frame fit into the suit without a wrinkle, just as ordered. Thick light brown hair, twinkling brown eyes, the round baby face that belied his fifty years. He looked in that moment like the father of yesteryear, jovial, optimistic.

She forced a thin smile and said quickly, "I gotta get my purse, Dad. I'll be right down."

She hurried back up the stairs, went into her bathroom, and splashed water on her face. Every word out of his mouth was an icy accusation.

A slippery lane, a burst of hail from the sky. And he had no idea. Not the slightest idea!

Never good enough! All your fault!

———

The old house smelled of roasting chicken and corn casserole as Ev came in the back door, passing by the kitchen. The garden's last ripe tomatoes sat on a plate, thick, pungent red slices covered with fresh ground pepper and oil and vinegar. Ev's stomach protested loudly. It was time to eat.

"Ev, will you get the plates out?" Annie asked, her back to him, bent over a pot on the stove. The steam was wilting her gray hair.

He stood in the dining room and tried to think what Lissa would appreciate. "Which ones do you want to use?" he called back to Annie.

He could hear her humming "The Way You Look Tonight." Annie never answered him when she was humming.

He started toward the china cabinet, then stopped beside the mantel above the fireplace and studied the clock, whose little twirling balls of gold seemed stuck. He lifted the glass orb and set them spinning again and checked the time by his watch. 6:54.

Annie rushed into the living room, an old apron wrapped around her waist. "For heaven's sake, Ev! Are you dreaming? She'll be here in five minutes!" Then, shaking her head exasperatedly, she added, "Men! Get the nice plates. Sounds like this girl would appreciate a well-set table."

"Stubborn woman! What do I know about fancy tables?"

It was their game, bantering back and forth as they prepared for guests. Despite appearances, they both knew a lot about fancy tables.

Never mind that.

They made a good team, and enjoyed having youth seated at the table. It reminded them of the years when their kids were teens.

Happy years, delightful years. Well, mostly delightful.

He wiped away the angst as he put the blue and white china plates on the table.

No, not always delightful.

He opened a drawer and took out Annie's sterling silverware, then carefully retrieved the crystal goblets she'd inherited from her grand-mother. He set the table, remembering the times when their family dinner discussions included more than schoolwork and grades and books, times when the kids discussed ideas, and even spirituality. Ah, he almost chuckled, remembering the fierce way his younger daughter judged her friends at school, her determination to reform them, and her ensuing frustration. He and Annie had nodded to each other and whispered, "Give her time."

Time! My goodness, what that daughter had become with time! A smile settled onto his face.

The doorbell rang, and he called out to Annie, "I'll get it, honey."

Well, that was good. The girl was prompt, despite the depression, the fear.

Ev opened the door, still holding a silver knife in one hand, a smile already on his face. He felt happy to see Lissa again, felt pleased, glad she could meet Annie.

"Hello, Mr. MacAllister," she greeted him.

She had on a casual black and white dress, loose and long. She wore her dark brown hair down—loose and long also—reaching past her shoulders. She had bangles on her tiny wrists, and she was wearing sandals, pretty black sandals. His eyes stopped there, focused on them for way too long. He didn't even recall later if he had said hello or not.

The blood rushed to his head; he felt the palpitations that his heart doctor warned against, his mouth dry. Sandals! The smallest detail could still send him spiraling back and back and back. Way too far back in time. Tate.

He needed to call to Annie. How long had he been standing there?

"Mr. MacAllister? Are you all right?"

He let out a breath, met her eyes, shook his head. "Yes, yes. Come in, Lissa. So nice to see you. Come in, come in." Trying to calm his heart, he called out, "Annie, our friend is here! Come meet her!"

Annie hurried to the front door in her apron and blue jeans, wiped a stray wisp of hair from her glistening face, and held out a hand. "Hello, dear. I'm Annie."

No-nonsense Annie had a forceful handshake that always took guests by surprise. Lissa's raised eyebrows told Ev that she was no exception.

"Nice to meet you, Mrs. MacAllister. Thank you for inviting me over."

"It's Annie. Only Annie. You can call him whatever you want," she said, winking, "but I'm Annie."

"Oh. Okay."

"Come on in the kitchen, and I'll get you something to drink. Hot enough for you? They say fall won't arrive for another three weeks. You like lemonade? Or iced tea?"

Ev watched them disappear into the kitchen and busied himself arranging the linen napkins on the table. He never got it right, but tonight it gave him time to recuperate.

For half a second Lissa *was* Tate, standing there in those silly black sandals, the ones Mother refused to buy. And so Tate had stolen them. He had pushed Tate's voice so far away in the past years he didn't hear her anymore, and honestly life was so much easier like that. He simply could not live with the voice of his dead sister whispering all the time.

Healing, grieving, yes, these things he had done almost thirty-five years ago. The anger was gone, and good had come from the tragedy. Years and years of good.

"What are you up to, Lord?" he whispered as he placed the silver knife with the little roses embedded in the handle beside a plate. Thoughts of Tate, though still present, did not interrupt him in the midst of every activity.

Until Lissa Randall had showed up in his life. When that happened, it was as if the Almighty shouted from heaven, "Ev, my boy, there are still a few things on this issue that we need to deal with. It hasn't been time until now. But now you need to come back to it. For Lissa. For you. For Annie. For the memory of Tate. For your girls."

The absolute gut-level truth was that he had no desire for God to interrupt him in this way. Ev felt that he had a close, intimate relationship with the Almighty. But going back in the past at this time in his life, with his weak heart and failing eyesight, seemed like sidetracking. Unfortunately, he knew all too well that when he dug his heels in too far, the Almighty had a way of sending him sprawling right down on his face.

"Ev! Mr. MacAllister, are you deaf? We're waiting for you on the back porch."

Annie's voice jostled him back to the present. He observed the table, fit for a queen, and headed through the living room, into the kitchen, and out the back door to where Lissa and Annie were standing, sipping their iced tea.

———

"Annie's the brains behind our business," Mr. MacAllister explained while they ate her homemade blueberry pie. "She does all the accounting, chases down the kids who don't pay, puts ads in the newspaper."

"Do some kids really not pay?"

"Oh, they never forget for long," Annie said, wiping the napkin across her face. "What Ev means is that if it weren't for me, he'd be giving free lessons all year long, and I'd be working at Big Mart as a cashier. Nothing wrong with Big Mart, mind you, but there's no sense in letting a perfectly legitimate business implode because the instructor can't do math and is as generous as your shadow is long at sunset. And that's *not* a compliment, Lissa. He'd give you his suspenders if he weren't afraid his britches would fall right off."

Lissa liked this odd couple: Mr. MacAllister and Annie. She knew she'd never be able to call her driving instructor by his first name, but "Annie" she could handle. The MacAllisters must have been quite a pair, she thought, when they were young. Even in jeans and a sleeveless cotton shirt, Annie was elegant. She bustled about like the nurses at Uncle Irvin's retirement facility, concise, abrupt, efficient. But there was something refined about both of them. Momma had called it "blue blood." Unpretentious, casual, but blue blood. Lissa could spot it as easily as Mr. MacAllister knew the make of every car in town. She'd been raised around prosperity at the Chattanooga Girls School.

It was almost as if Annie MacAllister tried hard to look ordinary, but she couldn't. A little round across the middle, thick silver hair, a silver that matched her husband's, which fell straight and neat on either side of a lovely sculpted face, brown eyes filled with mischief, and a speech that was as blunt as the silver knife by her plate. Lissa studied them carefully during the meal, relaxing into their hospitality like warm buttered rolls in a basket. She wished she could stay here until the heaviness of life lifted, until she could climb into Ole Bessie and drive up and down the steep, curving road to Lookout Mountain at night.

Driving Lissa home to East Brow Road took Ev twenty-five minutes. She sat silently beside him in Ole Bessie as he reviewed the evening in his mind. Thank heavens for Annie, animating the dinner conversation with her stories of other students who had failed the test, stories that couldn't help but make Lissa laugh. Ev had only managed about fifty words the whole evening while Lissa and Annie chatted about everything from Betty Crocker to Limoges china and then switched to a lively discussion on Latin declensions and the Latin Festival Lissa had attended three years ago. No doubt about it, the girl was bright. When she mentioned Herodotus, Ev was tempted to join the conversation. He loved history; he absorbed it. But not tonight. Tate's history was crowding in.

"I hear voices."

Lissa's voice surprised him. She divulged this information in the muggy blackness as a mosquito buzzed in the corner of Ole Bessie's windshield, as if she were telling Ev that she liked raspberry jam or fried zucchini.

"That's why it's hard to drive. I hear voices, and I see images of the wreck. And they won't go away."

Ev kept looking out into the moonless evening, concentrating on the white line down the middle of Nickajack Road. Not another car in sight. He felt the slight pull of his lips into a frown, but before he could erase it, Lissa added, "You think I'm crazy?"

He glanced at her and shook his head. "No." Ole Bessie's engine purred, filling up the silence between them. He digested the confession. "No. We all hear voices."

"Really? You think so?"

"Yes, Lissa, I'm sure of it. Different voices, but we all hear them. I used to hear one all the time that said, 'When are you gonna change jobs and get a respectable career?' I also heard 'Be the best, no matter what' quite a bit—came straight from my dad."

Her eyes grew wide. "*You* hear voices? You mean you don't think I'm nuts—schizophrenic or something?"

"If you are, so is the rest of the world. Problem is, you've got to learn which voice to listen to and how to shut up the other ones. That's all."

"Yeah. I guess that's basically what my therapist says too. Anyway, I thought I should tell you. I figure you found out about the wreck, and if you're going to help me, you might as well know the rest. I hear voices. Also . . ." She hesitated. "Also, my dad and I don't get along very well right now."

After Lissa got out of Ole Bessie, waving good-bye and saying "Thank you so much" for the fourth time, Ev drove a short way down the road to another of his favorite haunts: Point Park, where the Union Army had defeated the Confederates in November of 1863. He cut the motor beside the castlelike stone entrance, walked into the park, passed a large monument, and leaned against the railing at the park's northern tip. Staring down to where the black outline of the Tennessee River snaked its way through Chattanooga at Moccasin Bend, Ev stood there thinking of Tate and Annie and the girls. Thinking far back to an arrogant but broken young man at an evangelistic crusade, closed up in his heart, hearing voices, so many voices, until that gentle whisper had shouted louder than all the other ones.

Come home.

CHAPTER SEVEN

MONDAY, SEPTEMBER 28

Ed Clouse was in panic mode, not a very fun thing to wake up to on a Monday morning.

"We are going to get the Green novel out in three months. Three! That means you go into high gear, sales staff. Ads in the papers, contact the reviewers, get the cover drawn up. I'm doing all the editing, as usual, so don't bother me unless it's an emergency. I want this book on the bookshelves in the stores a week before Christmas. I want crowds lined up waiting to purchase it, convinced it will be the perfect gift. Is that understood?"

Ten heads nodded a nervous yes—the marketing team, the publicity team, the editorial team. No one said a word, but everyone was thinking exactly what Silvano was: *The boss is cracking up. Has he bothered to look at the fall catalog? We already have thirteen titles—more than ever before—and he wanted these to get heavy promotion.*

"Look, I know I'm asking a lot. How many of you were here when we published Miss Green's last novel, back in '82?"

Two hands went up, Leah's and Jim's.

"That's what I thought. Most of you don't remember the results of that campaign, because you weren't here. That's why I've asked Leah to fill you in on some history."

Leah, in her plain gray skirt and too-tight blouse, stood. "Miss Green's 1982 novel was received on June 22 of that year. Edits took one month. Galleys went out in early September, sales teams contacted the stores, and the book was released on December 3. Big Christmas advertising publicity scheme. First printing was 120,000, sold out in a week. By January 15 there were 500,000 copies in print. The book evened out at a million copies, and everyone at the publishing house went home with a big bonus that year."

She smiled. "It's a lot of work, but it can be done. We'll need a big push at Frankfurt in October and at all the smaller trade shows this fall."

"But you had five months to prepare. If we're aiming at a before-Christmas release, that's . . . that's twelve weeks max. Sir, that's impossible. *Publishers Weekly* won't even look at it." This came from the top marketing guy.

Ed Clouse boomed, "Listen, *PW* will look, and so will every other reviewer in America. With a name this big, it'll work."

"But wouldn't it be better to take our time, do a really slick job, cover all the bases? Give the book the best possible promo?"

"We will give it the best possible promo. Every parent will be buying this book for their kid's stocking stuffer. We'll aim at the high school and college kids—a great read over Christmas break. But it's got something for parents too. If we get it out just before Christmas, with the right publicity and marketing, it'll take off. Miss Green's newest novel will be in the back pocket of every kid in America, just like the first one."

Ed smiled, and his presence took up the whole room. "Remember, the stats show that every year we put out a Green novel, the staff take home fifteen percent more than their average salary. This time will be no different, I can guarantee you. A little extra work, long hours. It can be done."

Silvano shook his head. The boss was nuts, but at least things would be moving around here now. He needed to finish editing Frank Blanton's novel *rapidamente*. He had a lot of work ahead if he was going to introduce the world to Miss S. A. Green before Christmas!

———

Annie slipped onto the porch, wearing one of Ev's old sweat shirts over her pajamas.

He gave her a smile, took a sip of his coffee, and continued staring out into the sunrise.

"Took you a while to get home last night, boyfriend."

"Yes, I'm afraid Ole Bessie and I kinda puttered around the back roads."

Annie sat lightly on his lap and laced her arms around his neck. "She reminds you of Tate, doesn't she?" she whispered.

Ev swallowed, but the catch remained in his throat. He closed his eyes, gave Annie a squeeze, but could not find any words.

"Her mannerisms are so similar—her laugh, those eyes that seem to see too far into life, the way she turns her phrases. Ev, you should have told me. I knew something was eating at you."

He nodded, chewing on his lower lip and squinting. "Yep. First time I saw her, I thought I was seeing my baby sister. Strange. Thirty-five years of life somehow morphs into ten minutes, and there she is again, alive, breathing, fragile, sharp, desperate, hurting. All I see is Tate."

Now Annie placed her face next to his, and her warm, smooth skin soothed him. She smelled of fresh soap and bacon, of breakfast waiting. "Maybe I was wrong, Mr. MacAllister. Maybe it's not your job to help this young lady. Maybe you'd best leave her alone."

"Can't do it, Annie. I want to, but I can tell the Almighty's up to something. I wish He weren't. I told Him I wasn't going back. What's done is done. Problem is—I don't think He's gonna let me get away with it."

Annie stood, fiddled with her hair, and made a little clucking sound deep in her throat.

Ev knew what it meant—she didn't agree and was preparing her rebuttal.

"You know I'm not one to argue with the Lord. . . ."

Ev raised his eyebrows and gave a half grin. "Really?"

"Well, not often." She winked. "But you've got a weak heart, and I'd like to keep you around for a few more years."

"Fine, Mrs. MacAllister. You explain it to the Almighty, and let me know what He says. In the meantime, I believe Lissa Randall is coming for a lesson on Thursday."

———

For the first time in over a year, Lissa heard no voices when she awoke. She had a smile on her face and stretched lazily as the alarm went off. As she thought of the dinner at the MacAllisters', her body relaxed into contentment. Then a thought came, warm and comfortable.

They understand me. Or at least, they are beginning to. And they want to help.

She did her sit-ups, and the imaginary spot on the ceiling did not accuse her. She washed her face and was surprised to see a little gleam in the dark brown interior of her eyes. She brushed her hair and glanced at her wristwatch. 7:15. She was early. Early!

After she dressed, she bounced down the stairs. Her father was still sitting at the little breakfast table, his face hidden behind the *Chattanooga Times*. Half a piece of buttered toast sat on a small plate with the raspberry preserves next to it, top off, knife sticking out.

"Hey, Daddy!" She went over and gave him a peck on the cheek.

He set down the paper, surprised. "Well, Miss Liss! You're up early. I thought I'd have to pull you out of bed after your late evening. When did you get in?"

"Oh, it was only a little after eleven, Daddy."

"And you enjoyed it?"

"Very much so."

"Well, that is fine. Still wish you would be hanging out with kids your age, but that's fine." He smiled at her. "I guess all the kids your age are off at college, aren't they?"

The hurt washed over her like a cold burst of water. Her father was already looking at the paper again. Lissa went into the kitchen, but instead of the hungry growling of her stomach that she'd felt a few short minutes ago, she felt sick and leaned over the sink in a silent gag.

Failure! Your fault! Never good enough!

———

Janelle listened to the report on the radio proclaiming the bombing in Algiers. She shuddered. Brian was scheduled to go back at the end of November. His heart was in North Africa, she knew. Two years ago the military-backed government, intent on ridding the country of any religious group that might pose a threat, had upped their security. Since then Brian's travel to Algeria had become clandestine and less frequent. Now, as regional director of the mission agency, he supervised a correspondence school and a radio station that was broadcast throughout the Arab world.

The doorbell rang, and Janelle turned off the radio and went to greet the women arriving for a prayer meeting.

Dahlila and Oumel entered her home, their heads covered with their *hijabs*. It seared her heart. Their husbands could literally kill them if they were discovered at a Christian prayer meeting. Infidels! Even in France. Compared to these women, Janelle had nothing to fear, nothing to complain about. And yet her heart felt heavy.

And why are you comparing, Janelle? Every person's burden is different. I am here to carry them all.

The faint voice of her Savior startled her in the midst of the prayer time. She felt for one brief second that old familiar thrill, that intimacy and security. *Savior.*

As they continued to pray, the burden lifted, the words of prayer from other lips became a balm. This time Janelle heard the words not as an accusation but as an invitation.

Come home.

TUESDAY, SEPTEMBER 29

"You're not doing well, dear. That much is obvious."

Brian and Janelle sat facing each other in a small café on *Place de la Comedie* for another of their rituals. As soon as possible, when he got home after a trip, they went out for morning coffee—one of the "perks" of the job, they called it. A flexible schedule. Their afternoon and evenings were filled with people, but sometimes Brian could get away in the morning.

Today she could barely meet his eyes. "I'm just tired, I guess. The *rentrée* always is such a hectic time. Luke is being a bit defiant, wanting independence. And Sandy is having a rough time with her French verbs."

Brian reached across the table and took her hand. "Nelli, it's not that. I know the *rentrée* is hard, but for a different reason. I know you're thinking of Josh."

Janelle's eyes brimmed with tears. They had decided shortly after Josh's death that never would they refrain from using his name, as if he had never existed. His name, no matter how painful, would be pronounced and cherished and spoken so that healing could come, for Luke and Sandy, for themselves. His pictures still hung on the walls of the house and sat on the bedside table. He was there with them, a smiling cherub, a part of the past. Family.

"I can't talk about it here," she managed, turning her head down as tears slid down her cheeks. Her coffee sat untouched.

Brian squeezed her hand. He left francs on the table and stood. "Then we'll go somewhere we can talk, Nelli."

They laced their way among the people along the open square, across the cobbled stones of centuries past. Brian waited patiently for her to speak, but she couldn't. She turned a hundred words on her tongue, but could pronounce none. She thought of the image of the vines, ripe with grapes. She thought of Brian's work at the radio station, of the thousands of North African people who were hearing a message of hope through this means. How could she dampen his enthusiasm?

She thought of the gentle whisper she had heard yesterday afternoon at prayer meeting.

After ten minutes of silence she finally blurted out what she could not say calmly. "I want to go home! I'm dying here. I have nothing in me. I'm as dry as the Sahara, with no oasis in sight. All I hear is *go home. Go home.*" She took a breath, swallowed, tried to collect her thoughts. "But how can I go home? Home is here! Josh is here! Why? Why, Brian? I'm sorry. I'm so sorry."

Brian led her away from the main square onto a little side street. His arm was tight around her, and she leaned into him. She knew he was processing. He didn't answer her heartache with a solution. He'd learned long ago that didn't work.

Finally he said, "Darling. I think you *should* go home."

Then silence soaked into the pavement.

"I think you need to see someone. Need to grieve. I've, I've talked about this with Norm at the headquarters. He agrees."

"You've talked about it?"

"Nelli, this is not new. It rushes on you at times and is dormant at others, but it isn't new. It's depression. You know it. I know it."

"We did get help. Six months of help where I kept you from your work, holed up at headquarters in Atlanta, bawling my eyes out, the kids going to that little elementary school, jerked back and forth in their worlds. I won't do it again."

"Nelli—sometimes it takes longer. Sometimes it takes years."

"You're over it! How can you never think about it, about him! How can you be fine!" The anger in her voice, the accusation, startled her.

"Nelli—I think of Josh every day of my life, you know that. I know I have the ability to compartmentalize life. It's not that the hurt isn't raw and real. It's just it doesn't bleed in front of me all the time. It's just a different way, Nelli. Just a different way. You know that." His voice cracked, his arm around her tightened.

They passed the open *marché* in front of city hall, stepping around people buying apples and figs and tomatoes and leeks. The red and green canopied stands of the merchants blinked happy color into the fall morning; the sounds of the vendors calling out their wares in the slow drawl of the Midi punctuated the chatter of the crowd. Brian turned onto a tiny side street that eventually opened into a small cobbled square with a gurgling fountain in the middle. It was empty of people. Benches sat under plane trees that were shedding their leaves.

They sat, and Brian held her as if she were a frightened child with a skinned knee.

"I've been thinking this through, Nelli. What if you spent a month with your parents, saw the counselor again? Had time to rest, sleep, wait, pray? Then we can decide together what our next step should be."

Janelle closed her eyes and tried to imagine long, lazy days at her parents' house. After a moment, she said, "I can't leave you and the kids here. You've got enough work without dealing with their schedules."

A long breath. "Nelli, the work keeps me going. You know that. I need it, and I enjoy it, and I think it's part of the healing for me. But maybe you need something else."

"Thank you" was all she could choke out.

"Think about it. The kids are okay in school. We could make the schedule work."

She stared down at the ancient stones and thought of home, with the red Georgia clay and maples and oaks and hickory trees displaying their bright fall colors against the backdrop of the mountain. "Maybe . . . not yet. Let the kids get settled. Not yet, but maybe at the end of October. Maybe then."

———

"Gina! Gina!" Katy Lynn rushed into the house, head throbbing. "Gina!" She took the steps two at a time.

Gina came from her room, eyes sullen. "I'm okay, Mom. Calm down."

Katy Lynn let out a sigh of relief, reprimanding herself for the panic that crept into her voice every time she left Gina alone for more than a few minutes. Good grief! This was worse than having a toddler.

"I made the appointment for the doctor, dear. He's evidently excellent."

Gina crossed her arms over her chest. "I don't want to go. I'll be fine. Just leave me alone."

"Gina, please. It's normal for you to be mad. But it's good to talk about it."

"I don't want to talk about anything! I've got my friends, and they are helping me! So leave me alone!" She went back into her room and slammed the door.

Of one thing Katy Lynn was sure. Her daughter was not fine. Gina looked almost scrawny, her thick brown hair unkempt, shadows under her eyes, and her arms always covered with a long-sleeved blouse. Katy Lynn wondered if she had carved any other message on those arms.

She went back downstairs and into the kitchen, kicked off her high-heeled pumps, and massaged her temples. She should think about dinner, but without a man to feed, she found she lacked inspiration. What to fix for two emaciated women?

Fifteen minutes later, as she stirred a pot of Campbell's soup, she heard Gina come into the kitchen. Turning, she found her daughter carrying a suitcase and her backpack.

"I'm going to Caroline's for a few days. Her parents said it's okay. Her dad's coming over to get me."

Katy Lynn opened her mouth to protest, but Gina beat her to it.

"Please don't argue. Her mom's gonna call you in a minute." Her angry expression softened for just a second. "I need to get away from all of this for a while, Mom. Please. I'll be fine."

She opened the front door and went outside, and the phone rang.

"Hello? Ellen, yes, hi. Yes, it seems our daughters have been scheming. You sure you don't mind? Just a few days. Yes, thank you."

Well, at least Ellen Lewis was not nosy. She'd doubtless heard the rumors; maybe Gina had spelled it all out to the whole family.

Oh, let her go. Katy Lynn was too tired to put up a fight. Her daughter would be safe enough at the Lewis house, and maybe this would give her a chance to talk to that investigator. The thought exhausted her. All she really wished was that she could just pack up her bags and disappear.

She heard the car drive up, the door slam shut, but Katy Lynn didn't budge from her spot in front of the stove, stirring a can of Campbell's Tomato Soup.

Katy Lynn searched for the phone number and found it stuffed inside an old phone directory. She made the decision quickly and dialed the number before she changed her mind. It took forever for the connection, and then it was fuzzy static.

"*Allô?*" It was her brother-in-law's voice.

"Hey, Brian. It's Katy Lynn."

A long silence. Then, "Wow! Katy Lynn! Great to hear your voice! How are you? Where are you?"

"I'm here in Atlanta, and I'm fine. Absolutely fine." She could not make her voice sound pleasant. Her crisp tone cut to the core. "Could I speak to Janelle?"

"Sure."

She imagined Brian finding his wife, whispering quickly that her estranged sister was on the line, calling for the first time ever in their decade of living overseas. She let out a sigh, tapped her foot impatiently, and tried to calm her fragmented nerves.

Get hold of yourself. Keep up the act. Don't go groveling to your little sister. Not now.

Thirty seconds passed. Then a minute.

"Katy Lynn?" Her sister's voice was a whispered surprise. The astonishment and worry zipped through the phone line like lightning.

"Hey, Janelle. Yes, it's me. Don't faint. And," she said quickly, "everything's fine. Don't worry."

"Okay. That's good to hear. What are you doing calling?"

Katy Lynn had memorized this part, after having dug around to find her sister's letter dated back in June. "I, I wondered how you're doing. Your last letter didn't sound too good."

"Oh, you know. There are always ups and downs with the work."

Janelle's voice was guarded. Her sister was no dummy. She wouldn't reveal her heart to a sister who, up until now, seemed completely unconcerned.

"We're hanging in there."

Katy Lynn wondered briefly how long she needed to sound interested before she could throw out her question. She almost asked about the kids, then thought of Josh and decided she did not want to touch that issue.

"Listen, I wonder if I could come over for a visit. I know it's spur of the moment, but I need to get away. Gina's been invited to stay with her best friend Caroline for a couple of weeks, and Hamilton has a crazy schedule this month. And I just finished the fund-raiser for the symphony, and the Christmas gala is well under way." She cleared her throat and made her voice light, cheery. "And, well, you've invited me for ten years, and I thought I might just finally take you up on it." She hoped her voice didn't belie panic, urgency.

Her sister hesitated. "Well—well, sure, Katy Lynn. You're always welcome."

"Could I come soon? A week from today? That'll be October 5."

She imagined her saintly sister on the other end of the line sending a prayer heavenward. *Help, God!* A phone call from the wayward sister, the black sheep!

"Next week?" Janelle repeated.

Her words were heavy, weighed down, but Katy Lynn could not worry about that. She needed to get away immediately. She did not know why, but she just *knew*.

"Sure, Katy Lynn. Come on."

———

Stella waited at the restaurant. She liked to arrive thirty minutes early so she could observe her client before he was aware of her gaze. She had an innate sense of time and space and people. She read them in their stride. She'd seated herself at the front window with a clear view of the street from all angles. Ted Draper glided in ten minutes early, looking perfectly professional, wearing a nicely cut gray suit. He was tall with neatly cropped brown hair and sharp features. Thin. An attractive young man, early thirties, she judged. Good posture, confident. She liked young men who were confident.

He stopped at the maitre d's desk, whispered a question, and was directed to where Stella sat.

"Miss Green," he said, walking briskly to her with an outstretched hand. "Ted Draper. A pleasure to meet you."

She stood and grasped his hand and looked him straight in the eyes. "The pleasure is mine, Mr. Draper. I hope." The handshake was firm, the intention communicated. All business.

She watched him register this, give a serious nod, and take a seat at the same time she did. "How was your flight?"

"Just fine, Miss Green. Although I'd forgotten how Chicago traffic lasts half the day and then starts over."

"Yes, it can be a bit unpredictable, even on a perfect fall day." She put on her glasses and studied the menu.

A waitress came over and filled Ted's water glass. "May I get you a cocktail, sir?"

"No, thank you. A Coke. Just a Coke."

He's being careful, doesn't want to shock the old curmudgeon, Stella thought with satisfaction, forcing her lips to stay in a thin, tight line. No curling up on the ends.

When their food arrived and they had finished with pleasantries, Ted began his subtle questions. "I understand you have a very unusual and successful career, Miss Green. May I go over your financial statement?"

"Of course."

"I would greatly appreciate you filling me in on any details that are lacking."

"I trust nothing will be lacking. Jerry Steinman has always been impeccable with my finances."

A soft pink stain colored Ted Draper's cheeks. "Of course, Miss Green. I just want to be sure I understand my new client. Thank you very much for taking me on—after Jerry. He's the best. I've studied your portfolio with him. Blue chips and mutual funds. Royalty checks come to me, and I handle them and send you a photocopied report. Twice a year it says, for the American royalties. Once a year for foreign royalties. Can be sporadic."

He fiddled with a file and took out a piece of paper with the letterhead *Stash Green Cash Foundation*. He saw her staring at the paper and said, "Interesting name for a foundation. Stash Green Cash." He gave a little smile.

"Do you have a problem with the name of my foundation, Mr. Draper?"

"No, not at all," he said too quickly. Then he recovered. "And I understand that all the royalties go into this foundation, unless otherwise specified?"

"That's right."

"And the statements are mailed monthly to this P.O. box in Chicago?"

"Right again. Jerry picked a sharp boy for me."

Ted Draper's brow creased, the pink stain deepened, but he did not lose his poise. He glanced down at the papers and asked, "Do you have a literary agent?"

"No. Never needed one. Eddy Clouse has always treated me well. I just hope he doesn't decide to retire like Jerry. That would be disastrous."

"May I have your permission to contact Mr. Clouse? Mr. Steinman has of course spoken about him to me."

"Contact him if you wish, but let me be perfectly clear. I do not want anyone at the brokerage house prying into my personal affairs."

"Yes, of course. But you do realize that the office manager and the administrative assistants know about all the accounts? It is part of their job."

"Yes, yes. I'm aware of how Goldberg, Finch and Dodge works. But I will not have personal contact with anyone besides you. If you have a question, contact me at this number." She handed him a piece of stationery with a phone number written on it. "Only in an emergency. Identify yourself immediately. Otherwise, for minor issues, talk to Mr. Steinman and Mr. Clouse."

Ted nodded, then asked, "May we discuss the foundation?"

"Of course."

"Created in 1967, I believe."

"Yes, after the publication of the second novel."

"You only want me to deal in mutual funds and blue chip stocks."

"Yes. Nothing risky."

"Are you interested in other bonds? Several very conservative new issues are coming out, and the market looks constructive for this type of investment."

She leaned forward and bore into him. "Mr. Draper, you may purchase what you like with the royalties. I trust you to invest well. Just be sure of two things. No junk bonds and nothing in computers, yet. I still believe in typewriters."

"Of course, Miss Green." He cleared his throat, looked down at the papers that sat beside an empty coffee cup, and shuffled through them. "I've spent some time studying your portfolio. It has grown considerably each year, with spikes after the publication of each novel. Your portfolio shows a gain of over sixteen percent last year. The total amount in the foundation comes to just over seven million dollars, of which you have specified seven percent each year be given away—well above what is required by law for charitable foundations."

"Exactly."

He twirled a pen on his fingers; Stella concluded it was his nervous twitch.

"I know that once a year we transfer whatever amount you tell us to your bank account in Switzerland. As your broker, it is my responsibility to inform you that the government is tightening restrictions on what can be considered 'charitable institutions.' Would you like to discuss where this money is going—to be sure it still qualifies?"

"No. I am fully aware of the law. And no one, absolutely no one, needs to know anything about where this money goes, Mr. Draper." She leaned across the table for emphasis. "Remember that your job is to invest well, build up the foundation. That's it. My job is to distribute the funds as I wish, no questions asked. Is that clear?"

"Yes, yes, of course."

"Good. Then that will be all." With one move she picked up the tab for the lunch and signaled to the waiter. She paid with a wad of bills, leaving a sizeable tip, and walked out the door, with Ted Draper catching up on her heels.

"Thank you, Mr. Draper." She shook his hand.

The tall, confident broker wore a startled expression that he changed quickly to a pleasant smile. "Thank you, Miss Green. So nice to meet you. Thank you for lunch."

Stella nodded, hailed a taxi, and got in, satisfied that she had gained the upper hand on this new recruit. The foundation was safe, for the time being. Everything was safe.

CHAPTER EIGHT

Eddy Clouse was out for the day. He had probably flown off to some meeting with good old Essay. At any rate, it gave Silvano a little more freedom with his phone calls. He dialed the number of the Atlanta firm.

"Goldberg, Finch and Dodge. How may I help you?" The woman's voice was young and professional.

"Yes, hello. I'm interested in finding a broker at your firm, and Mr. Jerry Steinman has been recommended to me. Is there a possibility I could set up a phone interview with Mr. Steinman?"

"I'm sorry, but Mr. Steinman is not taking on new clients at this time. He is actually in the process of retiring."

"I see. Would he have another broker he could refer me to?"

"Well, I know that he has turned over some of his accounts to Mr. Ted Draper. Would you care to speak with him?"

Silvano thought through his options and said, "Yes, yes, that would be fine."

"Excuse me, who may I say is calling?"

"Mr. Rossi, from Youngblood Publishers, at the First National Bank Building at Five Points."

"One moment, please."

Silvano drummed his fingers impatiently, or perhaps nervously, on his desk.

"Hello, Ted Draper here."

"Mr. Draper, hello. My name is Silvano Rossi. I'm an editor with Youngblood Publishers here in Atlanta. I've been asked to write an article on authors and investments in the stock market. I was referred to Goldberg, Finch and Dodge because one of our most illustrious authors is represented by your firm—Miss S. A. Green. I was wondering if I might have an interview with you and get information for other authors who are looking to us for financial planning."

Silvano made his voice as smooth as his greased-back black hair. "I know you cannot discuss Miss Green's affairs. The whole publishing house knows the legend of S. A. Green. We know that case is closed." He chuckled good-naturedly. "I'm wondering if we could set up a time for an interview somewhere downtown. Maybe over lunch. I actually think it might be good business for your firm. When it's published, this article will be read by authors all over the country."

"Funny that you should call right now, Mr. Rossi. I actually have a meeting scheduled at Youngblood early next week to meet with Edmond Clouse. We'll be busy all Monday morning, but perhaps I could work in your interview in the afternoon—or over lunch, if you prefer."

A smile, which eventually became a full-fledged grin, spread across Silvano's face as the broker spoke. "That would be fantastic, absolutely fantastic. I'd really appreciate any time you could give me."

"Yes, well, I'll look forward to meeting you, Mr. Rossi."

"Silvano. Call me Silvano."

"Certainly. See you next week, Silvano."

Buono!

Well, that was easy.

Play your cards right, Silvano, and it will all work out just right.

He made another call.

"Frank? Yes, Silvano Rossi here. Yes. Yes, I'm sorry that we seemed to get started on the wrong foot. All my fault. I've been looking over the manuscript again, and I believe there are several less drastic things we could do to make this work. . . ."

———

Ted loved driving through his new neighborhood—in the deep green Mercedes, no less—and turning onto his street. Tuxedo Road—*his street*. Where some of the wealthiest Atlantans lived. Yes, he was proud of himself! Life was good! Even better, now that he'd met Miss Green. Maybe she had a screw loose, but that was no problem. Weren't all artists a bit crazy? Genius and insanity were just two words to describe the same condition. It didn't matter. She liked him. Wary, yes. But it had gone well.

Ted entered the house on Tuxedo and knew immediately what Lin Su had fixed for dinner. Pork and vegetable stir-fry with cashew rice. A family favorite. He set down his briefcase and overnight bag in the hall and let out a deep breath. It felt so good to be home—the black and white tile floors, the high ceilings, the ambiance that Lin Su created seemingly without effort.

"Daddy!" It was Sammy's three-year-old voice he heard before the little guy scooted into the hallway in his pajamas, the kind with the feet in them that made him slip and slide and giggle as he went.

"Hey, buddy! Man, is it good to be home!" He picked up the child and swung him around while Sammy's perfect toddler giggles reverberated, as beautiful to Ted as any rendition of Bach by the Atlanta Symphony.

"Where's Mommy?"

"Wif Weeanne. Changin' da stinky diaper."

They both laughed and, with Sammy stuck on Ted's back, traipsed through the house, past the kitchen and master suite to where they could hear Lin Su humming as she patted powder on LeeAnne's perfect little bottom.

He came from behind and kissed his wife on the neck. "Hmm, you smell good," he whispered in her ear.

Lin Su turned around, black eyes beaming, and said, "You made it back in one piece!" Hoisting the baby on a hip, she planted a kiss on

Ted's mouth while Sammy peeked over his shoulder. "So tell all. What is this mysterious Miss S. A. Green like?"

Ted laughed out loud. "Crotchety old thing, that's for sure. Jerry was right about that. I don't care a bit for her. But I won't look a gift horse in the mouth. She's going to be a wonderful client—easy, in some ways. As long as I don't get on her bad side."

Sammy wiggled off his back, and LeeAnne crawled after her brother to where the VCR was set up.

"Now, you've got a choice," Lin Su said, giving him her best tiger-eye look. "We can eat dinner now, or we can let the kids watch the new Disney video I picked up at the store while we have dessert first." She winked seductively.

Ted grinned. "Wow. What an offer! I think I'll choose that dessert." He held her around the waist. He could tell her about the China trip later, over dinner. For now, with LeeAnne safe in her playpen, peering out at the TV, and Sammy lying beside her with his blanket, Ted pressed the Play button and escaped to the bedroom with Lin Su while a Disney melody played in the background.

Later, when the kids were tucked into bed, he held Lin Su close and said, "I've got a little surprise for you."

"Really?"

"Ever heard of the Million Dollar Club?"

She made a face, the one he loved where she scrunched up her button nose and pouted with her lips. "Nope, but it sounds like a club it might be fun to join." She flashed a smile.

"It's a great club to join—except you have to qualify. And to qualify, you have to do a million dollars' worth of business in a year for Goldberg, Finch and Dodge."

"Not bad. Know anyone who's done that much business?" she teased.

"You're looking at him!"

"Is that so? And here I thought all you did was meet for lunch with slightly crazy old women."

Lin Su was acting nonchalant, but he knew she was thrilled for him.

"And if you qualify for the club, they give you a free trip."

"Now, that sounds interesting."

"All expenses paid for you and your wife. And guess where the firm will be sending the ones who qualify this year?"

"No idea. Disney World?"

"Guess again."

"The Grand Canyon."

"Think a little farther away, a little more exotic."

"Europe."

"Exotic."

"Oh, I don't know, Ted! Tell me!"

"China."

Lin Su's eyes grew wide, the perfect, startled expression. "No. You're kidding."

"I'm not kidding. A weeklong, all-expenses-paid trip to China. Only we won't stay just a week. We'll be taking the kids to see your family—the aunts and uncles and your grandparents—while we travel with the company. And then we'll spend another week with your family after the trip."

"Is this already a done deal?" Lin Su asked, incredulous. "Oh, Ted! Are you serious! This is real?"

"This is real, sweetie." *Almost for sure*, he thought. His numbers were right on track for this far into the year. "You are going home for a visit."

The first time in eight long years. This was what he had dreamed of offering to his wife. This made all the headaches worth it.

He loved that his wife was gorgeous *and* tough. She'd never had anything handed to her on a platter. She deserved this. He thought back to their first meeting.

MIT. Second semester sophomore year, economics class. Two hundred students in the amphitheater. He had noticed her immediately. Petite, Asian, beautiful, dedicated. Over the months he observed her in the library way past the hours of most students. Asian tenacity, he called it. Finally in March, he'd gotten up the nerve to speak to her.

"Hi, I'm Ted Draper. I think we have econ together."

"Oh, I hadn't noticed." She didn't even look up from her books.

"Do you ever take a study break?"

"Rarely." She kept her head buried. "And I don't lend out my notes. Or go on dates."

"That makes two of us, then. I'm here to study. I plan to be top in my class."

She gave him a sideways glance, slightly intrigued. Lifting her eyebrows, she said, "Well, that's interesting. I'm planning on being the top in *my* class."

They became inseparable. Never a date, just grueling hours in the library, quick coffee breaks, and a gradual understanding that they were both after the same thing. Success.

Eventually, he learned about her background. Her father was American, her mother Chinese. Lin Su had lived all her life in Oregon with her parents and siblings, twice visiting China in her childhood. Money was always tight.

"My family has all their hopes placed in me," she confided late one night. "Failure isn't an option. Distractions aren't either."

"You won't fail, Lin Su. You may have an American father, but inside you're pure Asian—hardworking to the core."

At that, she seethed. "Don't you ever stoop to such a low stereotype again, Ted Draper. You understand?"

He remembered how he had blushed. He liked her grit.

Lin Su graduated first in their class and got a full scholarship to business school; he was third with his own scholarships offered. His buddies assumed his pride was hurt, but Ted knew that celebrating and encouraging Lin Su's success was the only way he could keep her. Theirs was a very rocky relationship: competition, drive, nasty fights, reconciliation. They both liked it that way.

They got married in the middle of grad school and spent their honeymoon in China, visiting all the relatives in a week of celebrations. They had not been back since.

She worked for a financial planning firm for five years, until Sammy came along. With much prodding from Ted, she had agreed to take a little break to stay home with the children. After all, with the market going straight up, they were making it just fine on his salary. Business was soaring—S. A. Green, a few other filthy rich clients and some bond issues, and an interview with an editor from Youngblood Publishers. Everything was going even better than he had dreamed.

———

"Well, there's irony for you," Janelle laughed dryly. "I think I need to get away, and instead my bitter big sister announces she's coming for a visit. Can you believe she wants to come now? What in the world would prompt that?"

"She must be hurting. You know your sister—she won't show it, but something is wrong."

"I know my sister, and if something is wrong, she will do everything in her power to pretend it is otherwise. She got a college degree in making sure everything appears to be perfect."

Brian gave her a squeeze. "Don't you think you're being a little hard on her?"

"Who knows? And what in the world do I have to offer now?"

"Maybe she just needs to see someone else's life. A change of scenery."

Janelle couldn't imagine really having her sister visit in Montpellier. She'd invited her for years. Once, back in the late seventies, Hamilton and Katy Lynn stopped by on their way to a cruise. Janelle made a face, remembering that very brief visit. Hamilton had thought they were nuts—fanatics trying to reform the French Catholics and convert the Muslims.

Of course, he hadn't said it exactly like that. He *had* talked all about *his* business and *his* plans for *his* company and made little condescending remarks about how small their house was and the strange bathrooms. By the end of twenty-four hours, Janelle was afraid her normally peace-loving husband was going to strangle Hamilton—"The egomaniac," he'd whispered, almost loudly enough for Hamilton to hear.

Afterward, she and Brian had both referred to that incident as the "visit from hell," and had laughed, albeit sadly. They cared about Hamilton and Katy Lynn, but they were on another wavelength, a completely different planet.

Katy Lynn had always shied away from any talk of faith. Raised in the church, something had gone stale many, many years ago. Janelle did not want to rehash old memories, did not have the mental strength to delve into that painful subject—how two sisters, raised in the same way, could turn out so very differently. Different interests, of course, were normal. But why had she embraced their parents' faith while Katy Lynn shunned it, blaming her father—*their* father—the gentlest man in the world? For so many years now, Janelle and Brian had prayed for Katy Lynn and Hamilton and Gina. But if the truth were told, the last person Janelle wanted to walk through her front door in four short days was Katy Lynn. Well, actually, perhaps that was inaccurate. At least she wasn't bringing Hamilton. Janelle could be thankful for small blessings.

————

When Lissa stepped out of the redbrick library building and walked across the spacious grassy courtyard, she had a smile on her face that to Ev looked like the sun's rays spilling through an opening in the clouds—a pleasant and unexpected shift in the weather.

"Hello, Mr. MacAllister!" she sang out. It seemed the heavens had granted her not only a sunny disposition but a new voice, a warm, rich voice of hope. She wore her hair down, and Ev noticed its bright sheen and the way it bounced lightly as she walked.

"Hello, Lissa!" He hoped his own voice communicated more warmth and optimism than he felt. Having Annie acknowledge Lissa's resemblance to Tate had not brought him relief. It only made him worry more.

"Um, Mr. MacAllister," she said as he started the engine, "I think I'm ready to drive through the park again."

"You sure? Remember, we're not trying to set any records."

"I know that, sir."

She talked easily as they drove across the Tennessee River and headed out of Chattanooga toward Fort Oglethorpe. She seemed eager to get in the driver's seat of Ole Bessie. Parked by the old house-turned-visitor-center, she hopped out of the passenger's seat and walked in front of the car, almost skipping. Ev barely had time to situate himself before Lissa was buckled in and revving the engine.

She backed the car out easily, pulled onto the wide road of the Military Park, and inched forward slowly but with confidence. Three deer from across the street perked up their heads at the sight of Ole Bessie.

"You ready to take the battleground loop?" Ev asked.

"Sure."

Another clear blue day, another perfect fall festival. Perhaps he'd been wrong about Lissa. Perhaps she could get past the block more quickly than he had expected. He'd been wrong before.

She handled the first part of the loop with ease. "There are so many monuments in this park."

"Over two hundred. Chickamauga was the bloodiest two-day battle of the war. Over thirty-four thousand men were killed, wounded, or missing."

Even as he said this, he noticed a barely perceptible change in the girl. The bead of sweat started on her upper lip—the way it had for Annie during her unpredictable hot flashes. But Lissa was nineteen. She cleared her throat three times in a row and leaned forward, squinting, then began to tremble, her fist in a tight coil, her breathing rapid, her brow sweaty. With only the deer looking on, Lissa pulled the car off into a small parking space meant for tourists who wanted to take pictures of a nearby military statue.

She leaned her head on the steering wheel and closed her eyes. "I'm sorry, Mr. MacAllister. I guess I was wrong. I just thought that maybe things would go more smoothly, but the monuments and all . . ." She couldn't finish her sentence.

"We're not in a hurry, Lissa."

The trembling stopped, but the girl looked devastated, surprised by her failure.

"I was so sure that today I wouldn't hear that voice—you know, the one that says it's going to happen again. That I'll have another accident . . . or worse."

Ev tried to think of something to say. Then he asked, "Do you remember what I told you the other night about voices?"

"That we have to figure out which ones to listen to and how to shut the other ones up?"

"Exactly." He patted the upholstery and squinted through the bright sun on the windshield. "Tell me what the nicest voice you ever hear says to you."

"The nicest voice?" Lissa's voice was thick with sarcasm. "Did I say there was a *nice* voice?"

"No, but I'm sure there's one in there somewhere. Think about it."

He was determined not to be in a hurry with Lissa Randall. They sat in Ole Bessie, with the monument in memory of the 35th Ohio Regiment looking over at them.

Lissa didn't say a word for a long time. Finally, she cleared her throat and said in a whisper, "The nicest voice I heard was my mother's. She's the one who would say, 'Let yourself enjoy things. Your life isn't all planned out, no matter what your father says. Dream, Lissa. Close your eyes and dream.' "

"And when you let yourself, Lissa, what do you dream about?"

She seemed to relax a little. "Not much these days. I dream that my father and I can have a real conversation. Something that goes a little deeper than the weather or work."

"Anything else?"

"Look, Mr. MacAllister, I really appreciate all your help, but I don't think this is going very far." She unbuckled her seat belt and shifted her weight so that she was facing Ev. Her voice was steady now, controlled. "My father and I are stuck. All he wants is for me to go to college. The best college possible. He cannot even begin to consider that I may not ever get there. That would freak him out big-time. So he just pretends things are going fine, that I am gradually getting better and that my 'little job' at the school library and my 'little time' spent with you learning to drive are just necessary—albeit embarrassing—steps to getting me ready for college. He cannot look at reality. The man absolutely refuses."

Vigor had returned to Lissa's voice, and determination. The word *gutsy* flashed in Ev's mind.

"I suppose you can't blame him really, Lissa. He wants you to move forward, wants the best for you. And he knows you've got the brains to get into a good school."

"Oh, yeah, I have the brains. But maybe I don't have the mental stability. Maybe I'm not going to get over all these panic attacks, and maybe his dream for me is never going to come true." Her voice grew louder, almost strident, her fists coiled tight in her lap. "He hates me because I killed my mother."

She said it forcefully, her deep brown eyes boring into Ev's, eyes filled with hurt and anger and conviction. "That's what he thinks. That's what I see every time I look in his eyes."

Ev massaged his chin with his hand and nodded. *Perhaps it's not accusation, Lissa. Perhaps it is grief and fear. Parents don't always know how to communicate the depth of their love and hurt.*

"I already have a car, and I'm saving up my money so that as soon as I can get my license, I can move out. We're just stuck right now. I need to be able to drive. It's urgent, so I can drive over to see— So I can drive. That's all I dream about." She had calmed down as she spoke, and now she cocked her head, stared at Ev. "I used to have other dreams, though. I used to dream of being a writer."

"A writer, you say?" That came from out of the blue, and he welcomed the tangent.

"Yes, sir. I was always making up stories in school, scribbling down ideas in my notebooks. My teachers said I had talent." She blushed. "I'm sorry. I'm talking too much."

"Lissa Randall, don't analyze. Just talk."

She frowned at him, almost a playful pout, almost—but not quite— annoyed. "But with the accident and everything, well, I've given up that dream. At least I've tried to. But the urge to write is still strong. It's just this . . . this need, I guess. You know what I mean?"

The crease in her brow told him she couldn't imagine that he did. *This old man doesn't understand much besides cars and drivers' tests,* he guessed she was thinking. "What about your stories?" he asked. "Did they go away?"

"Huh?"

"You said they were always crowding in on you. Do they still?"

"Oh, I still hear all kinds of stories in my mind—when I'm not paying attention to the other stuff. But I don't seem to have enough time to write them down. The only thing I write down is in my journal—for the therapist."

At last he had something to grab on to. "Lissa, that's your homework for next time. Write down whatever story you hear in your head. Write it down."

The annoyed frown again. "I don't see what good that's going to do, Mr. MacAllister."

"You don't have to understand it, Lissa. Just do it. Now drive us back to the visitor center, will you?"

———

Ev swallowed the little yellow pill quickly, refusing to think about it. The pill defied mortality, for a few more years at least. He did not fear death. Of course not—he anticipated it—*for to me to live is Christ and to die is gain.* Still the pill was bitter. Weakness.

The horrible pain shot through him like a blast from a shotgun. Ev grabbed his chest and called out for help. "I'm a young man. I can't be having a heart attack. . . ." But he was.

A quick-thinking friend had saved his life all those years ago. Another ten minutes, and Everett MacAllister would have been history. Now a pill and a good diet and exercise kept him healthy—healthy enough that no one asked questions like, Are you sure it's safe to be teaching driving lessons with your heart condition?

He went over the conversation with Lissa and thought of the agony in her eyes, so reminiscent of Tate. And there he went with the memory.

The white house was lit up with candles, hundreds of them so that it looked almost on fire. People were buzzing on the lawn, adults with cocktails, a happy, slurred noise of too much alcohol.

"Congrats to you, Mr. MacAllister!"

Ev saw himself in the tuxedo, his hair greased back, a cigar hanging from his lips, a martini in hand. Boisterous laughter. Annie on one arm, in her slinky dress, laughing, laughing.

A lovely redhead caught his eye from across the yard. She gave a wink, then, eyes dancing, turned and walked toward the house.

"Excuse me a moment," Ev said to his guests, kissing Annie on the cheek.

He hurried into the house and up the steps, following after Frieda—the redhead—in her low-cut white dress, her hips swinging. On the second floor landing, he grabbed her around the waist and kissed her hard, passionately, both of them laughing in their drunkenness. They pushed down the hall to a bedroom. Laughing, carrying her, he flung the door open.

Tate sat with her back to them, retching. Ev set Frieda down and shooed her out without a sound.

"Tate! Tate, what's the matter?" His words slurred with the simple phrase.

She turned red-rimmed eyes to him. "Is it true? Mother and Father are crooks?"

"Tate?"

"And you with Frieda! Is that true too? I hate this life."

Tate, fragile, porcelain china doll Tate. Striking brunette. Perfect curves at sixteen. Innocent and yet wise beyond her years. Hating life, hating the parties.

He came to her side and saw the blood on the wrists. "Tate!"

"Let me go! Let me die! Don't you pick me up. You selfish cheat! Leave me alone!"

Ev was carrying his little sister down the steps, her wrists wrapped in linen napkins, his eyes blurred, not from alcohol but from tears. Tate.

Lissa flopped on her bed, glad that she had spoken truth to Mr. MacAllister. She did dream of writing. She dreamed of many things. No, she *had* dreamed of many things. No more.

The gelding's head was high, his ears pricked forward as they headed into the final line of fences. Only one more line and they would have a clean round. Up and over the intimidating oxer. The in-and-out went smoothly. No problems. And the last fence, the brick wall. He sailed over, his hooves not anywhere near the jump.

"And another clean round for Lissa Randall and her gelding High Caliber," the announcer was saying.

She left the ring, collapsed on the gelding's neck, arms on either side. "Good boy. Good boy. We did it!"

Momma was laughing, rushing up to them both, eyes sparkling. Dad was even there, with a look of distinct approval in his eyes. He was holding the new camcorder, and had doubtless filmed the whole sequence. "For your college applications," he said with a wink. "They like to know that you have lots of different interests."

I have no interests now! She might have said it out loud, but it didn't matter. Even if he heard it, her father would swiftly put it out of his mind. He could not accept reality.

Helena had not replaced the photos. No picture of her standing beside High Caliber, the ribbon attached to the gelding's bridle, rippling in the wind. No smiling Momma in her sequined dress.

"Just call me the girl who can't quiet the voices." This she did say out loud. With no other transition, the story twirled in her mind until she made her way to the desk, took out an old notebook, and began to write—anything and everything that came into her mind.

Thirty minutes later, she laughed to herself. For whatever it was worth, Lissa had done her homework.

CHAPTER NINE

Discretion, they called it in the stock market. All those years ago she had given Jerry Steinman permission to choose the stocks, the bonds, and the funds in which to invest her money. Implicit trust. Now it was Ted Draper's turn. The young man had handled himself well—gotten to know her portfolio, taken the time to reassure her that he understood what type of client she was—only interested in the blue chip stocks and mutual funds. In the months to come, she knew she would feel as safe with him as she had with Jerry. It would take a little time, but that was fine. He respected her demands: no questions asked about the foundation, no information revealed about her to others, complete anonymity.

Stella looked at the folder he had left for her. The young man was thorough, much more than competent. A little cocky, she thought, but she trusted Jerry's judgment. Once again she signed the form.

She had not studied her portfolio for several months. It was time, with the new novel coming out much sooner than she had expected. The foundation was worth over seven million. Amazing what the years of careful investing had done for her, for them.

Young Mr. Draper was curious about the Stash Green Cash Foundation. She smiled at the name. Jerry would set him straight. It would all be okay.

But worry seeped into her mind, so slippery and devious. Before she could stop it, a scene from yesteryear played itself out in her mind once again.

"Stella?"

"Yes?"

"Who was it?"

"Eddy Clouse, saying the New Yorker *called him. Same request as always. An interview."*

She let the screen door shut on itself, turned, and went into the study, where her husband was bent over his desk. She studied him from behind. She had always loved the way his sandy hair curled up to the right whenever he was in need of a haircut. She placed a hand lightly on his back, leaned forward, and kissed him on the top of the head.

He swiveled around in the metal chair, his face erupting into a dimpled smile. "Sweetheart," he whispered and enlaced her with his arms. She settled softly in his lap, threw her arms around his neck, and pressed herself into his chest, her face against his, her attention on the steady beating of his heart.

An image from the first review flashed before her, a newspaper opened to the headline Stella Is Stellar! Debut Novel a Jewel.

*The second novel—*Stella Is Stellar Again, Anonymous Author Just Gets Better.

"I don't know if I can keep doing this," she whispered, nodding to the half-finished manuscript. "If I should. I'm sorry."

He hugged her tighter. "You're the strongest woman on the planet, and if you think it's time to quit, then you'll quit."

"But what about you?"

"I'll figure something out. Don't worry about me, darling."

But she did.

They held each other for another minute, neither of them speaking. Then she hopped off his lap, kissed him briefly, playfully on the mouth, and said, "I've got lunch to fix, and the kids'll be home in a sec."

She started off; he caught her arm, pulled her gently backed to him again.
She met his eyes, letting herself smile into them.
"Thank you," he whispered.
"You're welcome."

Stella reached for the phone to call her daughter. She needed to hear a friendly voice. She could not dial the number. Instead, she saw the notebook filled with Eddy Clouse's suggestions. She was getting too old for the charade. A long time ago it had all been right. But now? Now she was not sure. Seven million dollars in the foundation. Wasn't that enough?

She knew the answer before she had even formulated the question. It was never really enough if she wanted to be sure the job was done right. Why did it seem like it always depended on her? She did not want to go down that woe-begotten lane. Better keep her mind on the present. But the lingering memory pushed through and she surprised herself by uttering his name out loud for the first time in so many years.

"Ashton."

———

Katy Lynn hesitated before tapping on the office door. Two days ago, Lanie's husband lawyer, Chad, had given her the reference for Cannel Corporation, Private Investigators, a firm with impeccable credentials, well respected—and feared—among the elite of Atlanta's Buckhead. He had assured her that this firm would do her right.

The meeting went smoothly, all things considered. Katy Lynn concluded her little speech. "I will want a full report when I get back. Photos, dates, history. Everything. I want an airtight case! If Hamilton expects to get away with this little adventure, well, he is going to pay through the nose!"

"Mrs. Pendleton, we will handle this with the utmost discretion. You will have your report for the end of October."

She let out a long sigh and mentally reviewed her list: plane tickets bought, Gina staying for two weeks with the Lewises. Jazz practices, check; piano lessons, check; visit to the psychiatrist, check.

That had been the trump card for Katy Lynn to agree to Gina's "break from home."

The appointment was for next week, and Ellen Lewis, a Southern belle if ever one existed, knew exactly what questions to ask and what to leave unsaid. "I'll be happy to get her to the appointment, and I'll be watching for any unusual behavior."

Already Gina seemed lighter, happier when she called her mother every evening after school. "That is so cool, Mom, that you're visiting Aunt Janelle and Uncle Brian. France, the beaches. Have a great time, and don't worry about me. Caroline and I are having a blast."

Katy Lynn congratulated herself on the plan. Everything was in order once again. Now all that remained was packing her bags for the south of France. Montpellier. Halfway between Marseille and Spain, on the coast. She closed her eyes and smiled, imagining herself stretched out on some beach surrounded by half-nude women. She remembered Janelle describing their first trip to the beach. It made Katy Lynn chuckle even now. Prudish little sister Janelle going to France to save the Catholics—or was it the Muslims? And there she was, flipping out over women's bare breasts on the beach. Poor Brian! Such a fine young Christian man. He probably loved going to the beach, although he couldn't admit it to Janelle.

Katy Lynn thought back to the brief visit she and Hamilton had made nearly ten years ago. Hamilton thought the beaches were divine. He could have packed up and moved to France in a second. Katy Lynn had simply rolled her eyes. Men. Perhaps she should have been paying more attention to Hamilton's roving eyes. She pushed the unpleasant thought away, got out of the car, placed her sunglasses back in the purse, and stood up straight.

"Okay, Katy-Kate"—that was her mother's nickname for her—"time to pack your bags. You're going to France!"

————

Nothing put Ted in a better mood than twenty minutes on the phone with Kenny White. The guy was a genius! Never mind that he worked for the competition. They'd been trading information on junk bonds for two years now, and they had both come out ahead. A true partnership, he chuckled to himself. The Million Dollar Club. His smirk spread all the way across his face, remembering his romantic evening with Lin Su, his surprise announcement, her delight. Now he had the icing on the cake. Three new companies that Kenny had researched issued junk bonds. Business was soaring, and Ted knew exactly which clients would love to hear the news.

He picked up the phone and whispered to himself, "Okay, fellas! I'm about to make your day!"

———

Lissa enjoyed the Friday afternoon tutoring sessions. Seated by the picture windows in the library with the stunning view of the river and mountains just outside seemed to inspire the girls to try harder. At first it had been only the junior high girls and simple things like reviewing Latin vocabulary or discussing *Romeo and Juliet*. Then Mrs. Rivers had suggested that Lissa tutor the senior high girls who were struggling with fourth-year Latin and AP history. This she found a bit more challenging—not the schoolwork but the "student work"—figuring out how to help each girl succeed.

Chattanooga Girls School was famous for sending its students into depression. One of the top girl schools in the southeast—some said *the* top school—it had money, money, money from the alumni, from the parents, probably from the governor himself. It all spelled one thing to the students: *You're the cream of the crop; you must succeed.*

Plenty of the girls had the brains to make it through, but perhaps not the nerves of steel to face constant pressure, constant competition. Freshman Holly Jenkins, for example, should not be at CGS. But here she was, and she needed help in beginning Latin.

"Okay, Holly, can you name the seven cases?"

"Nominative, genitive, dative, accusative, ablative, vocative . . ." Holly blanked.

"Good. It was kind of a trick question. Locative is only used in special cases. But Mrs. Gruder will ask you about it, so tuck it away for good measure. Now the endings for the first declension?"

"*A, ae, ae, am,* and *a.*"

"Fine. Now can you decline the Latin word for *girl?*"

Holly obediently began reciting, "*Puella, puellae, puellae . . .*"

Very, very simple stuff that Holly should have memorized the first week of school. But by the end of the hour-long tutorial session, Lissa felt a bit more hopeful. "We'll meet a few more times together, and you'll be right on track."

"Thanks, Lissa!" Holly beamed at her. "See ya next week."

Lissa waved to Holly, then reached down and picked up the thin, hard-backed volume. *First Year Latin.* Just looking at the textbook brought a sudden pang to Lissa. She loved Latin. It made sense. It fit together. It was a puzzle, a lovely, ancient puzzle. What she would give to travel back in time, before college visits, to be sitting in Mrs. Gruder's fifth-year Latin class.

Eleventh grade. The Latin Festival. First Lissa had won the city-wide contest, then the regionals, and finally she had gone to the national tournament. After her performance, she was chosen as one of twelve students from across the country to spend two weeks in Rome. She had fallen in love with the ancient city. Every college she applied to, she determined, must have one thing: a study abroad program in Rome.

Lissa felt a chill and a pinching and an excitement, all mixed together in her heart. She longed to study again. She *longed* to! Why was she so afraid? Maybe this was just salt in the wound, these tutoring sessions. She herself should be studying.

She thought about this as Mrs. Rivers drove her home, taking the familiar route from the north shore across the Tennessee River and going through town on Broad Street. The words pounded in her mind as the car curved up the steep road to Lookout Mountain. When Mrs. Rivers dropped her off at her home, Lissa climbed the steps to her room and went to the desk where she had left the spiral notebook, tucked under several books. She took it out, and with the taste of Latin still on her lips, the memory of Rome fresh as new snow, she wrote:

How can I go to college when that act would mean moving on without her? College is the nail in her coffin. Even thinking about it reminds me of our last trip, the hail, the sliding, the fear, then terror, then relief. Then death. Everything that has to do with college is agony! I cannot go there. I do not have the right to move in that direction. Another, perhaps. Perhaps a future, but not college. Never.

She reread the words like a prison sentence. In her mind, she knew her thinking was somehow very flawed. But in her heart she hurt, a literal, agonizing pain, every time she thought about college. How to get beyond it? She did not know.

———

Silvano studied the manuscript carefully, comparing it with the other novels—all five of them—that sat on the floor beside the little desk in his apartment. The workweek was over at last! But now the real work began, and he honestly had no idea what he was looking for, besides a clue, any clue that could direct him to the whereabouts of Miss Green. On a scrap of paper beside a small ashtray brimming with cigarette butts he had scratched:

Miss Green's publisher: Youngblood
Miss Green's editor: Edmond Clouse
Miss Green's royalties deposited in a P.O. Box in Chicago
Miss Green's new broker: Ted Draper at Goldberg, Finch and Dodge,
*   an Atlanta brokerage firm*
Miss Green's former broker: Jerry Steinman, semiretired from Goldberg, Finch and Dodge
Miss Green's bio:

Here he was stuck. Every dust jacket had the same three sentences written on the back flap, following the description of the novel.

S. A. Green is a novelist who prefers complete anonymity and writes somewhere in the United States. Previous novels include (and here, depending on the order of the novel, the titles varied). The novels have all been bestsellers in America and Europe, with Eastern Crossings winning the coveted Penn-Warren Award, and Cautiously Optimistic having been nominated for a Pulitzer Prize.

Nothing more, nothing less.

Silvano drew in on his Diana and toyed with a pen. His best chance at nabbing information was the meeting with Ted Draper on Monday. Now what could he ask to glean a little more about Miss Green? Something the new broker wouldn't think of as secretive. He wracked his brain for five minutes while in the background Tom Brokaw narrated a news story about the Reagan administration. And then he had it.

Of course! Of course!

He didn't need any other information.

He had the post office box, and with that he'd provide bait to lure out Miss Green!

In Rome, the bait his family used was offering the cheapest postcards available next to St. Peter's. Cheap but good quality, and the best gelato within a two-kilometer radius of the Vatican. A deal for those obnoxious Americans, overweight, loud, dressed in the strangest color combinations and even daring to wear shorts into St. Peter's.

And now, here, the perfect bait was a letter sent to the post office box! Yes, that was it. A carefully worded letter—not threatening, exactly, but something disturbing, to make a neurotic writer shiver in her shoes and venture out of her little hole. Bait.

He smiled. He'd catch up on his reading this weekend. He felt confident that, after having reread all six of these novels, he would know just what was needed to coax dear Miss Green out of her hole.

MONDAY, OCTOBER 5

"Okay, kids!" Janelle called up the stairs. "We leave for the airport in ten minutes."

"Sure, Mom!" came Luke's reply. At least he seemed excited to see his aunt.

Janelle sat at the table in her yellow and white kitchen and read the letter—one that she kept stashed in a drawer in her desk—for the hundredth time.

September 14, 1979
Dear Janelle,

I know that life does not feel fun right now. More like an oppressive cloud hovering, ready to spill its bad news like water from the sky. I know, dear. What you and Brian are doing is tough. And it takes time. You felt a calling, you obeyed, you are there. Don't doubt the calling, sugar. You are in the ample and loving hands of our Father. Stay put, Janelle. Stay put.

You know it would be much easier for me to write other words: Come Home! in big, bold letters. Your mother and I need you. Please come home. Honestly, this is how I feel much of the time. But I will not argue with Almighty God. He called you.

And about Katy Lynn. You cannot change your sister. Heaven knows, if prayers could guarantee quick changes, she'd be galloping down the straight and narrow path like a mare at feeding time. Prayer works, Janelle. Never stop praying. But let God decide on the timetable.

Just love her, sugar. Somewhere along the line, Katy Lynn decided I was against her, that I disapproved of everything that was important to her. That I considered her ideas liberal and rebellious and plain wrong. How many nights have we stayed awake wondering what we could have done differently, why she shut me out?

I'm sorry to say I'm not surprised by the turn of their visit. Hamilton is so focused on his business and Katy Lynn is focused on getting everything out of life while being completely in control. Paradoxes. It can't be very appealing to see all you have given up, especially when they don't understand the reason.

Don't be too hard on yourself, sugar. You never know what God has planned for the next chapter. You just never know.

Mother sends mounds of hugs, as she says.

> *With love,*
> *Dad*

She folded the letter, placed it back in its yellowing envelope, climbed the stairs, and went into the office. She opened a drawer, slipped the letter inside, and gave Brian a peck on the cheek.

"Ready, Nelli?"

"As ready as I'll ever be, I suppose."

She grabbed her purse from the bedroom. Luke raced down the

stairs, with Sandy following close after. The sound of pounding young feet on wooden stairs made Janelle smile briefly. Brian followed behind, and soon they were on the way to the airport.

———

She was completely exhausted. It had been years since she'd traveled to Europe, and Katy Lynn had forgotten what jet lag felt like. Thank heavens for first-class tickets. She pitied the poor people scrunched together like a bag of vacuum-packed Georgia peanuts in economy. But even so, she hadn't slept a wink on the flight, and the food was atrocious. All she wanted was a nice bed and a bath.

Katy Lynn spied them waving at her through the glass doors as she waited to retrieve her luggage in the Montpellier airport: Janelle, Brian, Luke, and Sandy. My, the kids had grown! She couldn't remember the last time she'd even seen a picture of them.

She followed the other passengers to the metal luggage carts. She cursed under her breath as she rummaged through her wallet to find a ten-franc coin. Thank heavens she'd thought to change her money back in Atlanta! She struggled to drag the suitcases off the conveyor belt. Her feet had swollen on the flight and her beige pumps were killing her.

"Katy!" Janelle said as Katy Lynn pushed her cart through the sliding glass doors. Janelle gave her an awkward hug.

It was a shock to see her baby sister—Janelle had gained weight, and her hair was all wrong. And no makeup. Her little sister looked exhausted.

"Well, hello, gang! How marvelous to see y'all. Goodness, Luke, you are half grown! And Sandy! What pretty blond curls!"

"*Bonjour*, Aunt Katy," Sandy said, planting a kiss on her cheek as Katy Lynn leaned down to receive a handful of wildflowers.

"How sweet."

Brian took over the cart. "Good to see you, Katy Lynn. How was the flight?"

They stepped out into the sweltering heat.

"It's hotter here than Atlanta! And what time is it? Barely noon!"

"Yes, we're having a real Indian summer," Janelle said.

Perspiring heavily, Katy Lynn limped behind them to the parking lot. "Oh, my goodness! How are we going to all fit in there?" she said with a nervous laugh.

She had never seen a smaller car. A Renault. But Brian didn't seem ruffled. Maybe he was used to stuffing luggage into that tiny trunk. In the end, she sat up front with Brian while Janelle and the kids held the biggest bag across their laps. Katy Lynn searched in vain for the air-conditioning and, admitting defeat, rolled down her window and let the hot breeze blow across her face while rivulets of perspiration ran down her back.

"How adorable! Just like a dollhouse!" It escaped before she even gave her comment a thought. Katy Lynn wasn't tall, but she almost felt she should duck to walk inside the little town house. She had forgotten how minuscule everything was in France.

She looked for something to compliment and found it. "Oh, I just love the tiled floors, Janelle. So practical. And that terra cotta color is perfect."

She surveyed the downstairs: one modest-sized room, which seemed to serve the dual function of living room and dining room, a small kitchen, and this entrance hall—way too small for all five of them to be standing in at once.

"Aunt Katy, you get to sleep in my room!" little Sandy enthused. "I picked out the sheets for you. I hope you like them."

"I'm sure they will be perfect, dear."

The stairway was narrow too. Brian carried one of the suitcases up without much problem, but Katy Lynn accidentally knocked a framed picture off the wall as she climbed the stairs. It crashed to the floor and the glass shattered.

"It's no big deal," Janelle called quickly from below with a nervous laugh.

Sandy's room was about the size of Gina's walk-in closet. Never mind. The room was clean and Janelle had stenciled cute little teddy bears all around the wall. Some things never changed. Her little sister had always loved teddy bears.

"What a nice room, dear," she said to Sandy, who was peering up at her with round, inquisitive blue eyes. "Thanks so much for sharing it with me."

She really couldn't imagine why Brian and Janelle didn't have a guest room, with all the people coming in and out. But this would do. It would have to do.

They didn't have a tub either, just a shower, and a claustrophobic one at that. Katy Lynn kept bumping her elbows on the handle, which caused the water to turn scalding until she could fumble with it and adjust the temperature again. Still, the hot water felt good, invigorating. She put on a lightweight sundress and felt revived enough to join the family downstairs for lunch.

The conversation lagged a little, but the kids always seemed to have another question to fill in the pauses.

"How is Gina? And Uncle Hamilton?"

She breezed through that one with "Working like a maniac, as usual."

Near the end of the meal, Katy Lynn announced, "Well, it's good to be here! Thank you for letting me barge in on you all." She flashed her smile and said, "And I've brought a few treats for the kids. Let's see, Luke. Here you go." She reached down and picked up a small wrapped present. "Gina said a nine-year-old boy could use one of these."

Luke tore off the paper and his eyes grew wide. "A Walkman! Man! Wow! Thanks, Aunt Katy!" Then he looked cautiously over at his parents. "Can I keep it?"

Brian gave a half smile. "That's fine, son. We'll talk about it later."

Sandy opened a box to find a doll almost half her size, and squealed, "Aunt Katy! She's beautiful!"

Well, good. At least she'd picked the right gifts. Janelle's eyes even filled briefly when she opened hers: a set of six white linen place mats and napkins and six exquisite Limoges napkin rings. She might be living like a pauper in France, but Janelle appreciated the finer things of life, of that Katy Lynn was sure.

"I'll be taking the kids back to school in a few minutes," Janelle said, glancing at her watch. "And they don't get out until four thirty."

"That makes for a long day, doesn't it?"

"Yes, it does. But they do have this break between noon and two. Anyway, I know you must be exhausted, Katy, with the flight and the heat. I have a few women coming over for a prayer meeting at two thirty. You're welcome to stay down with us if you'd like, but if you'd rather read or take a nap, please feel free."

That announcement caught Katy Lynn off guard. A prayer meeting! "Yes, well . . ." She cleared her throat. "I'll just meet your friends and then go upstairs."

Three of Janelle's friends wore veils. They were *Arab* women. The other two must have been French. In any case, none of them spoke English.

Hamilton had been right about Janelle and Brian. "They have no business meddling with the beliefs of the Arabs," he'd said. "Trying to convert the Muslims to Christianity!"

If they asked her opinion, Katy Lynn would tell them they were playing with fire. Fire!

She certainly had no interest in a prayer meeting and a Bible study. But to be polite, she stayed until all five women had come inside and she had greeted them just as Janelle showed her, with a kiss on each cheek. She even stayed long enough to drink some awful sugary-sweet mint tea. Then she excused herself to find refuge upstairs.

Later, as she helped Janelle prepare dinner, she asked, "Why do your friends wear the veil?"

"Their families are practicing Muslims, and most don't even know that they have converted to Christianity. It's for safety."

"Safety?"

"People have been ostracized from families and even killed for converting. It is a serious matter. Terribly serious."

"And these women *want* to study the Bible and pray—in spite of the danger?"

"In spite of the danger, yes."

"I find that . . . fascinating. Simply fascinating, Janelle." In truth, she found it *incomprehensible* or *insane*. Or maybe *fanatical*. She'd never really thought too much about what Brian and Janelle were doing in

France, but being with them again brought it all back. They were just plain strange.

As soon as possible, she needed to check out the hotels around here. Surely the hotels had air-conditioning. She simply couldn't survive for two weeks in this little broiler house. She wouldn't hurt their feelings. Obviously, they barely had room for the four of them. She'd simply suggest after a few days that she was moving to a hotel so as not to impose on their hospitality.

Before turning in for the night, she made a quick call to Gina, promising to leave cash for the call when she saw Janelle's darting glance at Brian. She felt a tiny irritation. Goodness! Such penny pinchers. Anyway, she knew that overseas phone calls were expensive and would not talk long.

"I got here fine, Gina. All is just perfect," she assured her daughter.

"Have you been to the beach yet?"

"Not yet, but probably tomorrow."

"Cool."

Cool it was not. Katy Lynn brushed the hair that was sticking to her brow out of her face. "Talk to you soon, sweetie. Love you."

"Love you too, Mom. Have fun."

CHAPTER TEN

The letter arrived at ten a.m., a lightweight blue rectangle, folded and sealed in such a way that Ev had to find his pocketknife to slit it open. He didn't mind a bit. It had been over three weeks, and he and Annie always worried, especially at this time of the year. He had heard the lethargy in her voice during their last phone conversation.

He cut open the aerogram and read it out on the porch with Annie hovering over his shoulder.

"She doesn't sound so good, does she?" he said at last.

"No. Homesick. Depressed."

"Missing Josh. Going crazy missing Josh." Ev's voice cracked the slightest bit.

Annie joined him on the front porch swing.

"I've been so caught up in my thoughts about Tate and Lissa, I've neglected my prayers a bit for Janelle and Brian and the kids. I've prayed. I just haven't—"

"You haven't let yourself hurt for them, Mr. MacAllister. And your daughter would be happy to hear it. She doesn't want her father having a heart attack from grief. She needs you. We all do. Not that you haven't been hurting over other things."

"How can we help them, Annie? Money's always so tight for them. Could we send a little more this month? Brian's weighted down with those financial worries in the mission. . . ."

Annie took his hand. "Ev MacAllister, my boyfriend used to say, 'There is no use worrying, Annie, dear. God doesn't want us to rescue our children. He's the Rescuer. There are two things we need to do right now. Trust and pray.' "

He put his arm around her shoulder, pulled her close, and nodded. "Your boyfriend, for all his faults, had some things right."

Then, together, they poured out their hearts in a prayer of thanksgiving and supplication to their unseen God.

————

The offices of Youngblood Publishers took up three floors, the nineteenth through the twenty-first, in the First National Bank Building at Five Points, directly across from the Commerce Club, where all the big deals in Atlanta were made. Walking onto the nineteenth floor, Ted calculated their assets, their profits, by observing the size of the offices, the furnishings, the overall appearance. Youngblood Publishers, though rather small, had an impressive reputation, always managing to put out several books a year that hit the *New York Times* bestseller list.

He recalled Jerry Steinman's words: "Edmond's a good man, Ted. He's made Youngblood what it is today. Thirty years of hard work with a shrewd business sense. I've always enjoyed working with him."

The secretary, a middle-aged woman with bright eyes, directed Ted to Edmond Clouse's office. "He's expecting you. You may go on in, Mr. Draper." She rapped lightly on the door, stuck her head in, and whispered, "Mr. Draper is here," then motioned with her eyes for Ted to enter.

Not bad, Ted thought to himself. *A coveted corner office that measures at least two hundred square feet, with windows on both walls giving a nice view of the Atlanta skyline.*

Even though he had done his homework, Ted was taken aback when the publisher stood up; he was at least six-foot-three. Edmond Clouse had the reputation of a formidable man—big in stature as well as in publishing status, serious, overpowering, eager to get his way, in control.

Ted was used to sizing up his clients quickly. Edmond, although not a typical client, was nevertheless a man he needed to understand. They needed to understand each other.

"Good to meet you, Mr. Clouse."

"Edmond, please." The publisher held out his big hand and gave a hard shake. "Jerry and I have shared a very warm working relationship for thirty years. Sorry to hear he's retiring, but he has utmost confidence in you."

"Thank you."

"Have a seat," Edmond said, motioning to a comfortable armchair. He launched into business, just as Jerry had assured Ted he would do. "So you've met Miss Green?"

"Yes, last week." Ted lifted his eyebrows. "She's quite a . . . an interesting lady."

Edmond leaned back and laughed loudly. "Indeed. Quite a woman. Thanks for coming over today, Ted. I called this little meeting because I need to be sure we're on track with her money. She can be hawkish and, excuse the pun, I don't want to ruffle her feathers."

He laid out several papers on the desk and began explaining his strategy for Miss Green's novel. "You need to be aware of our time crunch. Miss Green is not all that happy with my game plan. It's a real stretch to get the book out for Christmas, but I've got the staff to make it happen. In general, we don't market books right at Christmastime, so that gives us a little leeway to put all our eggs into this basket. I'll admit it's a bit of a risk, but I think it'll pay off in big earnings for Miss Green and the publisher . . . and you."

"I know all about risks, Edmond. I think your plan sounds shrewd."

"I hope so. I've been communicating with Miss Green, and she agrees to have the edits back to me by mid-October. As usual, there's not a lot to be done. Her manuscripts are clean. Brilliant. Have you ever read one of her novels?"

"No, no, I must admit I haven't."

"Well, you should. Get Leah to give you copies. They'll help you get a handle on Miss Green." He picked up an envelope and handed it to Ted. "The advance."

"Ah, this goes directly to me? Does Miss Green even see the check?"

"She gets the receipt—already mailed out. She doesn't want the money to go through too many hands. Always preferred I send the advance and royalties directly to Jerry."

"I'm not very savvy on book deals, but I've read up a little. Usually the advance comes in two to three payments, right? The first when the contract is signed, the second when you receive the manuscript, and the third when the book is published."

"Typically, yes. But of course, Miss Green is anything but typical. She always signs a contract with us after the latest novel is released, stating that the next book comes to us. But she doesn't want any advance until she sends us the manuscript. She doesn't want the pressure. So we give her the advance all at once—when I've read the manuscript. And we settled a long time ago on the amount. When she turns in the manuscript she gets three hundred thousand."

Ted whistled. "Not bad. You must have a lot of confidence in this novel."

"She's never let us down. This one is a gem. The reviewers will love it. I've already heard back from *PW*."

"PW?"

"*Publishers Weekly*. They usually take three months to review a book. Try three days with this little beauty."

Confident, that was Edmond Clouse, with his thinning gray hair and broad shoulders and affable smile and steel gray eyes that held wisdom and intelligence.

"This thing is going to fly, and you need to be ready, Ted."

"Tell me what to do."

"I'm sure Jerry has filled you in. Stella is protective, hypersensitive, para-noid. You'll get a call from her every few days once the book is out."

"Why me? I don't have anything to do until she gets those royalty checks—twice a year, right?"

"Wrong. I'll keep you up on the sales figures, and you are to keep an eye on her foundation. Protect it. Make sure she is reassured. Do a little investing. A little, mind you, not a lot. The best way to get on her good side is to show Miss Green that you know everything about her account, you watch it daily, and there is nothing she needs to worry about on that end."

Ted lowered his voice. "What is this foundation? Stash Green Cash? Kind of strange. Seven million bucks, and she controls it all? You think it's legit?"

Edmond Clouse sat back in his chair and folded his big hands behind his head. "I think that it's none of our business. My business is to give the novel the best marketing plan possible, and yours is to take good care of her money. She can spend it however she wishes. But you reassure her, you hear? That's your job while we make sure the marketing plan is working and we keep enough books in stock to supply the demand."

They talked strategy, looked over her accounts, then Edmond gave him a tour of the offices. By noon the meeting was over.

"Can I buy lunch for you, Ted?"

"Thank you for the offer, but actually I'm having lunch with one of your editors. Silvano Rossi."

"*Assistant* editors," Edmond said, and Ted noted the slightest irritation in his voice. "Why did Silvano ask you to lunch?"

"Something about an article he's writing on authors and the stock market—how to help your midlist authors choose a broker and make wise investments with their money."

"Really? I had no idea he was working on something like that. Well, good for him."

They shook hands, and Edmond called his secretary on his intercom. "Leah, can you please take Mr. Draper to Silvano's office? Oh, and pick up copies of the S. A. Green novels for Mr. Draper, please."

———

Silvano took Ted Draper to Emile's, a popular French restaurant among Atlantans, only two blocks from the Youngblood offices. He certainly didn't want Edmond Clouse or Leah spying on their conversation. They needed privacy.

One thing was immediately apparent. Ted Draper was dressed for success. Good taste in clothes. Gregarious personality that doubtless helped him garner clients.

The restaurant was crowded, but the tables were well spaced, making it an appropriate setting for informal business meetings where conversations could be exchanged without having to shout to be heard.

"Your boss is an interesting man," Ted offered, after drinks had been served and they had both ordered the lunch special.

"Very. And persuasive."

"Overly so?"

"No. No, Edmond Clouse knows the publishing world. He's as good as it gets."

No need to say anything negative about the boss. Put Ted at ease.

"He's worked with the best in the business. I've handled some of the bigwigs for him—you know, lunch with Conroy, drinks with Wolfe. Updike has stopped by on occasion to chat. We're a medium-sized publishing house, but only because Clouse wants to keep it that way. We've earned the respect of the larger houses, that's for sure. And the finest authors. And Clouse is careful about whom he hires."

Ted looked sufficiently impressed.

"So where are you from, Ted?"

"Born and raised up East. Boston. Went to MIT, met my wife there. We both went to business school at Columbia. Best offer after business school was way down here in Atlanta."

"I thought your accent was nothing like the Southern drawl. And have you acclimated to Atlanta?"

"Yeah." He smiled, and his dimples spread across his face.

Silvano imagined he had success not only with stocks and bonds but with the ladies too, even if he was married.

"Yeah. We like it a lot. Atlanta's a great place to raise a family. Good private schools, good sports, the mountains and the sea not too far in either direction. And it's becoming more cosmopolitan by the year. We do take a trip north once or twice a year just to see old friends. And what about you? There's an accent I perceive that certainly isn't Southern—maybe not quite American?"

"I'm from Rome. Rome, Italy—not Rome, Georgia."

They both chuckled.

"Rome. Wow. Okay. So what brought you to Atlanta, Silvano?"

"I received a scholarship to study here, and my family saw this as an excellent opportunity." This was not the whole truth, but the story always sounded impressive. "I came to the States at the beginning of ninth grade, lived with my father's sister in Decatur throughout high school, then worked my way through Emory University with a degree in journalism. Landed my first job here eighteen months ago."

"So you came to the States and learned English and put yourself through college—a good school, no less. Not bad. Do you ever get back to Rome?"

"Oh, yeah. My mother couldn't handle not seeing me at least once a year. In August. The hottest time of the year is when I go home."

And help them sell postcards, rosary beads, and gelato.

"Last summer, while I was in the Holy City, I hosted a small affair for Armani and Gucci."

Well, not exactly hosted—a waiter at the restaurant, helping out a friend of his mother's.

Ted raised his eyebrows and nodded, again sufficiently impressed. "Wow. So tell me what you're thinking, Silvano. You said you're writing an article on authors and investments?"

"Exactly." He plunged into his list of questions, careful to avoid any reference to S. A. Green for the first fifteen minutes. Eventually he ventured into that territory as they discussed the different ways to invest: stocks, bonds, CDs, mutual funds, and, for more speculative accounts, options.

Cautiously, Silvano probed. "Of course, Miss Green is not your usual author. She's guaranteed a huge sales figure for her books. What do you advise for most of our authors—midlisters whose books sell between ten thousand and thirty-five thousand?"

"Honestly, Silvano, S. A. Green is my first author client. I stumbled on to her by good fortune. So maybe you should talk to Jerry Steinman. But for what it's worth, I'll give you my gut feeling—the way I handle all my clients. You have to *know* them first. Have to understand their personalities. And do what they say. I don't believe in pushing too hard.

If they're risk takers, then by all means go for it. But if they are blue chip conservative, like Miss Green, well, you honor that."

"I'm afraid I'm not familiar with the terminology."

"Some clients like to take big risks with stocks that aren't as stable. If they invest and it goes up, they make big bucks fast."

"But Miss Green isn't like that?"

"No. Very protective of her foundation . . ." Ted's face paled. He fiddled with a fork, twirling it on his fingers. "What are your other questions?"

Silvano pretended not to notice. "So could you explain the procedure in procuring a broker?"

"Often the broker makes the initial contact. But I also receive calls from a potential client, and best of all, referrals from a present client. We talk over the phone and then I arrange a meeting. Face-to-face if at all possible. As I said, my job is to know my clients."

"And you know Miss Green? You've met her in person?"

"We've met, yes."

"Lucky you."

"I suppose you could put it that way."

"Pretty odd bird, isn't she?"

Ted frowned. "Silvano, we are not here to talk about Miss Green."

"No, of course not. All right. Just a few more questions. How about a quote or two—something along the line of what a brokerage firm could offer an author? Something to use as bait."

"Bait? I'd prefer to have clients who want to be investing with me. Completely aboveboard."

"Of course. Of course. Now, about that quote . . ."

———

Ted didn't much care for Silvano Rossi. An opportunist was his evaluation. Those beady black eyes, the slicked-back black hair, the top-of-the-mark suit, probably something Italian. He looked like an actor wannabe or an advertisement for Gucci or some other fashion designer whose name he had dropped during the conversation. And he looked hungry—overeager. In fact, Silvano's constant name-dropping was annoying.

Ted tossed his briefcase, now filled with three novels by S. A. Green, into the back of his Mercedes, got in, and drove out of the parking lot onto Peachtree Street. Something was bothering him. He did not like this feeling, especially since he could not put his finger on it. The meeting with Edmond Clouse had gone exceptionally well. They would work well together. The interview with Silvano might get him a few new clients too. Maybe not another S. A. Green, but still, it could prove profitable.

But why did the Italian get under his skin so? Why did he suddenly feel so deflated?

The answer came at once.

Because you're staring at a younger you—Silvano Rossi doesn't have your natural graces, but you see through him. You see through him straight to your heart.

That unpleasant thought flashed across his mind like ticker tape. And like ticker tape, within a few seconds it was off the screen, removed. Gone.

TUESDAY, OCTOBER 6

Silvano brought his steaming cup of espresso to the little table at the back of the bookstore. Surrounded by the smell of old leather and musty books, he read the last pages of S. A. Green's fourth novel, *Passage from Nowhere*. He closed the novel, satisfied. The lady sure could write!

Silvano could have spent all day every day huddled in the back of The Sixth Declension. It was a small private bookstore, a relic of sorts in this part of Atlanta. The people frequenting the store were Latin teachers and lovers of Greece and Italy and ancient history. The shelves were stuffed with histories of the Roman Empire by Herodotus, Plutarch, and Livy; Greek classics by Homer, Euripides, and Sophocles; stories of the Renaissance; old art books with beautifully reproduced photos of the works of Da Vinci and Raphael and Tintoretto and Caravaggio and Carracci. Some of the same reproductions lined the walls of the shop, so that he could look around the room and be back in Rome, standing in front of St. Peter's or staring up at the Sistine Chapel and compliment-ing Michelangelo.

He had discovered the little bookstore years ago when he was in high school. Well, actually, his aunt had recommended it to him. Tucked between other little shops on Church Street in downtown Decatur, a stone's throw from Atlanta, Silvano had claimed his spot. When the horrible tentacles of homesickness strangled him, he slipped inside the store, greeted owner Evan Jones—who, in spite of his vanilla name, knew more about Latin and ancient Rome than the pope himself—and found a seat in the corner to study literature and political science.

Evan and The Sixth Declension deserved a lot of credit for the fact that Silvano Rossi had stayed in America, stayed in Atlanta, Georgia, when every fiber in him had wanted to return to Rome. To *Italia*. With Evan, he spoke Italian and even read week-old copies of the Italian newspaper *Il Corriere della Sera*, to which Evan subscribed.

Today, as Silvano smoked his Italian Diana and sipped the espresso that Evan made expressly for him—their little pun—he composed a let-ter to Miss S. A. Green. Ted Draper had managed a face-to-face meeting with the eccentric novelist. By gosh, he would too. He would.

———

"Dad, Mrs. Gruder invited me to drive with her to Atlanta on Sat-urday. We want to check out a bookstore there—the one I used to go to when I was in all the Latin competitions. She's taking three students to the regionals, and asked if I could help her get some books to prepare them."

"Mrs. Gruder. I remember her. Sounds like a great idea, Liss. I know how much you like that little store. It'll do you good to go to Atlanta."

"And I've asked her to drive me out to see Caleb on our way back to Chattanooga." She said it quickly, throwing out the information before he could protest. "And she's fine with that too. So I won't be getting home until late Saturday evening."

For a moment the tempest held at bay; the storm in Dad's eyes brewed, but she thought it might not erupt. She was wrong.

He cursed. "Melissa! Are you just plain deaf? I've told you not to go see him! It is too dangerous. I forbid it!" His fist thundered onto the table, and a plate sitting too close to the edge fell off and shattered.

Lissa ran up the steps, taking them two at a time, and slammed her door. She felt the perspiration above her lip, the trembling of her hands. She wished Mr. MacAllister were there to calm her. As it was, she huddled on the needlepoint rug near the bed, where she did her sit-ups. Only today she held herself tightly, rocking back and forth and crying and sucking in deep gulps of air. She hated him! Hated him!

That thought punctured the panic attack, and she grabbed the spiral notebook and began to write.

My life is separated into two parts and only two parts: before the accident and Now. Now is a curse, Now is an endless black spiral into despair. Now is condemnation.

I try to look around the Now, the accusation. I think of the horse shows, or Momma singing in the church choir, or of the Latin competitions—but then I hear the whisper. I can't think of that because it propels me to Now. Now without her.

I try to lose myself in a novel, but the strangest things bring me back to Now, without her. Any word, any reference can do it—the mention of a mother or a happy family. I am back to Now.

At the library, sometimes, when I'm with children who are lost in their little worlds, I get lost too—before or after, but not the present. That is what I live for. Away from Now.

Away from Dad. I cannot help it. If I cannot escape the guilt, the haunting voices, I will drag him into the hole with me. This is what I hear. This is what I tell myself.

Why did it have to be her? Why not him? If he had died in that grisly accident, Momma and I would have sobbed for days, holding on to each other for strength, for life. Cried until no tears were left and then slept and cried again. We loved him!

But eventually, eventually, we would have talked. We would have sat silently and then cried and then talked, remembering the good times, maybe even giggling, so worn out from grief that the silliness of fatigue would settle on us. Crying and giggling and holding and mourning, and it would all have been healthy and right and horrible and necessary.

But with him, it is silence and fury!

I used to love him. I know I used to love him. But once the past is lost, what does it take to reinvent a life?

If only I could get past the Now.

———

When Ev MacAllister picked up Lissa for her lesson, she wore an expression that Ev called "being busy in her mind." She was brooding. They didn't talk on the twenty-minute drive from Chattanooga Girls School to the Chickamauga Military Park. Perhaps anger helped her drive, he considered, as she handled the car skillfully along the battlefield tour route. Twice she did the loop with not one problem. When she parked by the visitor center and cut the engine, the thoughts that had been preoccupying her spilled out in a rush of words that surprised him.

"I realize how much I want to learn. I love studying. History and learning, this is life to me. But I just can't do it. That's all. I can't."

"Do you know why?"

"I'm trying to figure it out." She looked over at him and asked, "Do you believe there's a reason for the things that happen, Mr. MacAllister?"

"A reason?"

"Yes. Do you think there's a reason my mother was killed in a horrible accident?"

He felt his whole face sag. "Oh, Lissa. That's a hard question."

"I know. But you seem like a reflective man, and I thought, well . . . I thought you might have something to say on the subject. Never mind."

Before Ev could formulate how he wanted to answer, Lissa set a spiral notebook on Ole Bessie's dashboard and said, "Here's my homework."

So that was it. "Good, Lissa. Thank you for doing this."

He drove her home, again in silence. The only sound was Ole Bessie's purring motor and the occasional piercing of a siren from somewhere along Highway 2. But when Ev started up the steep, curving road to Lookout Mountain, she broke the silence.

"I might as well warn you that it's not very light reading. It's just me venting. But you can read it if you want to."

"I will do that, Lissa. Indeed." He pulled into the driveway of the white manor house. He could imagine its breathtaking view off the other side, perched way above the city. "See you on Monday."

"Yeah, on Monday. Thanks."

Ev read Lissa's scribbled pages out on the porch with the heat of the day, along with the sun, receding behind the mountains. He could almost feel her anguish—the tormented soul, the angry adolescent. How could he help her?

He contemplated calling her father and trying to talk to him. Could this man not see what his flippant comments and sudden bursts of rage were doing to his daughter?

Long ago, he and Annie had agreed that he would not meddle in the private lives of his clients. Pray, invite them for dinner, offer advice, pray some more. The Almighty could handle the problems much better than he could. Occasionally it became clear that he had another role to play. But not immediately. Only after objective consideration and prayer.

Pray. Yes, he prayed for the girl. Prayed for her anger to melt away. For healing. For redemption. For getting past the *now*, as she put it.

Ev did not know how to encourage her past grief. After all, thirty-five years later, his still felt fresh, like dew on the morning grass, like a sudden chill, like a creaking of the stairs at night. Somewhere inside he carried the slow ache of missing Tate. Janelle carried the ache of losing Josh. How could he promise Lissa that her ache would heal, go away, even lessen?

He longed to declare that God Almighty could do a miracle, would bring good out of bad, would give her a future. This he believed with all his heart. He knew it to be true in his life. But he could not promise her the ache would go away. He could not promise her she could ever go back to *before*.

A reason? Was there a reason? He did not know. He did not dare pronounce a judgment.

But he held her papers in his hand and knew one thing. Lissa Randall was a butterfly, a delicate beauty, and her words, her prose, would settle softly on hearts and grace the lonely and the hurt because she dared to express all that she had suffered.

This was not the reason. But this was the outcome. It could be redeemed if she would let it.

———

Thank heavens for the breeze. It wasn't fall weather, but at least the heat wave had passed. Katy Lynn kicked the sand as she headed through the dunes of Carnon and out onto the beach. The Mediterranean shimmered like diamonds in front of her. The sand warmed her bare feet. The beach held scattered bathers at three in the afternoon. Nice, firmly packed sand, a wide beach that went on and on. She could walk for hours! Ah, now *this* was more like it. She planned to walk straight to La Grand Motte, the vacation town about three miles down the beach—unmistakable with strange geometric buildings rising on the horizon, looking like a child's Lego configuration.

A warm breeze was blowing across the beach and she breathed it in. Finally, a few minutes alone to herself, without Janelle's sad eyes following her, without the awkward pauses in conversation, without little Sandy coming into the bedroom at any time and asking a hundred questions. It felt grand to be outside, out of that claustrophobic little house, walking along a wide expanse of beach!

Gina would be thrilled to hear. Katy Lynn decided she wouldn't mention the fact that dogs actually defecated on the beach, or that it was virtually impossible to find a restroom. She would tell her daughter that there were plenty of bare breasts lying open to the wind and sun, even in early October. Gina would giggle at that tidbit.

Katy Lynn felt sorry for her sister. That was it, plain and simple. Truth be told, Janelle seemed to be a bigger wreck than she herself was. She might be going through a divorce, but Janelle was dying on the inside. Katy Lynn knew the awful signs of depression very well—and despite all her baby sister's religious faith, Janelle showed them all. Somehow this made Katy Lynn cry.

She thought of her miscarriage at four months—their first baby, the first pregnancy—and the horrible shock, the eat-your-insides-out grief. She couldn't imagine the pain of losing a living child. A precious three-year-old, blond-haired blue-eyed toddler. She had made the trek to the cemetery with Janelle the day before. No words spoken. Janelle had not exactly invited her into this private grief, but for some reason Katy had felt compelled to go.

Janelle did not want pity, of course. Katy Lynn considered this and decided she didn't feel pity. It was something more like a perplexing admiration. Katy Lynn's heart—her mother-heart—hurt for her baby sister, and that surprised her. It almost comforted her. How nice—no, *different*—to have someone else to worry about for a change.

She sloshed out into the water, refreshingly chilly, and continued along in the shallow tide. Brian said she could walk to La Grande Motte in twenty-five minutes. Once there, she'd find a seat at a little café and treat herself to a strong coffee and some ice cream. Janelle had offered to pick her up at five. Katy Lynn wasn't about to ride the bus back to their house. Yes, it was too bad they only had one car, but Janelle assured her that after she picked up the kids at school and let them off at home, it would be no problem to come and pick Katy Lynn up.

Katy Lynn breathed in deeply. Maybe she would just stay with them after all. The weather had cooled while her concern for this family had warmed.

Strange. How very strange.

CHAPTER ELEVEN

Ted hung up the phone, almost slamming it down onto the receiver. *Keep your cool, man*, he told himself. Why weren't these clients interested? The first guy on Friday had been delighted with the idea of the three new junk bonds.

Yesterday's trip to visit Youngblood Publishers had kept him out of the office all day, away from the phone. Now today, this was his fourth call to a high-risk client, and again it was the same nervous tone in the voice, the hedging "Let me think about it, Ted," concluding with his promise to call back in a few days.

His commission run showed 635,000 dollars, year to date. Things that had looked absolutely airtight only two weeks ago had come to a screeching halt. He still had time. One quarter, three months left. No need to panic, but suddenly 365,000 dollars' worth of trading to do was making him nervous. He should have never breathed a word to Lin Su. Now all she could talk about was China! She was singing the kids Chinese lullabies, looking at the map. She'd even called her grandparents and giggled with them about how wonderful their time together would be.

The meeting with Eddy Clouse had been important. Extremely important. But S. A. Green's royalties wouldn't, *couldn't*, help him make this year's Million Dollar Club.

So what if he didn't make it? He'd break the news to Lin Su. There would be a nasty scene, tears, accusations, even a few threats. But nothing more. Surely nothing more.

Anyway, he *would* make it. Junk bonds were still selling like hotcakes and paying the customers handsomely for taking the extra risk. Time to make a few more calls. It was just that simple.

He dialed another number. "Coleman? Hey, it's Ted Draper here. How are you on this fine morning in October?"

He listened, the fake smile plastered on his face.

"Listen, I've got some great information on a couple of new junk bond issues, and it looks like the rates on these are going to be as good or better than the last ones we bought. . . ."

But the end of the conversation was the same. Not interested.

SATURDAY, OCTOBER 10

Lissa enjoyed the drive along I-75 South from Chattanooga to Atlanta, memories of former drives rolling in her mind like the gentle hills on the horizon. A short hour and forty-five minutes away, Atlanta had beckoned her often for horse shows, for shopping, and for *this*, a little bookstore tucked into downtown Decatur. From I-75, Mrs. Gruder veered off onto I-85 and took the North Druid Hills exit, driving through the well-established neighborhood boasting stately, well-preserved old homes, wide open streets, and a luxurious tree-filled median separating the traffic. Driving through Druid Hills was like a trip around Lookout Mountain, minus the breathtaking views into the valley. It boasted prestige and quiet, respectable old wealth.

Soon they arrived in Decatur, best known for Emory University and its medical school and Agnes Scott College. Lissa had visited both of them two years ago. Applied to both, been accepted at both. She pushed those thoughts away as Mrs. Gruder parked the car along the street in front of The Sixth Declension.

Walking in, Lissa let herself be transported to *before*. It felt heavenly; the crowded shelves brimming with history, the smell of the old books with their cracking covers. She remembered bringing in her Neatsfoot oil once and offering to rub it into the leather.

"It works miracles on my saddle," she told the aging store owner.

And Mr. Evan, as he liked to be called, had chuckled and said, "My clients come here for old, Lissa. It's part of the charm and the authenticity."

On this morning, Mr. Evan was stooping down behind the counter, lifting a box off the floor.

Mrs. Gruder stepped beside the cash register and proclaimed in the authoritative voice that had gained compliance from her students for years, "Hello, Evan! Your Chattanooga neighbors have come back for a visit."

He stood up, pushed his wire-rimmed glasses back on his thin face, and squinted at them, then broke into a smile. "Well, the pleasure is all mine. Deb Gruder! And Lissa! Lissa Randall, I believe. Long time no see."

Mrs. Gruder and Mr. Evan continued chatting, but Lissa headed to the shelves, not wanting to have to answer his questions about what she was doing with her life.

She gradually made her way farther back in the store where Mr. Evan kept the modern histories of Rome, the textbooks, the travel guides, and the coffee-table picture albums with the photos of Italian art and piazzas. The only other customer in the bookstore was a young man who sat at the back table, sipping a cup of coffee, his head lost in a book.

Lissa smiled to herself. Mr. Evan used to offer her coffee too when she sat in that spot, feverishly reviewing her Latin, poring over Horace and Virgil and Caesar and even the Bible. It seemed a lifetime ago.

She slipped between the table and the shelves, beginning a methodical search for the list of books she and Mrs. Gruder had compiled. She bumped the table and murmured "*Scusi*" without thinking, reverting to the Italian she enjoyed using with Mr. Evan.

The young man looked up, surprised. "*Parla Italiano?*"

"Oh, barely. Not well." She blushed, staring at the shelves. "I'm better in Latin, which of course you can't really speak."

"Oh, but you can! *Puella!* And if you put the two languages together, you get *bella puella!*"

Lissa glanced around. Something about his voice was familiar.

He beat her to it. "We've met before, haven't we?"

"Yeah. I think we have. A long time ago."

"You used to come in here with a group of girlfriends."

"Yes, we were getting books to help us study for our high school Latin competition."

"*Si*, I remember. You were good—going to the nationals, weren't you?"

"Uh-huh." She needed to change the conversation before it headed toward dangerous territory. "Mr. Evan was a lifesaver more than once. He used to serve me coffee too."

"Well, it's nice to see you again," he said, as if they had truly known each other.

Lissa could have closed her eyes and been back in Rome. This young man was Italian in every way, from his leather loafers and well-cut suit to his cigarette and espresso and his beautiful accent with its rolling melody and his dark eyes and hair and Roman nose—like one of the horses at the barn. Of course she'd never voice that thought—but it actually didn't look bad at all on this young man.

Yes, she did remember him, an Emory University student who spent his days at The Sixth Declension. Her friends made fun of him, called him a flirt, but she had liked him just because he was Italian. They'd spoken three or four times at most.

"So did you?"

She had missed the question and blushed to admit it. "Did I what?"

"Did you do well in the national competition?"

"Oh, pretty well. I got to go to Rome." She leaned back against the bookshelves, holding a textbook for fifth-year Latin students across her chest, almost protectively.

"Really! Well, yeah, I'd say you did *pretty* well. *Niente male!*"

"I loved it, every single ounce of Rome: the Coliseum, the Vatican, the Sistine Chapel, the piazzas. All those wonderful piazzas—di Spagna, del Popolo, and my favorite, Piazza Navona with the jugglers and the musicians and the artists and the tourists sitting to have their portraits made. And Bernini's Fountain of the Rivers. And the obelisk! We used to wander around the piazza, choose a little restaurant, and feel like life could not get any better." She stopped suddenly, embarrassed by her overly enthusiastic monologue.

The young man didn't seem bothered. Instead, he smiled and asked, "*Come si chiama?*"

"*Mi chiamo Lissa.*"

"Well, it's nice to know your name, Lissa. I'm Silvano."

She felt her face growing hot and could think of nothing to say except, "It's nice to meet you too."

He stood. "I come here every week, know this place like the back of my hand—or as we say in Italy, *le conosco a memoria*. Perhaps I can help you find what you're looking for."

Lissa glanced down at the list she had set on top of the textbook. "Oh, yes. Thanks. Um, I'm having a hard time finding the translation of Horace that we used a few years ago. It had the best footnotes. And I don't seem to be having much luck with Plutarch either."

When they had located the books, they stood in the back of the store talking about Rome. Lissa found herself laughing, almost tasting the creamy gelato and fresh bread. Without realizing it, she had traveled back, and it felt so good.

When the conversation lagged, she filled in quickly with a question. "Last time I saw you, I think you were a student at Emory. What are you up to now?"

"Well, I finished up at Emory two years ago. Landed my first job as an editor at Youngblood Publishers. I spend a lot of time reading the manuscripts of hopeful writers."

"Mmm."

"But there are lots of perks to the job—like meeting with the big names every once in a while. And right now"—he lowered his voice—"can you keep a secret?"

Lissa furrowed her brow, not sure she wanted to hear a secret from a stranger.

Silvano seemed undeterred. "We're putting out a novel by S. A. Green."

She shook her head. "I don't believe I know him."

"Her. She's the nutty lady who insists on complete anonymity and writes bestsellers every five or six years."

"Oh. No, I don't know her."

He seemed disappointed.

"I don't read a lot of modern literature. I tend to keep going back to the classics."

"Well, you can't go wrong there. So what's kept you away from The Sixth Declension for so long?"

"The main thing is that I live in Chattanooga. And after the Latin competitions were over, well, I didn't need to come as often. I'm just here helping my former Latin teacher pick up some books for her students. A trip down memory lane."

"Chattanooga."

"Yep. Well, actually, Lookout Mountain."

"See Rock City and Ruby Falls!" he said, mimicking the billboards.

"Yes. It's a lovely spot, in spite of the tourists."

Lissa glanced toward the front of the store where Mrs. Gruder was setting a stack of books beside the cash register. "Um, hold on a sec— looks like my teacher has just about found everything she needs."

Lissa took the textbooks and Plutarch's history to the cash register, then came back to the table. "Well, it was nice to see you again, Silvano."

"The pleasure was all mine, *bella puella*. Perhaps we'll meet again before two years pass?"

"Perhaps."

"For a pizza and bottle of Chianti?"

Lissa blushed again and shrugged. "*Ciao*, Silvano."

"*Ciao*, Lissa."

———

Lissa wrapped her arms around the gelding's neck and buried her head in his mane. "Caleb. Caleb. I'm so sorry. I'm trying. I swear I'm trying."

The chestnut nickered softly, ears pricked forward. Lissa knelt down and ran her hands along his front legs and fetlocks, instinctively feeling for any swelling. Nothing. The thoroughbred looked in perfect shape, albeit a little rounder around the barrel.

How could her father disown Caleb? Momma had loved this gelding, loved him like the second child she could never have. She relished accompanying Lissa and High Caliber—Caleb for short—to the competitions, even when it meant rising at four in the morning to help her braid the horse's mane and tail.

Lissa pictured her mother waving from the bleachers or standing beside the white fences and wishing them well with her eyes. She had always rejoiced in their success.

Why did her father blame Caleb? Perhaps it was easier to blame the horse than let it all fall on Lissa's shoulders. If they hadn't stopped at the barn to visit Caleb on that May afternoon, if they'd gone straight home, the hail would have beaten down on the house on Lookout Mountain with Lissa and her mother and father all snuggled safely inside.

Didn't her father understand that Caleb meant hope for Lissa?

Of course he understands. That's the whole point. Squelch the hope. Punish the perpetrators of the crime. Separate them. Condemn them.

During the first months after the accident, she had come to the stable and simply brushed Caleb, brushing, crying, grieving. Her father hadn't seemed to mind back then. Perhaps he'd simply been numb with grief. But when Lissa had wanted to start riding again, he had flipped. That was the only explanation.

"Lissa, I don't want you riding anymore."

"What?"

"It isn't safe."

"Isn't safe? What do you mean? Caleb and I are great together, Dad. You know that. You've seen us. . . ."

But the more she argued, the more stubborn he grew. His anger flared often. After she tore up her license, he refused to drive her to the barn.

If she found a ride with someone else, he exploded. The very mention of Caleb became a huge boulder in their relationship, something much harder to scale that the steepest side of Lookout Mountain. Eventually he refused to let her see the horse at all.

Lissa could not understand his logic—his "illogic," as she called it. He had stopped paying the board a year ago. Most of Lissa's small salary from the library went to pay it now, despite her father's vehement protests. He had put Caleb up for sale, and only Lissa's desperate phone calls to Cammie, the middle-aged owner of Clover Leaf Stables, had kept Caleb from being sold.

Now Lissa found Mrs. Gruder sitting in the tack room, reading Plutarch. "Are you in a big hurry to get back to Chattanooga?"

Her teacher smiled at her. "Take your time. I've got plenty of reading material."

Lissa grabbed her saddle and bridle, left Mrs. Gruder with Plutarch, and went into Caleb's stall, quickly tacking up the gelding. Out in the paddock area, she pulled herself onto his back, landing effortlessly in the saddle and patting Caleb's withers. He tossed his head impatiently as she coaxed him out of the barn into the bright October day, her kind of day, with the azure blue sky, the crisp fall weather, the leaves tinted in orange and yellow. The barn sat on ten acres of flatland twenty miles south of Chattanooga, and she intended to ride through the whole property this afternoon.

She trotted Caleb by the two large riding rings and rode into the open fields alone. Galloping across the bare terrain, Caleb's hooves kicking up dirt, they went faster and faster until Lissa felt barely in control. She closed her eyes, enjoying the sting of her hair flapping wildly in her face as Caleb picked up speed.

She wondered if they galloped fast and far enough, if perhaps they could move beyond the *now*, move beyond fear and failure and *All your fault!* She didn't need a little bottle of pills by her bed. She could ride away into nothingness, into some future hope that rose off the plain like the sudden appearance of Signal Mountain when they emerged from the woods.

She bent forward, almost lying on Caleb's neck. How she missed the competition, the horse shows, the thrill of the jumper classes where the fences were set up higher and higher until only a handful of horses remained in the competition. The fastest to complete the course with no faults won. Caleb was easily the fastest. Even though he measured only fifteen hands three inches—small for a jumper—he was compact, with a spring in him that could jump the moon. He took the turns, cut corners, leapt like a puma from a spot so tight the spectators always gasped to see it. Together Lissa and Caleb had won their share of jumper classes, had gathered the long-tailed, multicolored blue, red, and yellow ribbons signifying Champion, the trophies and silver platters engraved with *Hunter-Jumper Classic, Champion, Junior Division*. She missed the competition—the adrenaline, the thrill, the satisfaction.

She had no idea how much time passed before she turned Caleb and retraced their tracks, eventually slowing him to a trot and then to a walk. She lay down with her back arched over the saddle, her head on his hindquarters, staring at the huge yellow-leaved hickories, and feeling the horse's barrel expanding, in and out as white foam covered his body. She too was soaked in perspiration. It beaded on her lips and all along her arms. She felt her shirt sticking to her ribs, her hair matted, her face wet. It felt like *before*.

"We've had an offer from a girl in Virginia, Lissa," Cammie said, meeting Lissa as she untacked Caleb. "A serious buyer. I think you should consider it. She's fifteen, I think, gutsy, talented, determined. She reminds me of you."

Lissa shot Cammie a frustrated glance.

"She came down to see him last week. Tried him out on Friday, then rode him again Saturday and Sunday. By Sunday they were jumping four-and-a-half-foot fences."

Lissa swallowed the ball of hate in the back of her throat. "I thought you weren't accepting any offers on him."

Cammie looked pained. "Lissa, I can't ignore your father forever."

"So that's why I got that letter from you encouraging me to come to the barn."

"Yeah. It's been a long time."

"It's not easy to get a ride out here, and if I dare pronounce Caleb's name to Dad, all I get from him is a bona fide tantrum."

Cammie put her arm around Lissa's shoulder. "Look, Liss. I know you think your father is being horrible. But I think he's just scared. I think his grief over your mother's death has caused him to be afraid of losing you too."

Lissa glared at her.

"At any rate, Caleb is getting fat and sassy. He needs exercise. You could just lease him for a year or two. Let her get him back in shape."

"He called you, didn't he?" Lissa spat out as if she hadn't heard a word of what Cammie said. "He's pressuring you to get rid of him."

"Lissa, he's right. You never come. You're not going to ride him anymore."

"I rode him today! I'm trying! I never come because *he* won't *bring* me. I had to beg my Latin teacher to take a trip to Atlanta, for heaven's sake, so I'd have some sort of excuse. Dad still blessed me out. I want to ride. I *need* to ride."

Cammie shook her head. "I'm sorry, Liss. It's been such a mess, hasn't it?" She gave Lissa a hug. "I wish I could promise you that I won't sell Caleb, but the problem is, your father is the official owner. He paid for him. I have to abide by his wishes. I *can* promise you I won't sell him without letting you know."

"Cammie, please! I'm paying to keep him here. Please give me a little more time. As soon as I get my license, I'll be here four times a week. I swear it."

"Got any idea how long that will be?"

"Not really."

"I'll do my best, Lissa. But I have to tell you the truth. Your father is bound and determined to get rid of Caleb, and I don't know how much longer I can put him off."

Lissa spent the drive back to Lookout Mountain staring out the window, counting the signs painted on barn roofs inviting every motorist to *See Rock City* and *Visit Ruby Falls*. She felt confused by the chance meeting with that young man, Silvano, by the way just talking with him had transported her back to Rome. Even now she could almost taste the creamy gelato, feel again the thrill of standing in the Sistine Chapel and craning her neck to stare at Michelangelo's masterpiece on the ceiling. The creation of man. God's finger reaching out to touch Adam's. Life. Hope.

The Fall. Just as quickly, she saw Adam and Eve crouching in their shame, covered with leaves. Banished. Rome vanished, and she was in the car with Momma chatting about colleges and Caleb, heading home. *Just like today.*

Her hands began to shake first. She knotted them into two tight balls, but the trembling continued. Her breathing became shallow. She felt the blood running out of her face, the beads of sweat on her brow and upper lip.

Mrs. Gruder glanced over, alarm on her face. "Lissa, are you okay?"

The hail, the fear, the bridge ahead on I-75. The bridge that they were getting ready to pass under . . .

Lissa grabbed her head in her hands and ducked down, as if she could hide behind the dashboard. She had no idea how long she remained in that position, nor when Mrs. Gruder turned off the highway and parked at a Texaco station. She hardly heard the teacher's voice or felt her hand on Lissa's shoulder.

Eventually the trembling stopped. She sat up with difficulty and realized she was sobbing.

"I'm sorry, Lissa. I didn't realize—I forgot . . ."

Lissa nodded, unwrapping her fists, forcing herself to take deep, slow breaths as the therapist had instructed. Slowly, in and out, in and out. She swallowed repeatedly, but could not dislodge the lump in her throat. Tears slid down her cheeks as she heard the insidious words.

All your fault.

And her soft answer, seething through her brain. *I hate you, Dad.*

MONDAY, OCTOBER 12

Lissa anticipated the driving lesson with Mr. MacAllister the next Monday afternoon like a little girl going to her first horse show: unbounded excitement and total terror. If she could wrap her arms around all that had happened this weekend, if she could put words on the feelings, perhaps he would have an answer, or at least some advice. But halfway through the lesson, as she drove along the tranquil road of Military Park, she still had not found the courage to broach the subject. Fortunately, Mr. MacAllister did not need her to take the lead.

"Did you have a nice weekend, Lissa?"

She felt her face go tense, her jaw clench, her hands clasp tightly around Ole Bessie's steering wheel as if she were back on Caleb, gripping the reins as he galloped out of control while she desperately tried to slow him down.

"It wasn't so bad." Deep breath, deep breath.

She pulled Ole Bessie over to the side of the rode, beside a huge rectangular stone monument with a woman in long robes—a figure from antiquity—carved into the stone. Underneath the woman, Lissa read the plaque: *26th Ohio Infantry, 1st Brigade, 1st Division, 21st Army Corps.* All dead. A memorial for a bunch of dead soldiers.

She cut the engine and looked at Mr. MacAllister. "There were good parts of the weekend and horrible parts."

He said nothing.

"I went to Atlanta with my Latin teacher. On the way back we drove past the . . . the . . ." She cleared her throat. "The accident site." Very deep breath. "I had another panic attack. She was driving, but I panicked. And all I could hear were those horrible voices telling me again it was all my fault and that I was never going to get past this. Never."

She looked over at the silver-haired gentleman beside her, noticing again the kindness in his eyes, and something else. A pain, an understanding. She wanted to reach over and take his wrinkled hand and clutch it, wanted his thirty years of helping scared teenagers to seep through her hand into her veins and travel to her heart. Instead, she crossed her arms over her chest as if she were very cold.

"How often have you been back to the accident site, Lissa?"

Surprised, she frowned, felt the ripples on her brow. "Never. Never until Saturday."

"Doesn't sound like failure to me, Lissa. Sounds like courage. Facing the unthinkable."

Courage?

"It's just I wasn't expecting it. It came out of nowhere—like the hail—and all of a sudden we were passing under that bridge and I was coiled up in a knot."

Mr. MacAllister had one arm across his chest, and he surrounded his lips with his other thumb and forefinger, deep in thought. Finally he spoke. "There's a lot of mental energy that goes into driving, whether we realize it or not. The trick is teaching kids to be defensive drivers, to be prepared for the unexpected, to acknowledge it will happen. It's the same in life, Lissa. I call it a battle plan."

"Can you explain?" Her voice was barely a whisper.

He said nothing for several long seconds.

"Let's use an example from history, Lissa. The Battle of Chickamauga. Right here, right on these fields. September 20, 1863. The Confederate General, Braxton Bragg, had a decisive victory right here at Chickamauga over the Union troops led by General Rosencrans. I'll spare you all the bloody details for now, but in spite of terrible carnage, Bragg won. The problem was that General Bragg failed to follow it up—he allowed the defeated Union army to retreat to Chattanooga.

"General Bragg's indecisiveness following his victory at Chickamauga led to defeat at Chattanooga two months later. And then Chattanooga, firmly in Federal hands, would become the base for a drive into the Deep South in 1864—you can read that very inscription at the museum in the visitor center. You see, Lissa, Bragg wasn't thinking far enough ahead. But you can. You can get past the *now.*"

She glanced at him and shrugged, unconvinced.

"You're taking positive steps—like doing your homework."

She gave a bitter chuckle. "I guarantee you *that* wasn't hard. It just spilled out—all the anger, all the pain."

"I've learned that getting things out into the open, saying the truth about what is inside, usually speeds up the process of moving forward. Admitting it, facing it, and then planning a way to keep moving in the right direction."

"So what are you suggesting, Mr. MacAllister? What is my battle plan?"

"I can't make it for you. What do you think it should be?"

"I have no idea!" It came out as an angry expression of incredulity.

"That's okay. Think about it. It'll come to you, I imagine." Then he unbuckled his seat belt and opened his door to climb out, instructing Lissa to do the same.

He began walking quickly toward the monument, and Lissa hurried to keep up.

"You said there were horrible parts to the weekend and good parts. Do you mind telling me about the good parts?"

She followed him through the grassy field. "Oh, well, I got to go to my favorite bookstore in Atlanta."

He nodded, still walking. "Which one?"

"The Sixth Declension."

With that, he stopped and turned around to face her. He looked pleased. "I know that store. In Decatur? Used to go there every once in a while myself."

"Really? You like Latin?"

"I like history. All kinds of history. And Mr. Evan Jones knows his history. Filled his store with the best books—ancient and modern—available."

"That's weird. I mean, I can't believe you know that store." She almost told him about Silvano, then changed her mind. "Yeah, I used to study like a lunatic in that bookstore, surrounded by all those books—you know, back in high school, for the Latin competition."

"I see. And did you like it? The competition?"

"I *loved* it. I craved it. Competition was my caffeine for the longest time. You name it, I competed. Grades in school, the Latin club, horse shows. Life *was* competition."

He stopped and leaned against the stone monument. She imagined him as a soldier, perhaps a lieutenant or a corporal.

"Were you good?"

"Good?"

"Good at competition? Did you win things?"

"Yes, I did. I was very good." Lissa adopted a similar pose, her back against the stone monument, her eyes staring forward at the empty battle-field. "I didn't use to make mistakes, Mr. MacAllister. That's the thing. I got it all right. Nothing intimidated me. So you see, it's very odd to be reduced to panic in the driver's seat of Ole Bessie. Humiliating. Not even that."

Now she put her hands on her hips and looked Mr. MacAllister in the eyes. "It's like I'm a completely different person. If you told me that I could win a million bucks if I learned how to drive up Lookout Mountain by Christmas, it wouldn't motivate me now. Wouldn't mean a thing. I've lost the fun, the joy of the challenge. Why get up in the morning if there's nothing to prove and no one to beat? I hate the void. And then the void is filled by something dark and thick."

"Depression. Depression's a mean master. Sucks you dry, doesn't it?"

When he looked at her with his pale blue eyes, Lissa was convinced he knew exactly how she felt. "Yeah. It's like you're smothering under a huge, heavy blanket, and you don't have the energy to throw it off."

"Maybe you'll just have to crawl out from under that blanket, Lissa. Maybe you won't be able to throw it off. But I believe you are going to get out from under it. Gradually."

She shrugged. "Maybe." She thought of her ride on Caleb, the break-neck pace, that momentary delight at being almost out of control. A taste, a fragrance of the past. "Maybe you're right, Mr. MacAllister. Maybe it will come back. I just hope it comes back in time."

"In time for what, Lissa?"

"In time for life." She knew without looking at his face that this old man understood.

CHAPTER TWELVE

TUESDAY, OCTOBER 13

Sitting at her desk, Stella reviewed the list of edits she had received from Eddy Clouse. He had combed through the manuscript and found only a handful of tangles, nothing that a little conditioner couldn't remove, Stella thought to herself, pursuing the metaphor. Combing out the tangles was the absolute least of her worries.

She stared at the letter on her desk and literally felt she might vomit, spit out the last twenty-seven years all over the desk. All over the world. *Someone knew.*

No, someone was fishing for her identity. For years she'd dealt with overeager fans and nosy reporters. She had kept every letter from a reader carefully preserved in her files. Youngblood Publishers forwarded them to her post office box every month, wonderful letters that almost made Stella tear up as she read them, testimonies of the way literature seeped into hearts and changed them. She cherished the letters, and every one of them was answered personally and then sent back to Eddy Clouse, who posted them from Atlanta with the Youngblood address on the back of the envelope.

But this letter was different. First, it had come to the post office box on its own—not forwarded from Youngblood. Eddy Clouse and Jerry Steinman were the only people who used that address. How had this reader found out about it? Second, the postmark was impossible to read—this guy was careful about covering his tracks. And third, it was obvious that this person had already read the manuscript of the new novel. Impossible! A dangerous breach of security that Eddy would never allow.

Others had tried to sneak around the protocol and force her into the open. It hadn't worked then. But then she had been younger and, although she hated to admit it, sharper. Keen. Now she felt the weight of secrecy and old age creeping up on her. She mulled through the phrases in the typed, unsigned letter, the envelope with no return address.

Have appreciated reading your newest novel . . .

Here the letter writer—somehow she felt sure it was a *he*—launched into a precise synopsis.

> *As with all the others, it is "stellar," Stella. . . . For many years now, I have wondered at your anonymity. Why is this so important to you? Are you a recluse? Or is there something you are hiding? What is the reason you don't want anyone to know who you are?*
>
> *Here's my offer. Meet me in Chicago at a little restaurant called Stefani's, West Fullerton at noon on October 19. You show up and give me an interview, and I'll discuss with you how I will use this information. If you choose to ignore this opportunity, I will be forced to write an article based on what I know and get it published as I see fit.*
>
> *It's your move.*
>
> *Hoping to see you on October 19.*

The letter writer was sniffing her out, searching for clues. One thing was for sure; he had read the new novel. But that didn't bother her. He wasn't trying to steal her words. He wanted to steal her identity and then show it to the world—an unscrupulous fiend who wanted a face-to-face interview. What in the world made him think she would fall for such a ploy? Her heart sank. She *would* go. What if he knew about Ashton, about the past? She had a lot more to protect than her anonymity. She would go.

She dialed Youngblood Publishers immediately, asking for Eddy's personal line. She felt a wave of relief when he answered.

"Eddy, Stella here."

He doubtless noticed her unusually crisp tone. She rushed ahead.

"No worries—the edits are coming along fine. But . . . but I have another question, a problem. Who in your office has read the manuscript?"

"No one, Stella. Just me, as always."

"Somebody's read it, Eddy. I just received an anonymous letter, threatening me—from someone who has obviously read the whole thing."

Eddy's voice faltered. "I . . . I just don't see how. The manuscript arrived as always in the box and then secured in the burlap bag with the address label on the twine. It certainly didn't look like it had been tampered with. And I've kept it under lock and key since then."

"Very strange."

Silence.

"Have you talked to Jerry lately?"

"No. He's going to be my next call. I wanted to start with you." She let out a long sigh.

Eddy Clouse was her friend of almost thirty years. He had learned to read the stress in her voice, even if she never admitted it.

"This person is demanding a meeting. Even threatening to write something and publish it. I have no idea what he knows. But, Eddy, you know how very much I value anonymity."

"I do, Stella. Listen, talk to Jerry and I'll check with my staff here— see if anyone seems to know something I'm unaware of. Anything else I can do?"

"I actually think there is."

She explained her plan quickly and once again felt relief when Eddy said, "I'll be there."

Next she dialed Jerry Steinman's home number. His congenial voice comforted her across the phone line. "Steinman residence."

"Jerry, it's Stella."

"Stella! Great to hear from you! How are things coming with the new book? I hear from Eddy that he's pushing for a before-Christmas release. Fabulous!"

"I don't know how he will do it, but that's Eddy's problem. He can move mountains with the force of his words. But . . ." She lowered her voice as if someone might hear. "I am not as convinced about your Mr. Ted Draper."

"Really, Stella? I'm sorry to hear that. I thought you said the interview had gone well."

"It went fine. But I received a letter today—an anonymous letter— from someone who has obviously read the manuscript of the new novel. He's threatening to publish an article about me and insists that I meet him next Monday in Chicago. Could this be Ted? Or could he have leaked information?"

"I don't see how. He hasn't read the manuscript—hasn't read any of your novels yet. That's his homework. I don't see how or why . . ."

She could hear Jerry ruminating.

"Tell you what, Stella. Let me talk to Ted, and I'll get back to you."

"Thank you, Jerry. Thank you."

She hung up the phone, reread the letter, and set it on her desk. She tried to push the worry away. She trusted her two old friends. They had never failed her yet.

———

Katy Lynn shuffled out of Sandy's bedroom in her pajamas, heading to the too-small bathroom for a shower. Finally, after a week, her jet lag was over and she could really sleep in. Vacation. She passed by Brian's tiny office, where her brother-in-law had his head in some thick book.

"Good morning," she said.

He glanced up at her. "Good morning, Katy Lynn."

Thank goodness Brian seemed to wake up on the right side of the bed morning after morning. A happy personality—unlike poor, depressed Janelle—although she couldn't see what difference it made in his line of work, whatever it was.

Curiosity got the best of her, and over a cup of coffee later in the morning, she asked Janelle, "What does Brian do all day?"

She could tell by the way Janelle's face turned pink that her little question caught her sister off guard.

"Well, he has his office upstairs, and that's where he prepares Bible studies and sermons. But the media center is downtown. He's in charge of the day-to-day management—supervising the radio programs that broadcast the Gospel into North Africa, and the correspondence course work—sending out Bible studies in Arabic throughout the Arab-speaking world."

"Hmm. Okay. So everything has to do with convincing those Islam people to change their religion. Is that it?"

"Muslims." Janelle got a far-off look. "Not exactly, Katy. You see, we can't convince anyone to 'change his religion.' It's God's Spirit who works in the people's lives and moves them to study, to ask questions, to get to know who Jesus is. So many of these people have a false understanding of Jesus, what they've been taught since birth. We try to give them correct information."

Katy Lynn winced at Janelle's syrupy words. She shouldn't have asked. Couldn't her baby sister see it made her uncomfortable to hear her talk so openly about God? It reminded Katy Lynn of her teenage years when her parents discussed religion as if it were something very personal.

"Jesus this, Jesus that! Janelle, doesn't it ever seem like a charade to you? A put-on, all this God talk? I'd go insane if I had to listen to it all day. Trying to convince yourself that some big Creative Force actually cares about us. I've only been here for a week and I can see it isn't true."

Her baby sister grew silent.

Oh, deary me, I've hurt her feelings.

Janelle always was the sensitive one, the sweet little thing with the heart of gold. Well, like it or not, Katy Lynn had a right to ask questions.

Ever afterward, she would ask herself what her two weeks in Montpellier would have been like if she hadn't blurted out her thoughts. For goodness' sake, she was the master at charades, the queen of appearances. It must have been the heat and the close quarters and the sad, sad eyes of Janelle, and all her own personal problems, all combined, that made her say these things.

The next sentence came out too quickly, and again, unplanned.

"Look, Janelle, I can see you are depressed. You can't hide it from me. Your God isn't helping, and you are desperate. Quit faking it! Just be miserable. I can see it."

———

Janelle was completely unprepared for the accusation. *Faking it?* How could her sister, her sister of the perfect appearances, call her a fake? She stared down at her teacup, mentally calculating how many days before Katy Lynn left. The same as the last time she'd counted, five minutes ago. Eight more days, *if* they were lucky. Katy Lynn didn't exactly seem to be in a big hurry to get back to Hamilton and Gina.

This would go down in her mental scrapbook as the *second visit from hell.*

Lord, I'd love to strangle her. Then Janelle imagined the headline in the *Atlanta Journal*: Missionary to Muslims Strangles Debutante Sister in Passionate Debate Over Religion. No, it wasn't worth it.

With a sigh and a sip of tea she said, "Look, Katy Lynn, I don't expect you to understand our work—why we do what we do. You and I have never been exactly on the same wavelength. And yes, you're right. I am depressed. But"—she turned on Katy Lynn, and her voice wavered—"until you've lost a child, until you've held that little lifeless form in your arms, I don't think you have any business chiding me for being depressed! You weren't there for me when Josh died, and you haven't given a thought to us or our work for a long, long time. It's okay for you to come and take your vacation here. So be it. But please keep your mouth shut about the rest. We chose this life and it isn't easy. You can't compare it to Buckhead and the club and all your well-intentioned charities. It's different. But that doesn't make it wrong or unimportant."

Two perfect crimson spots appeared on Katy Lynn's cheeks. "You don't have to get all defensive, Janelle. I thought you'd be happy to see me after all these years. You have no idea what my life is like either. The pressures of Hamilton's job, my responsibilities, Gina as an adolescent. My life isn't a cakewalk!"

"Of course not," Janelle replied, hoping to end the conversation.

"And every bit of what we have, we earned the hard way, through long hours and sacrifice. At least we aren't begging for handouts from people—getting money from Americans so you can come live by the beach in Southern France!"

The words stung. But how could she explain it to Katy Lynn? How could her sister understand the concept of missionaries receiving their salary from Christians interested in their work, who felt it was important and pledged to support them with their monthly checks? It did sound like a handout. Janelle didn't have the mental energy to argue. She got up from the table, put her cup in the sink, and, without turning around, said, "I've got a few things to do before we go downtown." She jogged up the stairs, wishing she had not offered to take her sister to visit the old part of town at noon.

Hang on, Janelle, only eight more days.

Well, that's just perfect! Just what I need! I come to France to get away from my problems, and here I am having to deal with my depressed, hypersensitive sister. Some vacation.

Katy Lynn opened Sandy's tiny closet, where she had hung up her nicest suits. Amazingly, Janelle had suggested that the two of them go downtown for lunch.

After the little disaster at breakfast, who knows what I'll have to put up with. But I'll go. For the sake of my sister.

She took out her lightweight, sapphire blue pants suit with the silk camisole and the matching shoes. Janelle had specified to wear comfortable walking shoes, and these had a medium high heel, but they were the only pair that matched her outfit. They would have to do.

"Yoohoo, Janelle! I'm ready!" She stepped into the bathroom to check her makeup.

Ready for lunch. Then she thought, with an exasperated sigh, *My treat, of course.*

"I can see why you wouldn't want to leave Montpellier, Janelle. It's a wonderful town."

They were standing smack in the middle of a huge open square called *Place de la Comedie.* Katy Lynn had come here by herself earlier in the week. The ornate opera building stood behind them, towering over a fountain with a statue of the three naked Muses. Off to the right was a covered mall—the only one in the city!—and farther up on the left was the majestic, tree-lined Esplanade with its fountains, parks, and kiosks. People were everywhere, sipping coffee at a crowded café with the bright Mediterranean sun warming their backs; chewing on sugar crepes and waffles as they walked along and talked; making their purchases of fruits and vegetables at the *marché* on the Esplanade. Open squares, fountains, people, sun. The beach right around the corner. Katy Lynn loved Montpellier.

They wandered in and out of the labyrinth of *ruelles,* known as the *centre ville,* narrow, cobbled streets with shops tucked into every imaginable space in stone buildings from the Middle Ages, stores offering children's clothes, shoes, postcards, and lingerie, all hidden behind centuries of stone. Eventually they stepped into a restaurant where Janelle greeted the owner with a kiss on either cheek. The woman led them down a stone stairway into the bowels of the building, which turned out to be a cozy room with a stone vaulted ceiling and tables set with white linen tablecloths and china. A tiny fountain on the wall trickled water into an ancient basin.

"How absolutely charming! How did you find this place, Janelle?"

"Brian found it and brought me here once for my birthday. We really enjoy it. I suggest you order the menu—you'll get your entrée, the main course, and a dessert. It's always delicious. And the meal is on me, Katy Lynn."

"Oh, no. I wouldn't think of it!"

Amazing! Penny-pinching Janelle!

"Please. It's my pleasure."

———

Janelle felt the meal had gone well. After her second glass, Katy Lynn proclaimed the wine divine, giggling at the rhyme, and she had devoured the *paté,* the duck, and the profiteroles. The sisters had found a few safe subjects to talk about—the Atlanta Symphony and the newest exhibition at the High Museum and what the French thought about the American cowboy president, Ronald Reagan.

Janelle silently thanked Brian for suggesting they pay for the meal. "A small sacrifice for a peacemaking mission" was how he had put it. That offer had certainly surprised—and pleased—Katy Lynn.

They stepped out into the sun, and a surge of wind swept past.

"Uh-oh. The mistral is here—that's the wind from the north. It sweeps down through the Rhône Valley. We're okay here on these little side streets, but out on the open *Place* or at the beach, it can be rather impressive."

"Oh, yes. Yesterday it was blowing so hard on the beach that it literally stung my skin. I thought I was going to get a rash!" Katy Lynn giggled again, then suddenly looped her arm through Janelle's, as if they had lunch together every week. "Well, Janelle, we may be as different as night and day, but I can agree with you on that restaurant. Delicious. *Merci.*"

"It really was my pleasure."

Katy Lynn leaned into her, stumbling once on the cobbled stones. "You know, Janelle, I've been thinking. You wonder why we're so different, why you embraced faith and I rejected it. . . . Well, maybe it's because of all that happened during those ten years before you were born. Things you have no idea about."

Janelle brushed the hair out of her eyes. It was true that she had precious little information about her family prior to her birth. Just a few words about how much the Lord could change any situation and what a blessing her arrival had been—"a confirmation of God's call on our lives" was how her father put it. Her mother said nothing in those rare moments of her father's leaking a clue to the past.

"You can tell me now, Katy, if you want. I'm sorry I never asked you before now. What was it like when you were small?"

Maybe the fact that they were walking, not facing each other, helped Katy Lynn speak. Maybe it was the two glasses of red wine. Or maybe it was the fact that after spending a week together, the ice of their relationship was thawing.

Whatever the reason, Katy Lynn blurted out, "It was pure hell, plain and simple. Our parents fought all the time. I have snippets of memories of them screaming—all dressed up for some fancy party, and Mama screaming at Daddy, and him laughing, half drunk. A little kid understands more than you think. They lived up East—New York or Connecticut—and moved among the intellectuals, an Ivy League crowd and fast moving. At least that's what I've pieced together from my memories and a little snooping. There were so many parties back then, Janelle. Music, drinks, laughter, skimpy dresses, and Daddy's roving eye."

"What?"

Her father was the most respectable man on earth—never a wayward glance. He only had eyes for her mother.

"It's true, Janelle. I know you think Dad is a saint, but he didn't use to be. He got the big head and became way too familiar with way too many ladies. And Mother had enough. Took me one day and off we went. She left him. Of course, at the time I didn't understand about the drinking and the cheating. Mother explained that to me one night a year or two later, when she was drunk herself."

Janelle had never heard this story.

"We lived in our own extravagant way. Mother was intent on making Daddy miserable and spending every cent of his money."

"His money? Do you mean they had lots of *money*?"

"Oh, they were well off, believe me. They must have inherited money from both sets of parents. I mean, think about it, Janelle. Sure, they live in that old Victorian piece of crumbling junk, but they have antiques, they have gorgeous china, silver, real oil paintings. Where do you think it came from? A driving school? There must have been family money.

"Anyway, apparently Daddy was devastated to have lost us. He started drinking even more and lost his job and decided to reform."

"He lost his job? What was his job, Katy?"

"I don't know. I was just a little brat. But whatever it was, he was good at it and made plenty of money. Then, according to Mother, he up and quit—or got fired, is my guess—and stopped partying, stopped drinking, and set out to find Mother and me. From what Mother says, it took him almost a year—looking all around North America. And in the meantime, he'd gotten religious."

"Religious?"

"Yeah, they were the best of pagans before that. Great pagans!"

"Why didn't they ever tell me any of this?" She said it out loud, but more to herself than to Katy Lynn.

"I guess the truth was a little too dark for you—or so they thought. I was four or five when they split and almost eight when they finally got back together. And by the time you came along, they were this really conservative, holier-than-thou couple who never took a drink of liquor and hated parties and forced us to go to church every time the doors opened. My life completely changed." She fished for a cigarette in her purse and lit it.

"You can say that Daddy started over and made a better life, but as far as I was concerned, there was way too much to forgive him for, and I couldn't do it. He screwed up my childhood, and by the time things got back together, well, I just didn't buy it. And you were the favorite—the baby conceived of their true love and religious awakening. It all sickened me. That's all."

"I didn't know," Janelle said, almost under her breath. Why hadn't her parents ever told her the whole story? Wouldn't their change be all the more believable and moving if they had given her the details of their former lifestyle, their separation, their reconciliation?

"And you know what, Janelle, I always loved the parties. Not the drinking and the screaming afterward, but the parties! Oh, it was like *The Great Gatsby*, I tell you, and I got to wear the most gorgeous little-girl dresses and parade around. I loved that part. So when they traded that in for an old Victorian house that was falling apart, and left the highbrows of the East to move to Hickville, I hated it all. I knew what kind of life I wanted. It had nothing to do with the life they reinvented. Not a thing." She sucked in on the cigarette. "Mother and Daddy aren't as squeaky clean as you imagine, Janelle. In fact, as far as I'm concerned, they qualify as some of the biggest hypocrites on the planet, that's what I say."

"I didn't know," Janelle repeated.

"Oh, quit saying that! I realize that. They should have told you. I guess they were just too intent on making a good impression, on protecting the younger child, on protecting their religious reputation."

"That just doesn't sound like them."

"Janelle, don't worry. I don't expect you to change sides—you've always agreed with them. I'm just giving you my version of the story. I'm not here to get any brainwashing or counseling. I'm just here to get away." She tossed the cigarette on the cobblestones of *centre ville* and crushed it out with her sapphire blue shoe.

Janelle sat by the stone marker of Josh's grave, picking off the wilted blooms of the geraniums. She absentmindedly brushed her fingers over the stone, letting them slip into the carved indentations.

Joshua Brian Johnson
Beloved child, gift of God
August 3, 1982 – September 16, 1985

Three short years. A breath, a flutter.

Her next thought surprised her: Katy Lynn at three years old, floating through extravagant parties in the East. Then Katy Lynn at five, following her mother, *their* mother, across North America, spending her father's money. Janelle tried to recall conversations that hinted at this unknown past. She could think of only happy memories:

Sitting on her father's lap, playing with a doll.

"What is your favorite place in the world, Daddy?"

"Right here with you, Nelli. Right here with you."

"In the big white house with the wapawound porch?"

"Yes, the big white house with the wraparound porch."

"Did you ever live anywhere else, Daddy?"

"Oh, sure. Long ago I lived far, far away."

"Where is far, far away, Daddy?"

"It's a place I don't ever want to go back to, little Nelli. I like it here
with you."

Janelle wanted to make a phone call to her parents and ask them all the questions in her heart. Perhaps Brian was right. Once she got rid of Katy Lynn, she'd make her plans to see Mom and Dad. Back there, in the shadow of Lookout Mountain, she could ask her questions. Another thing to grieve—her parents' past that she had never known about.

Go home.

Katy Lynn was taking a nap, the kids were still at school, Brian was at the office. In the silence of the late afternoon, Janelle took out a blue aerogram and began to write:

Dear Mom and Dad,

I don't quite know how to begin. Katy Lynn is here visiting with us. She called out of the blue, asked to come alone, and showed up on our doorstep one week later.

As you can imagine, this was a huge surprise, and one I wasn't ready for. Granted, we've invited her to come with Hamilton numerous times, but I think I was always relieved when she turned us down. This visit has proven my assumptions true. She doesn't have a clue about our work, doesn't care, and is still the self-centered sister I've always known.

Then yesterday, she suddenly began sharing things about her past, things of your past before I was born, things I had never heard before. Troubling things. And I wondered why you had never mentioned these things to me. I don't want to discuss this in a letter. Brian had already suggested that I come back for a month-long visit, a time to get away, see the counselor again. He's worried about my depression. I might as well say the word. Depression.

So could I stay with you? Katy is supposed to leave in a week. Then I'll stay here until the end of October to get the kids back on a normal schedule. But after that, in early November, could I come?

I love you both. I am just confused. Very confused. I hope you won't worry. Just pray. Pray.

Janelle stopped by the post office on the way to pick up Luke and Sandy at school and mailed the letter. She watched the light blue rectangle slide into the slot on the yellow postbox marked *Etranger*. And as it disappeared out of view, she wondered to herself, *What have I done?*

———

With a sigh Ted ran his hand through his thick hair, leaned back in the swivel chair, placed his fingers together, and thought. The last thing he needed right now was to have Jerry Steinman worried about the crazy novelist's account. He hoped their conversation had placated Jerry's concern. Of course he had said nothing to anyone about the foundation. It irked him that Jerry would even suggest such a thing.

He didn't have time for this; he had worries of his own. Goldberg, Finch and Dodge was a well-respected, fairly large regional brokerage firm, mainly in the southeast. They were known for their research particularly on southeastern companies. The firm received plenty of old Atlanta money from its investors, whose source of wealth came from Coca-Cola, Genuine Parts, and Trust Company of Georgia. Goldberg, Finch and Dodge would weather any storm.

But he had to admit that a storm was definitely brewing in the market. Even though the market had shown amazing economic growth over the past five years, shady IPOs and conglomerates were proliferating. Yes, the bulls had been driving the market for the past few years, but Jerry Steinman wasn't the only one who sensed trouble ahead. Leveraged buyouts and hostile takeovers were rampant, with junk bonds financing many speculative deals.

Earlier in the year, the Securities and Exchange Commission had conducted numerous investigations of illegal insider trading. That was the problem now, Ted reasoned. His clients still remembered those investigations, and they were wary of more high-risk trading. And due to the extremely strong economic growth, inflation was becoming a concern. The Fed had rapidly raised short-term interest rates to temper inflation, but now that was hurting the stocks. Like many other institutional trading firms, Goldberg, Finch and Dodge had started utilizing portfolio insurance to protect against further stock dips. This was absolutely legit—using futures contracts as an insurance policy for their clients. In case the market crashed, they could make money, offsetting the losses in the stock holdings. But with the rise in interest rates, many of the large institutional firms were all using portfolio insurance at the same time. This perhaps was not the best thing.

He admitted something else. He was nervous. October 13 and he was at 640,000 on his commission run. Only one of his sure-fire clients had bought into the junk bond idea. Ted felt the perspiration breaking out on his forehead.

Why did Lin Su have to mention the Million Dollar Club to his parents? Her parents were living on the West Coast and her grandparents were thousands of miles across the ocean, but his parents lived only five blocks away. His father slapped him on the back at the meal at the club on Sunday night and congratulated him. That had felt good, coming from the man who had assured him that he didn't have a chance in the stock market, the man who had made his life miserable during all the growing up years. A slap on the back. A smile.

Trouble was, it wasn't a done deal yet.

He'd been right on track to do his million-dollar business. But his clients—even the highest risk ones—were sitting on their hands and not doing much because they were scared. He knew the junk bonds were going to pay big. So if his clients weren't interested, he'd invest some himself.

He rummaged through the new clients from Jerry, stopping at the portfolio of Dr. Harold Kaufman. Jerry had told him that this man never followed his account. All he cared about was glancing over his statement once a quarter and seeing that the stocks were going up. Hmm. There was a possibility. Ted would make them soar! No, it wasn't authorized by the doctor—heavy trading—but he'd still trade within the blue chips and mutuals. No junk bonds. Yet. Then with the return he expected on these trades, the doctor wouldn't have one thing to complain about.

Ted winced only once, remembering Jerry's words: "I'm trusting you with my biggest clients, Ted. Do them right." And then that lecture on junk bonds.

Ted prided himself on many things, but perfect integrity was not one of them. So far his illustrious career at Goldberg, Finch and Dodge had not necessitated any fudging. He tried to push one unpleasant memory from long ago out of his mind, the make-it-or-break-it course at MIT. The ticket into grad school. He had known then, and he knew now what to do and how to cover his tracks. Nothing dishonest. An adjustment. A simple adjustment.

He sat at the desk and typed out the orders for trading. The way he figured it, five days of heavy trading in Dr. Kaufman's account would increase the surgeon's portfolio and bring Ted pretty close to that million-dollar goal. It was definitely a risk worth taking. And with a little luck, Dr. Kaufman wouldn't even notice the trading. All he would look at was the result. A lot of profit.

But he sure wished that annoying little voice would go away.

Know your client.

CHAPTER THIRTEEN

WEDNESDAY, OCTOBER 14

To break the monotony of the silence on the drive home from work with her father, Lissa reviewed the day: the kids in the library, little Amber begging for another book by Marguerite Henry, an impromptu tutoring session with Holly, Mrs. Gruder checking on her for the third time in three days.

"Are you okay, Lissa?"

What was she supposed to answer?

Yep, doing great, Mrs. Gruder. Feeling very up and positive after I freaked out on the highway, after I learned that my dad is going to sell my horse. . . .

Ev MacAllister's words *battle plan* floated somewhere in the back of her mind, but she had not found any concrete steps to take, in spite of her efforts to scribble ideas in her journal.

Then a bright memory, one that almost made her blush, flashed in front of her: lunchtime earlier today, huddled in the corner of the teachers' lounge with her head stuck in one of the books Mrs. Gruder had purchased from The Sixth Declension. She told herself she was simply brushing up on Latin to prepare for the tutoring session on Friday. But it was more than that. Latin and Italian swirled in her mind. She kept smelling the espresso and feeling the connection between Silvano and her.

"Look at those leaves, Liss!" Her father's loud voice interrupted her thoughts. "Gorgeous colors. They'll be at their height in a week—two at most. Nothing nicer than driving up good old Lookout Mountain in the fall."

Lissa heard her father's upbeat mood, but her thoughts were a jumble of Latin and Silvano and Caleb and Cammie's announcement about a possible buyer.

"You think you can get along tonight, Liss? I've got a dinner appointment."

"Sure." Then in an attempt to make conversation she asked, "With whom?"

Her father glanced over at her with a little nervous smile. At fifty-two he was still a handsome man, full head of light brown hair, a round babyish face. "Just a few friends. You remember the McCalls?"

"Sure. They own the store where Momma bought the Oriental rug, right?"

"Exactly. Well, they wanted me to meet a friend of theirs, so we're all going to dinner together."

"A friend?" Then it registered. "A woman?"

"As a matter of fact, yes. A lady they've known for years. She lost her husband to cancer a few years back."

"Do you *want* to meet this woman?"

Dad looked over at her. Lissa met his eyes, then looked past him, out the window where she could see the edge of the mountain through the trees. Far below in the valley lay the town of Chattanooga.

"I think so. I figure we both need to move forward, don't we? You're learning to drive again. I guess I need to try something new too."

Lissa hesitated. The wrong word and their relationship would once again careen off the side of the mountain. "Hmm. Okay, Dad. Sure, I'll be fine. Maybe I'll just fix myself some French toast."

She surprised herself with that comment. A smile spread across her lips.

"You wouldn't dare fix our favorite while I'm out!"

"Just kidding. I'll probably settle for something boring and nourishing, like liver and broccoli."

Her father gave his trademark guffaw. "That'll be the day, Liss. That'll be the day!"

They settled back into silence as her father turned the BMW off of Ochs Highway and onto Ochs Boulevard, and wound around to East Brow Road. By the time he parked the car in the garage beside the yellow Camaro, Lissa's thoughts had returned to Silvano. But later she wrote in her journal: *Dad and I had the very barest of beginnings of a real conversation. A hint of emotion, a teasing like long ago. Is this hope? I hope so.*

Lissa made the French toast after all, two pieces, slightly crispy, the way she liked them, smothered in real maple syrup from Quebec, a yearly gift from dear family friends who lived on a farm outside Montreal. The radio was playing a pop song with a heavy beat as Lissa used the last few bites of the toast to sop up the syrup. She'd just stuffed an unusually large bite in her mouth when the phone rang.

Swallowing it down with a gulp of milk, she answered on the fourth ring. "Hello, Randall residence."

"*Ciao!* Is this Lissa Randall, Latin lover and Rome romanticist?"

Lissa swallowed again, to no avail. Her heart began thumping in rhythm with the strong beating of the drums on the radio. "Silvano?"

"*Si*, indeed. Am I catching you at a bad time?"

"Oh, no. No, not at all. I was just finishing up dinner."

"I was at The Sixth Declension earlier today. Evan and I were discussing things—notably your impressive ascent in the Latin Festival a couple of years back. I asked him for your phone number. I guess he knows me well enough to have agreed to give it out. I hope you don't mind."

"No, not at all." She said this too fast. "I really enjoyed being at the bookstore on Saturday. And it was fun to meet you—see you again. Made me miss Latin and Rome."

Her words were jumbled, and she realized she was clutching the phone, not unlike the way she clutched Ole Bessie's steering wheel. She forced herself to breathe slowly, wondering if this exercise helped with silly nervous jitters as much as with panic attacks.

"Look, I have a business meeting out of town on Monday, and Chattanooga is right on the way. I thought I might drive up your way on Saturday, spend the night there, and continue my trip north on Sunday. I was wondering if I could take you to dinner Saturday evening. Someplace fun and Italian."

"Oh, wow. Well, um . . ." She wiped the extra syrup off her mouth and tried to keep her voice from squeaking. "Sure. Why not? Saturday evening? About what time?" She reached over to grab a pen and pulled the phone off the table. It crashed to the floor. Retrieving it, she said, "Hello? Silvano? Sorry—I dropped the phone."

He chuckled. "I wondered what that was. May I pick you up at seven? I know a nice little restaurant in Chattanooga. How does that sound?"

"It sounds good. Thank you, Silvano." She gave him directions to her house, all the while telling herself *Breathe, girl. Breathe.*

"Great, Lissa! See you on Saturday, then. Looking forward to it. *Ciao.*"

She found herself blushing and smiling as she hung up the phone.

———

"*Auguri*, Mr. Rossi!" Silvano congratulated himself, holding the wineglass high in the air and then taking a long sip of Chianti. He had done it! Done it! Scared Miss S. A. Green out of her hole! At least he could be pretty sure. Why else would Eddy Clouse have questioned him that afternoon about the burlap bag and the manuscript? Surely it meant that Stella had contacted Clouse about his letter. *Buono!* Chicago, here we come! Eleven hours of driving one way, but it was worth it. He jotted in his agenda to call in sick the following Monday, October 19. Let Eddy squirm and wonder. He could handle Eddy just fine.

What a week! Silvano had finished reading all of Green's novels and had a notebook filled with thoughts, ideas, and questions to ask the lady next Monday. And he had a date! *Another reason to celebrate, Silvano!* He smirked. Lissa Randall had been taken with his charm, his Italian, his knowledge, his Roman citizenship. He chuckled, proud of himself.

According to Mr. Evan Jones, Lissa Randall was a catch. Latin competition finalist, accomplished equestrian, one of the top in her class. And he was glad she didn't live here in Atlanta—he didn't need anyone else around snooping into his business.

He frowned momentarily, recalling a few of the bookstore owner's other words. "Silvano, that girl has been through a lot. I love you like a son, and I know you like a son. If I give you her number, you treat her right, you hear me? She is not another girl to list in Silvano Rossi's Italian book of American conquests."

Good old Evan! Of course not. Lissa Randall and he had similar interests. This girl, attractive, pensive, intelligent, had the potential of friendship written across her face. Friend, conquest, stepping-stone. As with everyone else in his life, Lissa Randall would serve some purpose in his goal of making it to the top.

"Auguri!" he said out loud.

THURSDAY, OCTOBER 15

Thursday afternoon meant another driving lesson, another chance to fail. No, she corrected herself. Another chance to learn, to listen, to talk with an older man who seemed to Lissa to hold secrets tucked in his pockets, perhaps like Zeus in his Greek robes, or Plato talking with Aristotle. All she really knew was that being with Mr. MacAllister seemed like an essential part of her "battle plan." When she was with him, she wanted to talk about the painful things in life; she felt an energy with the old man, something she couldn't describe, but something good.

As Lissa walked from the library past the main building, what all the girls called "the rotunda," she spotted Amber waiting outside for her car pool, along with several other third graders. They sat on the steps, skinny legs sticking out of their blue plaid skirts. The rest of the waiting girls were in high school, but they too wore the familiar CGS blue plaid uniforms.

The nine-year-old was clutching the copy of *Born to Trot* that she had just checked out from the library. "I'm going to start reading it as soon as I get home," she confided to Lissa.

"Good girl," Lissa said.

Oh, to go back to those days of C. W. Anderson and Marguerite Henry, to flop on her bed and lose herself in the pages of a horse story. How many afternoons had she spent this way? And then she always felt such inspiration that she would get out her spiral notebooks and write. Lissa felt for just a moment the old thrill of creating her stories, horse stories written in her nine-year-old cursive on wide-lined paper. *That* had been her dream—to be an author, the youngest author ever! The memory made her smile momentarily. The past, before *now*.

Mr. MacAllister arrived, parking the blue car by the curb between station wagons and Suburbans. Lissa got in the passenger's seat of Ole Bessie, patting her cracked upholstery almost affectionately.

"She kind of grows on you, doesn't she?" Mr. MacAllister asked.

Lissa nodded. "Yeah. Ole Bessie reminds me of my horse. Well trained, dependable, steady."

"So you have a horse, do you?"

"Yeah. A beautiful chestnut gelding. He's the one I showed in all of those jumper competitions I was telling you about. He's small and trustworthy, and he can jump the moon. A bundle of talent in just fifteen hands, three inches of horseflesh." She blushed. "I guess I sound like an advertisement."

"You sound like a kid who loves her horse."

"Yeah. You're right, Mr. MacAllister, I love my horse." They were halfway down the street when she added, "My father blames me for the wreck. But he blames Caleb even more."

"Caleb?"

"My horse."

Lissa drove four laps around Military Park without one hesitation, without one bead of sweat on her brow. This felt like progress. Granted, she didn't surpass thirty miles per hour, but she drove with confidence. When she pulled into the parking lot of the visitor center and looked over at Mr. MacAllister, his long face wrinkled with pleasure.

"Not bad, Miss Liss. I didn't even think about pushing on my brake. I was just enjoying the foliage. Good job. Give me a high five."

What a strange thing for an old man to say, but then Ev MacAllister was a bit strange. And fascinating. She lifted her hand, reached over, and slapped his. "Thanks, Mr. MacAllister. Thanks."

He turned to unlock his door.

"Wait, Mr. MacAllister."

The urgency in her own voice surprised her, embarrassed her. She didn't want to get out of Ole Bessie; she had so many things she longed to discuss with this man.

He cocked his head to the side, his big hand with the long fingers holding the door handle. "Yes, Lissa?"

"I was just wondering. What is your favorite period in history?"

He didn't laugh at her or make a face as her father would at such a non sequitur. He dropped his hand in his lap, and his expression told Lissa his thoughts. *I get it. You need to talk.*

He settled back in his seat. "I like it all, Lissa." He motioned with his eyes to the large panels of information sitting outside the hexagonal glass entrance to the visitor center. "I've studied just about everything I can get my hands on that has to do with the Civil War, of course. Lots of history around here. And up on the mountain, right near your house too."

She nodded. "Yeah. Point Park."

"And I have always been fascinated by Rome and the early church period. What about you?"

She had guessed right. Anyone who spent much time browsing through books in The Sixth Declension had to like Italy. "When I was in Rome, I imagined that I was living in the days of the gladiators, or Nero. I could see the Coliseum filled with cheering crowds of citizens in togas. I walked under the trees on Palatine Hill and looked down on the hippodrome, and it was so real."

Now Mr. MacAllister was cradling his chin in his left hand, and his eyes had traveled far away. "The city grabs you, doesn't it? When I last visited, we went down below in the Coliseum where the wild animals and the gladiators were kept. And the Christians."

Lissa nodded. "All those martyrs, refusing to renounce their faith. Like Polycarp. I've always had a fondness for him."

"Beloved Bishop of Smyrna, burned at the stake under the regime of Emperor Marcus Aurelius."

If he had been her grandfather, Lissa would have leaned over and hugged him. This man knew and cared about the same things she did. "And he was old—over eighty—when they seized him and demanded that he renounce his faith or die. I don't think I could choose death."

"I've never fancied myself a martyr either," Mr. MacAllister said, "although there are many modern-day martyrs. My daughter and her husband work with North Africans who have converted to Christianity from Islam—or are considering it. These people know persecution. Many have fled their countries precisely because of death threats. Sometimes we aren't that far away from Nero and his human torches or hungry lions."

He had been staring out the windshield of Ole Bessie at a row of cannons. Now he turned and looked straight into Lissa's eyes. "Sometimes it seems to me that history does draw itself into a wide circle and come right back up, knocking on the door. And what have we learned? Are we any different because of it?"

Looking into his pale blue eyes—eyes that held a history of their own, of wisdom and experience—Lissa asked a question that had been bothering her for a week. "Why do you do this job, Mr. MacAllister? You should be a professor."

He laughed out loud. "A professor, you say."

"Or a famous guest lecturer, or, I don't know, a man who archives old books. Why a driving instructor? That seems so . . ."

"Menial?"

"No, not menial. It's a fine thing to do, but it just doesn't exactly fit you. Don't get me wrong, you're good at it. But . . ."

"I could be doing something a lot more interesting than sitting in Ole Bessie all day helping scared teenagers."

Lissa felt the heat rise in her cheeks. "Yeah. Something like that."

"Vocation." He pronounced the word almost reverently.

"Vocation? What do you mean?"

A slight frown creased his brow, and Lissa noticed the moment the pale blue eyes lost their sparkle. She wished she had not asked.

"I guess you could say it was something I felt called to do."

"Called—to start a driving school?"

"Yes. A conviction, deep in my bones, planted there, I believe, by the Almighty himself."

Lissa could think of nothing at all to say to that, but she had the oddest feeling that perhaps she was in the presence of someone important, another Polycarp, who had floated down from heaven on a cloud and landed right beside Lookout Mountain, inside an old blue Ford.

———

The afternoon sun slipped behind the mountains as dusk settled gently over the valley. Ev looked at his watch, surprised. "I'm afraid we're running a bit late, Lissa." He opened the door and went around Old Bessie.

"Oh, gosh!" She hurried out of the car, her thin face red with embarrassment. "I'm sorry I made you late."

"It's no problem," he chuckled as they exchanged seats and he started the engine. "I like talking about history too, as you can tell."

"Do you have another student waiting?"

"No. I'm done with the students today. Actually I'm visiting a rehabilitation center."

"Really?"

"Yes, for accident victims. Para- and quadriplegics. Many of them very young."

"Wow. That's, that's pretty heavy."

"Yes, sometimes it's very heavy."

"Do you go there a lot?"

"As often as I can. A couple of times a month."

Driving along Highway 27, they crossed out of Georgia and over into Tennessee, heading toward Chattanooga. Lissa seemed lost in thought.

"Is one of your former students there? I mean, do you go there because one of your students was in an accident—something that left him paralyzed?"

"No, Lissa, thankfully I've not had any students in that condition. No, I just go to encourage some of the kids, to help them see it isn't the end."

"It's another vocation for you, isn't it, Mr. MacAllister?"

"I guess so."

She was smiling when he left her by the entrance to CGS. She looked frail yet resolved, a gleam of hope in her eyes, as though determined to try on life.

"I don't know much," Ev said, opening the door on the passenger side of the red Buick and motioning for Annie to climb in. "But I know when my girlfriend has something on her mind. Come with me to the center. It'll do you good. Get your mind off our problems."

Annie scowled. "Oh, quit being so smart, Mr. MacAllister." When he leaned over and pecked her on the cheek, she relaxed slightly.

They left the town of Fort Oglethorpe on Battlefield Parkway, heading toward Ringgold. He turned the Buick onto a road a few miles west of I-75 and drove for a while, then made a right onto an old country road. At the end of the winding road sat a redbrick building surrounded by fields, with horses grazing and tall trees providing shade and, on this day, a vibrant canopy of color. A sign proclaimed *Good Shepherd Rehabilitation Center.*

Ev pulled the car into the parking lot beside several vans, the kind specially equipped for handicapped drivers. He cut the engine, got out of the car, went around, and opened the door for Annie.

The moment they walked into the building, Ev watched the tension leave his wife's face. He spent a good bit of time at the center, playing a game of chess with one patient, helping another learn to drive the specialized cars. He enjoyed his afternoons there and applauded the courage and grit of the patients, many of them so very young.

When Annie had started accompanying him several years ago, she was never content to sit and chat or play cards. She was as determined as the patients themselves that they would make progress, and she became a stubborn and vocal cheerleader. Now he watched her bustle down the white corridors, knock on a door, and slip inside the room of a young woman who had been paralyzed in a boating accident. An hour later, he found her in the cafeteria, talking animatedly with a young man who was leaning on crutches. He smiled to himself.

As they walked back to the car, Annie said what she always did after a visit. "There are a lot of courageous kids in there. God bless 'em."

Annie was silent on their ride back to Fort Oglethorpe. He knew she had a hundred thoughts and a thousand memories swirling in her mind behind the gray hair and the softly crinkled skin—the face he could stare at for hours. He'd been watching this woman for the better part of fifty years, and he still had not figured her out.

Parking at the house and stepping out of the Buick, he spoke. "You're worrying about something. What's on your mind?"

"You know good and well what's on my mind, boyfriend. Same as what you're thinking about right now."

Ev placed his hands gently on his wife's shoulders. "Look, Annie. We're going to get through this time, just like all the others. With the Lord's help. Trusting Him. He always comes through at just the right time."

Annie squeezed his hand and nodded. "Life can get so complicated, can't it?" Then she drifted off into another thought. "But it'll be fine, as you say. I don't want you to worry, Ev—let me do the worrying. You take care of your heart."

"You don't need to protect me, Annie. Doctors always exaggerate. They need our money."

She frowned at him. "Stubborn old man."

"Shall we?" He took both of her hands in his.

"Yes, of course."

It was their habit; when one of them felt weighed down with life, the other initiated prayer. Together they took a seat on the porch swing.

Ev's rich voice began. "Heavenly Father, Almighty God. We thank you for life. For the brave kids at Good Shepherd and for our girls too. Holy Father, our hearts ache for our children. For Katy Lynn, who is so close in distance and so very far away in her heart. For Gina, who is hurting. We want to help, we *could* help, Lord. But we cannot force our way back into their lives. And so we wait.

"And for Janelle, whose heart keeps breaking. Oh, Lord. Put people in her path to help her move forward, to help Brian and Janelle keep believing in your love and goodness. Be with Sandy and Luke.

"And, Lord, we give you the other things that seem so hard right now. Amen."

———

When Ted Draper checked his sales numbers at the beginning of the day on Thursday, a self-satisfied grin spread across his face, like a thin line on his son's Etch A Sketch. With the heavy trading of the last two days in Kaufman's account, he was up over the 700,000-dollar mark in commissions. Things were looking up again for him, even if the Dow Jones was slipping slightly. Nothing to worry about. Savvy brokers knew all about these adjustments, the ups and downs, the bull and the bear. His obvious next step was a bit riskier, but necessary. It was the perfect time to do a little more aggressive trading for Dr. Kaufman. When the upswing came—which Ted predicted for the following week—Dr. Kaufman would be all the richer and Ted all the closer to the Million Dollar Club.

Options. That should work—even if it wasn't exactly legal, since no option papers were on file for the doctor. Not exactly, but close enough. He reviewed again Dr. Kaufman's blue chip companies. If the market didn't stay down long, his best bet was buying call options on a number of stocks that the doctor already owned. No need to explain it all to Dr. Kaufman. When the market went back up, Kaufman and Ted would both make a lot of money. "Leverage," they called it. This, Ted told himself, was a perfect scenario. So good, in fact, that Ted decided to buy options for himself as well.

Gambling. Yes, and so what? He had made a reputation by gambling money. He had an uncanny way of reading the market. All the brokers said it. This was just another chance to prove it. He envisioned Lin Su smiling, his father slapping him on the back, his mother's expression, relieved and proud.

Go, go, go! China, here we come. And don't you dare look back, Ted. Don't you dare!

CHAPTER FOURTEEN

THURSDAY, OCTOBER 15

Katy Lynn made a quick collect call to the private investigator's office at two p.m. on Thursday afternoon, French time. That meant eight a.m. in Atlanta, and she wanted to be sure that the PI was up and running. What he related in a confidential voice made Katy Lynn squirm. Every one of her suspicions about Hamilton was confirmed. After five minutes she said she'd heard enough and hung up. No need to completely ruin this vacation. Next she dialed the Lewises' number. It was embarrassing to have to call collect, but she'd reimburse Ellen just as soon as she got back home. She'd kept a close count on her minutes. At least Janelle couldn't accuse her of spending any of *their* francs on phone calls!

"Hey, Ellen! It's Katy Lynn." A pause. "Oh, yes. Marvelous. Absolutely marvelous. The weather is hot. Been to the beach three times. Divine." She lowered her voice. "Listen, Ellen, I am so sorry for these collect calls, but my sister and brother-in-law are on a tight budget right now. I'll pay you back just as soon as I'm home." Another pause. "Well, that's certainly sweet of you. Is Gina there?"

For the third time in three days, Ellen gave her the same answer.

"No, she and Caroline had some early meeting today. But she's doing great. No trouble at all. I'll be sure to tell her you called. Now you just keep on enjoying the beach, Katy Lynn. We're fine here."

Katy Lynn hung up the phone and felt a stab of self-pity. *I am all alone in life! Gina has no idea what I'm going through. She can't be burdened with any of my problems. Not Hamilton, not finances, not all the unknowns of the future.*

For a split second, Katy Lynn wished she could spill out the whole mess to Brian, who seemed to have good advice. If only he didn't have to throw in religion with every other breath.

She realized that her hands were shaking ever so slightly. She needed a cigarette. No, what she needed was a shoulder to cry on, a sister who would take her in her arms and tell her that it was going to be okay, after Katy Lynn had spit out the whole ugly truth.

Well, that is not going to happen, girl. Quit dreaming. Just keep up the charade. Keep it up.

The ever-present sun had suddenly left Montpellier's skies, and the day felt humid, gray, dreary.

Never mind. I have to get to the beach.

So what if Brian had taken the car to Marseille for two days of meetings? Katy Lynn would get to that beach somehow, even if it meant riding on a bus. Reduced to public transportation! For heaven's sake!

She waited over fifteen minutes at the stop and then, when the bus finally came in view and stopped and she was almost stepping on, she saw the number in the window: 12. She didn't need bus number 12. She needed number 26. Another ten-minute wait. Finally it appeared, and she handed the driver a small rectangular ticket, given to her by Janelle. Baby sis was becoming positively extravagant with her money!

By the time the bus left the stop and headed out of Montpellier onto the beach road toward Carnon, Katy Lynn expected the sky to dump barrels of rain on them at any minute. It didn't matter. She could not stay in the house one more second. She could not plaster a happy smile on her face after her call to the private investigator. She wanted to throw up.

The bus let her off at the roundabout, the Grand Trianon, and Katy Lynn stepped into the wind, drew her parka around her, ducked her head, and began to walk along the beach. The tears came immediately, hot and humiliating. How could he! How *could* he?

I wanted it to be a lie. I wanted to be wrong. I wanted him to be asking for a divorce because he was worried or tired or mad. I wanted it to be anything but this.

Proof, staring her right in the face. Hamilton and *her*. A blond secretary from the office who wore her sweaters so snug that Katy had wondered how the girl could breathe.

She could not bring herself to say it out loud, but in her heart that felt tight and squeezed, she admitted the truth. She loved him. She still loved him, no matter what he had done. She did not want to live alone in that big house on Habersham Road. Nor did she want to sell the house and move to some high-scale condominium for divorced women. She wanted her life back, *their* life, with parties and laughter and tickets to the symphony and meals at the club and easy money.

My life is splitting down the middle, just as my parents' lives did.

That was the thought that struck her, suddenly, like a flash of lightning, on the trek down the beach. She laughed bitterly at the irony—she had run off, just as her mother had all those years ago, to escape the pain.

But would history repeat itself? No. Hamilton would not drop everything to get his wife and daughter back. Hamilton Pendleton was not Everett MacAllister.

He'd stopped loving her years ago, wrapped up in business deals and travel and who knew what else—perhaps the arms of other women, although she had never suspected it. With Hamilton's attention cooling, Katy Lynn found that her whole reason for existence was heaped onto Gina. To ease the pain of the truth, she had simply transferred her crazy adoration from Hamilton to Gina.

When the skies opened and poured rain on Carnon and the gray-blue Mediterranean Sea, Katy Lynn barely noticed. The rain fit. She just kept walking and remembering.

She was hurrying to keep up with her mother, who was lifting several leather suitcases into a yellow cab. "Mommy, where are we going? When is Daddy coming? I want Daddy to come with us."

Her mother answered impatiently. "Shh, Katy-Kate. Don't worry about Daddy."

"But Daddy's sick, Mommy. I saw him, stretched out on the bed. That nurse was trying to wake him up."

"He's better now, but he needs to rest. And your father has a lot of work. I am going to take you on a wonderful trip far away where we'll see castles and beaches and go to fancy parties and ride ponies. You'll be happy, little Katy-Kate. We'll be happy."

But she had not been happy. She had missed her father, the way he held her in his lap and read her wonderful stories or made-up ones of his own. Life with her mother meant constant moving, from house to apartment to estate to farm, a journey to fancy places with strange foods. All Katy Lynn wanted was to go home and be a family of three again.

A crash of thunder surprised her, and she watched, mesmerized, as far out over the sea a brilliant flash of lightning split the sky in two with its fierce jagged white line. Just as suddenly another scene flashed before her.

Mommy led Katy Lynn to the bassinet, where a tiny baby lay wrapped in a blanket. "Look, Katy Lynn! Your baby sister! Isn't she beautiful?"

Katy Lynn did not think she was beautiful. She didn't want this baby. Katy Lynn finally had what she had dreamed of—the three of them, together, happy. Mommy, Daddy, and Katy-Kate. Now her father looked adoringly at Mommy and baby Janelle. Not fair! In her nine-year-old heart, Katy Lynn decided she would do whatever it took to win her father's affections back to her.

By the time Katy Lynn found refuge in a café in La Grande Motte, she was soaked to the bone and her mind had replayed several other distasteful memories of the past. She had hated her baby sister, treated her as an intruder, watched jealously all the attention her parents had lavished on the new baby.

"Sweetie, listen to Daddy. Nothing in the whole wide world can replace my Katy-Kate. I love you with everything in my heart." Here he swung her around and around until her giggles filled up the room. "Baby Nelli requires

a lot of attention right now, but that doesn't mean we love you any less. You are our wonderful Katy-Kate."

Katy Lynn did not want to remember the rest—the way everything had changed, the way her capricious fits wiped the joy from her father's face, the way her parents were forced to hire baby-sitters to watch Janelle because they could not trust teenaged Katy Lynn with her little sister, the jealousy that had clung to her just the way her damp hair was sticking to her face and neck as she bent over her hot chocolate.

It took two hours to get back to the house, and when she opened the door, Janelle greeted her with a hug.

"Katy! I was so worried. I had no idea where you'd gone, and I had no car. And look at you! You're sopping. Where in the world have you been? Are you okay? Oh, I'm so glad to see you. Now run take a shower and get on some dry clothes, and I'll fix you a cup of hot tea."

Katy Lynn felt numb from the cold and the reality of her life. She climbed the steps obediently. Her sister was treating her like a child, but Katy Lynn did not mind. It felt good to be worried over, pampered, and cared about by someone else.

Katy Lynn stood in front of Sandy's closet, naked and clean. She reached for her pajamas, needing their comfort, but settled on the worn pair of jeans she had thrown in her suitcase at the last minute, in case she needed something casual.

Casual! Everything about Janelle's life was casual! No parties except the ones she gave for veiled women and bratty kids. Even at their little church, Katy Lynn had been way overdressed. Never mind, today she needed casual. She pulled on the jeans and a sweat shirt. No sense putting on makeup; she couldn't cover up her red eyes. Well, who cared? Janelle certainly was no queen of fashion. She probably didn't even own an eyeliner.

Katy Lynn took a breath and walked down the stairs.

Janelle had set a teapot on the scratched coffee table, along with two mugs and a plateful of those delicious cinnamon cookies Katy Lynn had discovered at the store. She was sitting on the couch—the one that desperately needed recovering—her legs tucked under her, a copy of *Southern Living* spread across her lap.

"You look nice and comfy," Katy Lynn said.

Janelle glanced up, took in her sister's appearance without comment, and patted the sofa. "Yes, it feels heavenly to be reading a magazine. Thanks for bringing it. Come on, sit down and have a cup of tea."

Katy Lynn sat on the opposite end of the sofa and watched as her sister delicately poured the tea, placing the mug on a coaster and offering her cream and sugar. She took a lump of sugar, then another, shrugging. "I shouldn't," she said as she reached for a cookie.

Janelle poured herself a mug of tea, stirred in the cream and sugar, delicately again. No, not delicately. Thankfully. Yes, as if this simple gesture were an extravagant gift, something she relished.

"Sometimes we just need a little comfort, don't we?" her sister said, taking a long sip of tea.

Katy Lynn felt her body relax, the tightness in her chest lessen. "Yes. I guess so." She reached for the cup and found herself curling her legs up under her. "Thank you, Janelle. For this. You're right; I needed it."

"Umm. Good." Her sister held the cup in front of her, and the steam seemed to warm her face. "I can't offer much, but it always surprises me how a good cup of tea will do the trick."

"You have lots of ladies over for tea, don't you?"

Janelle gave a shrug and her round cheeks grew pink. "I guess it's just my way. The women need a shoulder to cry on, someone to listen to them. So we drink tea, and I listen."

"That's it?"

"Well, eventually, after they tell me about their lives, they start asking questions about my life, about my beliefs. If I listen long enough, they don't seem to mind when I talk about the way I do things and about God." Her cheeks were glowing now. "You know, faith. But it's all so gradual. Just takes time. A lot of time."

Katy Lynn turned over these words. France had stripped her sister bare, but not in a bad way. Bare of the trappings of life, but full of relationships. Sad, depressed Janelle nonetheless made tea and listened. Katy Lynn had accused her of being a fake, but the truth was that Janelle did not hide her pain, neither did she hide behind it. She used it. Yes, that was it. Tragedy was part of her life.

"You visit his grave every day, don't you?"

Janelle looked straight at her sister. Katy Lynn had never really noticed that her eyes were such a deep brown, a soothing color.

"Almost every day, yes."

"Does your, your faith help you, Nel?"

"Sometimes it does." Janelle gave a sad smile. "And then sometimes I feel so very low and even angry, and nothing helps." She set down her cup on the coaster and stared out into the tiny backyard where rain was pelting the grass. "But even then, I know God is holding me. He's not expecting me to be some strong woman. I don't think He minds my tears. My friends are patient, but they want me to be over it. Two years, you know . . ."

She looked at Katy Lynn almost apologetically.

"Oh, Janelle. How could you ever be *over* it! People say the stupidest things! I don't know how you've kept going. Losing a child must be the worst thing on earth. You should just keep grieving for as long as it takes." Her eyes misted. "I'm sorry I didn't know how to help. I should have done more."

Janelle shrugged her shoulders and gave a weak smile.

What do I expect her to say?

"You're brave, Janelle."

At that comment, Janelle rolled her eyes and gave an exasperated sigh. "Right."

"No, you are. I mean it. And I can tell how much the people love you. Don't feel bad about hurting." The next sentence she needed to say quickly. "I think it scared me—the horror of it—you losing Josh. And it happening to you—a missionary, devoted to God's cause. I couldn't figure that one out."

Janelle nodded and bit her lip. "I guess finally I stopped trying. The Bible says it rains on the good and the evil. I had to accept that our tragedy wasn't going to fit into some neat little category about God's will." She ran her hands through her hair, pulling it back into a ponytail, then letting it fall free again. "I guess I just wanted my friends to listen and cry with me, the way I had done with them. Instead, they tried to make it better. I know they meant well, they still do, but people can say such shallow things."

"That's for sure. My group of girls—good friends, mind you—are the queens of gossip. Sometimes I wonder if they would listen if one of us ever brought up anything serious."

"I think it's something we have to learn—we have to feel the freedom to tell the truth. That kind of atmosphere comes with time, with trust."

Katy Lynn took another cookie, dipped it into the tea, and watched the cookie change color, parts of it disintegrating into the liquid. Tears were right behind her eyes; she dared not speak.

Gently Janelle asked, "Katy Lynn, how's Hamilton? You haven't really talked about him much. Are things okay?"

The tears trickled down her cheeks. She said nothing, occasionally brushing them away with the back of her hand. Finally she whispered, "Hamilton has gone off with a cute little secretary from the office. He's filed for divorce."

Janelle reached over and took her sister's hand. "No. Oh, no."

"Yep. Just got a full report from the private investigator this morning. Plenty of pictures, if I want to see them when I get back." She took the Kleenex Janelle offered and blew her nose. "That's why I'm here. I was trying to escape. Your big sister's life is falling apart."

"I'm so sorry."

Katy Lynn blew her nose again. "You'd think I would have caught on earlier. I was too busy pretending everything was okay, making it seem okay . . ." Another sniff. "Anyway, I'm glad I came. I really am."

"Me too."

"Thank you for letting me barge in, a silly sister who has no clue about what your life is like. You're a saint."

Janelle looked at her wryly. "You know *that* isn't true. I can't say I was jumping up and down when I found out you wanted to visit. But I really am glad you're here."

Katy Lynn took a sip of tea and smiled. "You've done it again—tea and cookies, and I'm spilling out my life. But there's something I want to say. You and Brian are great parents. And the kids are fantastic. They really are. And I want to say something else. What you're doing matters, somehow. I can tell it matters."

Spontaneously, they reached across the couch to each other and squeezed hands. Then each took a Kleenex, blew her nose, and laughed.

FRIDAY, OCTOBER 16

Janelle didn't know what to make of the sudden change in her sister, but she accepted it with gratitude, like an unexpected hug from one of her children. When she returned from walking Luke and Sandy to school on Friday after lunch, Katy Lynn announced, "Janelle, you need to get ready."

"Ready for what?"

"I'm taking you shopping. And to get your hair cut."

"Oh, no, Katy. You don't need to do that."

"I *want* to do that. It's the least I can do. You've kept me for almost two weeks, free room and board, yummy food."

"In the dollhouse," Janelle said with a smile.

"I've grown quite fond of your dollhouse. Come on, Nel, let me treat you to a haircut and a new outfit. I guarantee it'll do wonders for you."

Janelle had to admit as she searched through her wardrobe for something appropriate to wear that she felt a sudden lightness and excitement at the prospect of shopping with her sister.

———

Amazingly, the coiffeur knew at once what Janelle needed to bring back a youthful appearance. Janelle could not help but smile and feel the heat coming to her cheeks when the hairdresser swished her neck with the duster and pulled off the plastic robe. She looked years younger!

Katy Lynn nodded in approval, paid with a wad of franc bills, and said, "Brian will go wild. But we're not done yet."

My sister is a woman on a mission, Janelle thought as Katy Lynn led her through Montpellier's mall to where the chic store Galeries Lafayette opened in front of them.

"Makeup. You need makeup. Subtle, but enough to highlight your strong points. You've got gorgeous big brown eyes and a perfectly creamy complexion."

Before Janelle could protest, Katy Lynn had located a saleswoman and convinced her with hand signals and bare-bones French to give Janelle a free makeover. Thirty minutes later, Janelle stared for several seconds before she actually recognized herself as the young woman staring back at her in the mirror. She felt like shouting *Hallelujah!*

"Next item! Lingerie!"

"Oh, no. French lingerie is expensive and it never fits me right."

"Don't be ridiculous! French lingerie is gorgeous and doesn't have to exactly *fit*." Katy Lynn gave her a wink. "The whole point is that it won't stay on for long!"

Janelle's face went scarlet, but then she said, "Lead on, big sister! Seduction, here we come!"

————

Katy Lynn had not had this much fun since she'd treated Gina and her friends to lunch at Neiman Marcus last year. It took a bit of prodding, but she managed to convince Janelle to purchase French lace undergarments, things Janelle had probably never even dared to look at before. Well, Brian would certainly enjoy looking now! And in the women's department at Galeries Lafayette, she found two pairs of stylish jeans that made Janelle look slimmer, as well as a nice fitting long-sleeved blouse in a soft brown that was the perfect color for her. Katy Lynn couldn't resist buying her sister matching pumps and a purse.

On their ride back home on the bus, each woman carrying several bags, Janelle looked at Katy Lynn and shook her head.

"I don't know what to say, Katy. Thank you so much. It's been a long time since I've had anything new. A long time since someone treated me like I deserved to look nice."

For some odd reason, Katy Lynn felt a catch in her throat. All she could do was nod and choke out, "My pleasure." Nothing else came. Next thing she knew, she'd be hugging her sister.

The truth was simple: it had been a pleasure, a great pleasure for Katy Lynn too.

———

"Ready, kids?" Katy Lynn called up to Sandy and Luke.

Janelle smiled to herself, hearing their enthusiastic "Yeessss!" as they came bounding down the steps. Sandy was wearing her favorite white lace blouse and bright pink jeans, and Luke had actually combed his hair and tucked his blue polo shirt into a pair of clean jeans.

"This is a big compliment to you, Katy Lynn. They're dressing up for their date with their aunt."

"You kids look great," Katy Lynn cooed. "Now let's get out of here!"

Janelle merely stared in wonder as they left the house with Katy Lynn saying, "Okay, I'm giving you each two bus tickets. You hang on to them, you hear?"

She shut the front door and leaned against it and closed her eyes. "Thank you, Lord. For little gifts. Lots of little gifts." She played out the wonderful afternoon with her sister in her mind. Then she remembered with a tinge of delight the astonished faces of her children when she had picked them up from school.

"Oh, Mommy! You look so, so beautiful! You are a princess!" Sandy had squealed.

Janelle had always heard that if you really wanted to know the truth, ask a six-year-old. Sandy had volunteered the compliment with absolutely no prodding. Even Luke had stopped, looked at her for a long moment, and smiled sheepishly before stuffing his mouth with bread and chocolate.

And now Katy Lynn insisted on taking the kids to the McDonald's that was housed in a beautiful eighteenth-century building on *Place de la Comedie* and then, after dinner, to see the newest Disney movie. The kids were beside themselves.

Janelle hoped her beet-red face had not scared the children when Katy Lynn whispered before leaving, "You and Brian need a night at home alone to celebrate his homecoming and your makeover. And you better wear the lingerie—at least for a few minutes! Promise?"

She went upstairs, checking her watch. Brian was due home in an hour. She showered quickly, then covered her body in lotion. Wiping the fog from the small bathroom mirror, Janelle tried to apply the makeup as the lady had shown her. Her hands were trembling. Obediently, she donned the beautiful lace lingerie and then pulled on a new pair of jeans and the blouse. She felt like a girl on her first date. Terrified. What if Brian didn't like her haircut?

She turned on the cassette player, listening to Amy Grant's new album as she prepared supper. She set the table with the linen place mats from Katy Lynn and the stoneware they'd inherited from other missionaries who returned to the States. She even opened a bottle of wine and lit several candles.

When she heard the car engine in the driveway, her heart started thumping ridiculously. Brian opened the front door, and she met him there. "Welcome home, sweetheart."

It took him several seconds to take in her new appearance. "Wow! Honey! Look at you."

"Am I okay?"

"Okay?" He shut the door. "You look like a twenty-year-old model. You're gorgeous." He set down his briefcase and gave her a long kiss. Then he noticed the soft music, the candles, the table set for two. "Where are the others?"

"Katy Lynn took the kids. She wanted us to have a night alone. She's the one who insisted on everything—paid for my haircut and new clothes and . . . other things." She looked up at Brian and lifted her eyebrows; his eyes registered surprise and complicity.

"Your sister? What happened?"

"I don't know. I just fixed her some tea, and she opened up and started sharing. It was hard, and good. Very good."

Brian took her in his arms and held her close for a long time. "Never underestimate the power of my wife and a good cup of tea! You're amazing."

The evening was a roaring success. Brian approved of everything, especially the French lingerie, which now lay on the floor beside the bed as she lay in his arms.

———

By Friday morning Ted could tell that his heavy trading in the Kaufman account was working, but not really fast enough.

Okay, this is truly against my principles, but I don't have a choice.

He'd simply move to the next logical step—doing a lot of trading in things the doctor had not authorized.

Be careful with the junk bonds.

He shut out Jerry's voice. If he didn't make the club, his difficult marriage was going to take a bigger downturn than the stock market. He knew the adage *Put your family first*, and he intended to do it. Junk bonds, it had to be. An adjustment, a bit of illegal trading in the account. The end would justify the means, Ted assured himself as he wrote out the orders for those three high-risk bonds and several other very speculative stocks for Dr. Kaufman. He believed in himself and the market. This downward swing was going to be followed by an upward spike. He'd been right before.

SATURDAY, OCTOBER 17

Silvano put on his best suit, slicked back his hair, splashed the Ralph Lauren aftershave on his face, observed himself in the mirror, and felt satisfied. He'd made it through the week with Eddy Clouse watching his every move. The boss didn't have a clue.

Let him snoop and stare. I've covered my bases. He won't find me out.

Buono! Now he could enjoy a date with the girl in the bookstore— "bright with a tragic past," as Evan had put it—who knew Latin and Rome and books. Evan trusted him—Silvano was like a son to the old shopkeeper. So when he prodded about Lissa's background, Evan shared the information that her Latin teacher had revealed to him on Saturday. "Bad accident, mother killed. The kid isn't going to college, although she should. She should be at Emory or Harvard. I tell you, she has a lot of potential. . . ."

Potential. Now that was a word Silvano liked. A girl with potential; a relationship with potential. All to help him reach his goals, to push him along in his quest for money and family honor. He mentally listed Lissa Randall's name beside that of Edmond Clouse, Ted Draper, and of course S. A. Green. Adding up all that potential spelled the word he liked best of all: *success*.

———

Lissa felt like dressing up for the first time in eighteen months. The last time she'd worn a dress was at the funeral, a black dress that she had stuffed in the back of the closet. But before that, she had worn dresses and enjoyed feeling feminine. Her girlfriend Jill had said long ago, "You look sexy in anything—riding pants, tight jeans, or an evening gown."

That was before the accident, before food had completely lost its taste, and she had lost her curves. She was too thin. But never mind. It felt good to want to dress up. She had no doubt that Silvano would be dressed nicely. Her friends used to laugh that he wore a suit to study at The Sixth Declension.

She washed her hair, blew it dry, and let it fall loosely on her shoulders, surprised to notice its healthy shine and natural red highlights. She recalled Jill's advice from a few years back: "You've got gorgeous eyes and long lashes. Add a little mascara when you really want to attract attention. And don't forget the lipstick—soft pink is best for your complexion." She searched in several drawers before she found the makeup and applied it.

Opening her walk-in closet door, she went in and studied her choices. Nothing too tight—that made her look emaciated. At the back of her closet she found a long-sleeved, off-white dress, the one she had worn to the fall banquet her senior year. It certainly had enhanced her figure back then. She pulled it over her head, then found an oversized belt and buckled it around her waist. Next came the brown leather boots and a cable-knit cardigan with great fall colors—red and orange and green. A gold necklace and earrings completed her outfit. Staring in the mirror, several words flashed in her mind: *attractive, pretty, classy.* What nice words to be hearing!

Last, she grabbed a jacket and skipped down the steps.

Her father was watching the news on TV in the den. He glanced up at her, then back at the TV and again at her. "Lissa, you look great, sweets. What's up?"

She tried to sound nonchalant. "I told you I ran into an old friend when I went to Atlanta. He's taking me to dinner."

"An old friend?"

"Yeah. He was an Emory student—he hung out at The Sixth Declension, and I got to know him a little when I went there to get books."

Her father nodded and turned back to the television program. Lissa wished he would leave. She didn't relish the idea of introducing the two men, as if she were fourteen and on her first date.

Silvano arrived on time and was dressed, as she had imagined, with impeccable taste.

"Daddy, this is Silvano Rossi. Silvano, my father, Gary Randall."

Silvano stuck out his hand and looked her father right in the eyes. His manner was confident and smooth. "Nice to meet you, Mr. Randall. Lissa tells me you work for Brock Candy."

She didn't recall giving him this information, searching in her memory so that she missed a little of their introduction.

"Yes, sure I know them. I see your ads all the time. As well known in Chattanooga as Gucci or Armani or Dior."

"Are you in sales or fashion?" her father inquired.

"No, no. I'm in publishing. I'm an editor with Youngblood in Atlanta. But I've been around fashion all my life. I'm Italian. Grew up in the shade of the Vatican. I worked for some of the top designers as a young teen before I came to the States. I occasionally do an ad for them when I go back in the summers."

They talked advertising, publishing, and fashion for thirty minutes, with her father offering Silvano a martini—which he accepted—as she sipped on a glass of Coke. Silvano seemed to know everyone. She was thankful when they escaped her house and headed to the restaurant where surely they could discuss Rome. Ancient Rome.

———

Silvano could hardly believe his luck. The girl lived in a mansion! A white mansion perched on the side of Lookout Mountain with a breathtaking view into the valley below. Sliding glass doors encompassed the whole back walls of their living room and dining area. Standing there at sunset, Silvano congratulated himself on having such fine taste not only in clothes and food but in women too.

"Lissa, you look absolutely ravishing. You're a princess," he complimented her as he held out his hand in the driveway. When she took it, blushing, he twirled her around. "Lovely."

And in fact she was. Perhaps Lissa Randall would become more than just a friend. In any case, Evan was right. She had potential.

Silvano made a split-second decision. With this much at stake, the family restaurant he had planned to take her to would not do. Fortunately, he knew of a pricey little Italian restaurant with great atmosphere and live music in downtown Chattanooga. He could afford to spend the money, he reasoned. This was an investment. *Buono!*

CHAPTER FIFTEEN

~

Ev read through Janelle's aerogram for the third time, his thoughts darting back and forth like frightened squirrels in the street.

Unbelievable. That was his first thought. Katy Lynn was in Montpellier, staying with Janelle and Brian. The estranged daughter would not drive an hour and a half to visit them in Fort Oglethorpe, but she had flown across the ocean on a whim to be with her sister.

Disastrous. That thought came next. From Janelle's letter, it sounded like a battle on the scale of Chickamauga was brewing.

The other thought, the one that made his jaw sag, had everything to do with Janelle's sentence: *She shared things of the past that I had no knowledge of.* Normally he would have received the prospect of his daughter coming to spend a month with them as a delightful blessing. But this felt more like a curse. He and Annie were going to have to face the past with her: their wealthy lifestyle, the separation, what it did to Katy Lynn, Tate, his depression.

Depression. Oh, how well he knew depression. He had seen the signs in Janelle long before tragedy struck, and he had cursed himself for passing down those genes. So often in the past he had used a "battle plan" to rid himself of those horrible lies, the whispers in the mind, the accusations that screamed self-hatred, that drowned-out hope. Now those old memories were threatening him again.

The phone rang and he reached for it, knocking a bottle of whiskey off the table.

"Son."

Even in his stupor, he recognized his father's stricken voice.

"Son, there's been an accident."

Without knowing quite how he got there, he was standing by the crumpled car, watching the ambulance's blinking red light carry away his crumpled sister.

Two days later, after the other mourners had left, he sat beside her fresh grave, reaching out to her and sobbing until, completely exhausted, he lay down beside the dirt mound, whispering over and over again, "Tate."

"Tate!" He said it out loud, pronounced the name with the same anguish in his voice as when he had lain by her grave in 1952, tears streaming down his face. Death was always just around the bend or visible out the rearview mirror. Who could escape it?

"Katy Lynn! Don't you look swell? You are so beautiful in that dress!" His mind foggy, he reached out to pick her up and stumbled.

"Daddy! Daddy!"

Little Katy Lynn with her flaxen hair, her eyes the color of irises, her laughter like the sound of the handbells in the church choir.

"Daddy, play hide-and-seek with me!"

Running, Katy Lynn following in her light yellow dress, running through fields of sunflowers and screaming with delight when the butterflies took flight.

"Wake up, Daddy. Please get up! Mommy's crying. Please get up and tell her everything is going to be okay."

Katy Lynn, leaning down by his face. "Daddy, who's that lady? Where are your clothes? Are you sick?"

Enough! If he let them, the memories would suffocate him, would nail him to a cross. Guilty, guilty, guilty. At his lowest points he wondered, what did it matter if God forgave him? He had lost his wife, his daughter, and his sister. Tate he could not get back. Annie he had won back with great difficulty. But Katy Lynn? He had almost single-handedly ruined her life. The next image landed in his lap as if the postman had delivered it along with Janelle's aerogram: Annie's letter from 1950, the letter he had read a thousand times, had memorized as a form of penance before he had set out after them.

I can't live any longer with the drinking and the cheating and the lies. Each time you sober up, you crawl back, begging forgiveness, only to start the whole cycle over again.

I'm taking Katy Lynn. Don't look for us. We aren't coming back. You've said you wanted freedom. It's yours. Annie.

No amount of praying made the image go away. Not even reciting that verse, that wonderful verse in Galatians 5: *If the Son has set you free, you are free indeed.*

He held the aerogram and knew what Katy Lynn had shared with her sister. She had every right; it was her life, her truth. Why she hadn't done it years ago was simply a matter of her cold refusal to be involved in her sister's life. But now . . .

Ev read the signs of holy intervention as if they were printed on the pages of his worn King James Bible. He had lived through decades of being squeezed by God, and now the Almighty had placed his finger on that old, old problem and was saying, if not audibly, nonetheless clearly, *I will rebuild the ancient cities that have been devastated for generations.*

His whole life had been one desperate attempt to cover up the mistakes of long, long ago. There. He'd admitted it.

Dear Lord, help me. Help us all.

———

Silvano watched from the store across the street as Stella Green entered the restaurant on West Fullerton in Chicago, with Edmond L. Clouse beside her.

Ha! She was no dummy, he thought, snapping several photos with the zoom lens. No dummy at all.

Well, neither was he. He wasn't about to show his face with his boss right there beside her. He observed them as they waited, checked their watches, came out in the street and looked up and down, went back inside and ordered lunch at the table he had reserved and to which he had paid the waitress a hundred bucks to attach the little microphone under the table.

This was much better than he could have possibly imagined! An hour's worth of recorded conversation between the boss and Stella. And when, exasperated, they got up and left Stefani's, he hailed a taxi and followed their car. He laughed out loud as they turned onto the exit for O'Hare. So Miss Green didn't live in Chicago! Not once in the crowded airport did they turn around to see him slipping in and out behind other travelers. They stopped by a counter to secure their return tickets. Silvano followed them far enough to see which gate they were headed for, then scanned the nearest listing of flights and destinations. Flight 327 . . . to Atlanta. Atlanta! Did Miss Green actually live right down the street from him? How very convenient!

He went outside and hailed another taxi. When he stepped into Stefani's, the waitress was waiting for him, the little tape recorder in hand and a smile on her face. She should be smiling. She'd just earned another hundred bucks.

———

"Interesting young man, Lissa, that Silvano. Seems to be bright, hardworking, wants to get ahead. You can hardly hear his accent. He's a bit pompous, though."

Her father looked up over the newspaper as Lissa munched on a piece of toast and gazed out the picture window in the breakfast room. A gray squirrel was posed on a tree, looking like he might leap into the air and fly off the side of Lookout Mountain.

"Yeah. You're right—interesting and pompous." She made her voice noncommittal, but the truth was that she had actually enjoyed her date on Saturday. They had laughed about Latin, spoken in Italian, had one of the best meals she could remember. She liked many things about Silvano Rossi—his beautiful Italian accent, his attention to detail, his knowledge of art and history. He had a fierce drive about him, a love of competition, which made them kindred spirits. Maybe if she hung around Silvano for a while, her own competitive drive would return.

The main drawback was his over-the-top cockiness. Pompous indeed.

A name-dropper. Determined to get ahead in life. Still, something made Lissa not write him off immediately.

He wanted to see her again, next weekend. He even offered to take her to see Caleb—that information, about her horse and her father, had slipped out over dessert. Well, why not? She needed to get to the barn.

She reasoned that she could handle Silvano Rossi's advances—he'd tried to kiss her two or three times—for the sake of Caleb and her love of Italy. She grinned even now, remembering his overtures. "Slow down, Mr. Rossi," she'd whispered in Italian when the arm over her shoulder had traveled down to her waist. "I guess Italians are a bit more forward on first dates."

"Maybe so. Or perhaps Southern belles just know how to make us wait."

She'd make him wait. She wasn't in a hurry for a boyfriend. Silvano had his faults, but he had a whole lot of pluses too: Latin and Italy and Rome and a car, a little car that could drive just fine from Atlanta to Chattanooga and back, with a stop at Clover Leaf Stables on the way.

On Monday afternoon, Lissa left the library with a smile on her face and a lilt in her step. For the first time since she had started driving lessons with Ev MacAllister, she actually felt a type of excitement and challenge at the thought of getting behind Ole Bessie's steering wheel. Cammie's words kept playing in her head.

Your father seems bound and determined to get rid of Caleb.

She answered back: *I'll be more determined. Driving lessons. I'll show him.*

"Mr. MacAllister, I swear I'm ready to try the highway. Please. After all, it's my eighth lesson, and I didn't freak out at all the last time—or the time before. I mean, I like the Military Park just fine, but it's getting a little boring."

The old man motioned with his head to the passenger seat. "Lissa, you've only driven past the accident site once, and that caused a panic attack. So, no, you can't drive on the highway, but yes, we will go there, and I will drive. Part of the battle plan."

As they drove along Interstate 75, Mr. MacAllister seemed lost in thought. At least that was Lissa's appraisal. Not once did he ask about her weekend or her journaling or her father or Italy. She had so many things she wanted to tell him, but without his gentle probing, she did not volunteer the information.

They were traveling south on I-75, which meant they would reach the accident site from the opposite direction from which it occurred. As they passed the exit Lissa physically braced herself, pushing her left leg into the front of the car, almost touching the instructor's brake. Her arms were stiff on either side, gripping the old upholstery. She forced herself to look out the window, to look at the bridge and beyond, at the emergency lane. *I can do this for Caleb. I can.*

"What are you thinking right now, Lissa?" Mr. MacAllister's voice startled her.

"I'm seeing the hail. My heart is beating so hard. I'm terrified." They swept under the bridge and out into the open again. "I'm thinking if only I hadn't panicked so bad, Momma would never have needed to offer to drive. She wouldn't have gotten out of the car. That's what I'm thinking."

Mr. MacAllister spoke calmly but forcefully, keeping his eyes straight ahead. "Anybody would panic if the car started skidding. And you remembered how to correct the skid. In the middle of panic, you had a good reaction, Lissa."

He had turned off at the next exit, driven across that bridge, and gotten back on I-75, traveling north. Once again they drove under the bridge, this time on the side of the highway on which the accident had occurred. "What are you thinking now, Lissa?"

"I'm still thinking it was all my fault. It was my fault, Mr. MacAllister. It was! We were driving that day because I wanted to visit more colleges, and then I wanted to see Caleb. Momma did it all for me. It was my fault."

He turned off at an exit and once again drove across the bridge, once again returned to the highway, now headed back toward Atlanta. When he drove under the bridge, he slowed the car and pulled into the emergency lane. "What are you thinking now, Lissa?"

"I, I don't know. Just the same old things. Kinda."

His intensity scared her almost as much as driving past the scene of the accident.

A final time he turned off at an exit and headed north, back toward

Chattanooga. A final time he drove under the bridge and pulled off into the emergency lane, in the exact spot she had found herself with her mother all those months ago. He did not ask her anything. Instead, Ev MacAllister looked directly at her and pierced her with his pale blue eyes. She didn't see compassion in them, but rather anger. *A holy anger*, she thought without knowing why.

"Lissa, it was *not* your fault. It was an *accident*. A horrible accident that no one, *no one* could have avoided. Hydroplaning happens when the highway is slick. Cars slide. It was horrible, but it was not your fault. It was an accident." Now he raised his voice and his eyes were blazing. "There was nothing you could have done differently. You hear me? Nothing!"

Lissa shuddered. She forgot momentarily the horror of her accident, because she was not at all convinced that Mr. MacAllister was talking to her. It seemed to Lissa that he was talking to himself.

———

What a weekend! Both kids had been sick and Lin Su was in one of those foul moods where every word from her mouth came out like the knives used in those Asian flicks. Even her teasing had felt like tiny stabs.

"Why are you so fidgety, Mr. Million Dollar Club?"

Ted certainly couldn't admit to her what the market had looked like when he had left the office on Friday afternoon. The Dow had lost a total of 260 points in the past three days of trading. Alarmed, Treasury Secretary James Baker had given a fine little speech outlining his concerns for the economy.

Well, isn't that helpful, Ted thought bitterly. Baker was simply giving all those already-jittery investors a whole weekend to worry.

As soon as the opening bell rang Monday morning, the trading systems were deluged with orders. Phones were literally ringing off the hook. Everyone was selling. Everyone!

By ten thirty every broker was cussing up a storm, loosening his tie as sweat proliferated under arms and on foreheads.

"We're headed for a crash," someone whispered, and all Ted could see were the hundreds of thousands of dollars he'd just traded in Dr. Kaufman's account. *Illegally.* His crisp blue cotton button-down was drenched in sweat.

At eleven, Bob Turner, the office manager, his face a pasty white, gave a brief speech as he watched the prices evaporate on the computer screens right before his eyes. "There's not enough liquidity in the market to handle all of the portfolio-insurance options. The credit is gone. Gone."

"What do we do?" several young brokers begged, as if the boss had the slightest idea, as if this happened every few years. But it hadn't *ever* happened before. Even the crash of '29 had stopped before completely sliding off the edge.

The computer programs were going wacky. That was it, Ted was sure. They were sending masses of sell orders to the NYSE's computer system. Trading volume was huge, having already surpassed the previous all-time record set on Friday. The delays in trading grew longer.

"The whole system is inundated," Ted said out loud to whoever was listening. "Any minute now that baby's gonna crash and burn." *And us with it,* he thought. The whole system was about to collapse in front of their eyes.

Ted recognized the problem, as did other brokers. The program trading with those automated portfolio-insurance strategies that Goldberg, Finch and Dodge and all the rest of the institutional traders had been using to hedge their portfolios against the downswing of the market were kicking in with automated short sales. The pressure to sell felt enormous, and chaos reigned. Pure chaos. The Dow was in a free fall.

"I've been in this business for almost forty years and I've never seen anything like it," a colleague muttered.

Several other traders were literally crying, bawling like babies before the ticker tape and computer screens. One of the brokers, a twenty-five-year-old already worth several million, suddenly let out an eerie, anguished scream. "I've lost two million bucks in thirty minutes!"

Ted half expected the guy to get out a gun and shoot himself. Instead, he ran toward the restrooms, but he didn't make it before he had thrown up right on the slick office floor.

Individual investors were in a panic; it seemed every one of his clients was trying to call him at the same time. As soon as Ted hung up with one, the phone rang with a similarly horrified-sounding voice on the other end.

And what could he tell them? "Sorry, Joe, I deeply regret to inform you that you've just lost four million dollars in the space of five minutes."

Stop selling! Stop selling! Ted wanted to scream, but no one would have listened anyway. The dam had burst, and the water gushed out. Every broker at Goldberg, Finch and Dodge was soaked, drowning. His clients begged him to sell, cashing in on their futures, grabbing for their insurance.

"Hold steady," he told each one, "and everything will turn out right." But he didn't believe it. Ted watched in horror as the effects of just one morning washed across the ticker tape. It was a bona fide stock market crash. The blue chips had taken a terrible tumble, but the junk bonds were in an out-and-out free fall.

By the end of the day, every broker at the firm—probably every broker in the world, for that matter—looked as if he had been battered to a pulp by Mohammed Ali. Frenzied radio reports tried to explain what had happened to an astonished, flabbergasted audience:

"After interest rates rose earlier in the year, many of the large institutional firms started using portfolio insurance. Because of the instability of the market from last week, worried clients, who had been brooding all weekend, decided to sell all at the same time. The futures market was taking in billions of dollars within minutes, causing the futures market and the stock market to crash from instability. Additionally, common stock holders all wanted to sell simultaneously. The market couldn't handle so many orders at once, and most people couldn't sell because there weren't any buyers left! Within one day, five hundred billion dollars evaporated from the Dow Jones index. Markets in every country around the world collapsed in the same fashion."

Collapsed. Ted felt he might collapse himself. This time he had been dead wrong. No upswing at all. Just a huge bear gobbling up everything he had put his faith in, a bear on a rampage. The phone continued to ring throughout the afternoon, long after the bigwigs had decided to close down the market. He heard later that some unstable individuals who had lost fortunes went to their brokers' offices and started shooting, and several brokers were killed.

"God have mercy," he mumbled to himself.

You deserve to be shot, came the voice out of nowhere.

He did. But he wouldn't go down with the market. There was always a way out, always a way to cover his tracks. He just needed to find it.

When he stumbled in the door late that night, the first words out of Lin Su's mouth were not "Honey, are you okay?" or "Darling, what a horrible day. I'm so glad you survived." Her first words were, "What does this mean for China? Will they still hold the trip? I hope none of this will affect you, Ted. I hope you were smart enough to see this coming."

He poured himself a double Scotch and stared out the window onto Tuxedo Road. All the neighboring houses were still sitting on their perfectly manicured lawns. The neighborhood was calm. He even heard a few birds. By the light of the lamppost he watched a chipmunk hop across the road. Just another day, another ordinary day.

He opened the front door and slammed it behind him, ignoring Lin Su calling out, "Where are you going at this hour?"

In a fog he walked down Tuxedo to where it crossed Valley, thankful to be away from his wife's accusing stare.

Don't you understand that everybody lost out today? Everybody?

But Lin Su did not want to hear reason. She was a fiercer competitor than any of the guys at the office, and she knew how to get what she wanted. He'd put the idea in her head, but now she would make it come to pass. She was going to China.

Their marriage worked as long as the money kept flowing. They had ridden for five years on the back of a strong bull, but Lin Su was not one to stay with a raging bear. He had known the stakes of marrying her long ago. He had to succeed.

TUESDAY, OCTOBER 20

They named it Black Monday. In one day, the Dow Jones plummeted 508 points. At the end of the day on October 19, 1987, the stock market had lost 22.6 percent of its value and over half a trillion dollars, making it the worst crash in history. A broker from Paine Webber said it best,

Ted thought: "The final hour was like a dream sequence. You knew what was happening, but you couldn't believe it was real."

Tuesday was just as surreal—the market was deathly calm, with absolutely no trading going on. Who could trade? All the credit had evaporated. The Federal Reserve tried to step in on Tuesday morning to prevent further losses. As the nation's central bank, it affirmed its readiness to serve as a source of liquidity to support the economic and financial system. Later on Tuesday, the Fed, led by newly appointed Alan Greenspan, held a conference call with members of the Federal Open Market Committee to discuss what role the Fed should play in trying to calm investors and the markets. Greenspan said, "I think we're playing it on a day-to-day basis. And in a crisis environment, I suspect we shouldn't really focus on longer-term policy questions until we get beyond this immediate period of chaos."

This immediate period of chaos. *Well, he's got that right,* Ted thought.

By Wednesday the papers were filled with quotes from important individuals, commenting on the crash. Ted read every one with a nauseous feeling in his gut. *You're right, Mr. Iacocca,* he thought. *We can't "keep romping forever on borrowed money."*

He set down the newspapers and cursed out loud, so loudly that several brokers looked over and gave him sympathy smiles. If they let themselves, every broker in the firm could shout out a string of profanity that would travel around the world.

Why had he invested so much of his own money in those lousy junk bonds? How could he have been so blind? After all, didn't the name spell it out in black and white? Junk. Not only had he lost hundreds of thousands of dollars for Dr. Kaufman in illegal trading, but his nest egg had shrunk by 75 percent.

When he awoke on Wednesday morning, he felt something he had not known in years. He was terrified. Not just scared. Fear pumped him up, got the adrenaline going. But terror drained him completely.

This was not the scenario he had imagined a few weeks ago. Then he'd been dreaming of the Million Dollar Club and China; today he was wondering how to stay out of jail. Jail! That's what he'd get if they caught him.

Ted reviewed the past weeks of trading in Dr. Kaufman's account. At first just a little hedging, a little more activity. Then he'd done it. Since the market continued to go against what he'd expected . . . down, down, down . . . he had made the step over into doing some illegal trading in the account. Ted wasn't sure how he'd convinced himself to start buying junk bonds and very speculative stocks with Dr. Kaufman's money. But he'd done it, and now the money was gone.

He had to get the money back in the doctor's account before he noticed. All of his investors were expecting a loss because of Black Monday. If he could cover over the illegal trading, he could weather the rest of the storm like every other broker.

He made the decision quickly, before he could change his mind. He'd take money from the crazy old writer's foundation. She wouldn't miss it, not for a while. Reluctantly he pulled out the portfolio of Miss S. A. Green. She hadn't even called in the frenzy of Black Monday. She'd held on to everything. Unfortunately, the good stocks went down with the bad. Even though her portfolio was much more conservative than others and had not been affected nearly as drastically, she had still lost at least half a million. All he needed was seven hundred grand. That would cover his tracks. Somehow he'd convince her that those blue chips had lost a lot too. He'd siphon off a tenth of her account and make Black Monday look like the culprit.

What did he have to lose? His marriage was rocky, and he'd already done enough illegal trading to spend a decade in jail. He had no choice, he convinced himself, but to take more risks.

Kenny White, his friend from the competing brokerage firm, called him late in the afternoon, whispering frantically into the phone, "I know Monday was bad, Ted, real bad. But if you keep your head, I think we can still make it work for us. The regular bonds are paying four percent at most. But look at our favorite type of bonds. They pay nine percent!"

"What are the companies behind them like?"

"What does it matter, Ted. Nine percent!"

"I need to know."

"Okay, they're not that hot, some are non-rated and some are

BB- to C-rated. But don't write it off. You can make a lot on these low-rate bonds. I swear it."

Even as Kenny was speaking, Ted reviewed in his mind the speech Jerry Steinman had given to the younger brokers six months ago about integrity, honesty, perseverance, steadiness, not panicking in the midst of a crisis. How to hang tight in a bear market. Refusing greed. *The thing that gets brokers in trouble is greed.* How many times had he heard Jerry give that little talk to the new brokers?

Was it greedy to want to make the Million Dollar Club? Was it greedy to want a nice house and things for his kids . . . or to want to save his marriage? Was it greedy to want to stay out of jail?

He rehearsed the speech in his mind for the fifth time that day, a speech he would give to no one but himself.

First of all, you've gotta understand how things work in this business. To succeed, sometimes you have to make a few compromises. But it always pays off in the end. Sure, I've made some enemies, but I've also made a bunch of money and a pretty good reputation along the way. I'm a hothead, I'll admit it. But I am loyal to those I love, and I love my wife. She deserves to have the best, and so do my kids. I'll do just about anything to get it for them. If you knew our background, you might be a bit more sympathetic. But I don't care what you think about me. I am not going to be found out. And heck, this writer lady is wacko and has a ton of money and all she does with it is to send it to some illegal foundation. She never sees the stuff herself, so what is wrong with taking some of that money and using it for a good cause? I mean, keeping a man out of the slammer is a good cause, isn't it? I'm not a bad man. Not a criminal. What would happen to my wife and kids if they locked me up for ten years? I'll do whatever it takes to cover my behind. And S. A. Green is heaven's gift to me, as far as I'm concerned. The batty old woman is going to keep me out of jail.

Stella Green was no idiot. In fact, she was brilliant. Some creative types didn't have a smidgen of business sense, but this lady was good, scary good. She didn't want anyone following her tracks. So it was immensely important that Ted plan his strategy down to the last detail.

S. A. Green's royalties all came to Goldberg, Finch and Dodge. From

there, Jerry deposited the royalties into that strange charitable foundation—Stash Green Cash. The name was as wacky as the lady herself. Then
once a year Miss Green wrote checks to her other bank account, the one
in Switzerland—the one he was sure was set up for tax evasion.

He reviewed the portfolio. She always transferred at least five percent—as stipulated by law—and sometimes up to eight percent from the
U.S. charitable foundation into the foundation's Swiss bank account of
the same name. In the end, no one at Goldberg had any way of knowing
to whom the final checks were written, or if in fact they were written.
All they knew was that the money was leaving the foundation and being
deposited into the Swiss bank account. What really happened to this
money? That was his question. Technically, it had to be distributed to a
charity, but in reality it could be going anywhere in the world. Illegally.
Ted figured she was avoiding taxes and no one ever knew. Who could
trace it? Certainly no one at Goldberg, Finch and Dodge.

Jerry had helped Stella create the foundation way back in 1967, with
the first deposit of two hundred thousand. A handsome royalty check at
that time, Ted imagined. Twenty years of conservative trading had brought
the foundation's worth up to seven million—although Black Monday had
taken its toll on the account. Every year, on the exact same date, Stella
mailed a check for at least five percent of the foundation's worth to the
Stash Green Cash Foundation bank account in Switzerland.

She was sly. But so was Ted. He had another card to play. He had read
about other brokers in trouble, who set up dummy accounts in which to
trade illegally. In the space of a few hours on Wednesday morning, Ted
set up another account for Stella Green—the Stash More Green Cash, he
called it—at the brokerage firm, using a P.O. box right there in Atlanta.
If anyone asked questions, he would say that Stella had called him up
and given him telephone instructions—that was the right wording—
to transfer 1.5 million to the new account because she wanted to take
advantage of the market being so low to do some riskier trading.

*It makes sense. Other conservative clients have done this before. People
will believe me.*

The bulk of Stella's money—now just under five million—would
remain in the old account to be used for the conservative investments.

Now was the time to make money quickly, while every stock was down low. He could purchase a number of speculative stocks, counting on their reputation to bounce back more quickly than the conservative ones. The purchase would generate a lot of commission for him and allow him to pay back the doctor's account.

He took out a document with Stella's signature and then placed a piece of lightweight paper over it, tracing the name. Then on the same sheet he practiced signing her name over and over, concentrating on the way she formed her capital *S* and then the *A*. At length he tore that practice paper into hundreds of tiny little pieces. Still he hesitated—a full thirty minutes—before forging Stella's name on the document authorizing the opening of the new account.

Illegal! Illegal! The words flashed in his mind.

No, Ted argued with himself. *Just another little and necessary adjustment. That's all.*

When it came time for him to compose a letter from Stella, requesting that 1.5 million be transferred to the new account, he typed it out quickly and then scribbled her signature at the bottom before he could convince himself that this was a big mistake.

By the end of the day, he had begun trading the 1.5 million in options and low-grade bonds. He felt a momentary thrill as he calculated the commission. All the closer again to the Million Dollar Club, and with just a little bit of luck he'd make enough to pay back both Dr. Kaufman's account and S. A. Green's. Now he had the false documents to justify himself.

Greed. Many brokers were tempted by greed. But his temptation was something much more basic. *Survival.* How had he plummeted from golden success to simple survival in just one week? He did not know, but he prayed to the God of Mammon that his plan would work.

CHAPTER SIXTEEN

WEDNESDAY, OCTOBER 21

The little scoundrel, Stella thought. *Some nutcase is trying to wrap me around his finger. Well, it won't work.* She was as mad as a rabid dog on the last day of his life! Who was toying with S. A. Green? She didn't have time for this game. Or the energy, she admitted to herself. This person was snooping into her life, and she'd been foolish enough to fall into his trap. No doubt he—or she—had been somewhere in Chicago on Monday, probably observing her every move. What did that mean?

It meant she had to outsmart him.

With the plane hovering somewhere over Raleigh, North Carolina, she had decided to spend the night in a hotel. What if this creep was on the plane and planning to follow her home? She wasn't going to lead him to her doorstep. She'd spent half the plane trip looking over her shoulder, with Eddy doing the same. They saw no evidence of being followed. Still, just to be safe, Stella had found a nearby hotel and checked in.

Now on Wednesday, back at home, she still felt nervous. Never mind. She wasn't buying into any more schemes. She had enough pressure on her with the editing of the manuscript. And the stock market. The news was all about the crash on Monday. The *New York Times* described the panic at the brokerage firms, of people losing millions in the course of one day.

She picked up the phone and dialed Ted Draper's number. He answered on the third ring.

"Ted, this is Stella Green."

"Oh, hello, Miss Green. How are you?" His voice sounded as smooth and confident as ever.

"Very well, but I need to ask how are *you*? And of equal importance, how is the foundation?"

"I was actually planning on calling you later today. You are one of only a few of my clients who haven't called me this week. Hold on a minute. I have your portfolio right here."

As Stella waited, she realized her temple was throbbing.

Ted came back on the line. "I won't lie to you, Miss Green. This has been the worst week of my life—the worst week for all brokers—as far as the stock market goes. People are numb with shock. Most everyone has lost huge sums. But I actually think it was fortunate that you held on to everything. Right now you're showing a loss of about nine hundred thousand dollars. But I urge you to stay calm. It could have been much worse."

Stella swallowed hard. *A loss of nine hundred thousand . . .* "So the foundation's worth has dropped below six million?" She was surprised at the raspy tone in her voice. She tried to clear her throat again.

"Not quite."

He was trying to reassure her.

"And with the advance from the new novel, I'm sure it will bounce right back up. My advice to you is to hold tight. Be patient. It will inch back up, maybe sooner than either of us expects."

He sounded so confident. What could she do besides trust him? While her account had lost hundreds of thousands of dollars, she had been standing on a corner in Chicago waiting for a neurotic reader to show up and ruin her day. He hadn't shown up, and the big bear of Wall Street had. Every way she looked at it, Black Monday had been a disaster.

The recording was not the clearest, but in between the scrape of knives and forks and the chatter of the restaurant, Silvano got the gist of the conversation between Stella Green and Eddy Clouse. The first twenty minutes centered on him—the jerk who was making them waste their day in Chicago. Silvano laughed out loud at every reference to "some neurotic reader." Eventually, they began to discuss other things that were much more interesting.

"Stella, maybe it's time to let your fans know who you are."

"Impossible. Not yet, Eddy. I can't yet."

"When?"

"I don't know. I'll have to think it through, talk to him."

"To Ashton?"

"Yes."

More static as Silvano scribbled down the name Ashton. Stella then made two references to places in Atlanta, after which followed a long period of Eddy and Stella talking about the editing. Once Stella grew quite agitated, but Eddy managed to calm her down. And then the lunch encounter was over.

He looked over his notes. With the information he had gleaned, as well as the photos of Miss Green and a recorded conversation between the author and her editor, he had plenty of scoop to dangle before a magazine. The identity of Miss S. A. Green should be worth a lot.

"And all I want to do is to make him suffer. Suffer terribly. I know you'll think that is just sinful, but it's how I feel."

The kids were in bed, and over a cup of coffee, Katy Lynn had finally managed to bring up the subject with Janelle and Brian.

"What are you hoping for, Katy Lynn?" Brian asked, his voice steady.

"What do you mean?"

"I mean, are you really looking for a fight and a way to ruin Hamilton's reputation, or do you want to go through this in the least painful way possible, trying to preserve some type of peace for you and Gina? Are you hoping to get all his money, or are you willing to split it?"

"Good questions." She had an old robe of Janelle's pulled over her pajamas and her feet tucked under her on the couch in their little den.

What do I really want?

"What I wanted at first was for him to come back to me. Plain and simple. To admit he'd made a huge mistake and been a fool and then come back."

"And what are the chances of that happening?" Brian asked, looking straight at her. He was concerned, compassionate without being emotional.

She took a sip of coffee and conceded, "Zero. He filed for a divorce, moved out. The only contact I've had since is by letter from his lawyer."

Brian leaned forward and, in that same soothing voice, said, "Maybe you don't want to rake Hamilton over the coals and ruin any chance of a relationship. Maybe you want to handle it like a businesswoman. Don't get me wrong, Katy Lynn. I know you feel horribly betrayed and justified in making him as miserable as you are. The wound is fresh and bleeding. I'm just wondering what might work the best in the long run."

"For Gina."

"For both of you."

Late on Wednesday night Katy Lynn sat in Sandy's bed, the pink sheets pulled around her, and listened to the mistral whipping outside, causing the wooden shutters to bang against the stuccoed walls of the little house.

Try being thankful, Katy Lynn. It works wonders.

Her father's voice from decades ago broke into her thoughts. She had rolled her eyes and mocked him back then, but on this night she followed his advice. She *was* thankful—for the honest discussion earlier in the evening with Brian and Janelle, thankful that they had insisted she stay another week, thankful that Ellen Lewis had laughed at her request, claiming Gina was adorable and like a second daughter. Even Gina had sounded pleased. "As long as you're having fun, Mom. Yeah, stay. That's cool."

Fun was perhaps not the right adjective. *I am enjoying being away from the pressures of home, receiving good advice, and understanding a little more about my sister and brother-in-law. Voilà.* That defined it well. She thought of the astonished look on Janelle's face when she had attended church with them last Sunday. Although she'd barely understood a word, the simplicity of the people, their sincere worship, and their devotion not only to God but to Brian and Janelle had touched some soft spot in her heart.

In three days she was getting on the plane and flying back to Atlanta to face lawyers and gossip and a teenage daughter with plenty of her own issues. Somehow Katy Lynn felt ready, or at least more prepared, than three weeks ago. She felt buoyed up by her sister and brother-in-law, knowing that all this way across the ocean, they cared. They would listen and pray, and for Katy Lynn that felt as refreshing as a long sip of iced tea on the porch of the country club.

THURSDAY, OCTOBER 22

Janelle and Katy Lynn bent their heads into the mistral, drew their scarves around their necks, and marched down the beach at Carnon, pushing themselves into the whipping wind while fine particles of sand pricked their cheeks.

"Such a pleasant stroll," Katy Lynn said, and then they both burst into laughter.

"Oh, yes. Divine! I love walking down the beach with my eyes closed! I'll have you know, sister, that I am only doing this for you. I usually come to the beach *after* the mistral has packed up and left."

"I know," Katy Lynn said, and wrapped her arm in Janelle's. "Thanks. Somehow I just needed one last walk on this beach before heading home."

Go home.

Janelle kept her head bent down as she said, "Speaking of home, Katy, I am seriously considering spending a month with Mom and Dad and seeing a counselor. Brian thinks it could help. I hate to leave him here with the kids, but he assures me he'll be fine."

"Really?"

Janelle waited for her sister to digest this information.

"Going back to Mom and Dad's for a month. You're brave." Katy Lynn kicked the sand and pulled her sweater around her. "No, I shouldn't say that. I actually think that's a very good idea. You need some time to be away from constant demands and take care of yourself. Maybe seeing the counselor would be another step in helping you to get past the depression."

"Yes, and I think I need some time with Mom and Dad. For lots of reasons—including what you've told me about the past."

"Yeah, you're probably right."

Her head bent into the wind, Janelle ventured the next question. "When was the last time you saw them?"

"It'll be three years this Christmas."

Janelle said nothing, watching her sister huddled under an oversized sweater, her hair blowing in her face. She wasn't wearing any makeup. Perfect Katy Lynn, Miss Etiquette and Miss Socialite and Miss Beautiful.

I've judged you all wrong, Janelle thought. *I've seen you as a snob with lots of money and a superficial, cushy life. Pretty, with a great figure and tons of designer clothes and very few brains.* Now one word came to Janelle's mind. *Generous.* Three weeks with Katy Lynn had shown Janelle the delightful generosity of her big sister. Not pretentious or condescending.

They found shelter at a café at La Grande Motte and ordered hot chocolate.

"Janelle, if you really do come back to the States and stay with Mom and Dad, I'll . . . I'll go back and see them too—if you are there."

"Would you really?"

"Yeah. I think it'd be a good idea. I know I need to forgive him, Nel. But I have no idea how to go about doing it. I could make my mouth say the words. I could probably even go to the house and carry on a halfway decent conversation. But I don't know how to uproot all the anger that is down so deep."

"Do you know why you're so angry?"

"Because Dad left; he treated Mom like a piece of trash. And then he got all religious and came back. And I'm mad at her for letting him."

"But can't you tell they love each other now?"

"I don't know. I just don't buy it. Not for them. But"—she smiled—"I see this faith stuff is real for you and Brian, and I think that is good. I'm proud of you."

"Thanks. I certainly don't have any easy answers. All I know is that I'm really, really glad you came, Katy."

"Me too."

FRIDAY, OCTOBER 23

Early on Friday morning, Brian, Janelle, Luke, and Sandy made a circle around Katy Lynn, each taking a turn to hug her. The kids had insisted on riding to the airport, even though it meant rising an hour earlier than normal. They thanked their aunt again for the gifts—the doll and the Walkman and the dinners and movies.

Janelle gave Katy Lynn one more squeeze and whispered, "We'll be thinking of you, Katy. Please call us and keep us informed."

"I will. I really will. And you let me know when you're coming."

They waved to her and watched her disappear around the corner with a final "Bye, y'all! Thanks for everything."

Sandy turned and followed Luke down the escalator, calling out, "Wait for me!"

Brian took Janelle's hand as she brushed away a few tears.

"What a very strange three weeks. I can't believe that I'm crying over Katy Lynn. I've prayed about a lot of things in the last few years, but I never even thought to pray that I'd get to know my sister."

"The Lord answers prayers in different ways, doesn't He, Nelli?"

"Yeah. But why? Why does He give you someone you never even knew you needed—you didn't even *want* to need—and take away someone you were absolutely convinced you could never live without? It doesn't make sense, the way Jesus answers prayer. Someone finds his keys, someone's child is healed, another child dies." She sniffed softly. "A child dies in an accident, and we didn't even have time to pray. We didn't know it was going to happen, so we never got the chance to ask Jesus to prevent it. It just doesn't seem fair."

She had said these things a hundred times before, and Brian had learned to let her vent without offering advice. He simply paid their parking ticket, and together they walked outside the airport into the dawning of an October day. Up ahead, Luke ran behind the metal luggage cart, pushing it across the parking lot, with Sandy hanging on and giggling.

"It's a lopsided faith, Brian. Sometimes it works—praise the Lord— and sometimes it doesn't. Paul and Silas prayed and sang and were miraculously released from prison. But John the Baptist was beheaded, and James died by the sword."

"The answers aren't always in the present. But they will be fulfilled in the future. In eternity. You know that, Janelle."

"But people say such foolish things!"

They had almost reached the car, where the children were waiting impatiently.

"They thank God for something so trivial and talk about how good He is. God is bigger than that. They tell me we could have another child. Who wants another child? I want Josh! I want Josh back!" She stopped in the parking lot and faced Brian.

"I know," he said.

"That was something that surprised me most of all about Katy," she whispered. "She understood. She really did. I felt like she truly grieved with me for Josh. I never expected that at all."

Sandy came over to her mother and hugged her tightly around the waist. "Don't cry, Mommy. Aunt Katy promised me we'd see her again soon. She really did."

———

The smell of her chocolate chip cookies permeated the area around the circulation desk, despite the foil that covered the plate. When the last child had left, Lissa brought out the plate from behind a stack of books and held it out to her boss. "Would you like a cookie, Mrs. Rivers?"

"Well, I thought you'd never ask. Their smell has been tempting me all day. Did you bake them yourself?"

"As a matter of fact, I did. I'm invited to my driving instructor's house for dinner, so I thought I should take something."

"Well, that's nice, Lissa." Mrs. Rivers took a bite of a cookie. "Mmm. Just what I needed to get me through the last hour." She winked at Lissa. "How are the driving lessons going, anyway?"

"Not bad. Mr. MacAllister is good at what he does."

"Yes, he seems like a very competent and kind individual."

"You've met him?"

"Didn't he tell you? He came in a few weeks ago."

"To the library? Was he looking for me?"

"No—no, it was after one of your lessons." Mrs. Rivers's face colored slightly.

"He wanted to find out about me, didn't he?" Then it registered. "You're the one who told him about the accident."

"Yes. I could tell that he truly cared. I'm sorry, Lissa, if I revealed something I shouldn't have."

Lissa finished her cookie and set the plate on the desk. "No, no. I'm glad you told him. It kept me from having to."

She was only trying to help, Lissa told herself as she reshelved a cart full of books: *Curious George at the Circus, Amelia Bedelia, The Berenstein Bears, Anne of Green Gables, Anne of Avonlea, Little Women, Little Men.*

She picked up the book that Amber had turned in earlier in the day, another story by Marguerite Henry. *Black Gold.* The cover showed a black foal lying in the grass, its ears pricked forward, a small white star on its forehead. The sky behind the foal faded from yellow to orange. Underneath the bold black title was a gold sticker: *The Sequoia Children's Book Award.*

Lissa thumbed through the pages lovingly, smiling at the illustrations. When she got to the back cover, she read: *Other Favorites by Marguerite Henry, illustrated by Wesley Dennis. Misty of Chincoteague, Brighty of the Grand Canyon, King of the Wind.* With each title Lissa felt a thrill, remembering the cozy evenings of her childhood when she snuggled in her bed and read her favorite books by flashlight. These books deserved much of the credit for her determination to become an equestrian. Walter Farley's got credit too, along with C. W. Anderson's.

She thought of Caleb, growing fat and sassy at Clover Leaf Stables. Like Black Gold, he was small. Like Black Gold, he was bold and determined. *And I was like Jaydee Mooney, "the boy who had no peace until he and he alone could ride Black Gold to glory."*

Only two more days until Silvano would take her back to the stable and she could ride again. Caleb was not for sale. She would make sure of that.

"Hello, Mr. MacAllister! How are you today?" Lissa slid into the passenger seat of Ole Bessie.

Ev MacAllister smiled and shrugged. "I am doing pretty well, Lissa. How about you?"

"Good. I've made you and Annie some cookies. Would you like one now?"

"Well, how nice of you. Thank you." As he munched on a cookie, he took the familiar route from Chattanooga Girls School back toward Lookout Mountain, driving down Broad Street. He began the tortuous drive up Ochs Highway.

"Are you taking me home, Mr. MacAllister?"

"No, of course not, Lissa. You're eating at our house tonight—I hope you remember."

"Yes, I know."

"But your life is all about coming up and down this mountain, so I figured we'd better tackle that at some point. I'll drive it today. The next time it will be your turn."

Lissa shot him a doubtful look. She knew every twist and turn of the road, the way it dipped down only to crest on a steep hill. Driving up Ochs Highway was one hairpin turn after another with brief interludes of curvy stretches. The mountain residents had perfected the skill of zipping up the curving three-mile stretch of road in under six minutes, while newcomers tended to putt along at twenty miles an hour.

Mr. MacAllister drove at a good pace, and Ole Bessie did not register a complaint. He didn't speak, and Lissa was content to watch the trees. Their leaves had deepened overnight, a kaleidoscope of fall colors, burnt orange, fiery red, golden yellow. She found her heart beating in anticipation as Ole Bessie rounded a curve and the splendid bright red oak burst into view.

"That's my favorite tree on the whole mountain in the fall. It's magnificent." Then, unexpectedly, as Ole Bessie rounded another hairpin curve, Lissa said, "Stop! Stop, Mr. MacAllister. Please pull over!"

On the right side of the road was a pull-off made specifically so that slower cars could get over and let the faster traffic move ahead. Calmly, Mr. MacAllister parked Ole Bessie in the niche. Without any explanation, Lissa got out of the car and fell to her knees, the damp of the dead leaves soaking into her jeans.

"Momma, all these cars behind me are making me nervous."

"Don't pay any attention to them. They can wait. You just take it nice and slow."

Lissa kept glancing back in the rearview mirror as the line of cars behind her increased.

"Okay, here's the little spot I was telling you about. Pull over here and let the other cars pass."

She pulled into the parking spot and waited impatiently. She was going to conquer Lookout Mountain. As soon as she got her real license, she'd go up it as fast as the rest of the residents.

Momma was chuckling. "Liss, you don't have to be the best in everything—at least not immediately. You're learning to drive. The important word in that phrase is learning.*"*

Lissa stayed there, head bent to the soil. She heard the swish of other cars' tires on wet pavement as they passed by Ole Bessie. Mr. MacAllister, wherever he was, made no sound. She didn't move, but said over and over, "I'm sorry, Momma. I'm so sorry."

Slowly Lissa stood up, wishing to disappear into that fall afternoon four years ago, a carefree fifteen-year-old with a learner's license, driving up the mountain for the first time.

Failure. All your fault.

She grasped in her mind for something else. A battle plan.

I can do this.

"Okay," she said to Mr. MacAllister, who was leaning against Ole Bessie, his back to Lissa. "I'm ready to go on." She wiped away a tear with the back of her hand.

Mr. MacAllister turned toward her. "Every step of the process is important, Lissa. I guarantee you it isn't wasted."

Once again, Lissa had the impression that she was in the presence of a mind reader and a psychologist. And a friend. A dear, trusted friend.

They passed the road that turned off Ochs Highway leading toward her house and continued along the ridge. As they reached the top of the mountain, the trees on the left disappeared to give a breathtaking view off the mountain into the valley below. Just ahead, the tip of the mountain jutted out into nothingness. Lissa took in the beauty of the scene, forcing herself back to *Now*. A moment later, Mr. MacAllister turned Ole Bessie into the parking lot of Rock City.

In answer to her questioning look, he asked, "Do you mind taking a little rabbit trail?"

"I guess not."

He parked Ole Bessie, then motioned to Lissa to follow him as he walked through the entrance to the park, saluting a guard with a smile and a handshake and calling out, "Good to see you today, Cal."

The uniformed man nodded and let both of them through the gate without paying a cent.

Lissa thought of the many barns along highways throughout the southeast, their roofs painted with the words *See Rock City.* It was a lovely park— literally a rock garden—with stone walls along walking trails that led tourists through impressive, ancient rock formations along a ridge of Lookout Mountain. For fifteen minutes Lissa followed Mr. MacAllister until they reached the familiar point called Lovers Leap where the mountain fell away, opening up to a panoramic view that seemed to go on forever. She had stood here many times before—as a child with her parents; with her classmates and teacher in elementary school; for her ninth birthday, surrounded by a dozen little girls; and most recently, after the junior-senior prom, when Brandon Hale had taken her to this very spot and tried to kiss her.

". . . There's Alabama, Georgia, South Carolina, North Carolina, Tennessee, Kentucky, and Virginia." Ev was pointing into the air as he referred to a large semicircular stone tablet with black arrows pointing in the direction of each state, along with its distance in miles from Lookout Mountain.

"See seven states from the top of Rock City!" Lissa quoted the advertisement she had heard since she was a toddler.

"Can't help but feel a lot of gratitude welling up in my heart when I stand here. Magnificent."

She wondered if he had a special reason for bringing her to this spot right at sunset. Indeed, the view inspired hope. Two other words floated into her mind. Magnitude and magnanimous. Three words that fit together perfectly in this spot.

Greatness of size, exceptional beauty, high-minded, noble, free from petty resentments. The mountain, the view, the man.

At length she asked, "Is there a point to our standing here, Mr. MacAllister? Does it have something to do with my driving?"

"I think so, Lissa." He was silent a moment, then continued. "Lissa, I know you hate failure. But failure isn't the final story. It's just a stepping-stone to success."

So he does have a point to make.

Ev MacAllister was leaning on the metal security railing, peering out into the sky with its palette of pastel colors, pinks and light lavender and violet blues and a tinge of orange. "When I'm tempted to go down that road of cynicism and analytical thought, I have to remind myself to start *thanking* instead of *thinking*."

Lissa joined him by the railing, bracing her hands on it and staring into the same painted sky. *Thinking and thanking.*

"Thinking too much just brings it back to me, me, me—but *thanking* takes my eyes off myself and my mistakes and puts them on others, on things bigger than myself. I can't stand here very long without being humbled at how small I am and amazed at how big and beautiful our world is. "

Me, me, me.

"Lissa, I know there are many things that haven't gone right for you, tragic things, hurtful things. But from what you've told me, you've had some very good events in life too." He was still staring out into the distance. "I've known a lot of heartache. Enough to weigh me down further than the valley below. So I have to concentrate on being thankful for the good things. It's an exercise that has surprising repercussions. At least for me."

Once again she wanted to move closer to Ev MacAllister and hug him around the waist as she might have done her grandfather. She wanted to grab his fine, wrinkled hands and say, Tell me about your heartache and how you survived. How you made your mind change.

Instead, they stood a foot apart, leaning on the rail as the shadows gradually overtook the valley, darkening the kaleidoscope of autumn colors on the trees below. Far out in front was a hazy outline of mountain ridges. Flags representing the seven states whipped in the wind to their right. In the silence Lissa physically felt a lightness infuse her, something akin to those adjectives—peaceful, content, *thankful*—as she stared out into the expanse while a rainbow of pastel colors lit up the horizon, boasting beauty to anyone in those seven states and beyond who cared to look up at the sky and see.

Dusk had fallen by the time Mr. MacAllister pulled Ole Bessie into the driveway of the white two-story house, with its wraparound porch and black gables, and parked the car beside the red Buick and the white Impala. Inside the dirt driveway was a carpet of green grass. Lissa wondered if a panicked youth on his first trial drive had ever run off the dirt into a tree or turned into the green lawn and left deep tire marks on the perfect grass.

On either side of the steps that led up to the porch were well-trimmed boxwoods, and in front of those, abundant flowers—pansies and day lilies and a few other varieties that were happily blooming in the fall. The front porch held two white wicker rocking chairs on the right side and a porch swing on the left. Like Ole Bessie, the house seemed to have a personality of its own, one that reminded Lissa of the couple who lived inside. It must have been grand in days gone by. Now it needed a fresh coat of paint and numerous small repairs, starting with the porch, which sagged a little in the middle.

Annie MacAllister bustled out of the house before they could even get out of the car. "Everett MacAllister, where have you been? Dinner is getting cold!"

Lissa watched Annie in her jeans and apron, a small, energetic woman, a little round in the middle, with flashing blue eyes and gray hair that fell straight and covered her ears. *Feisty*, Lissa thought, remembering with pleasure her first meal at this house.

Ev planted a kiss on Annie's forehead. "We got detained looking at the sunset at Rock City."

Lissa wondered what Annie would do with such a pathetic excuse.

"So he gave you the *think* and *thank* speech, did he?" Ignoring Lissa's surprised expression, Annie wiped her hands on the apron and held them out to Lissa. "So good to see you again."

"It's nice to be back. Thank you for having me." Then, remembering the cookies, Lissa went back to Ole Bessie and retrieved the foil-covered plate. "I baked these for you."

"Well, that was very thoughtful, Lissa. Thank you."

Ev grinned, and Lissa imagined what he was thinking. *She's making progress, doing something for others, making cookies. This is good.*

Annie had prepared meatloaf, mashed potatoes, and green beans, a simple meal that reminded Lissa of something her mother might have fixed. She forced herself to think of something else. Thankfully, Annie asked her a question about Latin and The Sixth Declension, and the conversation began to flow smoothly.

"Ev was the king of languages in college. He routinely embarrassed his professors by quoting lengthy passages from Virgil in Latin."

"You studied languages in college, Mr. MacAllister?"

Ev wiped his mouth with a linen napkin, creased his brow, and cleared his throat. "No, I didn't study languages—just liked them. I had taken five years of Latin in high school, so I just kept it up, along with some literature classes. I was a bit of a first-class jerk in school."

"You can say that again!" Annie confirmed with a nod.

"Where were you in school, Mr. MacAllister?"

"Oh, up East. Annie and I both went to school up East."

"There are lots of schools 'up East.' Which one?"

"Princeton."

"Princeton! I visited there! It was my first choice for a while. I loved the campus. Those beautiful gray-stoned buildings and the way you could just feel the weight of years of learning . . ." Lissa stopped in mid-sentence, embarrassed.

The MacAllisters looked equally uncomfortable, and Annie changed the subject. "Ev says you really enjoy Latin. That little bookstore in Decatur is a jewel, isn't it? We haven't been there in the longest time."

Eventually the conversation turned to Rome and its museums and piazzas. But later, Lissa wondered why Ev and Annie MacAllister tried so hard to disguise their fine education, their northern roots, which were embedded in the way they pronounced some words.

No, *disguise* was not the right word. *Camouflage?* Was that it? And if that was the right word, what in the world did they have to hide, and who was the enemy?

Late that evening, Lissa sat down at her desk and wrote in the spiral notebook.

There are two things that happened recently that are noteworthy. First of all, the only time I've heard the voices in the past three days was driving up Ochs Highway this afternoon. Momma just invaded my thoughts. It was horrible, but Mr. MacAllister says nothing is wasted. I hope he's right.

I really like them both, the MacAllisters.

The other thing is that twice this week I actually went back to Before and felt excited about college—especially tonight when Mr. MacAllister mentioned Princeton. I could practically smell the spring air of that weekend in April when I visited the campus. I realized that Mr. MacAllister is right. If I can get my mind off myself and on to other people, I feel a lot better.

She sifted through the letters from colleges and read again the latest letter from Jill.

. . . I absolutely love three of my classes, Liss. I wish you would come for a visit. I know you would love it here. This place is so you, Liss. I swear. Please come.

Before she climbed into bed, she had another thought: *I am thankful for Ev and Annie MacAllister. They really care about me. I can tell that they carry a weight of heartache, just as Mr. MacAllister said, but somehow they still manage to live a happy life. They're studying the sky and thanking their God and hoping for something. I have no idea what, but I want to know how and why.*

CHAPTER SEVENTEEN

"I'm outta here!" Lin Su flung a bottle of formula at Ted as soon as he stepped into the house. "And don't stand there staring at me like you have no idea what is going on!" She grabbed her purse and pointed to her watch, her black eyes flashing. "LeeAnne has *not* eaten, and her teeth are driving her crazy. She's got a fever. I gave her children's Tylenol at four, so you've got to hold out until eight before she gets any more. And Sammy has deposited his you-know-what in his pants four times today. You try to potty-train that stubborn child!"

Ted imagined his shoulders sagging a little more with each tidbit of information Lin Su spit out. But for some reason, the last sentence brought a half grin to his face. "I'm sorry, sweetheart. I'm sorry I'm late. You go have fun with the girls, and Sammy and I will deal with the— the *poop*."

Lin Su's eyes softened, then she smiled too. "Another rough day?"

He pecked her on the lips. "Don't even get me started." He patted her on the rear end and said, "Go on. Have fun. We'll be fine."

Ted watched Lin Su breeze out the front door, and he wanted to cry.

Maybe he would. Maybe he and LeeAnne could just both scream at the top of their lungs while Sammy pooped on the floor.

Ted set down his briefcase in the entryway and took the bottle of formula to where the baby was whining in her crib. He picked her up and held her fiercely to his chest, then walked across the hall. Sammy was watching a video in the den.

"Hey, buster! What's up?"

Without turning his head from the screen, Sammy stood up from his place on the floor, backed up a few steps, and plopped himself down beside his father and baby sister.

"Hey, Daddy," he whispered. "We have to be quiet. This is the good part."

As LeeAnne contentedly sucked the bottle and Sammy sat snuggled beside him, Ted watched cartoon dinosaurs trampling across the parched earth. He stared at the screen and literally felt pain for these beasts, desperately searching for water in a scorched desert.

Soon they will be extinct, he thought to himself. *And if I get caught, I could be history too.*

It took him an hour and a half to get the kids to bed. Now he stood by LeeAnne's crib and watched the little pink blanket rise and fall softly with each breath. Only LeeAnne's black hair shone out from under the blanket.

"Baby girl," he whispered. "I have so many dreams for you, baby girl."

Back in his bedroom, Ted picked up little Sammy from where he lay splayed out in his Batman pajamas, finally having given in to sleep after the third reading of *Goodnight, Moon.* Ted lifted his son and took him to his bedroom with the walls that Lin Su had painted bright blue interspersed with white, fluffy clouds. He gently laid his son in the bed, pulled up the covers, and put up the railing. Sammy had a dance all his own in the night, and all too often he ended up with a thud on the floor. The security railing helped Lin Su sleep more peacefully.

After a long, hot shower, Ted warmed up the leftovers in the microwave and carried the plate back into the den, flipping on the television. The kids' bedtime routine had kept him from hearing the voices that had shouted and screamed at him all day.

You are going down, Ted! You've been found out! Too late! Too late!

For the past two days he'd imagined hundreds of sets of eyes on him, expected the office manager to call him in at any moment and lay it on the line. Fired for illegal trading and summoned before the arbitration board—every broker's worst nightmare.

CNN narrated the disasters in the world, focusing primarily on the stock markets around the globe. After five minutes, Ted switched off the TV. His nerves could not take any more bad news. Instead, he thought he'd try one of S. A. Green's novels that Eddy Clouse's secretary had given him over two weeks ago.

Ted never read novels. Ever. His reading consisted of the *Wall Street Journal, Barron's,* the *New York Times,* the *Atlanta Journal and Constitution,* and a dozen books on the stock market. But tonight he needed a break. He went into the bedroom and picked the shortest one, a book called *Eastern Crossings,* fully expecting it to lull him to sleep within minutes. When he heard Lin Su's key in the door, he glanced at the clock and was surprised to see the time. 11:53. He was on page eighty-five, and he had not noticed the time go by. Even as he set down the book on the nightstand, he was still picturing a line of orphans waiting by a train in Eastern Europe.

"How were the kids?" Lin Su asked, coming into the room.

"The kids were great. LeeAnne screamed for an hour and Sammy pooped three times in his pants." He flashed her a smile. "Just kidding. They were really great. How was your night out?"

"Fun. It was a lot of fun."

He forced himself to concentrate as Lin Su recounted her evening. When she snuggled up next to him in bed, he felt thankful for her words.

"I think we're both too bushed tonight."

He turned off the light and kissed her on the lips. She fell asleep almost immediately, but Ted stayed awake for a long time, with scenes from that novel drifting in and out of his mind.

A line of orphans waiting and waiting for a train that would never come. The image of their hope evaporating like the steam from the engines as the trains left the station without the children inside.

Ted thought of the way he had felt a lurch in his gut as he read about those poor children who were stuck in a place where no one could rescue them. Stuck in a physical place, but much more importantly, stuck in the emotional clutches of a past that had discarded them and a future that looked as promising as the blur of the trains passing by.

Stuck. He felt stuck, alone, and terrified. Hope was evaporating. As he drifted off to sleep he wondered, *Who can help me out of this mess? I don't want to go to jail.*

SATURDAY, OCTOBER 24

At least she found something to talk to her father about over their lunch of soup and salad. Though he didn't ask, she volunteered the information, cutting through the silence like her knife cut the ripe red tomatoes on her plate. "Dinner last night with the MacAllisters was great, Dad. They are a really fun couple."

"I'm glad to hear that, Liss," her father said, not looking up from the Saturday edition of the *Atlanta Journal,* which sat by his plate. "Glad you are getting out a little, even if it is with an older couple."

She ignored his innocent jab and asked, "And guess where they went to college?"

"I have no idea." He was reading the financial page, as he'd done all week, yet another article about Black Monday and the crash of the stock market.

"They met at Princeton."

"Princeton?" He set down his fork, turned from the newspaper, and furrowed his brow. "Are you serious?"

"Absolutely. They both graduated from Princeton."

Her father met her eyes. His round, boyish face looked pudgy and soft, his eyes tired and only vaguely interested in what she was saying. "This man went to Princeton, and now he teaches kids how to drive? I find that a bit odd."

"Maybe so, but it's true."

"I suppose it could be. Perhaps he had another job for years and decided to slow down and do this little thing."

"He's been doing this 'little thing' for thirty years, Dad!"

"Strange," her father said, turning back to the paper. "I'd like to see his diploma."

Fuming, Lissa stood up from the table. "I've got to get ready for my date."

"Your date?" He chewed on a bite of lettuce. "Ah, yes. With that Italian fellow. Silvan."

"Silvano."

"Yes, Silvano. He's a bit of a character, isn't he?"

She hurried up the stairs, not replying. When the doorbell rang ten minutes later, she ran out the door, carrying a bulky sports bag and calling out, "Gotta go, Dad!"

She wanted to scream at him: A cocky young Italian who drives a sports car, and a seasoned Princeton grad who drives an old blue Ford. Figure that one out, Dad. And while you're at it, figure out how your daughter fits in the puzzle too! Instead, she simply imagined her father still sitting at the table, deep in thought about the stock market and anything else that would keep his daughter far away from touching his hard, wounded heart.

Silvano was wearing a pair of jeans—perhaps designer jeans, but nonetheless he was trying to look casual.

"Hey," she greeted him nonchalantly.

"*Ciao*, Lissa. It's a delight to be with you again. Thank you for consecrating this lovely Saturday afternoon to me."

She rolled her eyes and laughed. *My pleasure, Mr. Rossi. I'll do anything to get to see my horse.*

When they passed the accident spot on I-75, Lissa did not flinch.

She fixed her eyes on Silvano's black hair, wondering what type of gel he used to glue it in place, and tried to concentrate on his words.

". . . After the business trip this week, things were pretty busy at the office . . . keeping up with the bigwig authors . . . asked me to personally handle all his editing and give suggestions. . . ." He droned on, dropping one name after another, like the trees on Lookout Mountain dropped their dying leaves on a blustery autumn day. When he tired of talking publishing, he turned to the stock market crash, which Lissa had heard way too much about from her father.

Finally, exasperated, she said, "Look, Silvano, can we talk about something a little more interesting than stocks and bonds?"

Silvano raised his eyebrows, glanced at her quickly, then back at the road, and said, "And what do *you* find interesting, Miss Lissa Randall?"

"I don't know. Just about anything would do. Books—let's talk about books. Not about the authors you meet or the trips you take. Let's talk about what you find that is thought-provoking in those books."

He glanced at her again, obviously surprised—and perhaps entertained—by her comments. "You know what I find interesting, Lissa? You. You are a fascinating young woman."

Yeah, right. She didn't answer.

"Tell me about your horse and your riding career."

Well, I'll be. Maybe he can show interest in another person after all.

Lissa spent the rest of the drive to the barn explaining to Silvano her life of horses and horse shows.

"Here we are," Silvano said, turning onto the dirt road with the sign marked *Clover Leaf Stables.*

Lissa was relieved to be at the barn, momentarily away from images of her father hiding behind his newspaper and Silvano painting his workday as something larger than life.

Cammie had already tacked up Caleb and hooked his bridle to the crossties. The chestnut pricked his ears and stamped impatiently when Lissa patted his muzzle.

"So glad to see you here again, Lissa! Looks like Caleb's pleased at the prospect of a workout."

"He and I both! Cammie, this is a friend of mine, Silvano Rossi. He offered to drive me here. I've told him all about this barn."

"Good to meet you, Silvano. If you want to come with me, you can find a spot outside the ring to watch Lissa and Caleb."

While Silvano followed Cammie toward the riding ring, Lissa slipped into the little bathroom behind the tack room in the barn and took out the bag she had packed with her riding hat, leather riding boots, jodhpurs, and chaps. She liked the feel of the jodhpurs, the way they stretched and clung comfortably to her legs. She pulled the chaps over the jodhpurs, the smell of leather and sweat taking her back to her former life. Dressing for the barn had been second nature, she thought, pulling her hair into a ponytail and attaching it with an elastic band. Then she tucked the ponytail under her riding hat and emerged from the bathroom.

"Hey, there, boy," she said, unsnapping the lead shanks from Caleb's bridle. He shook his head twice when Lissa took the reins over his head and led him out of the barn. She blinked in the bright October sun and tightened the girth. Her heart was pumping as hard as before a real competition as she swung onto Caleb's back. The minute she felt him beneath her, she forgot Silvano and her father and driving lessons and the library. She was back! Back!

For thirty minutes Lissa worked Caleb at the walk, trot, and canter, guiding him in both directions in the large riding ring. Every once in a while she glanced over to where Silvano was sitting in the bleachers beside the ring. He was following their every move.

"This is just the warm-up," she called out to him. "I know it's boring, but just give us a few more minutes."

Cammie had her arms draped over the fence. The sight of the large, middle-aged woman standing precisely where she had stood on hundreds of other afternoons comforted Lissa. She pulled Caleb to a trot and then a walk, loosened the reins, and came up to where Cammie was standing. "I think I'm ready. I really do."

Cammie's brow furrowed and she frowned. "Okay, but start off slowly, Miss Liss. You haven't done this in a long time, remember."

For the next fifteen minutes, Lissa took Caleb over fences made of bright red- and white-striped poles, no more than two feet off the ground.

Then she nodded to Cammie. "I'm ready for a short course. Can you raise them for me?"

Silvano helped Cammie raise the poles on eight fences, set in lines of two. "I'm putting them at three feet max, Lissa. And don't you make a face. You haven't done this in a long time, so we're starting slow and low. Got it?"

Lissa nodded with a grin. *Slow and low.* That was Cammie's dictum, had been for years. Work your way up, take your time. As in the old days, Cammie pointed out the course of eight fences, showing Lissa the order in which they were to be jumped.

"And I mean slow. I want you to think as you go into each line, count his strides, look for the small spot, not the big one."

"Got it, Cam. I promise." Lissa felt the soreness in her thighs as she squeezed them into the saddle—the wonderful confirmation of hard work on the back of a horse. Caleb eagerly obeyed. Every move seemed at once natural and completely foreign, as if she were speaking Latin again after years away from the language. She knew the things to do, the way to encourage Caleb with her heels and hands and by squeezing the saddle. She still had the instinct, but the practice was rusty. Caleb was impatient to jump, bolting out from under her after the last three-foot fence.

"Whoa there, horse! He's definitely feeling his oats! Good job, both of you."

"Put them up higher, Cammie."

Cammie put her hands on her hips and shook her head. "No, Liss. That's enough for today. Caleb's a mound of froth. He's out of shape, and so are you. You need to take it easy." She patted the chestnut on the neck and gave Lissa a hard stare.

No, I don't. A hint of that former competitive drive coursed through her. But she said, "Okay, Cammie. Thanks. Thanks for being here. I'll walk him out."

"Sounds good. I'm gonna start feeding—call me if you need anything."

Lissa waited for Cammie to leave, then called to Silvano in the bleachers. "Can you put the fences up?"

"But the lady said—"

"Silvano. Don't worry." She thrust her left leg in front of the saddle, leaned over, and tightened the girth. She gave Caleb a pat and nodded to two jumps. "Just that line, there. Set the poles up two notches on both jumps."

Silvano gave her a skeptical look. "How high are you jumping, Lissa?"

"Not high for us. For heaven's sake, Caleb can jump the moon. This is barely over three-six. It's nothing."

Silvano raised the poles as Lissa instructed, calling over his shoulder, "How long did you say it's been since you've ridden?"

"Two weeks. I was here two weeks ago."

"I know that, but I mean before."

"Almost eighteen months. Now get out of the way. We're going to jump."

Silvano obediently retraced his steps to the bleachers.

Lissa turned Caleb and cantered him in a few circles. Then she headed him to the two jumps. Three-foot-nine was definitely a respectable height, but they'd gone as high as four-nine. Today she was back in the saddle in more ways than one. Leaning forward, squeezing hard with her legs, she urged the little chestnut gelding forward.

He sailed over the first fence, took two long strides, and then sailed over the second.

"Good boy, Caleb!" She let go of the reins, and he galloped around the ring while she held her hands over her head, straight up in a gesture of victory. She was back.

Lissa showered at the barn, just like times past, and when she came out in her jeans and an oversized sweater, Silvano nodded in approval.

"You look great, Lissa, whether you're on a horse's back or just standing there in a pair of jeans. *Mervaviglioso.*"

She grinned and shook her head. "Please, spare me the flattery. It really won't get you anywhere."

She stopped by Caleb's stall, where the small chestnut was munching his hay, his flanks still wet from where she had hosed him off and then slid the sweat scraper across his belly to remove the froth. He came to the stall door, tiny ears forward, and nickered.

As if on command, Lissa produced a carrot, rubbing his muzzle as his oversized teeth crunched into the raw vegetable. "Thanks for bringing me here, Silvano. It means a lot to me. A whole lot."

What prompted this guy to drive from Atlanta to Lookout Mountain, then back toward Atlanta to this barn? And later he was taking her back up Lookout Mountain. Was he lonely? Surely he could find a date in Atlanta. Then on second thought she imagined that most girls got tired of his banter after a first date.

They drove along back roads on the return trip to Chattanooga, and Lissa was thankful to be off the highway and bypass the accident site. She still felt the pumping of adrenaline, the thrill of being on Caleb's back and watching the fences being heightened.

"You are a competitive young lady, aren't you?"

"Is that a problem to you?"

"No, of course not. I just hadn't seen that before."

She smiled at him, lifting her eyebrows. *I hadn't seen it in a long time either.*

The restaurant was definitely Italian, but a sharp contrast to the expensive, intimate atmosphere of the week before. Here, people crowded in the foyer and waited their turns, happily talking and laughing to pass the time. Palvoni's had a warm family style, with red- and white-checked tablecloths and waiters bustling in and out, carrying plates overflowing with pasta.

"So you want to talk about books, Lissa. Go for it. What are you reading right now?"

"I'm rereading Virgil's *Aeneid* in Latin—to prepare for a tutoring session next week with the girls in the Latin competition."

He seemed duly impressed. "The *Aeneid* in Latin. Do you ever do anything for *fun*? Light reading?"

"Sure. I'm in the middle of a novel that came out last year by Tom Wolfe—I think you said you've met him. Anyway, it's fascinating. *The Bonfire of the Vanities.*"

"Yes. I read that last year. Wolfe is great—very provocative. And quite a character. And speaking of characters, remember I told you about the anonymous writer S. A. Green? I've been working on her stuff."

"The new novel, right?"

"Exactly. I tell you, you should read this lady's work. It's good. She has a way of getting into your soul." He sounded almost embarrassed. "I read a lot of stuff, you know. And sometimes I can't get through the first five pages. But she's amazing. The way she uses her words is like poetry in prose. It's like . . ." He searched for the right words. "It's like being back in Rome, Lissa. You're surrounded with something that appeals to your senses. You can taste and smell and feel and hear it. Somehow she makes her stories palpable."

"Wow. That's quite a recommendation."

"Yeah. I don't know what it is. The lady gets to me, like a fine bottle of wine or an opera where the music soars." He stopped. "Sorry. You're right. I do get carried away."

"Hey, it's okay. You've convinced me. Tell me what she's written."

"Five novels—not counting the new one. If I were you, I'd start with the first one—it's short and poignant. *Eastern Crossings*. It came out back in 1960, but I'm sure you can find it in a bookstore or the library."

"Actually, I think I've seen it at our school library. I'll look it up."

By the time Silvano drove her back to the house on East Brow Road, Lissa had changed her mind about the cocky Italian. He had depth. He was interesting. He could even show concern for someone else. He just needed a little guiding. And guide him she would. A free ride to the barn, a good dinner, and conversations about books. For a deal like that, she could lead him around for a long, long time.

———

Two a.m. How she hated jet lag! Katy Lynn wished she'd bought the sleeping pills that Lanie had told her about.

She'd arrived in Atlanta yesterday afternoon. Gina and Ellen and Lanie were waiting for her at the gate at the Atlanta Hartsfield Airport.

Gina had rushed over and given her a rare warm hug. "Hey, Mom!

Welcome home!" And she'd actually seemed happy to return to their house together.

Katy Lynn had been so exhausted that she'd tumbled into bed at ten. But now she was wide awake, staring at the ceiling and reviewing the past three weeks, especially her conversations with Janelle. It felt good to get to know her sister, truly know her, for the first time.

When the clock showed two thirty, Katy Lynn got out of bed and dialed the number in France. Six hours ahead meant Janelle would be up.

"*Oui, allô?*"

She felt a rush of warmth at the sound of her sister's voice.

"Hey, Nelli. It's me."

"Katy Lynn! What in the world are you doing, calling in the middle of the night?" Then she laughed. "Jet lag, right?"

"Exactly."

"Well, how are you? How does it feel to be home?"

"I'm okay. Gina's here, so that's good." She almost let it go with that. Everything under control. "Actually, I'm scared to death. Overwhelmed. I don't want to go through with this divorce. I feel so alone."

She could almost hear Janelle measuring her words, determined not to spoon out superficial advice.

"I'm sorry, Kat. I can imagine it seems overwhelming. Give yourself a few days to get back on schedule before you do anything rash. Trust me. In all my traveling back and forth, the best thing I've learned is to give myself a little time in transition. No big decisions. No major changes. Take a deep breath."

"Thanks, Nelli. I'll try that. I really will."

"And grab a good book."

"What?"

"Find a good novel to read if you can't sleep."

"Really? Yeah—maybe I will."

"And Katy Lynn—you can call me any time of the night or day, understand?"

"Thanks, Nelli. Thanks for being there."

Katy Lynn shuffled out of bed and into the office down the hall, where shelf after shelf was lined with hardback books, most of them well read. Flipping on the light switch, she reached for one of her favorites, finding comfort in the worn feel of the cover. Her mother had given it to her on her fifteenth birthday, back in 1960. *Eastern Crossings.* She loved that book. It had grabbed her, touched her heart, made her laugh and cry. Somehow Miss Green had known what was going on inside her fifteen-year-old soul.

Katy Lynn brushed her fingers across the other novels by S. A. Green. She'd read every one. Good friends. She shuffled back to the bedroom, flicked on the lamp on the bedside table, and snuggled under the covers. At three twenty she switched off the light and drifted to sleep with a scene from the third chapter settling gently in her mind.

Vasilica, the young hero of the novel, was close to giving up, when his younger sister came beside him, assuring him that they weren't stuck. Little Tonia promised her big brother that someone would come for them.

Katy Lynn had always loved the conversation between brother and sister. She loved how the youngest character in the novel pronounced the wisest words. *And somehow, she made me believe them,* Katy Lynn thought. Now, in the middle of the night, she could almost hear Janelle pronouncing the same words, offering comfort to her older sister, who also felt like giving up.

———

Silvano tossed and turned in his bed. Why had he waxed eloquent about S. A. Green to Lissa Randall? He'd hardly believed it was his voice talking, listing her literary acuity. All of it true. Problem was, he didn't need to be finding virtue in the woman he was planning to expose. And he did not want to be reminded of the way her books jabbed him in the soul, the way phrases from the new novel floated out to him, breaking into his thoughts. He didn't need this. He needed to think straight. Already he was having trouble concentrating with images of Lissa Randall in his mind. She was no pushover. She'd called his bluff in a minute. So he needed to proceed with caution. The *Aeneid* in Latin, of all things!

He got out of bed, found a notebook and pen, and began to compose the letter to a couple of major magazines—a letter that was going to buy him fame and attention and a better job. He had to word it perfectly, leaking just enough information to let the editors know his offer was for real. And then he would see who offered the most for such a scoop.

After struggling with it for half an hour, he got back in bed. Drifting off to sleep, he thought of another scene from Green's manuscript. He heard his own voice transcribing the words in his mind. *Can't you see you're going too fast, Silvano? You are going to get into trouble! Deep trouble!*

MONDAY, OCTOBER 26

The first thing on Lissa's mind Monday morning when she arrived at Chattanooga Girls School was the novel that Silvano had recommended. His description of S. A. Green intrigued her. As she straightened a few things at the circulation desk, she asked, "Mrs. Rivers, have you ever heard of an author called S. A. Green?"

"Oh, sure. She's very well known. Not very prolific, though." She left the circulation desk, with Lissa following. "Her first book came out when I was about your age. *Eastern Crossings*. I loved that book. I had the choice of reading it or *The Red Pony* by Steinbeck. I knew Steinbeck would be sad, so I chose Green—and bawled my eyes out over it. I tell you, that little novel changed my life."

She scanned a shelf. "Here it is."

"It changed your life?"

Mrs. Rivers laughed good-naturedly. "Figuratively speaking, of course. But, yes, at the time, that novel touched something in me that needed touching."

At Lissa's skeptical gaze, Mrs. Rivers handed her the book. "Don't believe me. Read it for yourself."

Lissa held the thin paperback novel in her hands. It had that comfortable feel of use, like her leather saddle. Many hands had held this book, had turned page after page, so that under the clear plastic cover, the corners turned up and the paper inside had lost its crisp, clean feel.

"Thanks, I think I will." She carried it back to the desk and signed it out.

At two in the morning, Lissa could not get it out of her mind. The novel was disturbing. She felt as though the writer had looked inside her own heart. How could this be, when S. A. Green was describing orphans on the other side of the world in the early twentieth century? Orphans waiting for a train that never came.

Silvano and Mrs. Rivers were right. The prose felt like a smooth cream on chapped hands. How could such beautiful words bother her so deeply?

One of the characters had told young Vasilica, the novel's hero, that sometimes the only way to move ahead was by looking back. Something like that. Something about the way to the future being found in the past.

Lissa groaned. She was stuck in the *Now*.

Silvano made her look back, that was true—back to happier memories of Latin and Rome and boys. Her ride on Caleb had certainly taken her back to the thrill of feeling a horse beneath her, the natural high she felt jumping those fences. Even now, the dull soreness in her thighs was a pleasant reminder of her workout on Caleb. Mr. MacAllister was forcing her back too—to the scene of the accident and then further back to the winding road up Lookout Mountain, when driving was just another challenge, another competition, something fun.

Her mother's ash blond head appeared around the corner where Lissa was sitting at the kitchen table. "Lissa, you are the most competitive girl I have ever seen. It's two in the morning! Will you please come upstairs to bed?"

"I want to be ready."

"You are *ready. You've practically memorized the whole book, sweetie!"*

Another night, and again her mother came into the kitchen where Lissa sat spread eagle on the floor, rubbing Neatsfoot oil into her saddle.

"Liss, you are going to be too tired for the show tomorrow. We've got to get up at five. Go to bed."

She was *tired. Exhausted. But the adrenaline always kicked in when she and Caleb rode into the ring. Two Cokes in the morning with a sausage biscuit and she would be ready to go. . . .*

With a satisfied smile, Lissa admitted to herself that she wanted to go back *and* she wanted to go forward. Eighteen months was long enough to be stuck. Another scene from *Eastern Crossings* flashed before her. Tonia, Vasilica's little sister, was trying to encourage her brother and reassure him that they were not stuck, that someone would come to get them. She loved the little girl's words, full of hope and faith. Yes, the faith of a child.

She surprised herself by saying out loud, "That's what I want. I want the faith to believe that I am not stuck."

CHAPTER EIGHTEEN

Every florist in Montpellier was selling chrysanthemums—yellow, gold, burnt orange, burgundy red—displayed in pots in front of the nurseries. Rows and rows of pots. For All Saints Day—*Toussaint*, as they called it in France; for the graves, for the dead. Janelle paused beside the vendor's stand at the *marché* where the mums were a better price and chose two, gold and burgundy, for Josh's grave. Of all the French traditions, this was the one in which she wished she had no reason to participate: visiting the little cemetery, carrying her bundle of flowers. She wished she could disappear into some French child's skin and traipse through the manicured paths of this graveyard and play peekaboo behind the stone statues, oblivious to the sorrow.

Life in a foreign country was all about adapting to the new culture. She'd been doing that for years.

Why, God, why do I have to adapt to this? *To death?*

The wine and cheeses and four-course meals and long walks on Sunday afternoons, these she enjoyed. She endured the crazy governmental red tape, the rudeness of the shopkeepers, the undisciplined way people crowded each other and broke into line. Even the constant criticism from neighbors, from the children's teachers, from churchgoers, she had accepted as another part of French culture. But not this! Not the way her heart was constricting as she held the pots of chrysanthemums in front of her like a protective shield.

"There you are, Nelli!" Brian appeared with bags laden with fruits and vegetables from the *marché*. His eyes settled on the mums and darkened. "Let me get those for you." He reached out for the chrysanthemums, but she shook her head.

"No, it's okay. Let me carry them."

They walked back to the little gray Renault in silence. Brian tossed the bags into the trunk and Janelle carefully placed the flowerpots on the floor, wedged in between the front and back seats. When Brian started the car and pulled onto the road heading home, she broke the silence with words that sounded even to herself as if they were pronounced by someone else.

"Let me get through the long weekend. Let me get us all through the first of November. Then I'll think about going back to the States." Her voice was thin, feeble, on the brink of breaking. "I'll think about it, Brian, but I don't want to get my hopes up. The airplane ticket isn't in our budget. It would put us under for months."

Brian held up his hand, wagging his forefinger as every Frenchman did to say *You're wrong*. "We already have the money for the ticket."

"What?"

"Katy Lynn made the deposit into our account as soon as she got back to Atlanta. She asked me not to tell you, because she wanted you to decide for yourself. But if you want to fly back to Georgia, we have money for the ticket."

Tears trickled down Janelle's face. She had no words.

Go home.

———

"... planning to fly to Atlanta on November fifth ... a month ... if that's okay with you and Mom."

The crackling in the phone line made his daughter's words barely distinguishable.

"Of course, Nelli, of course you can. We would be delighted."

". . . kids and Brian through *Toussaint* . . . the flowers . . . the grave. I always do that."

Ev was sure that Janelle's voice was cracking, more than the telephone line.

"Of course. Of course."

The conversation lasted no more than four or five minutes. After he said good-bye to Janelle, Ev pushed back his desk chair, stood up, and let his eyes travel around his office—their office. It was spacious, with a window that looked out on the front porch and into the distant mountains, and furnished with furniture he had inherited from his mother and father. Books were crammed into every available space of the mahogany bookshelves that took up one whole wall. No, not crammed. Lovingly inserted. Every one of them chosen with care, history books from his Princeton days, classics, modern novels, picture books on France, travel guides, books on economy and politics, biographies. The stuff of a lifetime.

The filing cabinets were Annie's domain, and they *were* crammed with the records of students, the bills and licenses and tax forms, drivers' guides and pamphlets, the paperwork for a small home business.

Ev walked around his office and let his gaze rest on the dozens of framed photos on walls and shelves. Black-and-white baby pictures of Katy Lynn and Janelle in beautiful silver frames. Beside them, another silver-framed photo showed Annie and Ev in wedding attire, their faces erupting in delight as they stepped out of a limousine. On a different shelf was an old color eight-by-ten pose of their wedding party.

He reached for that photo and stared at the smiling face of little Tate. At eight years old she had held the honor of flower girl. There she stood, a big openmouthed grin showing several missing teeth, her shining brown hair falling to her shoulders, two tiny braids crowning her head. She wore a long sleeveless dress, the same color as the bridesmaids—a soft blue—and short white gloves. She held a small white straw basket in front of her, filled with real rose petals.

It was 1943. A fancy wedding in the middle of a war. Six months later he'd flown over the Atlantic to fight Hitler and fascism. By the time he got back, a mere two years after the wedding, Tate seemed so grown-up—much too grown-up for a ten-year-old.

"Tate," he whispered through the catch in his throat.

Katy Lynn probably did not even remember her young aunt. No, surely she did, for Tate had loved baby-sitting her niece. Janelle, though, had heard her name mentioned only a few times, and that many, many years ago.

There's so much they don't know, Lord. How do I explain it now? Why should I? Will they understand? Will it make sense? Then out loud he asked, "Will they forgive me?"

Ev replaced the framed photo of the wedding party and left the office, closing the door behind him.

"Janelle's coming home, Annie."

Annie, arms filled with groceries, lifted an eyebrow as Ev took one bag from her. Then she gave a stilted laugh. "Well, she couldn't have picked a better time."

Ev took the eggs and milk out of the brown paper bag. "Annie, anytime is the perfect time to see our daughter."

"I know, dear. I know. And I will be all excitement when the day arrives." She handed him a tub of low-fat margarine to put in the fridge.

Her eyes were anxious. Ev wanted to erase the worry that had taken over in the past weeks.

"Of course she would pick this time. Everything happens at once so that we're forced into depending on the Lord even more than usual. Has it ever been any different?"

"At least we've learned to recognize it, Annie."

"And make our battle plan, Mr. Ev." She gave him a wink, but the worry lines remained on her forehead.

"We're going to have to tell her. Tell them both, Annie."

"I know. I know. You think we'll lose her too?"

"Possibly. I can honestly say that I cannot predict how she will react."

"That's very comforting indeed, boyfriend." She gave a sardonic smile. "So remind me again, how are we going to handle this?"

"Just like every other time. On our knees."

———

Hunker down and hide. And pray that you don't get caught. This was Ted's mantra for every second of every day after Black Monday. *Don't let me get caught.*

And the good news, no, the great news, was that so far it seemed to be working! Those speculative stocks were inching back up. Heck, one was shooting skywards. *Well, hallelujah!* He ran his hands through his hair and grinned. Maybe he was going to get away with it! Ten days after Black Monday, no one had said a word to him. And just one week after creating that phony account, his year-to-date commissions were at 803,000 dollars.

Good job, Ted. Still a ways to go, but things are looking up again.

He thought of the way Lin Su's face had lit up when she talked about throwing a neighborhood Halloween party. A party in Buckhead was no small gesture. After all, the kids on Valley and Tuxedo lived in mansions, big enough to turn into extravagantly decorated haunted houses. He'd heard the stories of past parties—complete with rented ponies, magicians, and parents dressed as ghosts, who hid in different rooms as the children paraded through in search of tricks and treats.

Lin Su loved planning fancy parties. He preferred that she get wrapped up in the details of entertaining, even if it did cost a small fortune, so that she wouldn't ask too many questions about his work or notice the strain he was trying so hard to hide. He'd get the money back before she knew it was gone.

And believe me, I'm concentrating on it every waking hour.

It was only when he got ready for bed that night, after LeeAnne was snuggled under her pink blanket and Sammy was tucked into his Batman pajamas, that he noticed that darn novel sitting on his nightstand. Stuck, were they? Well, he'd read a few more chapters and find out what happened. Surely, if it was that good of a book, it would have a happy ending. He certainly hoped so.

THURSDAY, OCTOBER 29

Lissa Randall was once again talking with the little girl, bending down to her level in an animated discussion. When she came over to Ole Bessie, she was smiling.

"That Amber is the cutest kid! She'll have read every book in the library by the end of the third grade at the rate she's going."

Ev chuckled. He'd bet Lissa had been just like her.

"What do you read, Mr. MacAllister? What are you reading right now?"

"Well, I have a few old faithfuls—the Bible's my daily bread. I've been toying with a few of Michener's sagas. Nothing in Latin, though." He smiled at her.

"Oh, I'm only reading Latin for my tutoring sessions. Which, by the way, are going very well. I expect at least one of the girls to make it to the finals."

Ev marveled at the confidence in her voice. A different Lissa.

"I usually check out a novel or two from the library each week. I'm reading one now that's really good. *Eastern Crossings* by S. A. Green. Have you heard of it?"

Ev thought about his office and its stuffed shelves. *Eastern Crossings* sat on one of those shelves. "Sure. Yes. That little novel was written quite a few years ago."

"I know. But it's so pertinent for today—at least to me. Anyway, a friend of mine suggested I read it. It's kept me up late two nights in a row."

He nodded. "One of the great pleasures of life is losing oneself in a good book."

"I agree."

Ev pulled Ole Bessie out on the road. "Today's the day, Lissa. You're going on the highway."

"Really? That's perfect. Today I feel ready." Then, her countenance changing, she asked, "If I do okay today, and if I pass my test, does that mean I won't have any more lessons?"

She suddenly sounded like a scared little girl again, unsure and anxious.

Ev patted Ole Bessie's upholstery with a grin. "Lissa Randall, I never make a limit on the number of lessons. Some kids want only one. Others hang around for quite some time."

"How long?"

He smiled. "I've never kicked out a student yet, Lissa. You are welcome to keep coming for as long as you wish."

"As long as I pay," she added with a grin.

"That, my child, you will have to take up with Annie."

At the Military Park, Lissa moved to the driver's seat.

"First we'll do a loop or two around here," Ev said. "Then we'll head out on Highway 2 toward I-75. We'll get on the interstate at the Battlefield Parkway exit. It's usually a calm stretch of the highway." He watched the young woman for traces of fear and worry, but all he saw was a pretty teen in blue jeans, long brown hair cascading past her shoulders and a playful glint in her dark brown eyes.

———

Driving Ole Bessie along Highway 2 felt natural, easy. Lissa wanted to open her mouth and shout *I'm back! I'm back!* She picked up speed gradually on the entry ramp without Mr. MacAllister saying a word.

He was right—there were very few cars on the highway. They were probably all stuck in rush hour traffic back in Chattanooga.

This must be a good sign. Traveling south on I-75, Lissa felt relaxed and calm.

Mr. MacAllister said nothing as she approached the site of the accident. She drove under the bridge, barely glancing across the median to where she had sat with her mother while the hail turned to sunshine.

She continued down the interstate for at least five more minutes before Mr. MacAllister said, "Good job, Lissa. Okay, are you ready to turn around and go back north?"

What he means is am I ready to face the past. "I'm ready."

She got off at the next exit and drove across the bridge, then down the ramp and back onto I-75, traveling north. At five o'clock the day was waning, the sun making its way behind the mountains. Lissa looked down at her hands, loosely holding the wheel.

So far, so good.

But only a few moments later, as the bridge came into view, she felt a slight tightness in her chest and watched her knuckles turn white in a death-hold grip on the steering wheel. Next came the shortness of breath and then the overwhelming fear.

A thin layer of sweat broke out on her upper lip and forehead. She shook her head to make the image of a sliding car go away. It did, replaced by the memory of the pavement, the hail, the graffiti on the bridge. The bridge!

She felt Ole Bessie skidding before she even realized what was happening. The landscape changed, and she saw the median coming closer. She vaguely heard someone speak. She was aware of a hand grabbing the steering wheel, of the sudden screech of brakes, the blur of trees in the distance, of Ole Bessie puttering to a stop in the emergency lane.

There was not another car in sight. Had Mr. MacAllister arranged it, called some highway officer and told them to block off the road so that Lissa Randall could panic without killing them both and whoever else might get in the way?

She felt the hard thumping of her heart and tried to pry open her fists, but they appeared to be glued to the wheel. Her breath came in short gasps, muted by the comforting voice of Mr. MacAllister.

"It's okay, Lissa. It's okay. We're okay. Just sit here a minute."

When she glanced over at him—she did not know how much time had passed—he had his eyes closed, as if in prayer. Her mother had prayed when they had come to a stop in the emergency lane. Did people resort to prayer when death threatened?

Her next emotion was anger, a horrible, accusing anger.

Your fault! All your fault!

When she was finally able to speak, her words came out in a stifled whisper. "I was so sure I was over it! I've been riding, Mr. MacAllister! Riding and jumping. Jumping fences is a lot more dangerous than driving on the highway!" To her embarrassment, she started to cry.

"Lissa, slide over. I'll drive."

Momma had said that too. *Scoot over, sweetie, and I'll come around.* She stared at him, terrified. "No, Mr. MacAllister. Don't ask me to do that. Please don't ask me. I can't."

"Lissa, I know what happened back then, but this is a different day. *You* are different. You are on your way to healing. Slide over. Trust me."

"I don't trust you! I don't trust anyone. Anyone!"

"So that's it, then," he said softly. "Go ahead, Lissa. Get it all out."

"Why did she insist on driving? I could have done it! She was always trying to protect me, to make things easier! She was always sacrificing herself for me!" She could barely get the words out in between the sobs. "Only this time, this time . . ."

Mr. MacAllister placed a firm hand on her shoulder. "You're going to be all right, Lissa. I promise. You are." Then he climbed out of Ole Bessie and came around the front of the car.

Lissa could not watch. Instead, she slid to the passenger's seat, eyes on her lap. She heard the driver's door open and then close as Mr. MacAllister took his place behind the steering wheel.

"It's okay," he whispered.

Lissa threw her arms around his neck and wept.

He drove her back to Fort Oglethorpe and stopped at an ice cream shop. Her eyes felt so puffy that she begged to stay in the car. She had no desire to eat, but she let him buy her a scoop of chocolate chip anyway. He chose orange sherbet for himself, coming back to Ole Bessie with a cone in each hand. A brisk October wind swept through the car when he opened the door, and Lissa thought they must look silly, shivering in the car while they licked their cones.

"Why do you care so much about your students?"

"I believe that each person is put on earth to do his part, to help others. I believe that God allows us to go through hurt and pain and tragedy so that we can be there to offer comfort to others after us who go through similar circumstances."

He took another bite of his cone and chewed slowly, thoughtfully.

"A long time ago I had a little sister, a wonderful kid sister, almost fifteen years younger than I. Tate was so full of potential—beautiful and smart as a whip and the kindest person in the world. But her world drove her down the wrong path. She was just too fragile."

Lissa licked her ice cream, concentrating on the chocolate bits embedded in the white cream. She felt afraid to hear the rest of this story.

"Annie and I grew up in a different world, Lissa—a world of intellectuals and parties and the pursuit of knowledge and wealth. We were on what they call the fast track. Tate was on that fast track too, as a young teen, but that track was killing her. I saw it, but I wasn't in any condition to be able to help." He cleared his throat.

If she could have forced the words out of her mouth, Lissa would have said, *You don't have to tell me this.*

"Tate wanted desperately to escape from her world. It was smothering her creativity, her passion for life, her gutsy, adventuring soul. But she was stuck. In a desperate cry for help, she tried to take her life, without success. Then a year later, she was in a fatal car wreck. They called it an accident. Her car hit a tree when she was driving home from another party. Alone."

With that confession Lissa understood his passion.

"She was seventeen, depressed, and drunk. I think she purposely ran into that tree driving fifty miles per hour. She'd given up. That was 1952, long before there were any laws about alcohol and driving and seat belts. Killed on impact."

He stared off into the distance, and she noticed the loose skin and wrinkles on his face.

"We were close. Real close. When she died, I was sure that the best part of me died too. It took me a long time to get over it, and when I did, I decided I was going to do something to keep other lives from being wasted." He cleared his throat again. "Tate didn't get a chance to reach her potential. . . . And you remind me of Tate."

They sat on the front porch, Lissa in a wicker chair, Ev on the swing, drawing their coats close, and watched the sun's descent behind the mountain, its orange glow seeming to set the leaves on fire. Lissa was in no hurry to go home, and for some reason Ev felt comforted to have her there. It was as if he were getting another chance with Tate, to watch her move past the fears, the pain and horror.

"You said you've been riding again."

"Yes. Riding, even jumping. I could feel myself coming back. I don't know how to explain it, Mr. MacAllister. It was this fleeting feeling, but deep. Really deep. It was hope." She stood up and walked to the edge of the porch, staring out toward Lookout Mountain. "I shouldn't have let myself feel that way. I mean, for the last months I've just made myself not get my hopes up too much so that I wouldn't be disappointed." She glanced at him. "You know—thinking that things will get better. That kind of hope."

"You need to find a hope that doesn't disappoint."

"As if that exists."

It does, Lissa, he wanted to say. But he kept his mouth shut.

She leaned on the wooden railing, facing him. "Did you know I was going to freak out again, Mr. MacAllister? Did you expect that to happen?"

"No. No, I would never have taken you on the highway if I thought you would 'freak out.' "

"Did it scare you? Did you think we would die?"

He searched his mind for the right words. "Lissa, I'm not invincible. Sometimes I get a bit nervous. But years and years of doing this have taught me not to panic. Ole Bessie and I can usually manage to get things under control." He cleared his throat. "I told you I wouldn't let you fail."

"But I *did* fail! I failed!" Her eyes flashed anger.

Anger is better than resignation, Lissa.

"You didn't let me wreck and kill us, but you couldn't stop me from failing. Freaking out is failure."

"I don't mean to be cantankerous, Lissa, but I disagree with you. It's a stepping-stone to success. It's more information to calculate and put into your battle plan, that's all."

What could he say to convince her? Standing there with fury and disappointment etched on her face, Lissa appeared stronger. Ev could well imagine her on the back of a horse, determined, mad, and willing to prove she could do better. "It's like in your competitions—with your horse. You prepare ahead of time. You learn what to do. Did you win every single time you showed your horse? Were you always the best?"

"No, of course not."

"So did you give up and call yourself a failure?"

"No. I just worked harder." She shrugged and turned her head down. "But that was then. That's the problem. Now with every tiny step forward I get afraid, and then I want to cover my ears and scream out *Stop!* because I know the voices are going to start again. They're going to tell me it's my fault and I really am a failure."

"Those voices are lying, Lissa. Don't listen to them." He replied so forcefully, he could imagine he was speaking to Tate, trying to convince her of a truth he had only learned years after her death. He rocked back and forth, giving his words time to settle. "Grieving and healing take time. Every time you open the car door, you tumble out the other side into the past of the tragedy. It's the way you grieve.

"Some people would never allow themselves to open the car door. They'd stay as far away as possible, so they wouldn't have to face the fresh pain. I believe what you're doing is healthy and will ultimately bring healing. It just takes a while. I'm not in a hurry, Lissa. You don't need to be either."

He thought he saw a glimmer of hope as she narrowed her eyes and looked up at him.

He stood and pointed to Ole Bessie. "I need to get you home."

FRIDAY, OCTOBER 30

Lissa stood at the door of the library and watched the elementary-school girls parade down the halls of CGS in their Halloween costumes, several waving at her behind their masks. A black cat, a witch, a princess, a leopard, a tiger, a handful of Disney characters, a bumblebee. The memories of doing the same thing as a child made her smile and then want to cry. Or scream.

Something in what she had said to Mr. MacAllister yesterday upset her. Yes, she was upset by her anger. Anger at her mother!

Man, she really did need help. How could she be angry at her mother? Her father, yes. But Momma? Gentle, energetic, ready-to-help-in-any-way Momma? Momma bent over the sewing machine, stitching that Raggedy Ann Halloween costume, Momma taking her to horse shows at five a.m., Momma helping her with the Latin vocabulary.

Her thoughts were interrupted by Amber, who, dressed as an equestrian and riding on her broomstick horse, stepped out of line and gave her a hug.

I didn't tell you how much it meant. I never got to say thank-you. You died, Momma, and I'm not sure you knew how much I appreciated all you did.

Oh, how I miss you, Momma.

SATURDAY, OCTOBER 31

A little phrase from the new novel—something about not rushing things—popped into Silvano's brain as he sat sipping his espresso in The Sixth Declension on the Saturday morning of Halloween.

Ha! Miss S. A.! Thanks for the advice. If not for you, I might have moved too quickly.

But she was right. Timing was everything in the publishing business. And it wasn't quite time to let the cat out of the bag, to use another worn metaphor. Once the ads about the Green novel hit the newspapers and magazines and bookstores, once everyone was familiar with her name again, and reminded of the mystery, once they had their appetites whetted, then he would launch his bombshell. He'd hurl it out into the universe for the whole world to see. For a price.

In the meantime, he still had work to do. He had not located her whereabouts in Atlanta, had no further leads as to her address or any other information to make his deal all the more inviting. He opened the aerogram he had just received from Italy and read through it, worry spreading across his overconfident face, his hands brushing absentmindedly through the greased-back hair.

Mamma mia, his family's problems were only getting worse. Finally, after all these years in the U.S., he had received citizenship. Now, with enough money, he could bring all of them to America! The land of opportunity. The land that would let them escape the terrible price they had all been paying for his dead father's mistakes. America! A new start for Mamma and his siblings.

He imagined his mother serving the customers, selling the postcards and rosary beads and trinkets of St. Peter's with that jolly smile plastered on her face, while inside she was crying out *Help! Help us!* And he was the answer. Silvano to the rescue. He fingered the letter. And as he did so, he felt that same crushing weight of pressure that had motivated him for the past ten years.

Pregate per noi, *Silvo, and do what you can. You are our only hope. Pray for us.*

His response was always the same. *I'm trying, Mamma, believe me, I'm trying. I'm sorry it's taking so long. I miss you. God knows I miss you, Mamma. I miss you all.*

SUNDAY, NOVEMBER 1

Thank goodness Halloween had not yet made it to France. When it did, with France's obsession with the occult, Janelle imagined it would only bring ghouls and ghosts and other scary stuff. She'd heard from friends that churches in America were boycotting the holiday due to incidents involving firecrackers and guns and razor blades hidden in apples. She was glad she wasn't there.

The Halloweens she remembered were times of dressing up as a tiger or a bear and going around the neighborhood with Mommy and Daddy and a few other families. Friends and innocence and lots of candy. Thank goodness she didn't have to make costumes for Luke and Sandy, with a knot in her throat, knowing she should also be making one for

Josh, his little blond head poking through a gray hood with pink ears attached to it.

Stop it! she scolded herself. Such thoughts only made the pain worse.

She carried the flowers to the cemetery on the first of November, along with the rest of France. From a distance, the cemetery reminded her of the Georgia mountains with the fall colors of the chrysanthemums dotting many of the tombstones. The church bells tolled nine o'clock, and she watched others in the cemetery, most of them elderly, coming to carry on the centuries-old tradition of remembering the dead. Christian rites and pagan rituals had blurred on this holiday so that the true spiritual significance was clouded or lost. Some in their church shunned the day, claiming that the misinformed were not only remembering their dead but praying for them. That was certainly unbiblical, Brian would say. But Janelle was not praying for Josh's soul. She trusted that he was safe with Jesus, one of His favorite little lambs. No, she went to the grave and *talked* to her dead son.

"I miss you," she whispered. "I miss you so much. I know you are happy there, but I just wish, how I wish I could have had you for a little while longer."

She refused to let herself ask the questions, for then the anger would rumble down deep in her soul. Maybe someday she could talk about the anger. But for now she simply knelt by the grave and whispered again, "I miss you, Josh."

CHAPTER NINETEEN

❧

SUNDAY, NOVEMBER 1

Lissa finished the novel with a deep feeling of satisfaction. Ever since the panic attack on Thursday, the voices had been screaming louder again.

Failure!

Now, cuddled under the covers at three o'clock on Sunday morning, she concentrated on the orphans in *Eastern Crossings* and the sweet innocence in Tonia's voice when the waiting was over—the way that childlike faith had proven true. The way her brother, good, strong Vasilica, battle-scarred and so tough, had finally woken up to hope.

She liked the message of the novel, subtle and yet surprisingly clear. Hope. Something about the book felt so familiar, Lissa wondered if she had read it—or parts of it—before. Perhaps her English teacher junior year had given them an excerpt from the book to read, as she was fond of doing. At any rate, Lissa determined to check out another one of S. A. Green's novels next week.

Her mind went briefly to her date with Silvano later in the day. He'd offered to drive up to Lookout Mountain again, pick her up, and then head down to Clover Leaf Stables. While her father was at the golf course, she'd ride Caleb and "guide" Silvano.

Failure!

Hope . . .

Wide awake, Lissa climbed out of bed and walked across the hall into the guest bedroom. There she searched for the big black leather Bible with fraying edges, something her parents received for their wedding and Momma had kept on the shelf. She wanted to look up a quote from the novel that she was sure had come from the Bible. Years ago, Momma had taken her to Sunday school, and she'd sung a song with those same words. *I will bring the blind by a way that they knew not; I will lead them in paths that they have not known; I will make darkness light before them. . . .*

Back in her bed, Lissa spent ten minutes flipping through the worn pages of the Bible. She was going to find that verse if it took her all night. Then she set down the book and laughed at herself. Old stubborn Lissa, determined to figure out the problem, translate the phrase, jump higher than anyone else. Maybe she could memorize speeches in Latin and win jumping competitions, but she was not going to find some obscure verse in the Bible by turning each page. What in the world even made her care?

The novel. There were parts that seemed so very comforting, in spite of the bleakness of the story. Very strange. She reached over and turned out the light.

Hope.

———

Their conversation on the way to Clover Leaf Stables centered on books. If Lissa wanted to talk about literature, well then Silvano was happy to oblige her. "You said you'd checked out one of S. A. Green's novels?"

"Yeah. Yeah. I finished it last night. I thought it was really good. *Eastern Crossings.*"

"Her first one. Well, you should read this new one. It's really great."

"What's it about anyway?"

"It's about driving lessons. A kid taking driving lessons. In fact, that's the title. *Driving Lessons.*"

"What?"

"I know it sounds like the most banal of things, but it's really good." Silvano looked at Lissa. "Are you okay?"

"Oh, no. No, it's nothing. It just seems so bizarre . . . such a coincidence—that's all. I'm taking driving lessons right now."

"Really? Well, that *is* a coincidence."

Silvano liked the way Lissa looked in her jodhpurs, so he didn't mind sitting in the bleachers and watching her ride the red horse in the ring at Clover Leaf Stables. She'd already spent forty-five minutes walking, trotting, and cantering the horse, and she'd even jumped it over a few low fences. Now the heavyset woman, Cammie, came to the middle of the ring and began explaining something to Lissa, pointing to the eight or nine jumps she had set up. A "course"—that was what Lissa called it.

Watching Lissa there, her hair pushed under her hard hat, her long thin legs tucked inside those high black leather boots and dangling out of the stirrups, her face serious, concentrating on Cammie's every word, Silvano admitted something to himself. He liked Lissa Randall. She had spunk and determination and a sense of humor. He hadn't seen it at first, but gradually the fullness of her personality escaped, like the subtle tastes in a fine wine. And she would not let him get away with anything. He wanted a woman to hold him in check. He liked her a lot.

She looked over to where he was sitting, flashed him a smile and waved, then nudged the horse into a canter. Everything Lissa did on the back of the horse looked smooth, like poetry, from the way she circled it before heading toward the first jump to the way she confidently guided it from fence to fence.

Cammie stayed in the center of the ring, calling out periodically, "Okay, pull him back. He's getting a little too strong. Slow him down going into that line, Liss."

Lissa looked in control, her arms holding firmly to the reins, and legs clamped tightly to the saddle. He could watch her all day.

He thought about the little restaurant he had chosen for tonight and the way she had smiled at him when he mentioned the "intimate atmosphere." She was falling for him, he thought, smiling a little himself at the memory. But maybe he was falling for her too.

". . . and slow him down, Liss! You're going too fast."

Something about the tone of Cammie's voice surprised Silvano, and he turned his attention back to the ring. The horse seemed to be resisting Lissa's direction, its head thrown up high, its red chest painted in thick white lather. Lissa was practically standing straight up in her stirrups, yanking back on the reins as the horse galloped toward a solid-looking wall with poles spread out wide as well as high over the top.

"Pull him out, Liss! Don't jump it!" Cammie was yelling across the ring.

With Lissa still seesawing on her reins and calling out "Whooaaaa!" the red horse sprang over the fence, shaking his head as he lifted off the ground. Silvano heard the cracking and splintering of the wood as the horse's hooves knocked into the fence and it stumbled in midair, jerking oddly to the side and throwing Lissa full force into one of the thick wooden posts holding the poles. She hit it with a thud and collapsed to the ground. The horse went down on its knees, struggled, and then regained its balance, coming to a halt a few feet away.

"Lissa!" Cammie said, hurrying to where Lissa had fallen. "Liss, you okay?"

Silvano rushed out of the bleachers, ducked under the railing, and knelt down beside Lissa. For a few seconds he thought she had been knocked unconscious. Then she groaned and opened her eyes.

"Where does it hurt, Liss?" Cammie asked.

Dazed, she said nothing for a few seconds. Then she murmured, "Just got the breath knocked out of me. I'll be fine." She tried to sit up, winced, then gave a sharp cry.

"Where does it hurt?" Cammie repeated.

"My shoulder and my wrist."

"I think we need to get you to the emergency room." Cammie looked over at Silvano.

"I'll get my car."

As he hurried off, he heard Lissa's plea: "Cammie, please don't tell my father."

There was no way to hide Lissa's injuries when she arrived home late on Sunday evening with her left wrist in a cast and her shoulder bandaged.

"He's gonna kill me, Silvano. Kill me."

"Tell me how I can help."

Lissa's eyes had lost every bit of spunk. "I don't think there's anything you can do."

Mr. Randall opened the front door as soon as he heard the car in the driveway, and hurried down the flagstone steps. "Where have you been? I thought you said you'd be back hours ago." Then he noticed her bandaged arm. "What happened to you, Lissa?"

"Just a little accident, Dad. Nothing serious. I just need to get inside and sit down."

In the entrance hall, Gary Randall turned an angry face to Silvano. "Was it a car accident? What happened?"

With a tone of complete resignation, Lissa said, "No, Dad. Silvano had nothing to do with it. I fell off of Caleb."

Her father's roar reverberated throughout the house. "What? You went to the barn?"

"Yes, sir."

"You are not allowed to ride! Not allowed! How could you?"

Lissa's eyes flashed fury at her father, but then she turned them down.

Silvano ventured to speak. "She's nineteen, sir. Isn't that a little old to be telling her what she can and cannot do?"

"You stay out of this! You have no idea! No idea!"

His face red with rage, Mr. Randall paced back and forth in the den. "I told you it was dangerous! I knew this would happen! Knew it!"

Finally he went into the kitchen, picked up the phone, and dialed a number. Silvano heard him blasting Cammie in a monologue that went on and on.

"You call that girl in Virginia, and you sell that horse," he stormed. "Do you understand? Get him out of here!"

Lissa sank down on the steps with Silvano beside her.

"What do you want me to do?" he asked again.

"Nothing, Silvano. There's nothing you can do." Her face was chalky white.

"I could help you get out of those boots."

She gave a half grin. "Yeah. That would be great."

He pulled each boot off as Lissa braced herself on the stairs with her good arm. "Thanks."

"Can you manage? Will he help you?"

She winced as she stood back up and nodded. "I'll be okay. Don't worry." She paused on the first step and added, "Thank you for everything—for taking me to the barn, for waiting at the ER. I'm so sorry."

"I'll call you tomorrow."

She nodded, and he watched her climb the stairway with the angry voice of her father still punctuating the air.

———

Failure! Failure! All your fault!

Lissa lay on her bed, staring up at the ceiling. She let the voices taunt her, a horrible throbbing ache in her heart that matched in every way the stabbing pain in her wrist and shoulder. She reached with difficulty and opened the little drawer beside the bed. The pills were still there, all thirty-two of them, prescribed by a doctor months ago to help her sleep. She had not thought of them since she had started taking driving lessons.

There would be no more driving lessons, at least not for four weeks, the time it would take for the shoulder and wrist to heal. Nor could she ride Caleb. Every rider knew that the secret to overcoming a nasty spill was to get back on the horse as soon as possible. But if her father had his way, in a matter of days she would not have a horse to get on.

Eyes still open, she let the scenes collide in her mind—Ole Bessie's tires screeching on the interstate and Caleb crashing into the fence.

Lissa, I know you hate failure. I know you're scared of it. But failure is just a stepping-stone to success. It's not the final story.

A stepping-stone to success! Ha!

Failure!

She took the bottle out of the drawer and held it in her hand. She had other medication now as well, which the doctor at the ER had given her, tucked in a foil-lined wrapper and lying beside the Bible on the bedside table. Hope and despair—right there together, tempting her.

Mix the pills all together and swallow them down. That should do the trick.

Was it Ev MacAllister's words or Silvano's black eyes that kept her from doing it? Her father wouldn't mind if she disappeared off the planet. He hadn't even come upstairs to check on her.

She put the bottle back in the drawer, then she punched one tablet out of the foil and examined the tiny cylinder between her fingers before swallowing it down.

"This should help the pain," the doctor had said.

Oh, no, sir, it won't. Nothing will help the pain.

Sleep eluded her.

Sometime later she heard her father enter the room and walk to her bed.

"Lissa?" he whispered, but she kept her eyes closed. His hand brushed her forehead. Still she did not open her eyes. She heard his breathing, heavier than usual, and imagined him towering over the bed, wondering what in the world to do. At length, he turned and left. She heard the click of the door as he closed it and then his heavy steps on the stairs.

———

Jet lag was long over, and it was time to face reality. Reality, in fact, sat on the desk in front of Katy Lynn in the form of two manila envelopes. One held divorce papers from Hamilton. The other held photos, plenty of photos, of Hamilton with the other woman. At least the photos were safe in her house, not displayed on the front page of the *Atlanta Journal*. At least not yet.

"Gina got to see Hamilton three or four times while you were gone. I know that's hard to hear, but I think it really did her good."

That piece of information, offered by Ellen Lewis, had done nothing to calm Katy Lynn's already shattered nerves. It would be just like Hamilton to try to turn their daughter against her. She felt her temples pulsing as if they would explode. She wanted to kill him. She wanted to drag him through so much mud that he'd never be able to hold his head up in Buckhead society again!

What are you hoping for, Katy Lynn? Are you really looking for a fight and a way to ruin Hamilton's reputation, or do you want to go through this in the least painful way possible, trying to preserve some type of peace for you and Gina?

She dialed Janelle's number for the fourth time in the eight days she'd been home. Her sister answered on the second ring.

"*Oui, allô?*"

"Nelli, it's me. Are you alone?"

"Katy Lynn! Yes."

"Brian's not there?"

"No, he's at the office."

"And the kids?"

"They're still at school. What is it?"

"Back away from the phone."

"What?"

"Back away from the phone, but don't hang up."

"Katy . . . okay . . ."

Holding the phone away from her, Katy Lynn screamed her lungs out. "*I hate him! I hate him* and I am going to *kill* him!" She let out a string of curse words she hadn't pronounced since her father grounded her for three weeks in the tenth grade.

She imagined Janelle's startled expression in the silence that followed the outburst. Finally her sister came back on the line. "Wow, Kat! I guess that's what's called venting."

"Sorry, Nelli. I needed to get that out. I had a choice between calling you or grabbing a kitchen knife and going after Hamilton."

Janelle gave a harsh chuckle. "You made the right decision. Glad I could be of help."

Katy Lynn whispered, "I think I'm losing my mind, Nel."

"Yes, I can well imagine you do. I'm so sorry." There was a pause, then, "For completely different reasons, I know what that feels like. It's horrible."

"I'm trying to take things one day at a time."

"You're right. It'll get better, eventually."

"But there are so many decisions to make now." Katy Lynn gave a long sigh. "Just keep praying for me, Nel. Please."

What a silly thing to say, and yet somehow she needed to be assured of their prayers.

"You know we are, Katy. And thanks to your gift, I'll be coming over soon. Your giving that money for my ticket was such a confirmation. Thank you so much."

"You've said that enough, Janelle. It was really my pleasure."

"Brian purchased the ticket yesterday. I'm flying into Atlanta on Thursday. Could I spend the first two nights with you and Gina?"

Katy Lynn actually laughed out loud. "I can't think of any better news you could have given me at this moment, Nelli. That will be great."

When she hung up, Katy Lynn went and washed her face, reapplied her makeup, and hurried out the door for her luncheon at the club. She felt new strength to face her friends. They did not need to know yet. Janelle was coming. Together they would figure out what to do next.

———

Lissa hadn't slept a wink the night before, between the pain in her shoulder and wrist and the voices in her head. At eight o'clock she called Mrs. Rivers and explained what had happened.

"Heavens, child! You stay home and rest. Rest!"

Maybe her body needed rest, but her mind needed to keep busy. Otherwise she might go down a very dangerous path.

Her father had brought her breakfast before he left for the office. He'd even offered to stay home with her, but her seething "No thanks" had chased him away.

A tray with a glass of orange juice and a cup of soggy cereal sat on top of the Bible. Throughout the morning she kept looking at the orange juice, wondering how many pills she could gulp down with that one glass of liquid. Not many. She forced herself to stay in bed, away from the sink with the running water. Thankfully she dozed off and on.

Ev MacAllister's calling card sat beside the Bible. She'd used it as a bookmark for *Eastern Crossings*. Seeing it lying there, she thought back to that day in September when she had chosen to dial his number instead of swallow the pills. Well, here she was again.

Her father had set the phone by her bed in case she needed to call him. She didn't need him, but she had to make a call. With a shaking hand, she dialed the MacAllisters' number. When Mr. MacAllister answered, she whispered, "Is there any way you can come get me?"

"Lissa? Lissa, is that you?"

"Yes. Yes, it's me. I had an accident yesterday and broke my wrist and shoulder, so I can't drive. I'm not at work. But . . . but I just . . ." She tried to clear her throat. "I'm having some bad thoughts. . . ."

"We'll be there in thirty minutes, Lissa."

She could hold on for thirty minutes. Surely she could do that. Thirty minutes and then maybe, just maybe, hope would walk back through the door.

———

Ev sat in a chair he had dragged over, and Annie perched right on the bed beside Lissa, holding her good hand.

"Dear me, child, what have you done?" That was Annie's first reaction.

"I fell off my horse."

"Ah," Ev said. "The horse that your father doesn't let you ride?"

"Mmm-hmm."

Annie had fluffed up several pillows so that Lissa sat up straight in bed, her bad arm lying across her lap.

Annie asked, "How did that happen?

Lissa shrugged. "I, I made a stupid mistake in judgment, and Caleb crashed a fence."

"And so your father found out about everything?"

"Yep, and he flipped. He's gonna sell Caleb for sure now."

Lissa was nibbling on her bottom lip, and her face was white. She looked again like the skinny teen Ev had met back in September, alone, frightened, anemic.

He said, "I imagine you aren't feeling too great about yourself right now."

Head still turned down, Lissa raised her eyes to meet Ev's. "I feel like this past week has been one huge step backward, and I'll never get any better. I . . . I'm having really dark thoughts."

"I'm sorry to hear that, Lissa. Can you tell me about them?"

"I hate my father," she whispered. "But I hate myself more. I just wish I could escape from all of this."

"How would you escape?"

"I'd stop existing."

Ev watched Annie gently squeeze Lissa's hand and softly rub her back. Lissa didn't shed a tear, but she looked destroyed.

"I know you'll say that all these failures are stepping-stones, Mr. MacAllister, but it doesn't feel that way. It feels like I should just give up."

With another pat, Annie said, "We're here to make sure you don't."

———

When Annie offered to help her bathe, Lissa accepted. The older woman had an easy way about her, direct, self-assured but with a gentle streak, as if she was used to helping out suicidal young women. Sitting in a chair with her head leaning back over the sink, Lissa let Annie wash her hair. The warm water running over her scalp felt soothing, as did the way Annie massaged it.

Annie then filled the tub with water and helped Lissa into it. "My goodness, child, you're black and blue."

Self-conscious, Lissa nodded in agreement. Angry bruises covered the left side of her body. "It was a pretty bad fall."

"I'll say."

Annie washed her as if she were a little child, and her gentle, almost methodical manner alleviated Lissa's embarrassment.

Lissa desperately didn't want them to leave.

Back in bed, she asked, "You think things happen for a reason, don't you, Mr. MacAllister?"

As usual, he didn't give a quick answer. His eyes studied her.

He's trying to see through me, to the reason I'm asking this question.

"I think there is Someone in control who knows all about us and works things out."

"I don't see how you can seriously believe that."

"You're here, aren't you? We're here with you. "

"Yeah, but I could have just as easily not been. I mean, a guy at the license bureau gave me your card, and I decided to call you. How random is that? I almost didn't. I almost grabbed a handful of pills . . ." She stopped and looked down.

"Exactly. But you didn't, and you're here."

I'm here.

"It's just random stuff, Mr. MacAllister. You can't really think it's arranged. I decided to call you that day."

"Why?"

"I don't know."

I was thinking about the pills and then I just pulled the card out of my jeans pocket. I was desperate for something to hope in.

"Why did you call me today?"

"I needed you. I was afraid of myself. Of being alone." Exhausted, she leaned back on the pillows and closed her eyes. "Here's another random thing. A few weeks ago I ran into a guy at The Sixth Declension. Turns out we'd met a few years ago at the same bookstore. We talked awhile and then he asked me out. He offered to take me to see Caleb. And he likes Latin and he's from Rome. Just a random coincidence.

"And then I find out he's in the publishing business, and he started telling me about a new book that his publisher is putting out, and it's called, get this, *Driving Lessons*. How random is that? It's just another stupid coincidence that doesn't mean a thing."

Ev MacAllister nodded. "Except that you're seeing a lot of coincidences lately, and you're thinking that maybe, just maybe, it isn't as random as you had believed. Maybe you shouldn't ignore the coincidences in your life."

She shrugged. There he went again, being a prophet or a saint or a psychiatrist.

"I see you have a Bible by your bed."

Lissa felt heat rise in her cheeks. "Oh, yeah. Well, that's random too. I never read the Bible. It's just that I was trying to find this verse— something I read in the novel I told you about, Mr. MacAllister. You said you'd read it too. *Eastern Crossings*." Lissa paused and shook her head. "It's by the same lady who wrote *Driving Lessons*." Then, remembering that the new novel wasn't even published yet, she hurried on. "Anyway, I couldn't sleep in the night, so I got the Bible and tried to find the verse. I couldn't, though."

Mr. MacAllister asked, "Do you have any scratch paper, Lissa?"

"Sure, on my desk."

The older man walked over to her desk, found a piece of paper and a pen, and began to write something on it. Then he handed the sheet of paper to Lissa. "This will keep you busy while you are recuperating."

"Thank you," she said.

Annie looked at her watch, then motioned to Ev. "I'm afraid we need to go, Lissa. We have another appointment. Will you be all right?"

"Yes, yes, of course. I'm so sorry I called like that. I'm so embarrassed for asking you to come. I'll pay you, of course, as if it were a regular lesson."

"Don't be ridiculous! And you call anytime you like, you understand?"

"Thank you, Annie."

The older woman reached over and asked, "Can I pray for you, Lissa?"

"Pray for me? What do you mean?"

"I believe God listens to our prayers and asks us to pray for each other, especially when we're going through hard things."

"Well, I guess. If you want."

Annie closed her eyes, touched Lissa softly on the arm, and began talking out loud to God as if He were right there in the room with them. "Dear Lord, thank you for Lissa. Please help her see that life isn't random. Take care of her. Give her what she needs so that she can trust you. Amen."

Ev echoed an "Amen."

When they had left, Lissa sat for a long time just thinking about the encounter; then she looked at the paper Ev had given her. He had jotted down a number of references—Bible references, she supposed. She took the Bible in her good hand and began flipping through the big book until she found the first one. Isaiah 42, verse 16. *And I will bring the blind by a way that they knew not; I will lead them in paths that they have not known; I will make darkness light before them, and crooked things straight. These things will I do unto them and not forsake them.*

She stared at the printed words while tears blurred her eyes. She kept hearing something completely new in her mind. *Life is not random.*

———

"You don't look good, boyfriend," Annie said as they headed the red Buick down Lookout Mountain. "Maybe we should cancel the visit."

"We'll do no such thing. I am fine." Nonetheless, he had agreed to let her drive.

"Your hands are shaking, Ev! The cardiologist said to pay attention to that. You heard him."

"I'm fine. It just unnerved me to see her like that. She had that same look in her eyes as when I first met her. It had disappeared for a while, but today it was back. A lost look. And a look of desperation. I'm worried about her."

"I know."

He reached over and placed a hand on Annie's shoulder, rubbing it lightly. "Thank you for coming with me. I couldn't have gone alone."

"She's not Tate, Ev."

"I know, Annie. I really do. But she's on a destructive path, just like Tate. Just like a lot of the kids we've known." He rubbed his eyes with two fingers. "Strange, isn't it? All her talk about life being random. And her examples."

Annie glanced over at him and raised her eyebrows. With a smile she said, "That was definitely not random, boyfriend."

"That's for sure." He knew they were both thinking the same thing. "Janelle is getting on that plane tomorrow and flying over. I don't feel ready. Do you?"

"Of course not. But that doesn't mean it won't happen. I figure the Lord will get us ready at the right time."

"He always does, doesn't He?"

Annie pulled the car into the parking lot of Good Shepherd Rehabilitation Center. They entered the building, and the familiar sterile scent accosted them. A young man wheeled his chair over to Ev, smiling. He held out a withered hand and Ev took it.

"Hey there, Lou. How are you?"

"Good, boss, doing good. I got the grant. I'm gonna have a car. A real car."

Ev's face broke into a wide grin. "Excellent. That is excellent news!"

———

The ringing phone startled Lissa out of a light doze. She reached for it, expecting to hear her father's voice. Instead, it was Silvano's.

"Hey, how's my favorite equestrian today?"

She made a face into the receiver. "Horrible. Sore, black and blue, in pain."

"What about your father?"

"Oh, he came in with this sheepish look on his face this morning and brought me breakfast. He asked if I wanted him to stick around, and I made it clear I didn't."

"I'm sorry, Liss. I wish I could do something."

"Thanks for calling." She hesitated, then added, "And I had two guests today—my driving instructor and his wife."

"They came to see you? Weird."

"Not really. I've been to their house for dinner twice, and I just get along really well with them. They came at the perfect time, when—" What was she saying? She wasn't about to admit her dark thoughts to Silvano.

"Well, I hope you rest better tonight. I'll try to drop by on Wednesday."

"Silvano, you work in Atlanta! I'm not going to have you driving back and forth to Chattanooga during the week. It's not worth it."

"Oh, yes, ma'am, anything you say," he teased.

"No, I'm serious. I'll be okay. But thanks for calling. It means a whole lot."

She hung up the phone, hearing the words *coincidence, random, planned*. Was there a sense to all that was happening in her life? She could not believe that there was, at least not yet. But just in case, she would keep the Bible close by.

WEDNESDAY, NOVEMBER 4

Janelle had never flown across the ocean alone. She'd always had Brian and the kids, and they spent the better part of the flight making sure the children were entertained and quiet. She hardly knew what to do with nine hours of uninterrupted time. The truth was that she wanted to sleep, but sleep always eluded her on airplanes. She tried to think about positive things, but her mind turned inevitably either to Josh or to her parents' past. Neither brought any comfort.

She reached into her purse and took out her Bible, the thin one she used when traveling, and began reading where she had left off a few days before. Psalm 126. *Those who sow in tears shall reap with joyful shouting. He who goes forth weeping, carrying his bag of seed, shall indeed come again with a shout of joy, bringing his sheaves with him.*

Brian would call these promises from God, but she wasn't so sure—maybe it was just wishful thinking. She had certainly done her share of sowing in tears. That was true. But the reaping?

Oh, Lord, I don't even have the energy to think about all of this.

Brian had suggested she go home for a break, but she actually felt like she was walking into another storm, something as heavy and oppressive as her situation in France. Katy Lynn needed her support as she dealt with the divorce, and her parents needed to talk about long-ago things

279

they had kept from her for some reason. Maybe she wouldn't even have time to talk to the counselor about Josh.

Was the Lord truly in control of all these things? She felt too tired to work it through. Instead, she flipped to the New Testament, Paul's letter to the Galatians, and stared at another verse, one of her favorites, underlined in blue ink: *And let us not lose heart in doing good, for in due time we shall reap if we do not grow weary. . . .*

But I am weary, Lord. I am so very weary.

Somewhere above the Atlantic Ocean, the Bible spread across her lap, Janelle fell asleep.

CHAPTER TWENTY

Per l'amor di Dio, Eddy Clouse had done it. With Leah looking over his shoulder, Silvano admired the full-page ad in the November 5 morning edition of the *Atlanta Journal*.

Coming Soon to Bookstores Everywhere! Driving Lessons, *the newest novel by beloved author S. A. Green.*

The novel's cover showed the back of a car zipping along a country lane. Underneath the cover were five short but glowing reviews from the likes of *Publishers Weekly*, the *Wall Street Journal*, *Library Journal*, the *New York Times*, and the *Herald Tribune*. Six weeks after receiving the manuscript, Eddy had accomplished a miracle.

"This is going to be great!" Leah said. "Every family in Atlanta will be clamoring to have the novel by Thanksgiving."

Silvano pointed to the newspaper. *Available in bookstores December 21.* "They'll have to wait just a bit longer."

"All the better. They'll be lined up outside the stores!" When Leah got excited about books, she giggled like a teenager. "Have you read it?"

"Her novel?"

"Yeah."

Watch out, Silvo. . . . "No, have you?"

She nodded, her bobbed hair dancing in a silly way around her round face. "Yes. Mr. Clouse let me read the edits. It *is* wonderful. So different. It's like a handbook on survival, but it reads like poetry—poetry you can understand and take with you."

Leah had described it well. Poetry you could understand. How in the world did Miss Green make a driving lesson in the country sound like T. S. Eliot? *The respecting of rules is a difficult matter; difficult, yes, but delightfully rewarding.*

Grrr. Silvano did not want to think about that silly phrase that spoke of respecting rules. Rules were made to be broken, and he had certainly broken a few. But soon everything would be perfect.

He'd spoken to several weekly magazines that all seemed eager to pay him handsomely for the exclusive story: "An Essay on S. A.: The Woman Behind the Phenomenon." Exclusive. Obviously he could only have one buyer, but that didn't mean he couldn't make them bid against each other. If he were lucky, he could make a good bit more than his annual salary at Youngblood! He had already scribbled out a page of notes for the article. But what did he really know that would interest a magazine enough to pay him big bucks? They *thought* he had enough scoop to be worth a fortune, but did he?

He had a photo of the woman. Several good head shots. Not surprisingly, she had gray hair. She was about five-foot-three and a little round, but quite attractive for her age. She looked even more diminutive beside towering Eddy Clouse.

He scrounged through his notes from that recording. What else had she said?

"This is a work of art, Stella. I felt I was in the car, riding with you the whole way. I loved it."

"Well, Eddy, this one came from the heart, from a long line of life experiences."

"It shows, Stella. Brilliant . . ."

". . . I can't come back to Atlanta right away. We've got some family obligations. Do you think the last bit of editing will necessitate a visit?"

"No. We're right on schedule. Go back to your mountain."

Laughter—Stella's. "My mountain. I believe I will."

He jotted a few more notes to himself:

Stella is about sixty.

Lives on a mountain? Not in Atlanta, not in Chicago.

Has a northern accent.

What did "This one came from the heart" mean? he wondered. That was a good question. He tapped the pencil on the desk, a staccato rhythm.

Leah looked over at him. "Would you mind? That's annoying."

He gave her his best smile. "*Scusa, amore.*"

Leah could not hold a grudge for long when he spoke to her in Italian.

That made him think of Lissa. She was working out well too. The flowers he'd sent on Monday had prompted her to call and gush her appreciation. Well, perhaps *gush* was a bit strong. Still, he could tell she was pleased.

He set down the pencil, reached for the phone, and dialed the number on the calling card for Atlanta Florists. "Yes, this is Mr. Rossi again. Can you deliver twelve yellow roses to the same address on East Brow Road? Yes. Put it on my bill. Yes, thank you as well."

Things were looking up.

———

Stella opened her copy of the *Atlanta Journal*. There it was, just as Eddy promised. A full-page ad for the novel *Driving Lessons*. Very nicely done. Thank heavens for Eddy's push to get the book out before Christmas. She made a few quick calculations. Yes, there had been a large setback in the foundation due to Black Monday, but the advance should build it back quickly. Jerry Steinman had not sounded panicked when she'd called him for counsel last week.

"Your conservative stocks are going to climb back up, Stella. Hold tight. And trust Ted. He'll get you through this."

She had less money in the foundation, but she still should be able to write a sizeable check to the Swiss account come December 31.

December 31. Her head was throbbing. That day. Why did she let the pressure build and get to her?

Someone is going to find out. After all these years.

Stop it! Everything is fine. No more menacing letters, no follow-up to the Chicago fiasco.

So what is the matter?

It was the statement from Goldberg, Finch and Dodge she'd received in the mail yesterday. She needed to ask Mr. Draper about all of the activity. Yes, she had authorized him to use discretion. He had the right to trade, but this much? And this soon after Black Monday?

She dialed Ted Draper's number. "Hello, Ted. This is Stella Green."

Why did her voice sound so flat?

"Hello, Miss Green."

And his so taut?

"I'm calling about the account. I got my statement in the mail, and I find it a bit perplexing. Can we go over it?"

"Of course, Miss Green, of course. But . . . could I call you back in a half hour? I'm with another client right now." His voice was a whisper, a hoarse whisper.

"All right. Thank you." She hung up the phone.

Smooth, affable Mr. Draper sounded as if he'd just learned that all the money at Goldberg, Finch and Dodge had evaporated. Two and a half weeks after Black Monday, the experts reported that the market was recovering well. Mr. Draper was probably just having a bad day. It happened to everybody.

She glanced at the statement again. Ah, well, he'd call in a few minutes and straighten everything out.

———

This is not good, Ted. This is not good!

He felt the sweat beading on his brow, rubbed his hands over his face, and tried to calm his racing heart. Every single one of the junk bonds had crashed. Crashed and burned. No longer in existence. He had scribbled figures all over his desk calendar. Money lost! Huge sums lost! Even though he had only been trading illegally for a few weeks, Dr. Kaufman's account was showing a sixteen percent loss overall. And Miss Green's . . . Miss Green's account had lost over twenty percent as of this morning. The statement she held in her hand did not show even half of the trading he'd done. Perplexing? She had no idea. He thought he had imagined the worst nightmare, but this topped it. He could not retrieve the money he had traded during the last weeks. It was gone. Gone!

How horribly ironic, he thought to himself. His commission on all the aggressive trading had just inched over 900,000 dollars. He would easily make the Million Dollar Club. Easily. But what good would it do from jail?

The *Atlanta Journal* lay open across his desk to the ad for the new novel. A great ad, a great marketing scheme to take this book further than any of the other Green novels. Great possibilities for investing if he would just wait. Wait? What could he do? Too late!

He tried to formulate a plausible excuse for all the trading on Miss Green's statement. He had thirty minutes to come up with something convincing. He felt nauseated, cold sweat on his brow as if he might faint. Maybe he was going to spill his lunch all over the floor, as the young broker had done on Black Monday. He could not keep his foot from shaking. He closed the door to his office so that he could collect his thoughts without being disturbed by a dozen other brokers who were jabbering on their phones. Perhaps he could handle Miss Green as he had Dr. Kaufman's secretary, Miss Endicott, whose first phone call had come on Tuesday, right after she had received the doctor's statement in the mail. Ted shivered even now, recalling all her questions about the trading.

A broker must know his client. He hated that sentence. Doggonit, he *knew* his clients! Knew them way too well. And he knew he had screwed up royally with all the heavy trading he'd done in the account of a conservative doctor who only spent money on safe things; he'd ignored the doctor's profile and then moved on to those call options. The account had plummeted over sixteen percent and those options were worthless. Worthless! Dr. Kaufman had lost a total of 300,000.

Ted imagined Miss Endicott opening the mail and seeing the statements, trying to decipher the crazy trading, and then hurrying to bring this mystery to the doctor's attention.

Dr. Kaufman, there seems to be a lot of activity going on in your account. I didn't know you traded options.

What options?

Options! Look at this!

Miss Endicott had called five times in the past three days. In each conversation, she'd sounded less cordial. Finally at one point, totally exasperated, she had said, "What you are saying makes no sense to me, Mr. Draper. This is disturbing."

The woman was meticulous and careful, but fortunately for him, she did not understand all the intricacies of the stock market, and he had placated her with bold lies and syrupy promises. But for how long?

And would this same reasoning work with Stella Green?

He'd succeeded in putting about 75,000 dollars of the lost money back into the doctor's account from Miss Green's foundation after receiving authorization to send money to that phony account. Forgery, lying, fraud. The list went on and on. And soon the transfer of money from Stella's fake foundation to Dr. Kaufman's account would show up on the paperwork.

What could he tell Stella Green? For the first time in many years, Ted felt stumped. Surely if he concentrated hard enough, he could come up with a good story. Surely the old novelist would appreciate a good story with a surprise ending. After all, hadn't she caught him completely off guard with her ending to *Eastern Crossings*?

Come on, Ted. Think of something. Think!

———

Janelle called Brian to let him know she'd gotten in safely and then slept straight through the first night in the States. When she opened her eyes, the little alarm clock showed 9:43 a.m. She couldn't remember the last time she had slept in so late. With a yawn she crawled out of bed, stretched, and looked around her. How long had it been since she'd stayed in Katy Lynn's guest room? Years. And since then, her sister had redone the room so that it literally looked like a photograph from *Southern Living*. Perfect, down to the matching curtains and bedspread and the marble-tiled bathroom with the fluffy oversized towels. It was like a four-star hotel.

She showered and dressed, coming down the steps a little sheepishly.

Katy Lynn was in the kitchen and turned to see her sister. "Well, now the tables are turned. Look who's Miss Sleepyhead!" She laughed good-naturedly and added, "Were you awake half the night?"

"No, I slept like a baby. That bed is so comfortable." Janelle sat down at the round table in the breakfast room. "Your home is lovely, Katy Lynn. You've done such a great job of decorating."

"Thanks, Nelli. I guess that's one thing I'm good at—decorating, for whatever that's worth." She shrugged. "Let me get you some coffee. I'm afraid I don't have any croissants, but I do have some freshly baked whole-grain bread and homemade jelly."

"That sounds perfect."

"I hope you can just take a little time and relax today. Nothing on the schedule."

Janelle reached for the *Journal* spread out on the table. "It's weird to see an American paper. It's been quite a while."

Katy Lynn brought over a tray on which sat toast, butter, jellies, sugar, cream, and two cups of coffee. She sat across from her sister, dropped a lump of sugar in her cup, and pointed to the opened page.

"Hey, I thought you'd get a kick out of this ad. When I was going through jet lag and kept calling you, you told me to find a good book to read. So I picked one of my all-time favorites, *Eastern Crossings*. You loved that book too, didn't you?"

"Yes, I did."

"Well, look. She's come out with another one."

Janelle looked at the advertisement. "*Driving Lessons*. Sure is getting good reviews." She took a bite of toast. "I've read every single one of her books. I remember thinking she wrote them just for me."

"Yeah. Somehow they are personal."

The sisters' eyes met. They smiled and sipped their coffee.

"I can't offer you a stroll on the beach, but we could go to the club tonight for dinner, if that sounds good."

Janelle was still staring at the ad. She looked up. "I'd like that. I haven't been there in ages. Is Tom still there?"

"Still there. Remember when we used to sit with him in the shade while Mom played tennis?"

"Barely. Remember, I was only three when we moved to Fort Oglethorpe."

"True."

"But I do remember always wanting to tag along wherever you were going. That lasted for years and years. I guess it was a pain to have a baby sister trying to keep up with you."

"It wasn't so bad." Katy Lynn stood up and took her cup to the sink. With her back to Janelle, she said, "I treated you horribly, Nelli. I was such a selfish jerk."

"I hardly remember." But she did.

Hey, Katy! Can I borrow your book?

You're too young, Nelli. Anyway, it's a sad story.

I'm not too young! I'm eleven, and I'm already reading things you just finished.

Read it then, brat.

Hey, Katy! Wait for me! Wait. I'm coming.

Do you always have to follow me everywhere? Why can't you just get lost, Nelli? You are impossible.

How Janelle had wanted her big sister to notice her, to admit that she was grown up. She wanted to use her makeup and wear her clothes and read her books.

Janelle shook herself back to the present and, munching on a piece of toast, said, "Well, when this new novel comes out, let's each buy a copy, and we can read it at the same time."

"Good idea."

———

When Mrs. Rivers brought Lissa home after a half day of work on Thursday, the second bouquet of roses was there by the front door.

"Someone certainly seems to be concerned about you, Lissa," the librarian said with a wink.

Lissa felt herself blush. Silvano. The guy was a regular Romeo. At least she had one bright thing in her life.

She waved good-bye to Mrs. Rivers and went into the house. Setting the roses on the kitchen counter, she found Momma's favorite vase in the china cabinet in the den, came back into the kitchen, arranged the yellow roses in the vase, and set it on the kitchen table where the paper was opened. At the top of the page, her father had scribbled in his barely legible cursive: *Thought this would interest you, since you've been reading a lot of her books lately.* There followed a full-page ad for S. A. Green's new novel *Driving Lessons.*

Her father had actually noticed what she was reading? Amazing!

She sat down at the table and read the ad and the reviews. Silvano was right. Another masterpiece by S. A. Green. How very strange that this author, newly discovered by Lissa, had written a book about driving lessons. Random.

Dear Lord, thank you for Lissa. Please help her see that life isn't random. Take care of her. Give her what she needs so that she can trust you.

She put the newspaper aside and carried the vase upstairs.

She got a chair, stood on it, and set the vase on top of the armoire. Then she took the framed photo from out of the desk drawer, brushed off a layer of dust with her sleeve, and set it next to the vase in full view: a picture of herself with Momma at the *Bal du Salut,* right before the accident. Next she walked back to the desk and took out the photo of Caleb and her after the Hunter Jumper finals in May 1985—right before the accident. She set it on top of the armoire, beside the other photo.

It's okay. I can look back now. It's okay.

Then she sank onto her bed, her shoulder and her wrist throbbing. On Monday, while she was recuperating in bed, Mrs. Rivers had brought her three more novels by S. A. Green to help her pass the time, and they sat by the Bible on the bedside table.

Lissa had already finished *The Equal Journey* and had started *Passage From Nowhere,* feeling again that she had heard these stories before. For sure she had a new favorite author.

A new favorite author who wrote a new novel just for me. I can't wait to read it.

What a very strange thought.

Picking up *Passage From Nowhere*, she caught sight of the Bible. Like the good student she was, she had read each of the verses Mr. MacAllister had jotted down, verses about God speaking to a prophet through a still small voice, others about God caring for lilies—that one was familiar—and individuals, and then one that said to think about things that were true and honorable and pure and lovely. And a bunch of them were about Jesus. She did not like reading about Jesus. Even pronouncing his name bothered her. It seemed so personal, so troubling. God made man.

She preferred S. A. Green.

She was engrossed in her thoughts when the phone rang. "Hello," she said, hardly paying attention.

"Liss. It's Cammie." This was the fifth time Cammie had called since her accident.

"Hey, Cammie. Don't worry. I'm doing fine, really."

"I'm afraid I have bad news. Your father got in touch with the parents of the girl from Virginia. They are still very interested in Caleb. They're coming this weekend to try him again, and if it goes well and he passes the vet's inspection, they are ready to load him into the trailer and take him back with them."

Lissa froze. "No!" It escaped like a sob. Then she whispered, "Cammie! They can't. What am I going to do?"

"You have to talk to your father."

"He won't let me say a word. It's worse than ever."

"You've got to talk with him, Liss. I can't stop him from selling Caleb. I'm so sorry."

———

"Hello, Miss Green. Forgive me for taking so long to get back to you." Ted prayed that his voice sounded calm, optimistic.

"It's quite all right."

At least the crazy lady did not bless him out.

"And may I offer my congratulations for all the great reviews in the paper. That ad was fantastic!"

"Thank you."

Stella Green did not sound like she was in the mood for small talk or accolades.

"Miss Green, I'm assuming you have your statement in front of you?"

"Yes, indeed."

"Let's go through it one trade at a time."

Do it right, Ted. Do it right.

"With your consent—from the discretionary clause—I did some trading before Black Monday—that's there for you to see—and then unfortunately the stocks went down a bit, and of course on Black Monday everything took a hit. So when the stocks were low, it was a perfect time to double up on some of your holdings and perhaps hedge your position with some bonds. But you've jumped back up on page three—you see that?"

"I'm not following you very well, Ted."

She sounded more confused than angry, which was good, very good.

"Can you tell me about my losses?"

"Miss Green, I'm afraid that the foundation has lost a considerable amount because of Black Monday, but not nearly as much as other accounts, I assure you."

"You know I write that yearly check at the end of December. What is the foundation's net worth right now?"

"It's just down a bit. Under six million." It was actually barely above five million as of today, but she wouldn't see that statement for three more weeks. "I know this is upsetting, but you've dealt with the stock market for years. You understand the ups and downs. We just need to ride this one out. Would you like for me to meet you somewhere so we can discuss this further?"

Please say no.

"No, Ted. That won't be necessary right yet. Perhaps we can talk in the next week?"

"Absolutely. Absolutely."

With a sigh of relief, Ted hung up the phone. The lady definitely sounded worried—or vulnerable. Perhaps she had concerns about the new novel. If only that would keep her busy, overwhelmed even, until he could figure out a solution. If only.

———

"Pronto?"

On the third try, Silvano answered his phone.

"Finally you're home from work!" By this time Lissa had composed herself and was able to speak without sniffing into the phone. "Silvano, thank you so much for the gorgeous flowers. They have been the bright spot in my week."

"My pleasure, Miss Equestrian. How are you feeling today? Did you go back to work?"

"I'm much better, thanks. Not nearly as much pain. And yes, I've gone back for half days, yesterday and today."

"And how are things with your dad?"

"Oh, gosh. Don't get me started. Actually, that's one of the reasons I called. I hate to ask you this—" she took a deep breath—"but do you think you could drive up here tomorrow after work?"

"Sure. I've already offered twice."

He actually sounded pleased.

"I know, but . . . I just didn't want to bother you, especially since it's not for a date. It's Caleb. I've got to see Caleb. My dad's going to sell him."

"*Che peccato*, Liss! I'm so sorry."

She tried to explain it to Silvano, but her words made little sense.

Finally, he simply said, "Look, try to calm down, and I'll be there tomorrow, okay?"

"Okay. Thanks."

She hung up the phone and thought again of taking all the medication at once. She saw in her mind's eye the concern in Annie's face.

We're here to make sure you don't.

She stood up clumsily, went to the armoire, and knocked over the photos. The vase tottered a little, sloshing water onto the floor without falling over. She paced around the room, trying to quiet the voices.

Failure! All your fault!

Everything was throbbing—her arm, her head, her heart. She squeezed her hands over her ears, ignoring the shooting pain in her wrist, and screamed, "Stop it! Be quiet!" But it didn't help.

She went back to the bedside table and, with shaking hands, pushed the three remaining pain tablets out of the foil and swallowed them quickly.

Call the MacAllisters.

No. She could not, would not, bother them again.

She sat down at the desk and quickly sketched several stick figures into her journal. In one she was being crushed by a huge rock; in another she was being dragged on the ground, her foot stuck in the stirrup as the horse galloped in front; in the last her hands were tied above her head and she was in the water as it mounted, drowning. She scribbled the words that came to her.

Everything I had imagined for my life is falling apart, smashed under a bridge with hail pelting down, cold, hard, crushing me. Everything I held on to is being ripped out of my hands. Everything I hoped for feels too heavy to hope for anymore. I want to disappear, I long to disappear, I will disappear. I conjugate myself like a Latin verb. I feel as though soon I will be as dead as that beautiful language. I reach for the pills, I reach and reach and it hurts inside. It pulls and tears and yanks and hurts. The pain is unbearable, and I cannot escape it. I will carry this pain forever. It is not worth it. I would rather disappear. I might as well write the words: I want to die.

She opened the drawer and took out the bottle.

———

Hamilton had his schedule, and in the seventeen years of their marriage, he'd kept to it pretty closely. So Katy Lynn did not expect to run into him in the downstairs dining room of the club on Thursday night, with Janelle by her side. But there he was, still dressed in his business attire instead of the khakis and polo shirt he usually changed into, talking in an animated way with another man. Her heart skipped a beat.

He is strikingly handsome, Katy Lynn. How often had she heard that phrase throughout the years?

Janelle saw him immediately. "Oh, Katy. Let's leave."

"No. No, I refuse to let him run me away from my life."

She headed toward the table the waiter indicated, only inches from where Hamilton stood. No way to avoid it. As they passed by, two things occurred simultaneously. Hamilton saw Katy Lynn and Janelle, his face registering surprise; and Gina, who had promised to meet her mother and aunt at the club after basketball practice, came down the hall, smiled at her mother, caught sight of her father, and froze, eyes darting back and forth between them.

"Hello, Katy," Hamilton said. His face had turned a shade of red.

Katy Lynn took three long breaths while the little world of family and friends looked on.

What do you want to do—ruin him or save the family?

"Hello."

Hamilton appeared ill at ease. Then he stepped across an invisible line on the carpet, brushed Katy Lynn on the arm lightly, and gave Janelle a kiss on the cheek. "It's been a long time, Janelle. Good to see you."

Katy Lynn waited for her sister's response.

Janelle's face was pinched and tight. "I can't say it's good to see you, considering the unfortunate circumstances. However, I'm glad I can be here with Katy Lynn."

Hamilton cleared his throat and gave an awkward smile and turned to Gina. "Hey, sweetie. How was practice?"

"Fine," she said shortly. "I'm going to eat with Mom and Aunt Janelle now, Dad."

"Well, we need to be going," Hamilton said. "I'll talk to you tomorrow, Gina."

The two men walked out of the dining room.

Once they were seated at the table, Katy Lynn felt tears filling her eyes. She blinked several times.

Gina saw it and said, "Mom, we don't have to stay."

"Yes, why don't we go somewhere else, Katy?"

"It's okay." She tried to keep from trembling. "They're gone now. I guess I have to get used to this."

She had completely lost her appetite and only picked at her food during the meal, pushing it around on her plate, while Janelle, bless her heart, told several humorous stories about Sandy and Luke.

When dessert was served, Katy Lynn finally spoke. "Aunt Janelle and I are going to see your grandparents tomorrow, Gina. I will probably come back on Sunday afternoon. Do you want to stay with the Lewises?"

Gina frowned. "You're going to see Grandmom and Grandad? In Fort Oglethorpe?"

"Yes."

"Wow! You haven't been there in ages." Then she rushed on. "Can I come with you?"

Dumbfounded, Katy Lynn smiled. "Of course. We'd love to have you."

Afterward, Gina found two friends and ran upstairs with them. Katy Lynn and Janelle walked to the main entrance.

"Hello there, Miz Pendleton," Tom said. "Just saw Miss Gina leaving with her girlfriends. How you doin' tonight?"

"Pretty good, Tom. Do you remember my little sister, Janelle Johnson?"

Tom got a broad smile and said, "Sho' 'nuf! Well, hello, Miz Johnson. Sho' is good to see you again. Bin a long time."

"Good to see you too, Tom. Thanks for looking out for my sister."

"My pleasure, ma'am. All my pleasure."

———

Lissa awoke, feeling groggy, and heard the sound of knocking and voices calling her name.

She pulled herself off the floor and opened the fist where she clutched the bottle of pills, expecting it to be empty. But the pills were still there.

She struggled to her feet and looked out her window. A red Buick was parked in the driveway. Ev and Annie MacAllister were at the door. They had come anyway, even without her calling.

Nothing is random.

She made it downstairs, still shaking off the heaviness and sleep, and opened the door.

Annie rushed in and hugged her, carefully avoiding the bandaged shoulder. "We tried calling twice and didn't get an answer, and I got worried. I'm sorry for barging in."

Lissa's body was stiff, but gradually she relaxed into Annie's arms. "Thanks for coming."

"How are you feeling, Lissa?" Mr. MacAllister asked.

"A little better, I guess."

Annie was guiding her into the living room. "How are you really?"

"Horrible," Lissa whispered, and felt gentle relief in saying the word. She opened her fist to reveal the bottle. "I'm having those horrible thoughts again."

Annie looked at her husband, then covered Lissa's hand with hers. "May I have that, please?"

Lissa hesitated. A scene from *Eastern Crossings* went through her mind: Vasilica was being forced to let go of something dear to him.

She nodded with her head turned down and released the bottle into Annie's hand.

Don't you feel better now?

Lissa sank into the couch. "My father is selling Caleb. He's determined to take away everyone and everything I love. He wants to kill me."

Annie sat down beside her, and Lissa leaned against the older woman's shoulder and whispered, "I wish I'd never been born."

She dozed off on the couch. When she woke, Mr. MacAllister was sitting in the leather armchair, his head bent. Maybe he was praying. Annie was standing by the fireplace mantel, looking at a photograph of Lissa as a small girl.

Lissa sat up, and the heaviness in her mind cleared a little. "You're here, even though I was too stubborn and afraid to call you. You're here. And I didn't take the pills—I thought I would, but I didn't. And the book is about driving lessons, and you're right. You must be right. Life isn't random. There has to be some kind of order."

She realized then that her hands were shaking, that her whole body in fact was shaking. While Annie held her hands, Ev MacAllister went to the kitchen and brought back a glass of water. Lissa sipped it in big gulps. "Tell me about it, please. Explain to me why life isn't random."

Annie nodded to her husband, who leaned forward, his elbows resting on his long, thin legs.

"I don't believe things happen just by chance. I believe in a creator God, a God of design and power. An omniscient and omnipotent God, who loves humanity and who loves the individual. A God who's in the business of redeeming."

"But those are just words. Is there a way to prove God exists, a way to prove He orders things?"

"We're here, Lissa. You're here."

They came even though I didn't call. I wanted to take the pills, but I didn't.

"Life makes sense when it is centered around the God of the universe who controls all and yet cares about each individual. We need Him. He created us to need Him."

I need something. That's for sure. I need something.

"I think you need something, Lissa." He spoke softly. "I think you need Him."

She jerked her head up. There he went, reading her mind again.

"Then please," she said, "tell me how to find what I need."

CHAPTER TWENTY-ONE

⌇

Thank goodness for Friday night, with Lin Su out with her girlfriends again. Ted held LeeAnne in his lap and watched her sucking at the bottle. At least he could satisfy his infant daughter. The involuntary shaking brought on by his jittery nerves probably helped lull her to sleep. Sammy was already cuddled in a ball in his bed, the guardrail waiting to protect him from his nighttime "bed dances," as Lin Su called them.

Lin Su. How was he going to tell her?

Yesterday, Bob Turner, the office manager, had called him into his office and stared at him, grim-faced. Finally he had spoken. "Ted, we've had some shocking complaints from a client, Harold Kaufman. He claims his account has lost hundreds of thousands of dollars in unauthorized trading. We're reviewing all of your accounts right now."

Ted said nothing. He felt sweat pouring down his back.

Bob continued. "Dr. Kaufman's secretary called yesterday and said that the good doctor had lost an astonishing amount of money. I sympathized with her and explained that many customers had suffered because of Black Monday. She said the doctor understood that, but there was a bigger problem." He put on his glasses and picked up a paper from the desk. "The doctor has never endorsed option trading, but it's been happening—right before Black Monday and continuing afterward. If you look at the doctor's profile it says, 'conservative, blue chip,' not 'speculative, high risk.' " Bob took off his glasses and looked up at Ted. "She said quite a bit more as well."

Ted swallowed. He couldn't get a single word out of his mouth.

"This is serious, Ted. You could go to jail, if you don't get restitution."

He nodded dumbly. Restitution. It meant going before the arbitration board. It meant being barred from the brokerage business for many years, with the firm having to pay off the client's losses. He realized that he was clutching his hands together.

"Do you have anything to say, Ted?"

What could he say? The evidence was printed out in black and white.

"I think that I, um, I think that, um, I would like to um . . ." He shook his head. "Listen, Bob. Could I talk to Jerry Steinman? Could I talk to him?"

Jerry had agreed to meet him at the club on Saturday afternoon. There had to be a way out. Surely. What did people do in times like this? Pray? A scene from that bothersome novel came to him again.

Vasilica was just about to give up, but that cute little sister of his . . . what was her name . . . Tonia. Yes, Tonia kept insisting that they needed to pray. And Vasilica retorted something about not believing in prayer or God, and if there was a God, He definitely wasn't on their side. But Tonia had insisted they should pray, that it couldn't hurt to try.

With LeeAnne asleep on his shoulder, Ted closed his eyes and said the only words that came to his mind.

"Help, help, help, help, help. Please, somebody, help me."

———

"Settle down, Ev."

"You're one to talk. You've been bustling around for hours."

"They'll be here any minute, and I want it to be nice for them."

"The house looks great. Smells great too, with that roast in the oven. Now come and sit down with me."

He took Annie's hand, and together they walked out onto the porch. They sat down on the swing and bundled themselves in an old quilt, holding tightly to each other.

"Both of the girls here. And Gina too. It's amazing, Annie. Can't remember the last time both girls were here at the same time."

"I can. Nine years ago. Brian and Janelle were back for a brief furlough because she was having complications with the pregnancy early on. They were here for three weeks, and Katy Lynn and Hamilton came to visit."

"Ah, yes. It didn't go so well, did it?"

"If I recall correctly, Katy Lynn called us superficial hypocrites and Janelle and Brian fanatics. Something like that."

"Are you afraid?"

"Terrified. I want so badly for things to get better. I keep telling myself that Katy isn't coming to vent her anger again, but I . . . I'm afraid she will." She squeezed his hand. "You know me and my mouth. I need to keep it shut. Just let her talk, let all the girls talk."

"Um-hmm." He held her around the waist, pushing with his feet so that the swing swayed back and forth, lulling them, like a baby being rocked by his mother.

"What are you thinking, Ev?"

"Thinking about those verses in Isaiah where God calls His people trees of righteousness and says they will repair the ruined cities."

Annie quoted: " 'And their seed shall be known among the Gentiles, and their offspring among the people: all that see them shall acknowledge them, that they are the seed which the Lord hath blessed.' I hope so, Ev. I certainly hope so."

The wind was chasing dry leaves to the ground, as was its habit in early November. And their habit was to sit there, holding each other in the chilly evening and reciting God's promises. It had worked for all these years, consciously saying out loud the truth of Scripture to erase the insidious lies, the worries and doubts that were part of every season of life.

" 'Fear thou not; for I am with thee; be not dismayed; for I am thy God: I will strengthen thee; yea, I will help thee; yea, I will uphold thee with the right hand of my righteousness.' "

"Good old Isaiah," Ev whispered, feeling a catch in his throat. " 'Fear not: for I have redeemed thee, I have called thee by thy name; thou art mine. When thou passest through the waters, I will be with thee; and through the rivers, they shall not overflow thee.' "

Annie took up again where he left off. " 'When thou walkest through the fire, thou shalt not be burned; neither shall the flame kindle upon thee. For I am the Lord thy God, the Holy One of Israel, thy Saviour.' "

Ev felt his wife relax in his arms. He rested his head on hers and let his eyes wander to where Ole Bessie was parked in the circular dirt driveway. The old property had not changed much in nine years. Katy Lynn was sure to reproach them about that. Janelle would look for positive things, would be encouraging. But she was tired. And full of questions.

Ev rocked back and forth, thankful for the millionth time in his life that Annie was beside him, ready to walk through the deep waters by his side.

———

On Friday, Lissa worked the whole day. The pain was considerably less and the routine definitely necessary to help quiet all the voices.

Failure!

Hope!

All your fault!

Forgiveness.

Time is running out!

Life is not random.

Like a butterfly, her thoughts flitted from Caleb to Silvano to her father and finally landed on the strange conversation she'd had with the MacAllisters the night before. An omniscient God. That she could accept. But a personal God, a saving God, a God of grace? These were new concepts. Part of her wanted them to be true. But the pragmatic, Cartesian part of Lissa, the part of her that needed to be in control, knew they were not.

At three thirty she welcomèd four girls to the library for their after-school Latin tutorial. When Silvano came into the library at a little after six, Lissa was still talking to the students. They giggled when he gave her a kiss on the cheek, and Lissa felt her face turn crimson. The girls gathered their books and scurried out of the library.

"See ya later, girls. Good luck this weekend."

"Thanks, Lissa," they chorused.

"The first round of the Latin competition is tomorrow, in North Georgia," she explained to Silvano. "They're scared to death and excited at the same time. Brings back lots of memories."

Silvano stood by the picture window at the far end of the library. "What a view! It's almost as great as the one from your house. You've got the river, the mountains—in their amazing fall colors, no less. Nice place to work."

"Yes. Yes, it is." Lissa got her purse and locked up the library. "You made it here fast."

"Anything for you, my dear," he crooned in an exaggerated Italian accent.

She couldn't help but smile. Then he put his hand on her good arm and smoothly guided her outside and across the spacious courtyard. She found she didn't mind, enjoying the smell of his aftershave and the momentary feeling of security.

"You look great. *Bella!* How's the shoulder today?"

"There's a lot less pain, so I imagine that's good."

"Ready for a drive?"

Was she ready to drive to Clover Leaf Stables and tell Caleb good-bye? Absolutely not. But she nodded and got into Silvano's little sports car.

As he turned out of the school parking lot, she said, "Silvano, I really appreciate your coming. I, I don't know what to say."

"*Grazie* will do just fine."

She went into Caleb's stall, where the fresh shavings gave off their cedar smell, covering the stench of the manure pile out back. She put her right arm around the little gelding's neck, rested her cheek on his warm, sleek coat, and breathed in the wonderful horse smell of sweat and dirt and life. Her life for so many years. Not for the first time, she wished Caleb could understand her.

"It's all my fault, buddy. I ruined it. I'm so sorry." She closed her eyes, letting memories of their jumping competitions float into her mind. Then she whispered, "But don't think I've given up. I won't give up. I'm still looking for a way out of this mess."

Momma led the chestnut gelding into the paddock, and Lissa pulled herself easily into the saddle.

"Just start off nice and slow, Liss. They say he can be a handful—lots of jump in him."

It was the day she had first ridden High Caliber, the day she, a budding princess at twelve and a half, had met her handsome prince. It had taken every ounce of her strength to hold the feisty little horse back between fences when she first jumped him.

"You made me work so hard. I loved that. We worked hard together."

Caleb had carried her through adolescence, demanding so much of her energy that she didn't have time for boys and parties and what her mother called "all kinds of mischief."

She remembered her first horse show, his mane braided, the horse shying and her mother saying, "He's dancing on pins and needles. You show him who's boss, Liss."

She had never really felt like the boss. Riding Caleb was teamwork, a perfect blending of horse and rider.

She remembered rising at five to prepare for the shows, having tumbled into bed at midnight after cleaning the tack. Hard work and tough competition.

The night that Caleb colicked, she'd walked him for four hours, yanking him up every time he tried to lie down and roll. If a colicking horse rolled, he would twist his intestines and die. Despite her mother's pleas, Lissa had refused to go home, so her mother walked beside them. When Lissa was too exhausted to pull Caleb back up, she had laid her head on his heaving belly and bawled.

Don't be stubborn, silly horse. If you give up and lie here, it's just going to make everything worse. Please get up.

She covered him with blankets, rubbed him softly, and she and her mother coaxed him to his feet. The vet came at eight in the morning and found her asleep in the shavings in Caleb's stall with the docile gelding standing beside her. Lissa had walked him out of the colic.

Your daughter is just about as feisty as this horse. They make a good pair.

"We still make a good pair, Caleb. I'm so sorry."

She left his stall and found a stepladder propped against the wall. Setting it up next to the gelding, she climbed it and carefully pulled herself onto his bare back. The horse stood still.

"We were so good, Caleb. So good. I thought maybe we could do it again."

While Silvano drank coffee with Cammie somewhere in another part of the barn, Lissa whispered a prayer out loud.

"God, if you exist, I need you now. Right now. The MacAllisters said I have to accept your forgiveness and grace and allow you to be in control of my life. That's a huge, huge thing for me, God. I can't do it yet, but if it's really you allowing these un-random circumstances, then show me and help me. Let me keep Caleb. Amen."

———

"Well, here we are," Janelle said as Katy Lynn pulled the car into the circular driveway.

It looked exactly the same. The same flowers in the yard, the same old blue Ford, red Buick, and white Impala parked off to the side, the same white house that needed painting. How she loved and missed this place!

Janelle thought of all the nights she had cuddled by her father on the porch swing, watching the stars and talking about life and faith and the future. Wonderful, comfortable memories. Happy memories.

Her mother hurried out of the house first. "Girls!"

She had aged a bit in the past two years, but she still wore her happy smile and the sparkling brown eyes that seemed ready for mischief. She had on loose-fitting jeans and a bright red sweat shirt. Her gray hair was cut in a way that became her. Dear Mother.

Her father opened the screen door and stepped onto the porch, right on his wife's heels. Daddy walked with a little stiffness in his joints, but he still stood tall and erect, ever the soldier. Heavens, sixty-seven was practically young these days. Jane Fonda was touting the advantages of turning forty and wearing a bikini.

Janelle threw her arms around her mother and then her father.

"Sweet Nelli," he said.

"It's so great to be home, Mom and Dad." She turned around and motioned to Gina, who was following at a safe pace.

"Gina! Look at you! You are gorgeous. How good of you to come!" Annie pulled her granddaughter to her chest, almost smothering her there.

Gina seemed perfectly content.

"It's great to be here again, Grandmom, Granddad."

Only Katy Lynn held back, still seated in the driver's seat of the car. Janelle prayed for the hundredth time that day, "Lord, please, please let it go well. Please."

———

Katy Lynn was sure she'd made a mistake in coming. Now, watching first Janelle and then Gina embrace her parents, she could barely make her body get out of the car. She fiddled with the ignition key and then put on some lipstick and her sunglasses. Her hands were shaking.

For heaven's sake, get hold of yourself. It's just your parents.

A full three years had passed since she'd seen them. They were not elderly, simply older. Her father still looked tall and thin, still wore a strange combination of business suit and tennis shoes. Her mother had on comfortable jeans and the bright colors for which she was known. Perhaps she had gained a few pounds, but not much. They looked good, casual yet elegant. As usual.

She continued watching them from the car as Gina hugged her grandparents and began talking animatedly with them. She seemed so happy to be back here. Imagine a fifteen-year-old wanting to spend a weekend with her grandparents! That girl was full of surprises.

Finally Katy Lynn took a deep breath, opened the car door, and stepped out. Her heels sank slightly into the soft dirt. A gust of wind swept her hair into her face, and she brushed it out of her eyes.

Good grief. I feel like I'm walking down death row. Get a grip, Katy. Just smile and nod and look pretty. That's all they expect anyway.

Her mother reached her first—as always. She liked her mother, her sensible ways, her quick humor. If not for her mother's fierce loyalty to her father, she and Katy Lynn could have spent plenty of time together.

"Thanks for coming, Katy Lynn. We're so happy to have you."

She gave her mother a quick hug. "Thanks for having me."

That was a nice, neutral comment. She could make sure everything looked all right, but she wouldn't give her father the satisfaction of thinking she was actually happy about being there.

He came down the porch steps and looked at her with those intense pale blue eyes. He was trying to smile. He did not offer her a hug or a hand, but stood a few feet away, lost in awkwardness. "Hello, dear. Thanks so much for coming."

Katy Lynn cleared her throat. "You're welcome, Dad." She felt the tension in her head ease a little, tried to smile, and said, "We have a few things to get out of the car." She turned back to the car and let the others go ahead into the house.

It desperately needed painting. How could they let it get so run down? And that old blue Ford in the driveway—surely he didn't teach the kids to drive in that outdated model.

At least Mother still planted her flowers. She had geraniums in window boxes perched on the sills of the second floor.

I always bring in the geraniums around the second week of November, before the first freeze.

Katy Lynn smiled involuntarily at the memory. The pansies and primroses were planted all across the front in their beds, their bright display of color interrupted for a few feet by the flagstone walkway. And there was the same old porch swing, its dark wooden finish faded by years in the sun.

She walked in the front door behind the others, and the smell of roast and potatoes hit her full in the face. The aroma of decades earlier. Mother had prepared her favorite meal from her growing up years. Katy

Lynn felt a little prick in her eyes, blinked, rubbed a finger underneath them to make sure no mascara had smudged, and let the screen door close behind her.

They had moved to this house when Janelle was a toddler. Her mind floated back in time.

She sat in her father's lap and he held her tight, rocking her back and forth on the porch swing while the doctor worked upstairs with little Janelle, sick with a high fever. Daddy set Katy Lynn down.

"You stay here, angel. I'm going to check on your sister. I'll be right back."

Jealousy overtook her as she watched her daddy going through the door and up the steps. "He loves her more," she whispered in tears.

———

By the time they left the barn, it was almost nine o'clock and pitch dark. On the way home, Lissa kept silent while Silvano talked on and on about several supposedly big-name authors whom she'd never heard of, an actor he had once helped on the set, and the latest fashions from Gucci. Silvano Rossi was, as they said around the barn, feeling his oats. Lissa wanted him to stop talking and let her think.

She surprised herself by blurting out the question on her mind in the midst of Silvano's monologue. "How can I keep Dad from selling Caleb?"

He frowned momentarily and then said, "Look, Lissa, I don't want to interfere, but I think you should talk with him."

She raised her eyebrows. "Really? That's what you think when you've seen for yourself how explosive he gets? I've tried, you know. Many times. It just doesn't get me anywhere."

"What other choice do you have?"

"I don't know. I'm trying to come up with another idea, but your incessant jabbering is making it very hard to concentrate."

Silvano scowled.

She shrugged. "Sorry—I didn't mean that. Let's not discuss it—it makes me feel horribly anxious."

"Okay."

She closed her eyes.

A few minutes later, Silvano said, "I brought you a surprise."

"A surprise?"

"Yeah, take a look in the back."

Obediently she glanced around. A small rectangular box was lying on the back seat. "What is it?"

"*Driving Lessons*."

"The manuscript? You have it here?"

"Yep. I told you I've been helping with the edits. Now that they're done, I thought you might like to have a peek."

"Isn't that illegal or something?"

"Not as long as I call you an assistant."

She smirked. "An assistant? How could you call me that?"

"I want you to read some of the passages about driving lessons and tell me if Miss Green got it right."

"You've got to be kidding. From what I've read of Miss Green and what you and others have said, she always gets it right."

"No, I'm serious. My boss asked me to check out a few details. Could you describe for me what your driving school is like?"

Silvano's questions annoyed her; she was not in the mood to talk. But she owed him something for driving all over creation just so she could tell her horse good-bye.

"Oh, it's not really a school. The MacAllisters—that's the couple who run it—have their office in their home in Fort Oglethorpe. You just call and make an appointment and then show up at the house. You barely drive at all for the first lesson. You just get in Ole Bessie—"

"Ole Bessie?"

"Sorry. The car. She has a name."

"*Vedo*."

"Anyway, the instructor, Mr. MacAllister, finds out how much you know about driving, why you're there, stuff like that. And then he takes you out on a short drive; it all depends on your competence—how much you've driven before. He likes to have students drive through the Military Park—you know, Chickamauga Battlefield. I've done that a bunch of times. He's working on getting me to drive up the mountain."

"The mountain?"

"Yeah, Lookout Mountain. You know, where I live?"

"No need to get sarcastic." Silvano blushed, then he recovered. "Yes, that makes sense. I guess you would need to know how to drive up and down that mountain."

"Exactly. Anyway, when Mr. MacAllister thinks you're ready, you go out on main roads and then the highway." She hurried along. No need to dwell on her experience on the highway. "He caters to the need of the student. I think he's a bit different from most driving instructors."

The information seemed to satisfy Silvano, and for once he remained quiet until he turned his little sports car up the mountain road. Lissa reached back and picked up the manuscript.

"Go on. Take it and read it. Just promise me you'll keep it safe and not let anyone else see it."

"Are you crazy—I'm not taking the manuscript of the next great work by S. A. Green!"

"Relax—it's just a copy. And no one's going to come snooping around your house looking for S. A. Green's new novel. It'll do you good to read it—get your mind off your other problems. I guarantee you'll like it; it's profound and simple at the same time. My secretary calls it 'poetry that makes sense.' It's about learning to drive a car, but it's not about that at all. It's about life. How to live life. I tell you, parts of it sound almost spiritual. Very e—"

"Ethereal."

"Precisely." He smiled at her. "You're reading my mind."

Ethereal. Why had she used that word? Lissa closed her eyes, trying to trace back to where she'd heard that word recently. Probably in another S. A. Green novel. "Okay, I'll take it home. You've convinced me."

———

Driving back to Atlanta, Silvano's mind fairly exploded with information.

The driving school is just an old house; the car has a name; there is a mountain nearby.

Something felt very, very odd. Uncanny, almost supernatural. Could it be that this girl, Lissa, whom he had happened to run into in an old bookstore and who happened to like Rome and Latin and who happened to be taking driving lessons at this very moment in time, was another link to the novelist he was searching for? How probable was that? Surely there was some statistic that proved those odds to be less than ten to the hundredth degree. It actually left him feeling strange, like he needed to keep looking over his shoulder to make sure no one was following him. He thought *he* was playing detective. Could someone else be spying on him? Know his intentions? Plant people in his path? He shivered.

And then it hit him full force. The novel! It was written in the novel.

When he got home he hurried into his bedroom, got down on his hands and knees, and slid an arm under the bed to where he had stashed another copy of the precious manuscript in a locked chest that held his most valuable and sentimental items: the rosary beads, his grandmother's quilt, his father's pocket watch, a thousand dollars' worth of lira, the tape recording from Stella and Eddy's conversation, the photos, and *Driving Lessons*.

Back in his little den he searched frantically through the pages. He vaguely remembered the place in the book; he definitely remembered the scene. Ah, there it was, on page 235.

The protagonist was talking to his driving instructor. *"Seems like so many things are all pointing in the same direction. I'd say it was coincidence, but it's more. I can't explain it. It's like someone is reading my thoughts ahead of time, before I even think them. And then he's following me around and making things happen. Random things that aren't random."*

And the driving instructor said, *"When too many coincidences line up, when you feel there is someone looking over your shoulder, you are probably right. Someone big and unseen and all-powerful is orchestrating events in your life to get your attention. Not coincidence. Divine intervention. The question you must ask yourself is this: will I listen to this voice?"*

Silvano set down the pages. He almost wanted to cry. He didn't even know why. Yes, he did. He was scared. Was God looking over his shoulder? Worse, was God *orchestrating* events in his life? Was that what was happening?

Naw. *Ma sei matto, Silvano. You're nuts.* If he followed that line of irrational thought, then God had given him the idea to steal the manuscript and search out the author and everything else. Impossible! But he wondered, *Could it be that this unseen Someone knew and saw everything?*

Silvano felt a surge of irritation. *That's insane! I'm imagining things. I'm tired and I'm putting too much pressure on myself. I just need a little sleep.*

He hadn't been to Mass in years, had not prayed in months, and had stuffed his mother's rosary, the beautiful hand-carved one she had given him in tears as he left for the States, in the trunk under his bed. He knew his mother prayed and worried and prayed some more. *God our Father, watch over my child. Care for him. . . .*

He supposed that at some point in his childhood he had believed in a powerful, punishing God, a God of good works and righteous judgment. But he didn't fear God now—not in any sense of the word. No reverence, no healthy respect, no terror, like those Israelites had felt while staring at a glowing mountain.

"I am in charge of my destiny, and that is that." There, he'd said it out loud. He thought back to Rome, Rome with the ancient Coliseum, Rome that persecuted Christians, Rome whose museums were filled with art proclaiming God's majesty and splendor.

He did not have time to play mind games with God. He had to get the interview and publish it, and soon! Then everyone in the world could read the words of the author and decide for themselves. Coincidence or divine intervention.

As for Silvano, he once again got on his hands and knees, unlocked the trunk, took out the precious rosary beads, and slid the trunk, secured, back under the bed. He crossed himself and set the beads on his desk. What could a little superstition hurt? He was hot on the trail of Miss S. A. Green.

———

The porch light was on, and her father met Lissa at the front door when Silvano let her off.

"Where have you been? It's almost ten o'clock!"

"Silvano and I had a date. I left you a note."

"I saw it."

She braced herself for the yelling.

"Why did he drive all the way up here on a Friday?"

"He likes me, Dad! I know it's hard to believe, but it's true. You've seen the flowers." Her heart was pounding, and she felt anger throbbing in her temples. This was not the time to confront him about Caleb.

"So where did you go?"

She'd already planned the lie. "He took me to a really nice restaurant in Ringgold. A little Italian place. Fancy." She looked down at her jeans. "I didn't know it was so nice. I felt way underdressed. Anyway, I'm bushed. See you in the morning." She gave him a kiss on the cheek.

In the morning. I'll talk to him in the morning.

CHAPTER TWENTY-TWO

It was no use. At five a.m., Janelle climbed out of bed. She'd already been awake for nearly an hour. She walked down the hallway, past the bedroom that used to be hers and where Gina was sleeping. The old house wrapped around her with memories. Yawning, she reviewed the last twelve hours in her mind.

Dinner last night had gone well. Polite conversation, nothing controversial. Gina talked about school, and Katy Lynn raved over her visit to Montpellier. It was obvious to Janelle that her parents did not know about Hamilton's demand for a divorce. Katy Lynn's excuse for her impromptu visit to France was simply, "I needed to get away."

Katy Lynn maintained her poised attitude all through the evening. At nine thirty, when Janelle announced she was heading to bed, Katy Lynn echoed the same. The sisters had shared the bedroom usually reserved for the grandkids. Lying across from each other in the single beds, they had whispered into the night . . . something age and personality had kept them from doing as children in this very house.

Janelle went down the creaky stairs, letting her hand follow the smooth wooden railing, the one she had slid down on her little bottom time and again as a child. She made her way to the back of the house, into her parents' office where the telephone sat. In her hand she held a little plastic calling card—a gift from dear friends, a new way to make long distance calls inexpensively. She dialed a string of numbers and then waited for the phone to ring.

"Allô?"

She smiled at hearing her husband's voice. "Brian?"

"Sweetheart, it's kinda early for you to be up. Can't sleep?"

"Just jet lag, but it's not so bad. I made it to four thirty. How are you? How are Sandy and Luke?"

"Fine. We miss you lots, but we're fine."

"Just wanted you to know that I got to Mom and Dad's last night—with Katy Lynn and Gina. So far there haven't been any major explosions."

They talked for ten minutes. Before they hung up, Brian said, "I'm praying for you all. Relax. Try to rest. I love you."

"Love you too."

Janelle flicked on the light and walked around the office. It had a comfortable, crowded feel. One wall held imposing mahogany bookshelves, what her father called the *bibliothèque*. The shelves were laden with ancient leather-bound volumes, paperback novels, thick photo albums, and framed photographs. Many framed photographs. Two sturdy metal filing cabinets stood against another wall. Her father's old typewriter, a manual Remington, sat on the desk. A stack of bills sat beside it.

She walked over to the shelves and took down a framed picture of her parents' wedding party. She remembered studying the photo when she was a child, enchanted by the glamour of the occasion. Her father wore a black tux with tails, her mother a white satin bridal gown and veil of pure Belgian lace, her train spreading out magnificently behind her. Eight bridesmaids stood to the left of her mother in shining, off-the-shoulder blue satin gowns, and eight men to the right of her father, in their black tuxes. In front of the bridesmaids was Daddy's sister, little Tate.

In the photo Tate was no more than seven or eight, a stunningly pretty child. Janelle had always wished she'd gotten to meet Tate. As a child,

Janelle made up stories about her beautiful aunt who died too young. Whenever her father spoke of Tate, it was with a mixture of pride and deep grief. She didn't think he had ever really gotten over losing her.

She's the reason I started the driving school, sweetie. For Tate. To give others the help she never got.

He had said this to Janelle years ago, but now, as she remembered the words, she felt that all-too-familiar lurch in her stomach, and she wrapped her arms around her abdomen, protectively.

Maybe it's true that you never get over losing a loved one. Perhaps the rest of my life will be a long, long grieving for Josh.

Her father had always been her hero, a quiet but firm leader, a gentle man of faith with a sharp mind and a love of history and literature. She could not imagine learning anything about him or her mother that would damage that relationship. She examined the photo again.

They were rich! Rich, I tell you.

Yes, obviously the wedding showed a display of wealth. Yes, she had seen this in other pictures. She vaguely remembered stories of the "house up East" and going to visit her grandparents in New York when she was quite young. If parties and alcohol and women were part of it, she would just face it with her father and mother. And she would forgive them for keeping secrets.

She took several of the photo albums off the shelves and settled into her father's desk chair. She lost track of time as she paged through the familiar old albums of her family's life a long, long time ago. In every shot of the two sisters together, Katy Lynn looked like a teenage model, and little Janelle like a pesky baby sister.

We were never close. And that hurt. Well, here was a little miracle. Katy Lynn and I slept in the same bedroom last night and whispered secrets and laughed. Not so little. A huge miracle.

When daylight began seeping through the window, Janelle left the office and went down the hall and into the kitchen. The idea had come to her quickly. She'd fix breakfast for everyone, and she knew just what it would be. Her father's favorite: eggs, bacon, and grits. Grits! She hadn't had grits in ages. You certainly couldn't find them in France. The couscous she ate with her Algerian friends was about the closest thing, and the texture was still way off.

Scrounging through the cupboards, Janelle found the familiar blue and white box. She put water on to boil, took the eggs and bacon out of the fridge, and put bread in the toaster.

By eight thirty the house smelled like her childhood. Coffee and eggs and bacon and grits. Toast with real butter and homemade jam. It was good to be home.

———

Someone was knocking on the door at nine o'clock. Lissa hadn't slept well, and she wished her father would answer it. But the knocking persisted. Then the doorbell rang twice. She groaned, got out of bed, found a robe to pull over her nightshirt, and traipsed downstairs. Her father had left a note on the kitchen counter: *Out early. Be back around noon.*

Silvano's face was peering in the window in the entrance hall.

Lissa's cheeks flushed, and she ran her hand through her hair and opened the door. "What are you doing here? Are you nuts?"

"Yes. Yes, I'm *matto*. I needed to see you. I want to see you. I've got something to say." He looked intense.

"Silvano, I'm not dressed. You woke me up."

"I'm sorry. Can I come in?"

"My father isn't here."

"All the better!"

She laughed and relaxed a little. The nerve. "Oh, come in. Please don't tell me that you drove to Atlanta last night and then got up and drove back here this morning."

"Okay, I won't tell you—but it's what I did."

"You're nuts."

"Maybe." He grinned, looking around the kitchen. "You go and get dressed. I brought my own coffee and machine so that I can make you some Italian espresso."

He held up a little red bag, and she got a whiff of the rich flavor of real coffee beans.

"You'll love it. Be ready in ten minutes."

In spite of feeling slightly irritated, she hurried to shower, wash her face, and throw on a pair of jeans—the nicer ones, the ones that enhanced her figure. She picked a pretty blue turtleneck and a yellow cardigan, a combination that her friend Jill called "flattering." Why did she feel so nervous?

Coming down the stairs, she breathed in the odor of freshly brewed coffee. "I see you've made yourself right at home."

"Do you mind?" He almost looked apologetic. "And I brought you *un panino* from the little bakery near my house."

She rolled her eyes. "You're impossible. But it does smell good."

He motioned for her to sit at the breakfast room table and set a cup of coffee in front of her. "I still can't get over the view. It's breathtaking."

"Yep. It's pretty nice, isn't it?"

They stared out the picture window at near-naked trees.

"But enough small talk, Silvano. Why did you drive back up here at the break of dawn?"

"I missed you." He gave her a puppy-dog look that he didn't pull off very well.

"I don't believe you."

"Well, it's true." He placed a plate of fresh pastries on the table and handed her a fork and napkin. "Eat," he instructed. "Can't a guy do a few crazy things for a girl every once in a while?"

She shrugged. "I guess. . . . Well, are you going to eat?"

"No, no. I already had breakfast back in Atlanta."

She sipped the coffee and took a bite of the pastry as he hovered beside her.

"You're invading my space, Silvano. Please, sit down and spit it out. What did you come here for?"

He finally sat down in a chair across from Lissa. Almost urgently he asked, "Have you looked at the manuscript yet?"

"Is that what you're so concerned about? You could have just called me on the phone, you know. Anyway, I haven't had a chance. I was bushed last night. I'll read some today."

"Good." He leaned over the table, eyes bright. "Thanks to Miss Green, I'll be working with bigger accounts in the publishing house really soon. It's good-bye midlist authors for me. I'll be negotiating contracts with the likes of Holmeyer, Brack, Fryling, and Weaver, to name a few. The house's biggest names. I'm moving up."

Exasperated, Liss asked, "Why do you keep doing that?"

"Doing what?"

"Name-dropping. It's annoying. And I'm not impressed. I have no idea who you are talking about. I'm not in the publishing business. Please don't tell me you drove all the way back here to tell me about some authors I've never heard of."

Silvano's face colored slightly. He said nothing.

"Look, I'm not dumb. You didn't come here just to make me coffee and tell me about your publishing accomplishments. What is it?"

Silvano leaned across the table. "I'll explain why I'm here, if you promise to hear me out."

Lissa tried to read his mind. What was this guy after? "Okay, go ahead."

"Can I ask you a few questions first?"

Resigned, she nibbled on the pastry. "If you must."

"What do you know about Ev MacAllister?"

"He's my driving instructor."

"But what do you *know* about him?"

"What do I need to know, for heaven's sake? I told you yesterday. He runs a driving school. He's old. Sixty-five, I think. And he's spent a good part of his life helping screwed-up teens get their heads back on straight, get over stuff so they can drive again."

"Where's he from?"

"I don't know. Georgia or Tennessee, I guess."

"Does he have a Southern accent?"

"What?"

"Does he speak with a Southern accent? Like everyone else around here."

"What in the world does it matter, Silvano? Why are you asking?"

"I think he's hiding something. Protecting somebody."

"Protecting somebody from *what*?"

"I have an idea."

"Well, let me in on the secret, will you?" Her irritation grew. "Look, he's an old man who teaches kids how to drive. I really don't think he's dealing drugs or robbing banks."

"I'm just concerned for you. I don't want to see you used by him."

"What in the world would he want to *use* me for? Silvano, you've got a screw loose."

"Have you ever met his wife?"

"Annie? Sure. She's great. They're a great couple who really love each other."

"Does she have a job?"

"Are you almost done with the interrogation? Yes, she has a job. She handles the business end of the driving school."

"I think she does something else."

"Yeah, well, she probably does. For one thing, she fixes dinner. In fact, I've eaten at their house twice. And it's good food. Satisfied?"

"I think she writes books."

"Oh, you and your books! You know, not everyone is as obsessed with authors and advances and moving up the ladder as you are."

He took out a photo and gave it to Lissa. "Is this Annie?"

Lissa took the photo and felt a little chill run down her back. "Where'd you get this?"

"Never mind where I got it. Is this Annie?"

"Yeah. Yeah. Although I've never seen her dressed up. She's usually in jeans and a T-shirt."

"This woman, my dear Lissa, is none other than Miss S. A. Green, the famous and anonymous novelist."

Lissa stood up with an angry look on her face. "You're insane."

"No. No, I'm brilliant. I've figured it out. And if you want to say something is weird, you can talk about how I just happened to run into you again at The Sixth Declension while I was looking for this woman. That's weird."

"You were *looking* for S. A. Green? You mean you were trying to find her in person? Why?"

"I have my reasons."

"Oh, please. I guarantee you, Silvano, Annie MacAllister isn't the

type of woman who writes novels, and she certainly isn't S. A. Green."
Lissa stood. "Leave. Just leave."

"Lissa, hear me out." He reached for her hand, but she pulled it away.
"Give me a chance to explain."

She sighed and sat back down. "And anyway, what if she were a
novelist? There's nothing illegal about that, is there?"

"No, of course not. But if your pen name is S. A. Green, and if you
don't want anyone to know who you really are, well, people start wondering. I've been wondering for a long time. And what I've found out is very
interesting. She has a little 'foundation' worth millions of dollars."

"What proof do you have of all this? This photo?"

"I found Miss Green's mailing address, wrote to her, and asked her to
meet me at a restaurant. This is who showed up. I would call that some
kind of proof, wouldn't you?"

Lissa felt tears pricking her eyes. "Silvano, why are you saying these
things? I happen to care a lot about this couple, so you'd better just leave all
that alone. It's crazy." She was trying to piece it together. Silvano had a recent
picture of Annie; Annie had responded to a letter to Miss S. A. Green.

"Listen to this."

He took a small tape recorder from his pocket and let the tape play.
It was a conversation between a man and a woman. Lissa recognized the
woman's voice as Annie's.

"Why are you taking pictures and taping these people? Are you some
kind of spy? The MacAllisters are great people. They're religious and real
and . . . and spiritual. They aren't crooks."

"I'm sorry to upset you, Lissa. But I think Ev MacAllister's wife is
our novelist, Stella Ann Green. And I think she makes a bundle of money
that she doesn't pour back into the driving school. I think they play some
pretty risky games with that money."

Lissa put her hands over her ears. "Stop it! I don't want to hear any
more." She felt a tinge of fear inside. But Silvano was wrong, and she
could prove it to him. "What you're saying is impossible! I *know* them.
Annie is *not* literary. She's nuts and bolts. Practical down to her toenails.
She does the math for the driving school. She's an *accountant*, Silvano.

How many accountants do you know who are brilliant novelists? Mr. MacAllister is the literary one in the family. He's the one who—"

"What, Lissa?"

"Nothing. We just enjoy reading the same books, that's all." She got up and went to the front door. "Please leave, Silvano. Thank you for caring about me. But I don't believe you. I need to be alone. I've got so many things on my mind—Caleb, my dad. I can't think about this. I'm sorry."

"All right, Lissa. But please be careful. I swear I'm here because I'm concerned for you. Last night after I let you off, all the pieces began to fit together. It was weird, all right. Very weird. But it makes sense. I could be all wrong, but I don't think so. Just be careful, okay? Please." He hugged her and kissed her lightly on the forehead. "I'll call you later. Good-bye."

She waited for Silvano's car to leave. Then, in a panic, Lissa ran up the stairs and opened the bottom desk drawer where she had hidden the manuscript under her journals. Shaking, she opened the box and took out the thick ream of typewriting paper.

Driving Lessons.

She knew for sure that Silvano was wrong. Annie MacAllister was not S. A. Green.

It was Ev.

It was *his* voice she'd kept hearing when she read the other novels, his poetic voice telling her about history and literature, his turn of phrase that made the prose in the novels sound so familiar. She swallowed.

She stared at the manuscript through blurred eyes. She sat down on the floor by her bed with her back propped against it and began to read. She had no idea how long she sat there—thirty minutes or three hours. She kept turning the crisp white typing paper, page after page. Yes, it was like poetry; yes, it was beautiful, almost spiritual. Heavens, some of it *was* quoted directly from the Bible! And the rest was quoted from Ev MacAllister's life, his philosophy of teaching. She closed her eyes and was standing beside the tall old man in a seersucker suit, looking out from Rock City at the seven states far in the distance.

I've known a lot of heartache. Enough to weigh me down further than the valley below. So I have to concentrate on being thankful for the good things. It's a simple mental exercise that has surprising repercussions. At least for me, it has.

He had said that to her, and here it was, almost verbatim, in the novel.

Ethereal.

She tried to block out the word. Such a beautiful word and now it was icy, stabbing, painful. He had used that word a few weeks ago. *The best poetry is ethereal. It points you to something better, higher. It calls forth your imagination and haunts you with its beauty.*

Ev MacAllister was S. A. Green. He had never blinked an eye or given her any indication of the truth, even when she had talked about the novels, *his* novels, the ones he wrote with his long, slim hands. He was the author of these books.

He never acknowledged a thing because he *knew.*

He knew that his whole thesis—about God's omniscience and nothing being random—was indeed being played out in her life—through him. It didn't make sense. Or made too much sense.

And Silvano Rossi, the name-dropping creep, was somehow entwined in the whole thing. Lissa wanted to throw up.

. . . She makes a bundle of money. . . . I think they play some pretty risky games with that money.

Silvano was wrong! The idea was preposterous!

She thought about the old sprawling Victorian house. Yes, they had beautiful china and crystal, antique furniture, oriental rugs. But they were displayed beside a sagging sofa and a cheap coffee table. The MacAllisters were not pretentious, not interested in wealth.

Then why did they keep Mr. MacAllister's identity such a secret? What was the point? A tiny stab of doubt pricked the back of her mind.

Be careful, Lissa. Please.

She didn't trust Silvano—he gave her the creeps—and yet maybe he had a reason to be concerned.

She felt hot and sweaty and afraid. She could not think about all this. She needed to concentrate on saving Caleb. Caleb was more important than the mystery of S. A. Green. Every bit of her energy needed to be spent on convincing her father to keep her horse. Then she would deal with Silvano and the MacAllisters. Somehow.

She held her head in her hands. Once again her life felt out of control, as if she were galloping on Caleb toward that high fence and could not get him to slow down. No matter how hard she yanked, he ignored the bit in his mouth and plunged ahead.

Is this what happens when I pray? My whole life falls apart? Is that it? God comes in with His almighty power and crushes me?

She didn't want a God like that. She had enough problems without Him stepping in and taking over. She preferred her little bottle of pills.

———

Silvano stopped his convertible in the first service station he found after coming off Lookout Mountain. He filled up with gas, all the while congratulating himself. He had done it! He had found S. A. Green. Amazing! A very big coincidence.

Silvano kept seeing Lissa's startled face when he showed her the photo—S. A. Green, alias Annie MacAllister. But now the truth was out. Lissa had helped him in many ways, but the best was admitting that Annie MacAllister could not be the novelist. So it was the old man. Ha! What a very nice setup. The wife takes on the role of the bossy, intimidating author so that her hubby can be free to write and hide behind his driving school. Not bad. Not a bad cover.

He went inside the gas station to pay, then headed to a phone booth where phone books hung on a metal stick. He flipped through the Yellow Pages. Driving schools. There it was, MacAllister's Driving School. The address was on Sunrise Road in Fort Oglethorpe. He looked in the white pages and found Ev and Annie's name listed right there. Same address, same phone number. He could not wait to give them a call.

First, though, he needed to get his camera and tape recorder, needed to jot down interview questions, needed to make sure all was ready. Then he would show up on their front porch and get the interview. Ha!

Good job, Silvo! Bel colpo!

Silvano thought briefly of Lissa. He had not been lying when he told her that he cared about her. He really did. Then he thought about a scene from the novel where the driving instructor challenged the protagonist: *Do you care about your friends, or are you simply out for yourself?*

He didn't know. But he'd have plenty of time to work it all out in his head on the drive down to Atlanta and back to Chattanooga. It seemed insane, but it was worth it. Well worth it.

The ringing jerked Lissa out of her thoughts. She pulled herself off the floor and grabbed the phone, her mind in a fog. Cammie was on the other end, and she sounded distressed.

"Liss, I tried to talk to your father this morning when he got here, but he's made up his mind. The buyers came at nine. The girl rode Caleb, and the two of them were brilliant together. The parents signed on the spot."

"No!" So that's where her father was. The selfish, cruel jerk!

"The vet is coming on Monday morning. If everything checks out, they plan to take Caleb back to Virginia that afternoon."

"I can't believe he's done this."

But she did believe it. She had seen it coming for a long time.

In a flat voice, the emotion drained out of her, she said, "Thanks for trying, Cammie."

"Liss, I really am sorry."

"I know. Bye." She could not get another word out. Her mouth had gone completely dry.

What am I going to do?

Immediately she knew. Lissa got out a suitcase and packed it with underwear, toiletries, jeans, sweat shirts. She threw in the journals, the manuscript, the two framed photos, S. A. Green's other novels from the library, and with one more glance around the room, the Bible.

She carried the suitcase down the stairs with her good hand. Who could she call to come pick her up, and where could she go? Her first thought was the MacAllisters, but did she still trust them? Definitely not Silvano. But she had to get away.

You drive.

She went to the kitchen and got the keys for the little Camaro that had sat in the garage for months, waiting for her to get up the confidence to drive it. The garage door was still open from when her father had left with his car that morning. Should she write a note or just disappear without a word?

As she contemplated this, his car turned into the driveway. When he came in the front door, she was standing there, frozen, like the lovers on Keats's Grecian urn.

"Hey, Lissa. How are you?" His voice was jovial.

She turned on him in a rage. "You can't sell him! You can't! Don't you care about me? Momma would never have sold him. She understood. Caleb is part of the family."

His voice changed, wooden, yet fierce. "Your mother is dead, and I make the decisions in this family."

"You can't sell him!"

"Liss, it's already done. The horse is sold. Get over it." He turned to walk away.

She grabbed his arm. "Get over it? Get *over* it? I love Caleb. I love him more than I love you! Caleb did not kill Momma! He's just a horse. It wasn't his fault. And it wasn't my fault either, Dad. It was an accident. A freaking, horrible accident. Quit blaming us! Quit it!"

The hate and fury felt so real, so palpable. It shot up from the ache in her stomach.

Lissa moved to within inches of her father's face. "I'm leaving," she announced. "I hate you and I'm leaving and I don't care what you think about it! I wish you had been killed in the accident instead of Momma. I wish it had been you! I wish you were dead!"

Astonishment flashed in her father's eyes, and he stood there, for once stunned into silence.

Lissa didn't wait for him to regain the power of speech. She turned on her heels and ran out of the house, slinging her purse over her good shoulder like a rifle filled with ammunition. She tossed her suitcase into the Camaro, jumped in and put on her seat belt out of habit, and winced when pain shot through her shoulder. Ignoring it, she slammed the car door shut, turned the key in the ignition, put the car in reverse, and let the tires squeal in protest as she screeched out of the driveway onto East Brow Road. She wanted her father to be terrified that she was getting ready to drive the car over some steep cliff.

The thought brought her a morbid satisfaction.

CHAPTER TWENTY-THREE

Atlanta's weather did strange things in November, like the sun shining almost seventy degrees on the city.

Lin Su insisted that they take the kids to the newly renovated Zoo Atlanta. "I'll fix us a picnic. It will be perfect."

Ted could not get a word out. He simply complied, following her instructions the way Sammy's Duplo figurines obeyed their pint-sized master.

Don't panic, Ted. You'll find the right time to tell her. Don't panic.

"Well, I told the girls!" Lin Su announced happily as she pushed LeeAnne's stroller by the tigers' territory. "I told them everything about the Million Dollar Club and China, and they are so excited for me! I think they are secretly jealous too, but that's okay with me. They've had fancy trips of their own."

Ted swallowed hard and unconsciously gripped little Sammy's hand too tightly.

"Ouch, Daddy! That hurts!"

"Sorry, buddy."

Lin Su glanced over at him. "Anything wrong? You're mighty quiet this morning."

He gave her a weak smile and cleared his throat. "Just tired," he said, but it sounded stiff.

How was he going to tell her?

Uh, you see, Lin Su, there is actually a little problem. Nothing much to worry about. It's just that I've done some illegal trading, and to top that I've lost about a million bucks for my two biggest clients. And then there's the little fact that the manager and company found out and called me in. No big deal. Really. Basically I'll be going before the arbitration board. The best-case scenario is that I'll get fired, lose my broker's license, and Goldberg will have to pay restitution to my clients. After they drain my account, of course. Worst-case scenario is that all of the above happens and then I'll get incarcerated—you know, for a misdemeanor, anywhere from six months to two years.

But don't worry, Lin Su. I'm sure it will all work out fine, and before you know it we'll be on our way to China.

When they got to the elephants' cage, the stench of their droppings made Ted literally gag.

Lin Su shot him a worried look. "Honey, are you all right?"

You've got to tell her, Ted. You've got to.

"Yeah, yeah, I guess I'm not feeling so hot. Must have picked up a bug at work. Several guys were out this week."

"Here, let's sit down. There's a bench over there. My gosh, you're pasty white!"

As soon as they sat on the bench, Sammy started whining, "Mommy, I want to see the snakes! Can we see the snakes now?"

"We're almost there. Let's just sit for a sec."

When Lin Su stopped pushing the stroller, LeeAnne started to cry. Lin Su plucked her out, put her over her shoulder, and while she patted her daughter gently on the back she instructed, "Eat something, Ted. You look faint. Or take a sip of Coke."

He popped the top on the Coke can and took a long swallow. Sugar and caffeine. Yeah, that might work until they got back home and put the kids down for a nap. Then he could take Lin Su's hands in his, look her in the eyes, and say, Sweetie, I'm afraid I have some bad news.

At any rate, he knew he could not tell her here, not in front of the kids. Standing up, he said with more enthusiasm than he felt, "Okay, guys, let's go! Off to the snakes!" He made a hissing sound and opened and closed his hand, imitating a snake's mouth.

Sammy watched transfixed until Ted reached over with the same hand and pinched the little boy at the waist. Sammy howled with fright and laughter.

"And then we'll go to the monkeys! The monkeys." Ted scratched himself under his arms and twirled around, making *ooh, ooh, ooh* sounds.

Lin Su, Sammy, and even LeeAnne stared at him, their eyes wide. Then they all laughed.

Yes, laugh! Laugh, little family. Your daddy is cracking up.

———

Ev, Annie, and Janelle sat at the kitchen table and finished their breakfast.

Her father wiped his mouth with a napkin and said, "What could be nicer, Janelle, than eating my favorite breakfast fixed by my little girl? Thank you."

"My pleasure, Daddy. Would you like another cup of coffee?"

"I believe I will."

Janelle took a deep breath and was surprised at the prayer that settled in her heart.

Thank you, Lord, for time to be with Mom and Dad alone while Katy Lynn and Gina are still sleeping. I needed this.

She had chatted with them about Luke and Sandy and told them things they already knew about Brian's work with the radio station. Her parents were some of their most fervent prayer partners for the ministry.

Now her mother filled each cup with more coffee, sat down by her daughter, pulled her robe around herself, and asked, "How are you doing, darling? Really? From your letters and phone calls, it sounds as though you're struggling."

Janelle blinked back sudden tears, gave a sniff, and admitted, "I *am* struggling. Struggling with dark thoughts, depression. The past two months have been horrible, the same blackness that I felt right after Josh's accident. I thought it would get easier, but . . ."

Her father, sitting across the table from her, reached for her hand and held it tightly between his own. "It rushes on you at the craziest times, doesn't it?"

"Yeah. I was doing better, and then the whole bottom dropped out. Brian says it's the time of year—the anniversary of Josh's death—that kicks it off. I guess he's right." She bit her lip. "How long, Daddy? How long does it take?"

Her father moved his long fingers over her hand. "After Tate had been gone four years, I started thinking I might be able to live again. But you've got to give yourself permission to keep grieving for as long as it takes."

"You never really get over it, do you?"

"No, sweetie, not exactly. But then, do we want to 'get over it'? The memory of Tate, the memory of Josh, is proof of their importance in our lives. I think we just hope to let the Almighty redeem the terrible scars. Eventually He gives us supernatural strength and the desire to reach out and help others make it too."

"The driving school?"

"Yes, the driving school."

———

Lissa felt thankful for the anger and the hatred that were momentarily replacing her fear as she careened, out of control, around the curves on East Brow Road. Her father refused to entertain the idea of a conversation. They were at an impasse, and she knew from therapy that you could not force another human to change.

Failure!

Terrified and furious, she screamed out loud, "I give up! I quit!" and pushed down so hard on the accelerator that she thought she might run the car right off the side of Lookout Mountain. Forget her father, forget Caleb, and forget the hope of healing, grieving, and moving on!

She wanted to go far away, away from life. She had no Plan B, just soul weariness as she sped along East Brow, came to an intersection, braked too quickly, and skidded to a stop. Recovering, she turned to the right, zigzagging along Scenic Highway, her heart pumping wildly, driving as if in a fog, much too fast for the small mountain road.

The stately homes with the well-trimmed yards and the pumpkins still sitting by the front doors blurred on either side of the road. Sweat poured down her back, her shoulder ached, her mind felt numb. Her life was sliding away from her, sliding down the mountain, out of control.

She screeched again to a stop and stared at the familiar little black-arrowed signs pointing in different directions: Point Park, Incline, Rock City, Ruby Falls, Covenant College. Yes, Covenant College, the back of the mountain. She'd drive by the college on Highway 157, turn down through Hinkle and toward Flintstone and Fort Oglethorpe. There would be less traffic, and she could avoid that drop-off by Rock City where the mountain fell off into nothingness and a car could be catapulted down to Chattanooga.

That was a rational thought. Keep looking ahead, Lissa, keep your eyes forward. Breathe, breathe, girl. Loosen your hands on the wheel. Concentrate. Brake slowly.

A poky driver in a Suburban was twisting around the bends in front of her. Lissa realized she was approaching too quickly, but she didn't brake. Closer, closer the Camaro came to the Suburban.

Slow down, Lissa!

When the Suburban turned right into the steep entrance of the college, Lissa let out a breath and zipped past, following the road to the left. The Camaro's wheels squealed as she rounded a hairpin turn much too quickly.

Slow down, slow down—you are going too fast.

Beyond the college, the road straightened, but it was still punctuated with a succession of small hills and valleys. At her speed, she literally felt like she was riding a roller coaster, and at one point the car bumped so high that she felt her heart in the pit of her stomach.

Slow down.

Her hands were shaking now, her breathing coming with difficulty. Why could she not get the car to slow down?

In the distance a pickup truck was coming toward her. Was she still on her side of the road? Was she swerving, or was it just her mind?

Lissa, concentrate! Mr. MacAllister's voice was urging her. Then she heard his voice again, speaking to her through that manuscript. *Sometimes you must take drastic action. Sometimes, to avoid tragedy, you must make a split-second decision.*

She yanked the steering wheel to the right and mashed on the brakes. She heard the blast of the pickup's horn as it swerved off the other side of the road, barely missing her sliding Camaro, and continued on. As Lissa pressed harder on the brake, the car screeched and then came to a stop, smack in the middle of the road.

She was trembling so violently now that she did not trust herself to move. She took her hands off the steering wheel and held them together in her lap, but still they shook uncontrollably.

Caleb is sold.

I hate my father.

Ev MacAllister is S. A. Green.

Silvano is a creep.

It wasn't my fault.

It's all my fault!

Failure!

But somewhere in the midst of the voices, she heard another one, Mr. MacAllister's, calm and clear, telling her how to live as she drove Ole Bessie.

Lissa! Lissa, you can do this. I won't let you fail. I'm here. I'm here.

He was instructing her as surely as if he were sitting right beside her in the yellow Camaro.

You can do this. Breathe.

The trembling lessened; she forced herself to breathe deeply. An approaching car slowed, veered to the right, drove around her. Then she heard the other voice whispering in her head.

You can't trust that old man. He's a liar. A liar and a fake!

She again felt the sparks of anger and hate, her heart rate accelerating.

Then a whisper, a gentle whisper, drifting on the breeze.

Nothing is random, Lissa. I am here with you. I am here.

The voice wasn't her driving teacher's.

Every ounce of strength drained from her, and she felt weak and light-headed. Out loud, she whimpered, like a small child in the dark, "Then help me if you're here. I'm so scared."

Something settled inside her mind, a dried leaf floating to the ground.

She put her hands on the steering wheel, pressed the accelerator gently, and moved forward, carried by the voice. Not another car was on the road. She followed Highway 157 to the left as it curved gently through woods and farmlands, rolling up and down the hills. At a small white church, she turned to head down the mountain. She noticed the way the sun was playing in the remaining leaves that twittered delicately on branches. A flock of geese spread out in V formation far ahead. She felt her face relax and her fingers less taut on the wheel.

Ten minutes later she was traveling along Highway 2 en route to Fort Oglethorpe. The shaking and trembling had stopped by the time she pulled the yellow Camaro into the MacAllisters' driveway and stopped it beside Ole Bessie. Lissa sat still for a long time, breathing deeply. Then she rested her head on the steering wheel and sobbed.

———

It was past noon, but after such a big breakfast, in which Katy Lynn and Gina had eventually participated, no one was hungry. The five of them had moved into the den, giving snippets of information about their lives in between awkward stops and starts. Ev and Annie sat on the old sagging couch. Gina was curled on the floor with a magazine.

Katy Lynn took the straight-back chair, saying, "Janelle, it looks like Daddy's big armchair is left for you."

"Finally I get to try it," Janelle joked, and Ev thought the sound of the sisters' teasing was more beautiful than the view from his porch of the fire-colored trees on Lookout Mountain.

He did not want to interrupt anything. Yet he knew it was time. He glanced at Annie, who gave him a quick smile and a wink. His hands shook the slightest bit, and he felt a pinching in his chest. He wondered if he would be able to say what he needed to. Swallowing, he lifted a silent prayer in his mind.

Help me, Father. Help me.

"I just want you girls to know how wonderful it is to have you all here. Your mother and I appreciate your coming, each of you." He looked down at his hands, noticed the light brown splotches, rubbed at them absently.

"Janelle, you mentioned that you had questions about our past— things that Katy had alluded to when you were together." He cleared his throat twice. He nodded to Katy Lynn. "You were right to bring these up. It was appropriate." Now he was fumbling with his hands in his lap.

"I need to tell you things that will be surprising for all of you, things you may even have trouble believing. Katy Lynn remembers some of the past, our other life. Janelle, you weren't born at the time, and we never really told you about it." He looked down at Gina. "You need to know too. Please hear me out to the end. Then"—he held out his hands—"then you can each decide what you want to do with what I tell you."

He took a breath, and Annie patted his hands.

"Katy Lynn and Janelle, you know that this old house belonged to your grandparents—we bought it from Mom's father when her mother died. That was in 1956. But your mother and I met up East years earlier, when we were in college. I grew up in Connecticut, in a milieu that valued wealth and intelligence above everything else. I was expected to be a success, and I was determined not to disappoint anyone. At eighteen I was the biggest jerk in the history of the world."

Gina gave a nervous giggle. "You, Granddad?"

He nodded. "Me. Of course, I didn't see it that way. But trust me, I was. I had one stabilizing person in my life—my little sister, Tate. Do you remember Tate, Katy Lynn?"

Katy Lynn frowned at Ev. "A little. I was only three or four when we . . . when Mom and I left. And when we came back, Aunt Tate was . . .

was gone. But I remember she was pretty and a whole lot of fun. I have this memory . . ."

Ev watched his older daughter travel back in time.

"A memory of Tate letting me finger-paint on this huge sheet of paper. We made dozens of handprints, hers and mine, in all kinds of colors, and then we took off our shoes and made footprints too."

Ev pressed his lips together and glanced down at his hands. "She loved playing with you, Katy."

This was even harder than he'd expected.

"Tate loved and admired me. When I was with her, I was at my best—a proud and kind big brother. And we both loved to write. When she was just six, she and I started making up the most whimsical stories together." He could not help but smile with the memory.

"Tate had a hard time with the social circle around which our family revolved—she was a sensitive soul. I wanted to protect my little sister from all the rotten stuff around us, but . . ." He shrugged. "But I went to college and only saw her on occasional weekends. I basically left her to fend for herself in a world she hated.

"In school, one professor in particular believed in my talent so much that he convinced me to publish my senior paper in a literary magazine. So I did, and it got some positive reviews. Of course that went straight to my head. I was moving in the fast lane. We"—he glanced at Annie— "we were moving in the fast lane.

"And Tate was miserable. She was about nine or ten at the time. She used to tell me that I was acting snobby, bigheaded. I should have listened, but I guess I was blinded by success . . . and love. When I met your mother, I knew she could go places with me. She was witty, blunt, gorgeous. And tough. We got married right after I graduated. We were happy back then, weren't we?"

Annie shrugged. "We were spoiled brats, living off our parents' money, but we were happy."

"Then the war came. I was drafted in 1943. I came home in '45, and nine months later you were born, Katy Lynn. The happiest day of our lives."

He paused and glanced at his daughter. Did she, could she, believe him?

"With the encouragement of that professor and the help of my parents' money, I started writing full time. I produced a short novel in 1948. My professor insisted I send it to a publishing house. After a few rejections, a big house in New York picked it up, put a lot of money into the promotion, and it became what they now call a cult book. College students especially liked it. I made a lot of money and was thrust straight into a spot I was not ready for—fame. Interviews, pictures in magazines, book tours, acclaim. I thought I was on the road to becoming the next F. Scott Fitzgerald."

"His publisher called it 'hauntingly beautiful,' " Annie said.

"You wrote a book, Dad?" Janelle said. "Why didn't you ever tell us?"

"You'll understand in a minute, Janelle."

Annie left the room and came back a moment later holding a thin paperback novel. She handed it to Janelle.

"*The Homegoing*. By Ashton Mack?"

"Back then everyone called me Ashton—my first name—and they called your mother Stella."

"Stella! Like in *A Streetcar Named Desire*? I just read that this year!" Gina volunteered.

"Exactly," Annie said. "I didn't mind my first name until Tennessee Williams wrote that play, and suddenly my being Stella wasn't too much fun. As you recall, she wasn't the swiftest chick in the play."

Gina laughed. "True. But she was nice."

"Anyway, fame went to my head. When I wasn't at parties getting drunk, or worse, I was off signing books." Ev did not want to pronounce the next words. His voice caught, but he pushed on. "I left my young wife and baby daughter for weeks at a time—signings, parties, speaking engagements, interviews. I was proud and self-righteous. I devoted all my time to those things and hobnobbing with the intelligentsia. I thought I hung the moon."

He lowered his head. "I saw other women. I wasn't . . . I wasn't faithful to your mother."

Silence invaded the room. Annie took his hand again.

"I failed your mother, and I failed you, Katy Lynn. After two years of it, your mother got fed up." He squeezed her hand. "And rightly so."

His daughters listened without a word.

"She took you, Katy, and left. I wanted to throw myself off the bridge. Life had no more meaning—all the recognition and money and fame meant nothing. I did what a guy does. I drank. And drank."

Katy Lynn looked first at Ev, then at Annie. "I remember that. I remember us leaving. It *was* awful."

"Yes, it was. And I was fully to blame. I've poured my heart out in shame and repentance to the Almighty and to your mother. Amazingly, they forgave me—a long, long time ago. But I need to ask your forgiveness, Katy Lynn. And yours, Janelle, and Gina, even though you weren't part of the story yet. I'm sorry for that heritage."

Janelle gave a tiny nod when he looked at her. Katy Lynn had her arms folded tightly across her chest. She did not meet his eyes.

"Your mother's leaving was a wake-up call, but I didn't really wake up. I just kept drinking heavily and socializing with the wrong people. That went on for another year or so. Then I had my second wake-up call. On New Year's Eve, 1952, Tate was in a car accident. She was killed on the spot. At seventeen. She was drunk out of her mind. My family's social circle had finally sucked her in too, and I had done nothing to stop it." He wiped a hand under his eyes. "I let that world destroy her. If I hadn't been so caught up in myself, I could have helped her, maybe prevented the accident—"

Janelle looked sympathetic; Katy Lynn seemed to soften a little. Gina turned her head down and fiddled with a page in her magazine.

"Tate's death pushed me over the edge. I stopped writing, secluded myself. I thought about taking my own life. So when my old war buddy begged me to go to hear this hotshot evangelist at a revival—they were very popular back then—what did I have to lose? Humor the poor kid. So I went."

His voice dropped to a whisper. "In spite of myself, I was electrified by the simple message of salvation. I discovered that God wasn't dead, and the message, so simple and yet so complex—something in it appealed to my mind as a novelist. I thought, I need this. I need this Man. This God. I left the crusade in tears and returned to my flat with a tiny flicker of hope inside.

"It takes a long time to get over yourself, but time was something I had plenty of. No family, no job, just hanging on to hope. I checked out for a while, like the apostle Paul, and with the help of a few new friends I got to know this Jesus. And things happened. I determined to give up drinking and find my wife and daughter. I spent almost a year looking for you both."

Again his eyes went to Katy Lynn. She glanced at him briefly.

Annie spoke up in her no-nonsense way. "I wanted nothing to do with him. I didn't answer his calls or letters, and when he finally caught up with us, I slammed the door in his face. But he was persistent. He kept at us for six months. I could tell he had changed. I guess you could say our love story took a long time to bloom again—through lots of tears and sacrifice. It took a long time for me to buy his conversion too. I wasn't exactly a God-fearing young woman at the time. Fortunately, the Lord had a lot of patience and grace. He let us go through some pretty awful stuff to teach us humility and dependence on Him."

Ev nodded. "After we got back together, we knew we needed a radical change. First we changed our names. I started going by Everett instead of Ashton, and your mother went by Annie instead of Stella. We moved south, to Atlanta. That's where you were born, Janelle. When Annie's mother died, we bought this house in Fort Oglethorpe, and with Annie as master administrator, we opened the driving school. One of our main goals was to help teenagers become more competent drivers. We also wanted to teach them more about the dangers of alcohol, drugs, speeding. We lobbied for seat belts in cars and a lot of other things. I couldn't bring Tate back, but I thought maybe the Almighty could use me to keep others from meeting a similar fate."

Annie started to speak again. "Things were good. We lived a much simpler life. But I could tell your father missed his writing. So I finally convinced him to send out his work again for publication. He refused to go back to the fame of the former life, preferring anonymity. I knew he had great talent, and together we decided that he would use a pen name and that I would be his 'voice' for the publishers. We chose my first two initials—S. A. for Stella Ann, and my mother's maiden name, Green."

Annie and Ev looked at each other for several seconds.

Finally Ev said, "My first book published under the name of S. A. Green came out in 1960. *Eastern Crossings*."

It took a few seconds for the revelation to register.

Then Katy Lynn stood up, hands on her hips. "What! You mean to tell me that you, Dad, are S. A. Green?"

"I am."

Katy Lynn and Janelle stared at their father, dumbfounded, but Gina said, "Cool! That's so cool. I just read that book in English! My grand-dad wrote *Eastern Crossings*!" She got up off the floor and went over and hugged Ev. "That is really cool."

"I don't know what to say," Janelle said. "I can't believe it."

"Well, I know what to say." Katy Lynn spun around and walked behind the armchair, putting distance between herself and her parents. "I told you so! I told you they were hiding things from us, Janelle! I told you they were lying hypocrites!" Then she stared at Ev and Annie. "But I never imagined that your whole lives were a lie!" She stalked out of the room.

"Katy!" Ev went after her. "Katy, please. I know I've failed you, and I've never known how to make things right. But can you please hear me out? Then you will be free to choose. If I'm going to tell you the truth, you need to hear all of it."

She turned around slowly and regarded him with a look that seared him. "Why in the world would you not tell your very own daughters that you are S. A. Green?"

Ev did not answer at first. He walked back into the den. After a moment, Katy Lynn followed.

"I didn't want my new novels to have any connection with my past. Fame had ruined me once—it terrified me, the possibility of repeating the past. So I . . . we . . . decided anonymity was best." He looked help-lessly at Annie, then back at Katy Lynn. "Please believe me . . . it wasn't to keep the truth from you—it was to protect you. I didn't want to leave you girls a legacy of extravagant parties and material wealth. I'd seen what it did to me, to many of my friends . . . to Tate."

Katy Lynn stood rigid in the door frame, her face hard and angry. He wondered if she had really heard him.

"You ruined my life. The life you brought Mom and me back to was worse than the one we ran away from, for me. I hated it."

"I'm so sorry you felt that way, Katy. I never wanted to hurt you— before you left or after you came back."

Gina burst into tears. "Why do you say that, Mom? How did Grand-dad ruin your life? It's not his fault about Daddy leaving us. Daddy ruined your life, not Granddad."

Sudden silence invaded the room.

Ev watched his daughter's face fall. He wanted more than anything to take her in his arms, but he didn't dare.

"It's true," Katy Lynn said without emotion. "Hamilton has left us. For another woman." She took a deep breath. "This is about all I can handle for today. I need to get some fresh air."

This time Ev did not try to stop her when she turned and walked out the front door.

———

Lissa walked toward the house, holding the manuscript in both hands with the library copy of *Eastern Crossings* stacked on top of it. She hesitated on the porch.

Suddenly the door flew open, and a short, blond woman burst out and almost ran straight into her.

Lissa mumbled, "Excuse me," and the woman gave a startled little cry and stopped.

"I'm sorry. I didn't see you there."

"It's okay."

"Are you looking for someone?"

"Yes, I . . . I wanted to talk to Mr. MacAllister. He's my driving instructor. But if he's busy . . ." The way the woman stared at her made Lissa uncomfortable. "I'll just go."

But she didn't move. The thought of getting back in that car and driving away terrified her.

The woman let out a breath and seemed to relax. "No, go on in if he's expecting you."

But he's not expecting me.

The woman looked irritated. Or mad.

"Look, I'm in a bit of a rush. Just knock on the door, and someone will come." She hurried over to a green Jaguar, got in, and drove away.

Lissa walked several tentative steps to the front door, reached out a hand to knock, and let it fall to her side.

Failure!

Don't bother him.

Life is not random.

She pressed the doorbell.

When Mr. MacAllister opened the door, he looked as if he had run Ole Bessie into a tree and just stepped out of the car, shaken and disoriented. Then he saw her.

"Lissa! What brings you here this morning? Are you all right?"

She drew the manuscript close to her chest and stared down at his old blue and white tennis shoes.

"Come on inside."

She didn't budge. In a voice cracking between tears and anger, she whispered, "Who are you? Tell me right now, who are you?"

The old man furrowed his brow as if he didn't understand her question. "I'm your friend. That's who I am. Your friend."

She began to cry. She hated her tears!

Mr. MacAllister walked out on the porch and looked over at the Camaro. "How did you get here?"

"I, I drove."

"You drove the Camaro here? By yourself?"

"Yes," she sniffed. "I had to get away. Daddy sold Caleb. He sold him."

"Oh, dear, no."

By now Annie had joined him on the porch. "Lissa! For heaven's sake.

What's the matter? You're shaking." She hugged her and said, "Come inside, sweetie."

Lissa shook her head. "I can't. I can't, because . . ." She thrust out the manuscript and the copy of *Eastern Crossings*.

"You wrote this book, didn't you, Mr. MacAllister?" It came out as an accusation. "And this one too. *Driving Lessons* by S. A. Green."

The old man lifted his eyebrows in surprise, but didn't answer.

"It's you! I know it!" Lissa flipped the loose-leaf pages until she came to one she had marked. She thrust it toward him. "You said these exact words to me last month. You wrote this book! And you wrote all the others too. You're S. A. Green!"

"Why are you angry, Lissa?"

"Because you lied! You're famous! I knew you weren't just some old driving instructor!"

She saw a look of sadness in his eyes, a beam of light that pierced her. She lowered her voice. "I didn't mean it that way. I meant that I knew there was more to you."

If she could have taken her words back, she would have paid handsomely to retrieve them. She had injured him. Ev MacAllister stood before her, wounded in the heart.

At last he cleared his throat. "Of course there is more to me than simply being a driving instructor. It is one of my jobs, one that I feel strongly, passionately about. And yes, I'm also a novelist."

"Why? Why have you kept it a secret?"

"It's a long story." He looked over at Annie, and she nodded. "Please come in the house, Lissa. There are some people here I want you to meet."

CHAPTER TWENTY-FOUR

~

Katy Lynn knew the back roads of Fort Oglethorpe and Chattanooga all too well. She zipped around the turns as she cursed herself for having offered to come here with Janelle. Maybe she could rebuild some type of relationship with her sister, but not with her father.

And leave it to Gina to blurt out the truth about Hamilton. Oh, who cared? They had to find out sooner or later.

Her daughter was certainly enthralled with the old man's story.

I used to love his stories too.

"Hey, Katy Lynn, my sweetie." *Her father's young, handsome face was next to hers.* "I've missed you so much. Daddy was wrong. Daddy was bad. I'm so sorry. Can you forgive me?"

"Of course, Daddy. I'm so happy you're back. We're back."

She could have sat forever in his lap, folded in his arms, laughing at the way he told the stories of Mr. Snodgrass and Shiny Green and Slimey Green, the friendly snakes, and Blackie and Angelfoot, the ponies. And the

342

Princess of the Story. She was the princess of every one of his stories. How she had missed them when she and Mommy had gone away.

"Tell me a story, Daddy."

And he did. But ever since he'd come back, Daddy also told stories about the ark and the animals and the big sea opening up so a million people could pass through and stories of a baby born in a manger.

Katy Lynn pressed on the accelerator, tears blinding her vision.

Why did she hate him so? She was acting like Gina, who had carved her hate for her father on her arms.

I carved it on my heart. I hated him because everything changed. Janelle was born and we moved away and everything changed, my place in the family, my parents' values, my father's discipline. He wiped out all the fun in my life, and whenever I protested he gave me a lecture and said, "Sweetheart, what matters most is the heart."

Katy Lynn hadn't wanted her heart to change. She wanted to keep pretending for the rest of her life that everything was in perfect order and that she was still the Princess of the Story.

My favorite books in the whole world are those of S. A. Green.

Katy Lynn cried harder. Unbelievable! Her father had still spoken to her, still written her love letters through his books. Hadn't she known, hadn't she said at times that those novels were written for her?

She had turned him away because she felt betrayed. She had wanted him all to herself.

We chose anonymity because we didn't want you to carry that heavy past. We wanted to protect you.

They wanted to protect her from what fame and power and greed could do.

But I never understood.

She had driven unconsciously to the Chickamauga Battlefield, the very place her father had taught her to drive twenty-five years ago.

She braked the car by a statue of soldiers. A deer, startled by her sudden appearance, leapt gracefully into the woods.

These soldiers paid a high price for peace, Katy Lynn. A high price. But Christ paid the highest.

Why did he have to make everything religious?

Katy Lynn sat in the car for an hour, crying, listening, thinking, even praying.

I forgive you, Daddy. But is there any way I can forgive myself?

———

Oh, Katy, Janelle thought. She wrapped her arms around Gina and said, "Your mother's going through a lot right now. Let her sort it out. She'll be okay."

"I've never seen her so mad."

"I think sometimes *mad* needs to come out."

"She doesn't believe Granddad, does she?"

"Oh, I think she will come around."

Janelle believed her father, but she hardly knew how to react. Her father an author? Why was she surprised? He spoke poetry, could he not also write it? As a child, her fondest memories were when she was cuddled on her father's lap while he invented yet another sequel to the wonderful fantasy stories he spun for her.

Her father, an acclaimed novelist. Years ago she had wondered at his profession. But then she had moved to France and had her babies and started the ministry and lost Josh. She admitted she had not thought much about her father's life in a long time, other than to utter a brief prayer each day for the Lord to watch over her parents.

She wished Brian were with her to talk over this revelation.

Gina helped Janelle carry their coffee mugs back into the kitchen. The front door was cracked open, and from the kitchen Janelle heard her parents talking softly to someone on the front porch. A few minutes later they came back inside, followed by a teenage girl.

Her father was making an effort to appear calm, but he was not convincing.

"Janelle, Gina, I'd like you to meet one of my students, Lissa Randall. Lissa, my daughter Janelle, and my granddaughter Gina. And that was Gina's mother, Katy Lynn, you met coming out of the house."

The girl—Lissa—looked disheveled and fearful. But that was not what Janelle noticed first. For a brief moment, Janelle thought she was seeing the ghost of her father's dead sister, Tate. This girl had the same thick brown hair, a thin face with full lips, and lovely brown soulful eyes.

Janelle collected herself enough to join her parents in the entrance way and give a half smile to the young woman. "Good to meet you, Lissa."

The girl barely nodded, ill at ease, clutching a thick pile of papers to her chest.

Gina offered a quick "Hi."

"Come into the den and have a seat, Lissa," her mother said. "Let me get you something to drink. A Coke?"

The girl sat down on the couch and murmured, "Thanks, Annie."

———

Lissa felt trapped. She did not want to sit on a couch with the rest of the MacAllister family looking on. She wanted to talk to Mr. MacAllister. Alone. She wanted him to explain the voices—especially that one on the road. She had made it down the mountain. Spurred on by feelings of fear, hate, anger, and betrayal, she had driven alone.

Failure!

Victory!

She set down the manuscript and novel on the couch beside her and slowly sipped her Coke. The air in the house felt heavy and tense. Thankfully, the daughter and granddaughter disappeared into some other room.

Mr. MacAllister stood staring out the den window, lost in thought. Annie sat next to her on the couch. Lissa gulped down the rest of the beverage and stood up.

"Thank you, Annie. I, I need to leave."

Where could she go?

"Leave! Heavens, no! You need to rest. You've had quite a shock, and then you drove over here alone! With a broken wrist and shoulder. No, you'll stay put. You're pale as a ghost. Come upstairs with me."

Lissa had no strength to argue. She glanced at Mr. MacAllister. He turned from the window, appearing to Lissa suddenly very old.

With a sad smile he said, "Rest, Lissa. We'll talk later."

She followed Annie upstairs.

"Gina's using this room, but she won't mind if you stretch out on the bed. Get a little rest."

"I don't know why I'm here. I need to go."

"You'll do no such thing. Rest."

Thank goodness Annie could be forceful.

Lissa climbed onto the bed, exhausted, defeated, drained. Everything was going wrong, but all she wanted to do was sleep.

———

Ev felt dizzy when he walked into his office, holding the manuscript of his novel that Lissa had left on the couch. How in the world did she get a photocopy of *Driving Lessons*? One more odd occurrence to prove to him that God was at work. He sorted through the events—his meeting with Lissa and his memories of Tate, the threatening letter that had worried Annie so and caused her to fly to Chicago, the news of the foundation being drained of money, and now his daughters back in his home and learning the truth of S. A. Green. All of these circumstances, and others too, held the Lord's fingerprints. God was nudging Ev forward into something new.

You don't give us more than we can bear at a time. You are amazingly patient, and clean out our closets slowly and methodically. I've got some pretty thick cobwebs in this one, don't I, Lord?

The truth was out—the parties and women, his conversion, their move, his secret life as a novelist. His daughters wanted to know why he had never let the world know about S. A. Green. Heavens, there were enough reasons to fill his library! He had to flee his past success as Ashton Mack. He and Annie desired to escape from his wealthy surroundings and live a peaceful life. He had made a promise to the Lord shortly after moving to the South, "If you allow me to publish again, I will write for you." This promise he had kept.

But there was another reason for the anonymity: his heart. Twice he had touched the footstool of heaven. Born with a weak heart, the stress and alcohol and tragedy of Tate had brought him close to death in 1952. The second heart attack occurred in 1954, soon after Janelle was born.

The doctors had been clear: "Mr. MacAllister, if you don't want to face an early grave, you must slow down." And so he had.

Throughout the years, Annie begged him to hide away from the world, long after he felt that his ego could handle the attention of a well-respected author. The Lord would keep him in line. But for Annie, he kept his anonymity while she insisted, "You write. I'll deal with the rest." She took the brunt of the publishing business, and whenever he expressed concern, she fired back the same remark. "Ev, the Lord gave you the genius, but He gave me the strong heart."

It was no secret to Annie that he looked forward to the other side of life with a singing in his soul. "Going up to Jesus," he called it. But for Annie, to stay with her a little longer, he happily sacrificed the pressures of renown.

The problem was that life's stresses could not be counted and measured like a cup of flour for a cake. The doctor had said it in September. *Mr. MacAllister, you're playing with fire. I heartily recommend you retire.*

Annie repeated it ad nauseam. *Ev, dear, let go of Tate, let go of the driving school. You've done enough. Let it go.*

The ringing of the phone startled him. He sat down at the desk and answered.

"Hello, Mr. MacAllister?" The voice sounded panicked. "This is Gary Randall. I'm sorry to disturb you, but I'm looking for my daughter. She left here in her car about an hour and a half ago. I'm worried because she was driving alone, and you know that could be . . . dangerous. I wondered if—"

Ev managed to interrupt the hurried speech. "Your daughter is here, Mr. Randall. She's safe."

The man gave a sigh. "Thank God. I'll come get her right now."

Ev rubbed his forehead. "Mr. Randall, perhaps this is no business of mine, but you may need to give her a little while to calm down. She's fine here."

"Can I talk to her? I need to talk to her. It's urgent."

"I think she's lying down. I promise she's safe."

"Please have her call me as soon as she wakes up."

"I will give her your message."

Ev hung up the phone, ran his hands over the worn keys of the old typewriter, and closed his eyes. He needed to lie down himself.

Gina appeared in the doorway. "Am I bothering you, Granddad?"

He shook his head and smiled. "Of course not. It's such a treat to have you here, Gina. Come in and tell me how you're doing. I'm afraid I've only added to your problems."

"You didn't know about Daddy, did you?"

"No. No, that was a surprise."

Gina stood with her back leaning on the bookshelf. She twisted a few strands of her hair together, not looking at Ev. "I think Mom is mad at you because your life works and hers doesn't. No matter how hard she tries, it doesn't really work." She brushed her hands through her hair. "And she's been really worried about me too."

"Do you want to tell me why?"

She shrugged uncomfortably. "No—it's okay. I'm doing better anyway. I see my dad every week, and we talk. It's not all his fault."

"It never is all one person's fault. Thank you for coming, Gina. I really am glad you're here."

She picked up the photo of Tate. "That girl—Lissa—she looks so much like Tate."

"Yes, she does."

"She's so pretty, but she looks really awful—like she's scared or something. Is she going to be okay?"

Ev felt thankful that his granddaughter was growing into a thoughtful and compassionate young woman. "I think she will, eventually. She's traveled a hard road."

"None of my business, right?"

Ev gave her a wink.

"Can I look at your novels? You know—your *real* novels. The ones you wrote."

"Be my guest."

Examining the books on the shelves, Gina carefully took out each of the hardback copies of S. A. Green's novels and lined them up on his desk, running her hands lovingly across each cover. "I can't wait to read them all. I'm so proud of you, Granddad."

She came beside him and threw her arms around his neck, and Ev could not stop the tears from springing into his eyes. God was a redeemer. Ev had never had the joy of a teenaged Katy Lynn spontaneously hugging him. But now he had Gina.

"Thank you, sweetheart. Thank you."

"I guess you don't want me to tell my friends?"

"I'd appreciate it if you didn't, sweetie."

"Don't worry. Your secret is safe with me. All my friends tell me secrets, and I just file them in my brain and never say a word." She gave him a kiss on the cheek, then said, "Grandmom and Aunt Janelle are going to take me to get lunch at Wendy's. I'll see you in a little while."

"Have a good time, Gina."

———

At two o'clock on Saturday afternoon, Silvano turned his car off the highway and drove toward Fort Oglethorpe. His third trip to Chattanooga in twenty-four hours was worth it—it was going to make him rich! He had loaded the car with camera, tape recorder, the papers, the books, and a notepad on which he had scribbled a dozen questions.

He actually enjoyed his trek back to Chattanooga and the home of Mr. Everett MacAllister, alias S. A. Green. He had the phone number, but he would not call.

Take the old man by surprise, catch him off guard. That would make the best story!

Bravo! Fantastico! He was going to make a lot of money off of this deal. He could almost taste it, like creamy gelato. He fingered the rosary beads that hung from his rearview mirror.

"*Bel colpo.* I'm on my way, Mamma. All the waiting has been worth it! Soon you will all have a better life."

The Rock City signs on the barn roofs made him think of Lissa. Yes, he had shocked her, and yes, he had used her. But honestly, was it his fault that an interesting, attractive girl had led him straight to S. A. Green? It was simply a case of being at the right place at the right time, a bizarre and timely coincidence.

When too many coincidences line up in your life, perhaps Someone big and all-powerful is orchestrating events to get your attention.

He groaned as that little jewel floated to him from *Driving Lessons*. He did not have time to listen to Essay's platitudes.

Anyway, he'd get Lissa back. Yes, it would take more than charm and name-dropping. He grinned self-consciously, thinking of her reproach. He liked that girl. Forthright, bright, competitive . . . and yet fragile. He liked her a lot. But he was prepared to sacrifice the relationship—at least momentarily—for the higher cause: the story, the money, the beginning of a brighter future for his family.

He turned his car onto the road marked with the Fort Oglethorpe and Chickamauga signs, and traveled down Highway 2. Slowly he continued until he came to Sunrise Road. Perched on a hill, a rambling Victorian house with a wide porch sat far back from the road. An old blue Ford, a white Impala, and a yellow Camaro were parked in the semicircle dirt driveway out front.

Silvano did a double take. A yellow Camaro? He knew that car! He'd seen it just this morning in the Randalls' opened garage. Was Lissa here? Had she warned Mr. MacAllister? He needed to think fast. He'd imagined ringing the bell and snapping a photo when it opened, the way the paparazzi did for movie stars. But perhaps he should take a calmer approach.

He put all the equipment in the briefcase, and the camera around his neck.

Ready or not, S. A. Green, here I come!

———

Ev shook himself awake. He must have drifted off sitting there in his office chair. The house was quiet, which meant that Annie, Janelle, and Gina were still at lunch. Katy Lynn had not returned either. Perhaps she had driven straight back to Atlanta and he'd never see her again.

From somewhere in his subconscious he heard the doorbell ringing. He pushed himself out of the chair, got up slowly, and walked out of his office, down the back hall, and across the den to the front door. His heart was dancing erratically. Would Katy Lynn feel a need to ring the doorbell?

What would he read on his daughter's face? Hate? Condemnation? Love? Forgiveness? He opened the door with a prayer in his mind.

But the young man standing on the porch was a complete stranger, a salesman, dressed in an expensive suit with a briefcase in his hand and a fake smile on his face.

"Everett MacAllister?"

"Yes. That's right. May I help you?"

"I think so. My name is Silvano Rossi, and I work with the *Chattanooga Times*." He stuck out his hand and shook Ev's with a firm grasp. "I'm sorry I didn't call. My colleague got sick, and they sprang this assignment on me late last night. We're doing a piece on teenage drivers, and we understand you're in the business of teaching them. I only need a moment of your time."

The last thing Ev wanted was to answer a reporter's questions. "Look, young man . . . Mr. Rossi, is it? This is not a good time. You'll have to come back later."

Completely ignoring Ev, the young man took the camera from around his neck and began snapping photos.

Irritated, Ev stepped closer. "Look here, Mr. Rossi, please leave. You are out of line. Call me if you want an interview."

The man did not move. He had a know-it-all smile painted on his face, and his dark eyes were gleaming. "I think you will want to hear my questions."

Ev did not appreciate the young man's brash manner. "I'm afraid you are wrong. Now please be on your way."

"I'll leave, but first just answer this one question." He produced a photo. "Is this your wife?"

Ev looked at the photo of Annie. She was dressed in a business suit, the only one she owned, the one she had worn three weeks ago when she went to Chicago.

His heart skipped a beat, and then he knew. This was the man who had written them, enticing Annie to Chicago for an interview, the scoundrel who had not shown up, the one who had Annie constantly looking over her shoulder.

"Leave now!" Ev bellowed in an uncharacteristically angry voice.

"All right! All right. I'll leave. But I happen to know that this woman *is* your wife, Annie MacAllister, and that she came to Chicago—to meet me, in response to a letter I sent—in the guise of the novelist S. A. Green. I know that is just a cover-up—she is not the novelist. You are."

"Please leave." Ev wished Annie was here. She had a knack for getting rid of nosy reporters.

"I'll leave. But be warned. I'm writing an article on you for a major magazine."

"Please leave." No other words came to mind. He could no longer ignore the pinching in his chest.

"You shouldn't force me away so quickly. Unless of course you want me to publish things the way I see it, complete with photos and quotes."

"That is illegal."

"No, it isn't. Either you can give me an interview and set the facts straight, or I'll just write what I know and guess at the rest—about your books and your foundation and your wife."

Ev felt the sweat on his lip, his heart begin to flutter. He needed to sit down. "What do you want?"

"Just what I said, Mr. MacAllister. I want an interview."

"Come inside, then." Ev's vision blurred slightly as he led Silvano into the den. He motioned for the young man to take a seat in a chair as he sank down into the sofa. Surely the girls would be home soon.

"Perhaps you're wondering how I know these things. I believe you have a student named Lissa Randall. She was very helpful—gave me all kinds of information."

Lissa! Isn't she upstairs?

Silvano Rossi produced another piece of paper. "I've also been in touch with your broker, Mr. Ted Draper, about that foundation."

Ev felt trapped.

Lord, you aren't surprised. You aren't trapped. Give me wisdom to know what to say.

He got up a little shakily. "I'm going to get a glass of water. Can I get you anything, Mr. Rossi?"

"Water would be fine."

His vision blurred again as he made his way into the kitchen.

Get your medication!

But the tablets were back in the bedroom. No way he could make it that far. Hands shaking, Ev took two small glasses from the cabinet and filled them with water. He jostled half of the contents onto the rug before setting one glass in front of Silvano. The young man didn't even look up when Ev set his glass on the end table so forcefully that it made a hard thud and the water soaked his hand. He collapsed onto the couch.

Rossi had set a tape recorder on the coffee table. He switched it on and began firing questions. Where was Ev from originally? When did he and Annie meet? When did he decide to use his wife as a cover-up for his career as a novelist? Why did he start the driving school? How did Eddy Clouse discover his work? What about the foundation—why was it so secretive? Perhaps there was something illegal involved?

Why isn't Annie here? She knew how to answer these questions. He had never been good at stopping an aggressive reporter. The pain was increasing, shooting down his arm. He needed to get his tablets.

"Why all the secrecy, Mr. MacAllister? I just don't get it."

"Fame is a strange bedfellow, Mr. Rossi. Pretty soon everyone wants a piece of you, and if they can't get it nicely, they'll resort to all kinds of foolery to get it. You must understand that—here you want a piece of my fame too. Foolery! Shame on you!" He took another deep breath, tried to calm his racing heart. "My pen name and my wife's participation and the foundation are merely precautions to protect those I love, nothing illegal. All we're trying to do is to protect our privacy. Can't you understand that we don't want or need the attention? I'm doing what I was created to do, and that is enough."

Silvano looked thoughtful and stopped writing. "So then, tell me, Mr. MacAllister. What do you want, if it isn't fame and power and money?"

"For me to live is Christ, and to die is gain."

"Is that from the Bible?"

"Yes."

Silvano scribbled on his notepad. "I heard you are very religious."

"I'm not religious. I have a living faith in a living person, Jesus Christ.

And I believe I'm called to touch lives one at a time, as they come to me, as He brings them to me. I do my best to help, in the fullness of the word, in all ways. And perhaps my books go out to thousands, but they are read by individuals, and they too touch lives one at a time. But ultimately, Christ is the One who convinces each of us of our need to change and who has the power to change us. I am a simple worker. I do not want notoriety. I have no use for it."

Something in Silvano Rossi's demeanor changed. The hungry reporter leaned forward, and for the first time there was a hint of authenticity about him. "But, sir, from what I understand of your religion, Jesus Christ uses a book to touch lives one at a time, as you put it. Isn't the Bible called the written Word? Jesus certainly didn't refuse notoriety. That book is about Him, and it happens to be the bestseller of all time."

"Please don't compare me to Almighty God, young man. You just don't get it, do you?" Ev's voice rose, and he winced at his constricting heart.

The dizziness returned. Ev needed to get rid of this man, needed to lie down. He leaned over and whispered, "Mr. Rossi, if the day comes when I feel it would be for the greater good for my readers to know who I am, I can assure you I will tell them. In the meantime, I would prefer to remain anonymous." He took two shallow breaths and squeezed his eyes closed as the pain shot through him.

———

Lissa awoke, groggy and disoriented. She gazed around the bedroom and remembered that she was at the MacAllisters' house. Had she heard a doorbell? She turned over, dozed off and on, then finally got up and splashed water on her face. The house seemed quiet, although she thought she distinguished soft voices coming from downstairs. She pulled on her jeans, deeply thankful for her nap. How long had she slept?

She came into the upstairs hallway and recognized Mr. MacAllister's voice, though it sounded gravelly and distant . . . and distressed.

"I'm afraid that is no longer possible," said another very familiar voice.

It took Lissa only a moment to place it. Silvano!

She raced down the stairs and found Silvano sitting across from Mr. MacAllister in the den. A tape recorder was on the coffee table. She marched over to Silvano and blurted out, "Why are you here?"

He gave her a syrupy smile. "For my interview, of course."

"You creep."

"It's all right, Lissa," Mr. MacAllister whispered. "Please have a seat with your friend."

"Silvano's not my friend! He's a name-dropping, good-for-nothing creep!" Then she saw how Mr. MacAllister was sitting, almost sinking into the couch, his complexion ashen. He was bracing himself with one arm.

"Mr. MacAllister, what's the matter? Something's the matter!" To Silvano she spat, "What have you done to him? Can't you see he's ill?" She hurried to the older man's side. "Help me, Silvano! Help me get him to his bed."

Silvano got up quickly. Supporting the older man on either side, they led him into the back of the house, past his office to his bedroom.

"Where's Annie?" Lissa asked. "Where are the others?"

"Just out for a while. They'll be back soon." Mr. MacAllister lay down on the bed, his breath irregular. "Lissa, I need you to get me my medication."

"Where is it?"

"In the bathroom there."

"I'll get him some water," Silvano said, and hurried back to the den.

The sink was lined with brown prescription bottles. Lissa grabbed them all and brought them back to the bed. "Which one?"

"Nitroglycerin."

Her hands shook as she fumbled with the white plastic top. She got it opened and handed the bottle to him. He took out one pill and slipped it under his tongue.

"Thank you, Lissa. Thank you."

Silvano set the glass on the bedside table and left the room as Lissa sank to her knees by the old man's side. His eyes were closed.

"Are you all right? Should I call the ambulance?"

"No, no, dear. I'll just rest for a while. I'll be fine. The pills always work their magic." His voice was barely audible. "Just let me rest."

Lissa tiptoed out of the room, closed the door, and walked to the den, where Silvano was pacing back and forth. In a fury she turned on him. "Are you satisfied? Did you get what you wanted? Couldn't you see he was ill?" She was shaking in her anger. "Get out of here, Silvano! I never want to see you again!" She marched to the front door and opened it.

Silvano followed and grabbed her arm. "Listen to me, Lissa."

"No! I hate you! Let go of me!"

He obeyed. "Lissa, I'm sorry I've upset you. I'll leave you alone, I promise, but first will you please just listen to me for a minute? I know you don't trust me. But I have been around a lot of writers. Mr. MacAllister wants his religious message to get out to people. Here's an author with good intentions, a message capable of transforming lives. He and I were just talking about this when you came downstairs. I think he was beginning to understand the positive side of recognition. We can make him bigger, more important. Surely you see that would be good, Lissa."

As he spoke, it registered: Silvano had figured it out—that Annie was not S. A. Green. And it was her fault. She had led him to the writer.

"Just go away, Silvano. You're going to kill him. Leave."

"Lissa, every writer wants more readers, more recognition, more money. I've never met one who said he was making too much or he felt he had too many readers."

"Mr. MacAllister is different. He doesn't care. If he's stayed incognito for so many years, doesn't that prove he doesn't care?"

"He was afraid of fame. That's not the same as not caring. And, Lissa, he has made a bundle of money, and he wants to keep making it."

"How do you know?"

"I've met with his stockbroker. I don't know what he does with the money, but I know he is afraid of losing any of it. And he's old, Lissa. For heaven's sake, he won't be writing forever. Whatever he needed anonymity for in the past, it's over. I'm ready to help him realize his potential. He has a great message. He can reach more readers. It's a win-win situation, Lissa."

Lissa imagined the MacAllisters on the front porch, the steady stream of driving students coming in and out, drinking lemonade, trading stories, gaining confidence.

"His whole life is about doing good. His whole life is a message. He doesn't need anything else. Just leave him alone. Please, Silvano, don't publish your story."

"Lissa, you can't understand. You grew up around wealth, luxury. I doubt you've ever wondered where your next meal was coming from or if you'd have a roof over your head in a week. But that was my life. My family is poor, and I am their hope. They sent me to America for reasons you can't understand, and you can't understand the type of pressure I'm under.

"I'm not doing anything illegal. I'm a sleuth, and I've got a scoop and a magazine willing to pay me handsomely for it. I need the money for my family. You've got to believe me."

"I don't believe you! I don't believe anything you say."

Silvano went back into the den, grabbing his tape recorder and brief-case. "I'll go. But you're making a big mistake. You'll see soon enough, Lissa, that I was right."

He slammed the door. She leaned against it, closed her eyes, and slid down onto the floor.

The voice whispered distinctly, *"All your fault."*

CHAPTER TWENTY-FIVE

~

Nursing a gin and tonic at the club, Ted sat across from Jerry Steinman. This was no friendly business meeting. He had interrupted Jerry's golf game on a perfect fall Saturday afternoon.

Jerry took off his glasses, put them back on, took them off again. He carefully hid his emotions, which frightened Ted more than having him explode. At last he spoke. "I am really disappointed in you, Ted. You turned your back on all of my advice. Not only have you ruined your reputation, you've caused two of my best clients great harm. I trusted you, Ted. I assured them you would do them right. What were you thinking?"

Ted's mouth was dry, and the gin and tonic did not help at all. He cleared his throat and squeaked out, "China, sir. I was trying to help my marriage with a promise of a trip to China with the Million Dollar Club."

"Greed."

"Yes, sir. Greed. For those I love."

Jerry was looking through a file of papers, reciting Ted's grievances as if he were reading the ticker tape at the office. "You've been suspended from the firm pending investigation of the facts. From what you've told me, it won't take much investigation. Your actions were completely illegal: you messed up on discretion, you forged a client's signature, you started a ghost account, you traded illegal options." He set down the file. "Wow, Ted. You've screwed up royally."

"I know, sir."

Jerry clenched and unclenched his jaw, head down, studying the file. "Dr. Kaufman is asking for full restitution. He realizes that some of his losses were no fault of yours—a consequence of Black Monday. But the rest, the 1.2 million or whatever it is, will have to come from your account."

Ted felt the perspiration break out on his neck. "I don't have that kind of money in my account. What do I do?"

"You write a letter to Dr. Kaufman; you crawl and beg forgiveness and make up his losses. Sell your house, your car—your wife's wedding ring, if that's what it takes—but you make it right. And then you wait to see what the arbitration board decides."

Ted swallowed several times. Chills replaced the numbness. "And what about Miss Green?"

"I'm actually meeting with Miss Green early next week. I wouldn't expect anything but a trip to hell from her." Jerry shook his head. "And it's exactly what you deserve, Ted. I'm sorry to say it, but it's true. A trip to hell and back."

They both stood. Ted held out his hand and thought for a moment that Jerry was going to refuse to shake it. Eventually, the retired broker took his hand and gripped it fiercely.

"You're making me come out of retirement, Ted. I'd lock you up myself, but I don't need to. The authorities will see that you get what you deserve. Good-bye, Ted."

Ted watched the older man leave and thought to himself, *There goes my future. He gave me the biggest break of my career, and I threw it away.*

He had failed everyone—his firm, his clients, his mentor. His trusted mentor, and friend too. And boy, could he use a friend right now.

He remembered reading a passage from that darn novel and being thankful they were simply words written on a page. The little girl—Toni or Tonya or something—stood with her hands on her hips and told her brother that someday the bad guys were going to get caught. He just needed to wait and see.

Boy, was she right, and he was the guilty party.

I am not a bad guy! Ted argued in his mind.

Then he gave a pitiful chuckle. Who was he fooling? He was a lousy, cheating, thieving crook.

He waited for the porter to get his car out of valet parking, handed the man a dollar bill, and got in the Mercedes. His whole life was evaporating. Should he pray? Or fight? Surely, surely he could fight.

Sell your wife's wedding ring, if that's what it takes.

He had to go home and tell Lin Su.

He *couldn't* tell Lin Su. Not yet.

———

Ev knew what was happening. It had come on him slowly this time—the cold sweat, the loss of breath, the gradual pain in his chest, arms, and jaw. The first two heart attacks had been fast. Ever since then, he had felt them coming and prevented them with the nitroglycerin. But this time he had waited too long, and the pill only lessened the pain momentarily. Now it was back. The pressure. He pulled himself up on the bed, wincing as the pain increased. He needed to get to the phone and dial those three little numbers: 9-1-1. He stood up, and the nausea washed over him.

"Lissa!" he called out. It was barely more than a whisper, and he fell back onto the bed.

Forgive me, Father. I'm a stubborn old man. Forgive me. I give you my books again. Thy will be done, even if it means notoriety. Or death. Thy will be done.

But please don't take me in front of Lissa.

———

Silvano knew he shouldn't gloat, but he couldn't help himself. In that brief interview he had gotten all he needed: confirmation of the true identity of S. A. Green and a photo of the old man standing on the porch, appearing surprised. It was perfect! The article was going to be worth more than he had originally calculated.

You did it, Silvo! You did it! Auguri!

Silvano turned over the events of the day again and again. He had to admit it. Lissa was right: the guy was for real, an old man with a head of silver hair to lend authenticity to the rumor of S. A. Green's wisdom. An old man who taught teenagers to drive, for goodness' sake!

Silvano felt the adrenaline pump in his ears. Releasing this story would be a major breakthrough for the publishing house. He could imagine the sales climbing as customers scrambled to get copies of the other books by S. A. Green. They'd reprint the whole lot of them and give them glossy new covers with an even better literary slant.

And after his story broke, Silvano would grant interviews with other newspapers and magazines. Heck, he'd heard that TV stations even offered fancy trips for good stories. Maybe the story would be good enough for his whole family to get a one-way ticket to the States! He would make a name for himself.

Yes, Eddy Clouse would be furious and would probably fire him. But Eddy wouldn't snub off the profits, and sooner or later he would acknowledge that Silvano had been right. The end did justify the means.

I'll quit before he fires me. I'll find another publishing house that will be happy to have me.

Even as he congratulated himself, he heard Ev MacAllister's voice saying, *I do not want notoriety. I have no use for it.*

Blasted novelist! He hated the way the man and his message got to him, the words yanking on his heart like a tug-of-war between his mind and the mind of S. A. Green. Sure, he could give the old man a good argument—prove to him the worth of renown. He had even used the Bible to make his point—now that was a stroke of genius! But was it really for the best? Every one of the man's books had gotten under his skin.

He thought of Stella Ann Green—Annie MacAllister—tough, wizened, shrewd, and according to Lissa, tender at the core. He liked her a lot, what he knew of her. He liked them both. Now that he'd met the old man, the famous recluse, the writings meant even more. Lissa was right again: he was just an old man who wanted to live a simple life, protect those he loved, and help hurting kids.

Silvano tried to shake the image of Ev MacAllister's pale, pain-stricken face. He was sorry for the old man's health. But it wasn't his fault.

He was sorry he'd dragged Lissa into this, sorry for the way he had left her at the house. But again, it wasn't his fault.

Sometimes the best thing you can do is admit that you've failed, and start over. Repair, forgive, start over.

Why did he keep hearing lines from that book!

He was not about to start over. Fifteen years of living in the States away from family was finally going to pay off.

Lissa had no idea of the pressure, month after month. Sometimes he wondered if his family even cared about him, or if all they cared about was the money. He pushed the thought away. Of course they cared! They loved him, and he was their savior! No longer would he send his mother measly checks for several hundred dollars. Soon he would be sending her thousands! With that money, she could buy the plane tickets—or maybe a TV station would *give* him tickets—and move them all to Atlanta, to live with his aunt until they could get started on their own. Legal immigrants. No more renting from that gang of thieves. And finally he could hush the voice that said, *If you don't achieve, you will be responsible for your whole family's fall into ruin.*

Silvano turned onto Fourth Avenue, rolling down the windows. Leave it to Chattanooga to provide seventy-degree weather in November. He was going to reward himself with a Frosty from Wendy's. He glanced over to the passenger seat, where pages of notes lay beside his camera. In his rush to leave the house, he had not even had time to put them in the briefcase. At a traffic light, a gust of wind swept through the car, lifted one of the sheets of paper, and blew it out the window. Silvano watched, mesmerized for a moment as it floated and twisted with the force of the wind before settling on the pavement.

Sometimes the best thing you can do is admit that you've failed, and start over.

"I haven't failed! I've won! Won!" He quickly put on the emergency blinkers, pulled to a stop, jumped out of the car, and hopped over a low metal railing, retrieving the paper. Back in the car, Silvano set the heavy camera on top of the stack of papers. Amazing how his heart had fluttered at the thought of losing the precious material.

He would do what he had to do! He would!

———

Lissa did not know how long she sat with her back against the front door. No tears, her mouth dry, defeated. The accusations bombarded her.

Wasn't it enough, God, that I lost my mother? Now I've lost Caleb and my father and my friendship with Silvano. I don't even know if I can trust the MacAllisters. And worse, because of me, Silvano is going to write an article and tell the whole world about S. A. Green, and that is going to kill Mr. MacAllister. He's going to die.

The last thought halted the pity party. She jumped up and hurried back into the bedroom to check on him. He was sitting on the side of the bed and clutching his heart.

"I think I need to get to the hospital, Lissa. I'm sorry."

Her face drained of color. "The hospital?"

He nodded. "My old heart." He let out a breath. "You've got to call 9-1-1—get the ambulance."

Lissa tried to remember what she'd read about surviving a heart attack. She ran to the office and dialed 9-1-1. When the operator came on the line, she said, "Please, send paramedics and an ambulance to 22 Sunrise Road in Fort Oglethorpe. An old man is having a heart attack!"

The emergency operator relayed the news, then came back on the line.

"What do I do? Tell me what to do," Lissa pleaded.

"Does he have medicine?"

"Yes. I gave him nitroglycerin about ten minutes ago. I don't think it's working."

"Give him another pill, and aspirin if he has it. Stay with him."

Lissa hung up the phone and ran back to the bedroom. A glass of water and the bottle filled with nitroglycerin pills sat beside the bed. "They said to take another one of these, Mr. MacAllister," she said, then went into the bathroom and found a bottle of aspirin. She held the glass to his mouth as he swallowed the pills and then lay down. "Oh, Mr. MacAllister, where's Annie?"

"I'm sure she'll be back soon," he rasped.

"The ambulance is on the way. It'll be here in five minutes."

People died in five minutes.

I will not let you fail.

She was back on her knees, saying, "I'm so sorry, Mr. MacAllister. It's all my fault that Silvano found out. I didn't know what he was trying to do. I told him too much and he guessed the truth, and now . . . I don't know what I'll do if something happens to you."

Mr. MacAllister reached over and covered Lissa's hand with his own. It felt clammy. "Lissa, I'm a stubborn old man." With that he closed his eyes and sank further down in bed. He tried to pronounce another word, but couldn't get it out.

"Don't talk. It's okay. The ambulance will be here soon."

"I . . . should have stopped . . . teaching a few years back. If something happens to me, it's my fault. You understand, Lissa . . . my fault! Not yours."

She clutched his hand, and the words came automatically. "God, I don't know you, but Mr. MacAllister does, and he loves you and he's spent his whole life helping kids. So please, please, don't let him die. I don't know what else to say. Please, God. Don't let him die." Then she bent over and kissed him on the forehead.

From far away, a siren screamed.

Lissa ran out of the house, feeling suddenly very alive; her mind was not on anger or failure. She was motivated by fear and something else. Love.

I love this old man. I swear I do.

The flashing lights of the ambulance came in view as the red and white vehicle approached the house. She rushed outside to meet the men in their white coats. They lifted a gurney—amazingly similar to what she'd seen on TV—out of the back of the ambulance. In a flurry of words she directed them up the porch steps and back to the bedroom. From the hall, she watched them transfer Mr. MacAllister to the gurney, guide it out the front door and down the porch steps into the back of the ambulance.

One of the medics said, "We're taking him to Hutcheson Medical Center."

The door slammed and the ambulance sped off, leaving Lissa standing in the driveway in a state of shock. With the squealing of the siren in the background, she heard the voice.

Your fault.

Then she heard another voice loud and clear in her mind, the voice that she had heard earlier that morning on the road, the voice of assurance, of peace, of help, a voice traveling with her along this unfamiliar road, a heartbreaking journey.

Life is not random, Lissa. It is not your fault.

––––––

When Katy Lynn turned into the driveway, the young girl she had practically run into earlier was sitting on the porch steps. It looked as if she was crying.

Before Katy Lynn could park the car, the girl ran over to her. "It's your father!"

"What? What happened to my father?"

"He had a heart attack. They've taken him to the hospital."

"What?"

The girl's words tumbled out in one long breath of explanation. "Your mother and daughter and sister left. A man came to do an interview and I was upstairs sleeping and the man upset your father and when I came down, I could tell he wasn't well and he went to lie down and took the pill—you know, nitroglycerin—and he said he'd be fine because the pill always worked. But when I checked on him a few minutes later, he was having an attack and I called 9-1-1 and they came—just about five minutes ago. They took him to Hutcheson. I'm so sorry. I didn't know what to do. I didn't know who to call, so I just waited here."

Katy Lynn took in the barrage of news with a gulp. "How bad was he?"

"I think he was in a lot of pain, and he said the pill didn't work, and then it all happened so fast."

Katy Lynn ran into the house and scribbled a note to her mother, leaving it on the kitchen counter. "I've got to get to the hospital."

"Can I come with you?"

"Of course."

Katy Lynn knew the way to the hospital, just down the street. She kept glancing over at the girl in the passenger seat who looked so much like Aunt Tate.

The girl continued babbling. "It was my fault that the reporter came and started asking him questions. I didn't mean to tell Silvano—but he was looking for S. A. Green. I guess he just pushed his way into the house and started asking questions, and by the time I got there, Mr. MacAllister was in pain. . . .

"But it's like he knew what was going to happen ahead of time. He probably even expected to have a heart attack. He's like a prophet or Jesus or something. He knows things, and he's been there for me, both your father and your mother have been there for me. . . .

"I had no idea he was that famous author, but I knew he was someone important—like one of those prophets in the Bible that no one really listens to but they should have."

Katy Lynn tried to make sense of this young woman's running commentary. Prophet. Yes, how many times had she heard that word used about her father, sometimes as a joke and sometimes whispered with a mixture of awe and respect. A prophet no one listened to. She certainly hadn't listened.

"He's not a prophet—he's just really religious."

"Yeah. The kind of religious where you can tell it means something. Real. Your mom's that way too. They believe what the Bible says. They believe prayer works."

"Yep! You've got him figured out all right." Katy Lynn surprised herself with her clipped tone.

"You don't like him very much, do you?"

Katy Lynn shrugged. "Let's just say we haven't gotten along well for many years."

"My dad and I aren't getting along either. It's horrible. We can't talk about anything. It's weird, though. I can talk to your father. I can tell he cares."

He cares about everyone else.

Katy Lynn was perspiring. The wheels of her car squealed as she braked too quickly and turned onto the road leading to Hutcheson Medical Center.

He cares about me too.

"I've been taking driving lessons from him for about six weeks. And it's helping. At least I think it is. Actually, my life is such a mess right now, but things he says make sense and . . . and I don't know. I think eventually I'll get better."

The girl suddenly stopped talking. Then she wrinkled her brow and said, "By the way, my name is Lissa.

"I'm Katy Lynn. I'm glad to meet you, Lissa." Without thinking, she added, "You look so much like my dad's little sister, it's uncanny."

"I know. He told me. I think it must be hard for him to see me."

Katy Lynn parked the car in the hospital lot.

As they hurried into the emergency room entrance, Lissa said, "I am so afraid he is going to die. I don't know what I'll do if your father dies."

Katy Lynn blinked back tears. *I don't know what I'll do either.*

———

Silvano couldn't believe his eyes. Annie or Stella or whatever she called herself was walking out of Wendy's with two other women—one around thirty and the other a teen.

Fantastico! This was divine intervention. The Blessed Virgin was giving him more information for the article! Impulsively, he grabbed his camera and shot a string of pictures from the car.

The three women got into a red Buick and took off. Forget the Frosty. He was going after them!

Silvano followed at a safe distance, retracing his path back to the old house. He parked out of sight down the hill and crept out on foot. The yellow Camaro was still parked in the driveway beside the Buick, Impala and Ford. The three women were laughing as they went into the house. He'd wait a few minutes before making one last attempt to get fresh information for the article.

The front door had barely closed when it opened again, and all three came rushing out and jumped back into the car. From the expression on their faces, he knew they'd received bad news. *Something happened to the old man.*

Silvano ran back to his car and pulled out behind the Buick. He trailed the car as it sped through Fort Oglethorpe and eventually turned into the emergency room entrance to Hutcheson Medical Center.

Oh, great! I sure hope the old man doesn't die! That's not the angle I need for this story. Not yet. I need him to be alive and well.

————

Waiting rooms made bonding places. At least Lissa felt that way. She felt buoyed up by these women. They had not condemned her, even when she tried to explain about her relationship to Silvano Rossi, even when she showed them the manuscript that she had brought with her to the hospital as proof of Silvano's scheming.

Annie kept squeezing her hand and saying over and over, "You saved my Ev. If you hadn't been there, he would not have had a chance."

Not that his chances were very high right now.

Lissa observed carefully how Annie handled this crisis, par for the course of how she seemed to handle the rest of her life—with pure practicality and rock-solid faith.

"I told him over and over to retire. I think he was afraid that if he retired he would dry up, and the stories would not be there either. He needed both jobs—the one with young people and the one hidden away writing. He was like an owl coming out of his solitude in the late afternoons to teach the kids."

Sitting in the metal-backed chairs of the emergency room, the four MacAllister women took turns explaining to Lissa about Ev and Annie's background and why they had chosen anonymity. Exchanging stories helped pass the time as the clock ticked interminably. The doctor's words clicked interminably also: massive heart attack, bypass surgery, critical condition.

For a few hours Lissa actually felt she belonged in this family with no-nonsense Annie and fragile Janelle and hurt Katy Lynn and honest Gina. For one brief evening, she was not an only child with a distant father. She had a sister and a mother and aunts. She soaked up the company of these strong yet scared women, a pieced-back-together family. Tragedy made her privy to their secrets—a little boy taken, a marriage breaking up, a confused daughter trying to find her place in the midst of divorce.

The sun set, and the wait continued. A little trash can, filled with empty paper cups that had previously held coffee, testified to the passing hours. Janelle paced back and forth, Gina tried to read some woman's magazine, and Katy Lynn leaned against the wall and stared at the clock. Annie came from down the hall where she had inquired again at the nurses' station.

"Nothing new yet," she said with a shake of the head. She sat down in a metal chair and motioned for the others to do the same. Abruptly she said, "Girls, I need to tell you about a foundation that your father and I started years ago. And I need your help."

Katy Lynn and Janelle exchanged blank looks.

"It was started in memory of Tate. Set up with the royalties from your father's books."

Tate. The girl I look like, the girl who died in a car wreck.

"Your father told you about developing the driving school after Tate's death—and after his conversion. It never made much money, but it kept us young and motivated and doing what God called us to do.

"But the novels made a lot of money. We used a small percentage of the royalties for salary—never more than five or ten percent. The rest we put into a foundation. This was another of Ev's dreams, using his royalties to help others. He called it 'the circle of the body of Christ.' Giving what we received in abundance to meet the needs of others so that they in turn could do the same when they had extra.

"Have you heard of the Stash Green Cash Foundation?"

Janelle gave a sharp cry. "It's the way we stay in France—the gifts we receive from it cover almost a third of our salary. We were told it was from a donor in Chicago who wanted to remain anonymous. . . . But . . . why 'Stash'?"

"Stash for Stella and Ashton, Green for my mother's maiden name. The royalties go into this foundation at Goldberg, Finch and Dodge, and then once a year—on the anniversary of Tate's death—I write a check and send the interest to Switzerland. From that account I send the money out to the various charitable organizations."

"Brian and I have probably written a hundred thank-you notes to that lady through the years, addressed to that Chicago post office box. I've sent gifts! Chocolates, nougats, books on France."

Annie was smiling. "We received them all. Your father knew about every kind gesture."

"But why wouldn't he tell us?" Janelle looked as if she was going to cry.

"How would he be able to explain where the money came from? You knew we weren't making much with the driving school." Annie shrugged. "Perhaps we were wrong. We were trying to do what was best. And as for the foundation, your father uses it to support a number of missions and literary endeavors. But his biggest contribution is to Good Shepherd Rehabilitation Center. He helped start it back in the early seventies."

"You're kidding! The rehab center you all visited every month?" Katy Lynn asked.

"Yeah, I remember going there with him when I was in high school," Janelle said.

I went by there with him last week.

"That's cool—Granddad helped start a rehab center. What's it for?"

"Para- and quadriplegics—mainly victims of accidents. Many of the patients are quite young."

Gina seemed delighted with this news. "Wow! My grandfather is cool. He does all this stuff in secret. I mean, how cool is that? It's radical!"

Annie nodded. "Yes, Gina. That's the right word for him, stubborn old man." She stood up again and walked over to a vending machine. "The rehab center was just one more part of his dream. The foundation provides a large part of its budget."

"So does Granddad feel a lot of pressure to write so he can keep up the money in the foundation?"

"No, Gina, he writes because he was born to write, because he is at his best when he is creating stories. That he's made a lot of money from doing what he was gifted to do is a continual surprise to him. He gets a kick out of it. And he gets an even bigger kick out of giving most of his money away."

Gina accepted that information as if she'd just been told that the sum total of the foundation was being given to her. "That is so cool. And we have to keep the secret—Granddad told me—no one knows he's S. A. Green. Right, Grandmom?"

"No one except those of us in this room. Even Eddy Clouse, the publisher, thinks that Stella—that's me—pens these tales. It was complicated. We wanted to leave our past behind and let the Lord direct. Granddad told you that part of the story.

"But another part of it was that Ev was born with a weak heart. Two scares when he was quite young were enough to convince both of us that he didn't need any of the business pressure. So I became his voice for the books. I answered the phone, talked with the publisher, and generally became a royal pain in the bottom to anyone who tried to get information out of me. I refused interviews. So the mystery of S. A. Green was born and nourished throughout the years.

"No one has ever traced S. A. Green back to the young author Ashton Mack, who was such a hit in 1948. And no one guessed the real identity of S. A. Green. At least not until this man Silvano sent me that disturbing letter. And now, unfortunately, it looks like he's gotten what he wanted. The truth."

Katy Lynn asked, "What else do you know about this man, Lissa?"

Lissa sat up, startled to be addressed. "Um, he's an assistant editor with your publisher—Youngblood. We met several years ago at a bookstore in Atlanta, and then I ran into him again about a month ago, and we started seeing each other." She shrugged. "I kinda liked him. But it was stupid of me to trust him. He's an opportunist. He was determined to figure out the mystery of S. A. Green."

She fiddled with a button on her cardigan. "It's my fault that he succeeded. I swear I didn't mean to tell him things. It was just so weird, so unbelievably weird that I happened to be taking driving lessons from the man he was looking for." Lissa looked over at Annie. "It's like you and Mr. MacAllister have been saying—that things aren't random."

Annie smiled back. There was no accusation in her eyes.

"He even took pictures of you, Annie, and tape-recorded your meeting with the publisher. And he came to the house today while you were out and questioned Mr. MacAllister." Lissa ran her fingers through her hair. "It's all my fault, but I didn't know! I was coming this morning to warn you about

Silvano, but everything happened at once. Now he has the information, and he's going to write the article and sell it to a magazine." Lissa let out a little sob. "And he caused Mr. MacAllister to have a heart attack!"

Annie took Lissa firmly by her good shoulder. "This is not your fault, Lissa. And it's not that Italian's fault either. Ev was born with a weak heart, and he's known for a long time that it was giving out. There have been many, many circumstances lately that have added stress to his life. We're not here to throw around blame. You understand me?"

Lissa nodded reluctantly.

Annie addressed her daughters. "I'm also having questions about my new stockbroker. Jerry Steinman has been a faithful friend and astute broker for almost thirty years. He recently retired and placed my account with a young man named Ted Draper. I met this man, and he seemed very competent and bright, but I'm afraid he's gotten into something way over his head. Somehow the foundation has lost quite a bit of money. Mr. Draper says it's related to Black Monday, but my most recent statements show a lot of strange trading. I'm meeting with Jerry on Monday. If these considerable losses are legit, I don't know what this means for the rehab center."

Katy Lynn suddenly perked up and seemed ready for a fight. "Mom, you need to get a lawyer. In fact, I know someone who could be just right. Get your statements together, and he'll dig up all the dirt on both of these men."

"Mom's right, Grandmom. Let her help you. She knows lots of good lawyers."

Lissa had to ask the next question. "What will happen if Silvano writes that article?"

"We'll just have to deal with it." Annie was pure practicality again.

But Lissa was not convinced. "And when Mr. MacAllister finds out that the world knows who he is?"

Annie looked away and shrugged, biting her lip. Finally she turned around. One tear slid down her cheek. "It'll kill him. If the heart attack doesn't take him first, that would do it. I'm really afraid it would."

Lissa gritted her teeth. *Then I've got to make sure that Silvano never writes that article.*

CHAPTER TWENTY-SIX

SATURDAY, NOVEMBER 7
EVENING

He had done it, told Lin Su the whole sordid tale in one fifteen-minute monologue after they put Sammy and LeeAnne to bed. At first she had been speechless, but as the details continued, her lovely Asian face hardened, her eyes narrowed, and then she started yelling.

"Stop it! I don't want to hear any more. What have you done, Ted?" She grabbed his shirt, yanked him hard several times. "Here I was thinking you were honestly working hard to provide, and I find out I'm married to a criminal! A thief! I don't know what to say!"

"Honey, you're going to wake the kids."

"Let them wake up! Our lives are collapsing! They might as well know it." She stalked out of the house at eight thirty, and an hour later she had not returned.

Ted walked into LeeAnne's room and placed his hand on her back as she slept. Then he went across the hall and sat on the foot of Sammy's bed and stared numbly at his son. What would keep Lin Su from throwing him out of the house, demanding that he leave and never come back?

Dear God, please. I don't want to lose my wife and kids.

Ted dozed off with his head resting on the wall beside Sammy's bed. He awoke with a jerk to the sound of the front door opening and slamming shut. This was going to be even worse than he'd imagined.

He came out of Sammy's room into the den and wondered if Lin Su could see how much his hands were shaking.

Her eyes were red from crying, but they were also smoldering. "How could you do this, Ted? You're going to be fired! They'll put you in jail!"

She marched into the kitchen and leaned over the sink, threw water on her face, and looked up at him. "They'll put you in jail, Ted, because that is exactly where you deserve to be."

Her hands began to shake slightly, then she brushed them over her face. "This is a nightmare. We're going to lose everything!"

"We'll still have each other."

It was absolutely the wrong thing to say, but it slipped out of his mouth. He waited for her to crush him with her words. He waited for her to storm out of the house again and never come back.

Instead, she just stared at him, looking almost, but not quite, fragile.

She shook her head. "No, Ted. I don't have you. You're someone I don't know, a stranger . . . a, a thief."

Ted's shoulders sagged, and he felt tears behind his eyes. Trembling, he reached for Lin Su. She backed away, and the distrust in her eyes momentarily took his breath away. He had to say something. "I'm so sorry, Lin Su. I wanted so much to give you the best. I was wrong—horribly wrong, but I swear it was because I love you. I love you and the kids." His whole body began to shake and then came real gut-wrenching sobs, something that had never in his life happened before.

Lin Su looked surprised, then almost sympathetic, and then hard. Her face held that same grit and determination that had attracted and scared him all those years ago.

"I don't know, Ted. I don't know what to do. I need time. We need time."

He understood.

He went into their bedroom and began to place his clothes in a suitcase. Again and again, he went from the closet to his suitcase and back to the closet. His life was on remote control. He took his things into the hall, stopped, and went into LeeAnne's room. He lowered the side of her crib so he could lean over and kiss her on the cheek. "Daddy loves you, LeeAnne."

Then he entered Sammy's room. He leaned over the bars and tousled his son's hair. Sammy squirmed, opened one eye halfway, and then flopped over on his back.

"See ya soon, big guy," Ted whispered.

He left the house, carrying the suitcase, and turned to see Lin Su watching him from the front porch. He raised his hand to wave, then let it fall to his side. He climbed into the Mercedes and drove out of the driveway and down Tuxedo Road, watching his life disappear in the rearview mirror.

In the chapel on the second floor of the hospital, Lissa found Annie on her knees, staring up at the stained-glass window depicting Christ on the cross, arms outstretched, head turned down. Annie was looking up at the colored window, and from the back of the room it seemed to Lissa that this feisty woman had had the life sucked out of her. She was speaking out loud, petitioning or pleading in a voice Lissa had never heard her use.

"Please, Lord, not yet. Not yet."

Lissa wanted to hug the woman, wanted to throw herself on her knees right beside her and promise the world to Almighty God if He would only let Ev MacAllister live. Instead, she stood in the back of the chapel and remembered the voice that had whispered to her as she sat in the Camaro on Highway 157 and her own spontaneous prayer on her knees beside Mr. MacAllister's bed earlier in the day. She wondered if he was right. He had said that God was not surprised by the turn of events, even tragedy. He called God the director, the one who orchestrated life. Exhausted by worry and fear, Lissa did not have the mental capacity at the moment to dig deep into spiritual mysteries. But some day she would.

She tiptoed out of the chapel and rode the elevator down to the cafeteria. She bought a hot chocolate and sat alone at a table. For the first time in hours, she thought about Caleb. Monday morning this new family would load the gelding into a trailer and drive off to Virginia. Then she thought of her father, her cruel words to him and the way she had driven away, recklessly, in anger.

Now, strangely, her anger against him was gone. She saw the horrified look on his face as she had yelled at him and then left him standing in the hall. He had looked afraid. For her.

Lissa, it's dangerous. . . . Lissa, I don't want you riding. It isn't safe.

The thought whispered somewhere in her subconscious: *I need to let him know that I'm okay.*

———

Silvano had drunk way too many cups of coffee in the hospital cafeteria. Each time he had inquired about Mr. MacAllister, the reply had been the same: "Still in surgery." It was time to go home. He would not intrude on the women in the waiting room.

He was surprised to see Lissa come into the cafeteria. He watched her for a full five minutes before deciding to go over to her. When he did, she looked shocked and then furious.

"You really don't have an ounce of inhibition, do you? You force an interview on a man who's having a heart attack, and then you show up at the hospital! Why? Are you hoping he's already dead? Or would that mess up your precious story?"

"You're right. I followed his wife here. But when I realized how bad a shape he was in, I decided against finding the family."

"Oh, you are so gallant."

"Look, Lissa, we've already established the fact that you hate me. I was only going to ask you how Mr. MacAllister is doing. Then I'll go."

"He's doing very poorly. He had a massive heart attack and has been in surgery for hours. Are you satisfied?"

Silvano said nothing.

"Don't you get it, Silvano? Everything you are trying to do is about getting more, more, more. And Ev MacAllister is about less—giving away what he doesn't need, choosing to live on less, sacrificing for people he loves and for people in need, refusing all the glitzy things the world offers." She took a breath. "And all because that old man is so convinced that there is a God and He is in control and that nothing, *nothing* in life is a coincidence. He believes it's all planned and allowed, and if we let Him, this God will take all the horrible things and use them for good."

Lissa looked more shocked by her outburst than Silvano. "You see, I've gotten to know Mr. MacAllister," she continued. "He and Annie live what they believe. They're different, Silvano. A really good kind of different. Keeping their anonymity is a part of that difference.

"So please, please don't publish the story. Just leave him alone. I'm sorry for your family, but surely exposing a kind old man to something he detests isn't worth it. He has good reasons to want to remain anonymous. Let it go." She stood up. "I don't know why all these things are happening right now. All I know is that I believe what Mr. MacAllister says is true. He says that life isn't random and that I shouldn't ignore coincidence in my life. It all means something, Silvano. Something important."

Silvano watched Lissa leave the cafeteria, her arm bandaged but a gutsy determination in her voice. He waited for five minutes, then walked out of the cafeteria, down the steps, and out the door to his car.

———

Janelle expected at any minute for the doctor to step into the waiting room, shattering the night with bad news, just as it had happened two years ago. She turned her eyes back down to the manuscript in her lap. She had felt compelled to take it when the young girl Lissa had offered it to her to help her pass the time.

She was a teenager, sitting in the car with her father. He was throwing in another one of his analogies. "Life is like driving a car, Nelli. You think you have everything figured out. You know how the car works, you are paying attention to the road, minding your own business, when from out of nowhere another car slams into you and you go reeling. . . ."

Yes! Yes, exactly! Life was like that.

Janelle and Brian had followed all the directions from the mission agency. They had gone through every detail of schooling and raising support and studying the culture and learning the language. They had given up so much and were ready, eager for the adventure of their life—reaching out to Muslims in France.

And then, out of nowhere, tragedy! At a church retreat with the Mediterranean gleaming in the background, while the adults sang and worshiped God, while the baby-sitters watched the children, Josh toddled off toward the hotel pool. Teenaged girls laughing and giggling together, chasing the kids in the field and then realizing that one was missing. Rushing frantically to search inside, then behind the hotel, until they found him, a three-year-old floating facedown in a sparkling blue pool.

No time to pray, no time to petition Almighty God. One minute Josh was laughing that cherubic laugh, the next minute Brian was pulling him out of the pool, leaning over that tiny lifeless body, pressing his lips to the little face.

Janelle threw down the manuscript, hurried out of the waiting room, and took the steps down to the ground floor. She ran out into the parking lot, anger seething in her mind. *You let him die, God! You didn't even give me a chance to save him through my prayers. You didn't give me a chance!* She turned her head up to the black sky and stared at the stars. *If only you had given me the chance to choose! I would have given up anything, Lord, to keep Josh here.*

In a flash, the oh-so-familiar Bible verse sprang into her mind. *For God so loved the world that He gave . . .*

The thought struck Janelle like the force of the mistral slapping her face on a windy fall afternoon in Montpellier. God *did* have a choice. He didn't have to let his Son die, yet He chose to. He made the most horrible choice a parent could ever conceive of and allowed His Son to die. That old familiar truth suddenly seemed to Janelle like a revelation as fresh as sheets drying in the breeze. God made His choice out of love for humankind . . . out of love for *her.*

She sank to her knees right there in the parking lot. "That is a love I know nothing about, Lord. My love will cover and protect and save, but your love will give up and sacrifice for something so much bigger. I cannot understand it." She stayed on her knees for a long time, until at last she whispered, "I don't understand. I never will. But I accept. I accept it, Lord."

She felt her Savior's eyes looking down on her, promising to care for her, even in her anger and all that did not make sense in this life.

She thought of something her father used to say: *In God's economy, even those who mourn are blessed.*

———

It was eleven o'clock when Lissa left the hospital with Janelle and Gina. Katy Lynn and Annie had agreed to take the first night watch at the hospital. In silence, with Janelle driving the Buick, the three women rode back to the MacAllister house. As they turned into the driveway, Lissa saw her father's BMW parked there. She braced herself for the onslaught of anger and humiliation.

He was sitting on the porch swing, his face partly turned so that the car's headlights illuminated it. She wondered how long he had been sitting there, waiting to drag her home against her will. She got out of the car and forced her legs to move forward.

He was at her side before she had taken two steps.

"Lissa. Oh, Liss, I was so worried."

But instead of anger, his voice sounded broken. Then she saw his face. There were tears sliding down her dad's pudgy face. He didn't try to hug her, but reached out in a pitiful gesture and brushed her arm.

"I'm sorry." He choked it out. "I never blamed you, Lissa. Of course it was an accident, a horrible accident. And I was afraid. I couldn't bear the thought of losing you too. I thought if I took the horse away, if I convinced you to do something safe and, and normal, then I could protect you."

He hesitated, then said it again. "I wanted to protect you, Lissa. I just didn't know how."

In the silence Lissa remembered the accident she'd had with Caleb years before.

Caleb stumbling before the jump, crashing into the fence, the bright poles splintering and dispersing around them. Caleb's hooves barely missing her face as she was thrown in front of the horse. Staring up into her father's horrified face as he knelt over her, crying, "Lissa! Lissa!" and "Get an ambulance! Somebody get an ambulance!"

She stood facing him now, but what she heard was her mother's voice.

"Lissa, I know you are disappointed that your father isn't here to see you, but you know how nervous he gets. He can't watch his little girl jumping those high fences. He's so proud of you . . . but it's hard for him to watch. . . ."

"The only way I could think to protect you was to forbid you to ride. Lissa, I couldn't bear to lose you and your mother both."

Lissa reached out and placed her hand on her father's shoulder to steady herself. His words came from another dream.

"You're all I have, Liss. You're all I have."

She did not know how he got his wooden arms around her, but when he embraced her, she let her good arm close around his broad back. Over his shoulder, Lissa saw Gina and Janelle standing back by the car.

After a moment she said, "Daddy, this is Mr. and Mrs. MacAllister's daughter Janelle and their granddaughter, Gina."

He nodded with a grim smile, and they exchanged brief greetings. Janelle unlocked the door and went inside, with Gina following her and calling out, "Bye, Lissa."

"Please call me in the morning," Lissa said. "Annie has our number. Let me know how he's doing."

To her father she quickly explained where she'd been.

He seemed dazed. Then her words registered, and he mumbled, "I'm so sorry." He hugged her again. "I thought you had run the car off the mountain. And it would have been all my fault."

All my fault.

"I'm sorry, Daddy. I didn't mean it. Those things I said."

They got in the BMW and drove back to Lookout Mountain in silence.

———

Silvano was driving over eighty on I-75. He wanted to get back to Decatur fast. What a day! What a long day. The old man might die in the night. What would that do to his story? Lessen the impact? Perhaps not, if he wrote the article immediately.

Beloved Anonymous Author Dies. Newest novel published posthumously with a surprising twist—the man behind S. A. Green.

Yes, that could work. He started writing the article in his mind.

But all he could hear was Lissa's voice.

Don't publish that article. Please. Please.

Man, he was tired. He needed more caffeine. He turned off the expressway at a truck stop, went into the little station, and bought himself a cup of coffee.

"I don't suppose you have any espresso?"

The heavy-set man at the cash register laughed. "No, we don't do Italian, mister. That's Rome, *Georgia*, just up the road a piece."

Several truckers laughed with him.

Silvano didn't smile. He got his coffee, grabbed a pack of gum, and paid the cashier. Beside the cash register, a metal rack was filled with paperback novels. Front and middle was *Eastern Crossings*.

What is a book published in 1960 doing on a paperback rack at a truck stop? Silvano glared at the novel.

Enough already! Leave me alone, will you?

Had he said that out loud?

Non ne posso piu! Was he cracking up? Couldn't he get away from S. A. Green?

He's told me I shouldn't ignore coincidence in my life. It means something.

He *was* cracking up.

What did it mean? What in the whole wide world did all of this mean?

———

The news came somewhere around midnight when the doctor met Katy Lynn and Annie in the waiting room. His face was grim as he said, "He's beginning to wake up, but he is very weak. The surgery didn't go as well as we had hoped. I have to tell you it doesn't look good. I think you should come in and see him. But you may only stay a few minutes."

Katy Lynn's fresh tears were completely unplanned. She went to her father's side and took his hand. "Please don't die, Dad, before I get to talk to you. There are so many things we need to say to each other. Please, Daddy."

He did not open his eyes, but acknowledged her hand in his with a squeeze.

Katy Lynn bent down low and whispered, "I love you, Daddy. I love you and forgive you. And I want you to know that I will always be your princess."

Later she slipped into the little chapel, got on her knees as she had seen her father do when she was a child, and prayed, "God. I haven't talked to you in a long, long time. Daddy always used to say that things happen for a reason. Make sense of this, God, and if you could spare us our crazy old father for a few more years, we'd appreciate it."

———

Ev came in and out of consciousness, hearing the whispered voice of his daughter. He tried to answer, but he could not. Instead, he could only listen. Katy Lynn's confession settled on him softly, peacefully. She forgave him. That was enough. He could go now.

When Annie bent down, he smelled the scent of the woman he had loved for forty-four years, the scent of hard work and flowers. She was struggling not to cry, but he could always tell by the way her voice rose a notch and she sniffed too often.

"Please hold on. You can be so stubborn. Won't you be stubborn about staying here, boyfriend? I know you're ready, but I sure would like to have you beside me for a few more years. And the girls would too. Don't worry about anything. Just rest and hold on."

He answered her in his mind.

You always say that, Annie. Are you planning on keeping me around forever? Girlfriend, don't you worry anymore either. Let that young reporter have his story. If we're found out, what does it matter? We had all these good years, girlfriend. All these good years.

He had always heard there was a bright light before death, but he didn't see one.

He was young and proud, surrounded by eager people, friends, fans, report-

ers, *all toasting his success—with literature, with ladies, with life. Adrenaline filled him up and bubbled over and delighted him, like champagne.*

Then the room started spinning, spinning away from him, out of reach.

He was a grown man, an old man. But he was so small, sitting in the lap of the Creator, holding on to Him as Katy Lynn had held to Ev when she was a little girl. They were having a conversation; Almighty God was listening to him as he admitted the truth.

"You know how much I loved the spotlight! I loved it! I'm glad I left it, but you know that deep down I still missed that other life. It's taken me a lifetime to get over myself, hasn't it? I'm so sorry."

And the Father was consoling him, whispering, "You used your gift; you kept your promise; you did a good job. A very good job. Well done. Well done, my child."

Ev felt warm and reassured. He was still crying, but it turned into a deep, burning laughter, a laughter that he felt might go on forever, uncontrollable, spontaneous, sparkling and pure. "Oh, Lord, it was such a small, small sacrifice. It was worth it, worth it, worth it . . ."

There was Tate as a little girl, laughing, giggling. Then Katy Lynn toddled over and then Janelle . . . children, happy children with the sound of laughter singing into his subconscious. And Annie was laughing too. She was spinning around in her blue jeans, her silver hair shining with sunbeams. She could not stop laughing, and as she laughed she kept saying, "Boyfriend, boyfriend, boyfriend . . ."

Words from his own pen drifted into his memory: *When the time comes, you will be ready. You'll be ready to drive off into a whole new world.*

Ev felt his mouth turn upward softly. *I'm ready, Lord.*

EPILOGUE

MONDAY, DECEMBER 21, 1987

Lissa could not stop yawning. The line of people hovering outside of the bookstore continued to grow. When she had arrived at five a.m. the line was already wrapped around the parking lot. Now, at nine, the bookstore had put up rope partitions, and people walked back and forth as if they were waiting for the most popular ride at Disney World. The whole town of Chattanooga must have decided to buy this book for Christmas.

Lissa had driven by herself in her yellow Camaro along East Brow Road and down the winding Ochs Highway to the bottom of the mountain, gotten on I-75, and traveled three miles until she arrived at the exit for this shopping center. She had done it alone, calmly, her new license in her wallet inside her purse.

Thank you, Mr. MacAllister.

Thank You, God.

When at last the bookstore opened and she walked inside, she felt her stomach lurch. Stacks and stacks of hardbound copies of *Driving Lessons* lined the floor.

I miss you, Ev MacAllister.

A flustered store manager was explaining something urgent to his staff. When the salesclerk handed Lissa a copy, she opened it and slowly flipped several pages. She stopped at the dedication page and read, *In memory of my sister, and for my daughters, with all my love.*

She put the book in the back of the yellow Camaro and drove onto I-75 toward Clover Leaf Stables.

———

"I don't suppose you're carrying the new novel by S. A. Green? *Driving Lessons?*"

Evan came from around the counter in The Sixth Declension and shook Silvano's hand. "Are you kidding? We just got in about a hundred copies. Greece and Rome and Latin always make way for S. A. Green." Evan laughed good-naturedly. "I wonder if someday we are going to figure out who that woman is."

Silvano shrugged. "I don't think it really matters, does it? I mean, the message is the same, even if we never see the face."

Evan looked at him carefully. "You're a sly one, Silvano. I don't know if I should trust you." He tossed a copy of the latest edition of *Persona* magazine on the counter beside the cash register. "I think you know a whole lot more than you let on in this article. I think you know who she is."

"Why would you say that, Evan? I think you know me well enough to realize that if I had discovered the true identity of Miss S. A. Green, I wouldn't keep it to myself. I'd tell the whole world and make a bundle of money off of it."

Evan laughed. "*Sì.* That's probably true, my Italian son."

———

Lissa walked into the bookstore still wearing her riding boots and jodhpurs. She greeted Evan and then headed to the back, where Silvano was seated at the little round table.

He felt a little fluttering in his gut, seeing her for the first time in so long. "*Ciao*, Lissa Randall."

"*Ciao*, Silvano Rossi."

"Thanks for showing up. I wasn't sure you'd come."

She sat down beside him. She looked confident and in control. "I never turn down free espresso."

Bella Lissa.

"How'd you get here?"

"In the little Camaro. Alone."

"Fantastico!"

"Yeah. Yeah, it is. I got my license just as soon as they took my cast off. It's the least I could do for Mr. MacAllister."

"I wanted to come to the funeral, but I didn't think it would be appropriate."

"You were right."

"How is Annie doing?"

"Managing—as she always does. Relying on some deep inner strength." She cleared her throat.

"I'm so sorry for all of you."

Lissa stared off toward the shelves of picture books of Rome.

There were so many things he wanted to tell her about all that had happened in the past six weeks.

Go slowly, Silvo.

"Well, Eddy Clouse fired me."

Lissa turned back to face him, relieved, it seemed, to change the subject. "That's exactly what you deserved. Actually, what you *deserved* was a huge kick in the seat of the pants to send you all the way back to Rome."

Now she was Lissa Randall, back in form.

"Thanks for the vote of confidence. I told him everything, you know."

"You only did what was the very least to be expected."

She was not making this easy.

"Did you get another job?"

"I'm working on it. Several promising interviews with big-name publishers—"

She had narrowed her eyes and was shaking her head.

"Okay, I'll level with you. I might have one interview next week. Until then, I'm helping Evan out."

"Now I believe you."

"Did you see the article in *Persona*?" He pointed to the magazine lying on the table.

"Yeah. I read it while I was standing in line for my book this morning. 'An Essay on S. A. What I learned from America's favorite anonymous writer. By Silvano Rossi.' It wasn't bad."

"They paid me for it. Nothing like what I could have made if I'd told them what I really knew." He glanced at her. "The magazine was disappointed at first, but after reading what I wrote, they decided it was worth publishing, even if it wasn't what I had promised." He shrugged. "I'll send the money to Mamma. We'll see if it helps get my family over here."

Finally, Silvano saw Lissa's face soften. She met his eyes.

"So what made you change your mind? Why'd you decide not to tell the world about the MacAllisters?"

"A beautiful woman begged me not to."

Lissa rolled her eyes. "You Romeo wannabe." She looked away quickly.

He wanted to reach for her hand, to squeeze it and tell her everything. But it was not time. "There were a number of very convincing reasons, Lissa. And it was obvious that I needed, as both you and S. A. Green said, to pay attention to coincidence."

She looked at him. "Thank you, Silvano." Now her tone was soft and sincere, and her lovely brown eyes sparkled with kindness.

"It was very strange, Lissa, but all of a sudden, on the way back to Atlanta in the middle of that crazy night, it became very, very clear what I was supposed to do. And then it almost seemed easy. Someday I'll tell you the whole story."

"Someday I'd like to hear it."

"So can I get you an espresso?"

"Of course. Why did you think I stopped by?"

"I was hoping it was to tell me you don't hate me anymore."

"Dream on, Italian."

She laughed, almost seemed at ease, but then she changed the subject abruptly.

"The girls got back from the Latin competition. One of them made it to the finals."

"A trip to Rome."

"Maybe. And I'm starting courses at a community college in January. And filling out applications for a 'real college,' as Daddy says, in the fall. He's thrilled, needless to say."

"*Brava*, Lissa. *Brava*." Once again he was tempted to take her hand. Once again he refrained. His heart was hammering steadily. He toyed with the magazine, got up his courage, and said, "Lissa, do you think there's any way that if I called you up and asked you out to dinner, you might say yes?"

She narrowed her eyes, leaned across the table, and whispered, "I think it wouldn't hurt to try."

———

Down, down, down. Ted reviewed the long list of damages in his mind: separated from his wife and children, living with his parents, the house on the market, the Mercedes sold, Lin Su back at work, his appearance before the arbitration board two days ago. Even now, it made him break out in a cold sweat just to think about it. He wouldn't wish that experience on his worst enemy. He had felt like he was standing in front of them stark naked, trying desperately to find a fig leaf to hide behind, but every question and every remark left him feeling all the more exposed. Exposed! Humiliated! Ruined.

The verdict: fired from Goldberg, Finch and Dodge, his broker's license suspended for two years, and he was responsible to pay back an incredible amount of money that he didn't have.

But even that wasn't the worst. The worst was the court decision: illegal activity, misdemeanor, forgery. Six months in jail.

Lin Su had taken the news with amazing stability. She had found a job, found a baby-sitter to help with LeeAnne and Sammy on the days Ted did not keep them, and found an apartment to lease when the house sold. Lin Su was in control.

Still, his last conversation with her had given him a tiny bit of hope.

"When you get out of jail," she had said, the mistrust less apparent, "I think there will be room for you too."

He'd lost her for now, but there was a glimmer of hope for later.

Now he was on his way to see Stella Green for the third time this month. What more could she take away from him?

Jerry Steinman met him at the entrance to the club and shook his hand briefly. Ted had not expectd to see Jerry again so soon after the last humiliation.

"Hello, Ted. Come with me. She's got a table in a little private room over here."

A room reserved for still more bad news, Ted imagined.

Stella rose when the men entered the room and stuck out her hand. He was always surprised by her powerful handshake. Business as usual. She motioned for them to be seated and picked up a stack of papers.

"Ted, I asked Jerry to come today to be a witness of this conversation. He has been kind enough to devote quite a bit of time to sorting out the mess you left my accounts in. He's also explained in painstaking detail my losses and what I can expect from Goldberg and from you."

Jerry pushed his glasses back on his nose.

Ted cleared his throat. "Miss Green. Please let me say again that I am deeply sorry for my mistakes, for my illegal actions. I take full responsibility for them and intend to restore in time what I have lost through fraud. I—"

"There's no need to grovel, Ted," Stella interrupted him. "You have already given me this little speech." She set the papers down, and a sly grin came to her face.

This is it. What else can she do to me?

"All of that is now in the past. Forgiven. What is in the future, your future, *our* future, is the reason I asked you here today. Jerry has approved."

Ted winced and nodded. The batty old lady was being her enigmatic self.

"Just so we're clear and up front, the Stash Green Cash Foundation—the one you tried to destroy—seems to be doing just fine. The giving will be down, of course, but I'll still be writing a sizeable check to the Swiss account—totally legitimate—at the end of the month. The charities—all of them also legitimate, I might add—have not suffered as much as I feared. By the time you get out of jail . . ." She looked him straight in the eyes.

Ted felt his face redden. She was enjoying rubbing salt in the wound.

". . . I expect the foundation to be stronger than ever. However, I am tired of dealing with all of these things. To put it simply, Jerry has agreed to manage the foundation for me."

Ted glanced at Jerry, who nodded.

Stella continued. "And, Ted, when you are . . . free to work again—next July, I believe—I would like to hire you on as Jerry's consultant. I'll pay you a very modest salary the first year. If you handle things right, I'll double it the next year. And then, if you're still doing things the right way, when you get your license back in two to three years you can start investing again. And perhaps take over the management of the foundation."

Ted wiped his brow with a handkerchief and looked back and forth at Jerry and Stella. "Why in the world would you do this for me, Miss Green?"

"Call me Stella."

He swallowed hard. "Stella." It came out as a squeak.

"Because I knew a man, a fine man, who made some bad mistakes when he was young and kept going down until he hit rock bottom and tasted complete humiliation. But once everything had been taken away . . ." For one brief moment Stella faltered, and a look of vulnerability washed over her face. She recovered quickly. "He came up against himself and had to decide, Am I going to start making good choices? He did change, and went on to live a very worthy life. He started using his mind and his talents for good.

"And I want you to answer those same questions with a yes, Ted Draper. I want to give you another chance. I think you've got it in you, and I'm willing to take a risk."

"You'll take a risk on me?"

Now Stella and Jerry looked at each other, and she gave a tight smile. "Yes, you heard me correctly. I'm putting my options on you, Ted. It's a high risk, but I don't think it's speculative. I think it will prove to be a sure thing."

Ted took a napkin and wiped his mouth, even though he had not taken a bite of anything. He placed the napkin back in his lap. His hands were shaking. "I, I don't know what to say." Without thinking he reached across the table and clasped Stella's hand.

She did not pull it away.

"Thank you."

———

Katy Lynn dialed her sister's phone number by heart. "Hey, Janelle. Am I calling too late?"

"Are you kidding? The kids are like little dervishes with all the things you sent. They're living on a sugar high. They won't be in bed for another hour. They like counting all the gifts under the Christmas tree. You cannot keep spoiling them like this!"

"Did Brian like his early Christmas present?"

Janelle chuckled. "Brian thinks that you are the best thing that has happened to us in a long time. He says you're always welcome to bring as much French or American lingerie as you want."

They giggled into the phone together. Then, after an awkward pause, Katy Lynn asked, "So how was it, getting back?"

Katy Lynn imagined her sister wiping her eyes. "It sure was hard to leave Mom with . . . with everything. I'm so thankful she'll be spending Christmas with you and Gina." She paused. "But it's a funny thing. As I said before I left, I feel like the Lord is giving me a peek around the corner. At the other side of grief. And on the other side, well, I see God in a much bigger way. My grief sent me back home so that I could be with Dad one more time, hear his story, know the truth so we could support Mom now. . . . I don't know. It's big."

"Yeah. I've thought about that a lot," Katy Lynn whispered. "I can't say it as eloquently as that, but the truth is that the horrible things going on in my life were what pushed me to France—to you and Brian. And then being with you pushed me back to them—to him—before it was too late. Pretty weird—or *big*, as you say."

Janelle sniffed. "Anyway, I'm here, and it's going better than I expected. It's great to be back with Brian and the kids. And the folks at church saved me a little role in the Christmas play. It sounds silly, but that helps me jump back into life over here." She lowered her voice. "And we took a poinsettia to Josh's grave. All four of us. We stood there and cried, and it was like the counselor said—another tiny step on the road of grief."

"You amaze me, Janelle."

"Oh, please. It's just taking one day at a time." The phone line crackled in the silence. "How is Gina?"

"She's doing pretty well. She has now read every one of Dad's books—his original copies. Cries through them and then she recommends them to all of her friends. She is very proud and protective of her secret. Very proud of her grandfather. And . . . so am I. Better late than never." She gave a stiff laugh, hesitated, and then said, "I called Hamilton."

"You're kidding."

"No, I did. For Gina. For Christmas. I suggested we try to have a meal—the three of us—not on Christmas Day, but before."

"And?"

"And he agreed. So it's tonight. Pray for us."

"Wow, Kat, I will."

Katy Lynn let out a breath. "Well, that is absolutely enough talk of sad things. Now don't forget, I gave you that money so you could get a haircut—go back to that woman we found in town. She knew just what to do. . . ."

———

Lissa left The Sixth Declension and headed back to Chattanooga on I-75. *Driving Lessons* sat on the passenger's seat. It was almost as if Mr. MacAllister were in the car with her again, telling her how to drive, telling her how to live life, helping her form her "battle plan." When she passed under the bridge and by the scene of the accident, her heart raced a little. Her knuckles tightened on the steering wheel and she felt tears prick her eyes. But she knew she was in control.

I'm in control of the car, and Someone else is in control of my life.

She took the exit to Fort Oglethorpe, drove past the Military Park and onto Sunrise Road, and turned into the driveway. She parked the Camaro, picked up the novel, and got out of the car. She walked over to Ole Bessie, and almost lovingly—as if she were patting Caleb—ran her hand over the writing on the blue Ford. *MacAllister's Driving School.*

Annie came out of the front door and waved from the porch. She had lost weight. Her face wore the traces of grief—fatigue and poise and hurt.

Lissa hurried over to her and embraced her friend.

"Look at you, young lady. Driving by yourself! Ev would be so delighted."

"Yeah. It's pretty cool, isn't it? Sorry I'm late. I didn't even have time to change."

"You look perfectly adorable in your riding attire."

Lissa handed Annie the novel. "I waited for four hours for this. I was wondering if you would write something in it for me."

Annie brushed her hand gently over the cover. "Lissa, you didn't need to buy a copy. I was planning on giving you one."

"I *wanted* to wait in that line and buy my own copy. I *needed* to. I don't know why exactly, but it felt important."

"Well, of course I'll write something. The last novel by S. A. Green." Her face clouded over briefly, then she said, "Yes, I heard there was quite a crowd in the bookstores." She opened the screen door. "Well, come on in. Dinner's ready."

Lissa inhaled the familiar smells of pot roast and potatoes, vinegar and garlic, warm rolls and butter—the fragrance of comfortable, well-worn love. She sat down at the table with Annie, glanced at Ev's empty chair, and then looked away.

He should be here. If I miss him this much, what does Annie feel?

Whatever Annie felt, she kept the conversation going during the whole meal. "You said on the phone that you're applying to colleges?"

"Yep. I've almost got all the applications done. I think I'm going to study English."

"Good for you. Ev felt you had talent. You know what he'd say to you—just remember to use your gift the right way."

"Yes, I remember." She would remember everything he told her. "I wrote something for you. And for him." She handed Annie an envelope. "It was inspired by things . . . you know. Things he told me, about life and God. You can read it later. You'll see."

"Thank you, Lissa." Annie stared at the envelope for a few seconds, then flashed Lissa a smile. "So how's your father?"

"He's pretty good. We finally got everything out—about the accident, about us and my future and Caleb. Dad worked out a compromise with the family in Virginia. They bought Caleb, but didn't take him back with them yet. I'm leasing him from them until I start college, so for now I can ride—as of two weeks ago when the cast came off." Lissa cleared her throat and took a sip of iced tea. "Dad still gets this awful look on his face every time I go to the stables, but he doesn't say a word. It's funny, he doesn't seem as worried when I drive. I guess he is just so relieved that I am handling things better. I actually think he's loosening up a bit."

"He wrote me a very kind sympathy note."

"Really? That's neat. He didn't tell me."

"As did your Italian."

"Silvano? He wrote you?"

"Yes, a few weeks ago. It was very interesting. He sent me a copy of the article that appeared in *Persona* magazine—wanted to make sure I approved. He apologized—in a roundabout way—for his 'lack of discretion,' as he put it. He assured me he wouldn't divulge our secret, talked about how much Ev's books meant to him. 'They have caused me to take another look at spirituality' is how he put it." She shrugged. "I know you said he was quite the charmer. He was probably just covering his bases."

"Maybe not. He's surprising me. Underneath all the bravado, he seems to feel an incredible amount of responsibility for his family back in Rome. It couldn't have been easy for him to give up his big scoop."

"Well, that's good to hear." Annie stood and took the empty dinner plates into the kitchen. When she came back out, she gave Lissa an almost sheepish smile. "Would you mind terribly if we had dessert on the porch? It was our habit."

"I can't think of anything I'd rather do, Annie."

Together on the porch swing, bundled under blankets, Lissa sat with Annie, watching the silhouette of Lookout Mountain and listening to the stillness of the evening.

Lissa drove up the mountain in the dark. Unconsciously she began to smile, and then she heard the voice. It was a whisper, barely even there.

Chosen, it said. She turned her head ever so slightly, as if she had really heard the word spoken out loud.

Valued.

Loved.

The words followed in quick succession, a gentle breeze blowing through her soul, words from the verses Mr. MacAllister had written on that sheet.

Whatever is true, whatever is lovely . . . think on these things.

She tilted her head again. Something inside of her seemed to be smiling—perhaps it was her spirit or her soul. She felt a bursting type of sensation, filling up and expanding outward. She thought of the photo of Caleb, head high, blue ribbon floating, and her own delighted face. That was how she felt. Again. At last. Only better.

Another word settled softly in her mind.

Forgiven.

No other taunting voice came in to steal away the joy of the drive. There was only this voice, the One she was learning to recognize and listen to, all-powerful and yet gentle, all-knowing without condemnation, a voice of hope.

ACKNOWLEDGMENTS

If we are honest with ourselves, we have to admit that we all hear voices in our heads. For many years now, I have been learning to replace the insidious lies I was so used to hearing with the truth, found in the Word of God. As I contemplated the beauty of learning to hear the truth, I wanted to create a story with colorful characters who hear voices and find out what happens to each character when he or she listens to those voices. And voilà! *Words Unspoken*. My prayer, as always, is that this story will get into your heart and soul, cause you to think, look for answers, and ultimately delight in hearing the truth.

My thanks for so many who have helped me:

A couple of years ago, my husband, Paul, asked me, "Why don't you use an older male as the main protagonist in a novel someday?" And so Ev MacAllister slipped into my mind. Thanks, honey, for everything: advice, encouragement, love, life together. Thank you for helping me recognize lies and hear God's truth.

Although eighteen when he moved to the States for college, our older son, Andrew, didn't know how to drive (long story) until he started taking lessons in a little driving school in Fort Oglethorpe, GA, in the shadow of Lookout Mountain. Hearing him describe his lessons got me to thinking, *What if I wrote about learning to drive and let it be a metaphor for learning to live?* Thank you to both of our sons, Andrew and Chris, for many an exciting "ride together" on the mountain, but especially for the way you inspire me in this "ride of life." Your zeal and enthusiasm for the Lord and His truth truly challenge me.

At the time I was writing this novel, I did not know that the U.S. would be going through a huge financial crisis that far outweighed the one I describe in 1987. I am often amazed at the Lord's timing—how He inspires me and what He teaches me as I write. *Beware of greed!* May we all pay attention to this warning. Thanks to my father, Jere Wickliffe Goldsmith IV, the world's greatest dad and stockbroker, for your patient explaining of Black Monday, blue chips and options, and what a "rogue broker" looks like. And thanks for being a real Jerry Steinman to so many other brokers.

Barbara Goldsmith, my amazing mother—you are tireless in your help with research, contacts, mailing books to readers, encouraging me, and much more. The rest of the Goldsmith and Musser families—Jere and Mary, Glenn and Kim, Grandmom, Harvey and Doris, H. A. and Rhonda, Janet and Steve, Scot and Carol, Beth and Bill: each of you has offered me words of wisdom and encouragement along this writing road. How sweet of the Lord to let us be together on several occasions during our stay in the States.

It's always helpful for a writer to get to be on location when writing. Spending the fall living on Lookout Mountain allowed me to drive up and down that winding road plenty of times as well as poke around downtown Chattanooga, Fort Oglethorpe, and the Chickamauga Battlefield Military Park. I'm thankful for the help of these people as I did my research: Hazel Bickerstaff, DeeDee Dunkerley, Starlett Speakman, Peggy Michaels, Marty Vaughn, Kim Leffew, Gail Pinchak, Lacy Thompson, Melanie Gowin, and Kristi Sippel.

Thanks to Jennifer Brett with the AJC, who cleared up some last minute info about newpapers.

To Vickie Oliver from WOTH for being willing to tell me the truth about your grief.

To Isabelle Kozycki, dear friend and precious sister in Christ, for modeling for me throughout the years courage and perseverance after tragedy.

Cheryl Stauffer, Cathy Carmeni, and Bob Dillon—patient pre-editors—your advice was invaluable.

Silvana Tuikalepa—many thanks for helping me with Italian, making me laugh and being one courageous young woman.

LB Norton—my priceless editor. My novels are better because of you. I am so grateful for your precision and professionalism mixed in with large doses of humor. How great finally to meet face-to-face, twice!

The ones who continue to pray for the work of my hands and cheer me on: Val Andrews, Margaret DeBorde, Kim Huhman, Laura McDaniel, Marcia Smartt, Cathy Carmeni, Odette Beauregard, Trudy Owens, Lori Varak, Cheryl Stauffer, Karen Moulton, Vivianne Perret, Michele Philit, Marlyse Francais . . . and many others.

My agent, Chip MacGregor—I am so privileged to be able to work with you. Your expertise, advice, and encouragement have really helped my perspective on this industry.

What a blessing to meet the Bethany House staff on their own stomping grounds! Dave Horton, as always, my deepest thanks for your wise and patient counsel throughout all the years. And to the others who work so hard and honor the Lord, *merci*: Brett Benson, Joanie Brooks, Noelle Buss, Carra Carr, Donna De For, Jim Hart, Paul Higdon, Luke Hinrichs, Debra Larsen, Dave and Sarah Long, Steve Oates, Jim Parrish, Charlene Patterson, Karen Schurrer.

To my readers: It is a privilege to be allowed to write stories for you and a joy to hear from you as you travel along this journey called life.

To Jesus, my Lord and Savior: When I listen to Your voice, the others are quieted, truth is revealed, and the "ride," no matter how bumpy it gets or how many unexpected turns I encounter, is worth it.

ELIZABETH GOLDSMITH MUSSER, an Atlanta native and the bestselling author of *The Swan House,* is a novelist who writes what she calls "entertainment with a soul." For over twenty years, Elizabeth and her husband, Paul, have been involved in missions work with International Teams. They presently live near Lyon, France. The Mussers have two sons. *Words Unspoken* is Elizabeth's seventh novel.

To learn more about Elizabeth and her books, or to find discussion questions as well as photos of sites mentioned in the stories, please visit *www.elizabethmusser.com.*

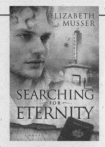